Mark Sargent

Ova the Moon

a novel

FAST BOOKS

Cover photographs by Xeni Taze

Fast books are edited and published by Michael Smith
P. O. Box 1268, Silverton, OR 97381, USA
Catalog at fastbookspress.com

ISBN 978-0-9982793-8-1

This is for the boys:
Alekos, Nikos and for
the memory of Yiorgos

Part One

1993

DAY ONE

J.M.W. at a lathe: $T\ U\ R\ N\ E\ R$. The bus wheezed, bumped to a start, and eased over the Korinth Canal. Sandra looked up from her crossword and sighted down the deep cut in the earth, a dark blue line at the bottom, a ship just entering from the Gulf of Korinth, another disappearing below. She smiled to herself at her ignorance of this feat of engineering—when had it been cut, by whom? With what tools and explosives, how many lives lost? She idly quick-sketched the view from the bus on the edge of the *Herald Tribune*—that cleft waiting to be filled, with air and watery mirror, a ship bound for Corfu, distances traveled.

She was in the Peloponnese now, and she craned her neck to peer out the bus window at the moving view of Acrokorinth, a bleak mass of rock topped by elaborate battlements and castlework. A year ago they'd been up there, all of them: Max and Briseis, the kids, Roberto. It had been a strange gray afternoon crawling about the mount, serpentine walls twisting over the harsh terrain, the wind whipping up, surprises of crocuses caught in the crotch of crenellations, wild oregano, the great aerial command of land and sea, just the brief isthmus separating the rippled bays. Only by treachery had it been taken.

She and Roberto had climbed a small tower through a narrow spiral staircase, shoulders brushing the walls of the passage as though you moved through a stone body, a parcel of warm, fluid flesh pushing through the channel, emerging from a small opening at the top. They could just barely stand together. Max and the kids were scrambling

3

along a broken battlement, shouting. Briseis was seated on another parapet gazing northeast toward the island of Aegina.

Roberto shuddered and admitted to a spasm of claustrophobia on the staircase. She turned, held the windblown hair from her face, and felt a cold glow of doubt begin to grow in the core of her—deeper than her stomach—as she reached up and stroked his face, squeezed out a faint smile. There would be no completion to their relationship. She saw this in an instant. He would not be able to push himself through to her—he would not arrive, finally, would not touch her center. Here on the top of this thin plinth of stone, his limitations rushed into focus and stunned her. She was completely unprepared for it. This was the man she had taken all of, her Latin lover, her romantic who had spent the past week walking the hills and beaches of Crete with her, swimming by moonlight, loving her in the long afternoons, octopus and ouzo, comic multilingual conversations with shopkeepers, hand gestures mistranslated, bargaining suspended to have a coffee. He was the same, nothing had changed but that she had gained an awful knowledge, had been allowed to see into what the two of them made. And it was not enough. Once again, it was not enough.

She turned toward the Saronic Gulf and looked, with Briseis, toward Aegina, then shifted her view to the dark greens and grays of the massed mountains of the Peloponnese. Something Max had said struck home. *Greece has been thoroughly lived. Whatever you think and do on this land has been done, in the same place, by others.* She took a deep breath, held it, and listened to the wind rush about them, listened for a whispered truth, a breath of insight, a heat to thaw this cold knowing; but it was all a long-drawn whoosh of lamentation. It was true. Others had felt the same here, but nothing had been solved on this lonely citadel.

They had started back down the tower. The shallow height of the staircase disallowed leaning forward, forcing you to descend erect, almost leaning backward. She led the way, Roberto just behind with a hand on her shoulder. Halfway down she quickened her step, broke contact, and came into the light alone. A moment later he came out grinning. It was easier coming down. It was too late.

Gerhard's quake: <u>R</u> <u>I</u> <u>C</u> <u>H</u> <u>T</u> <u>E</u> <u>R</u>. The bus turned onto the road to Argos. Sandra chewed her lip, resigned, free of longing, gently working the empty spot that only she could touch. Roberto was disappearing. She was climbing the tower again.

Calder in Alabama: <u>M</u> <u>O</u> <u>B</u> <u>I</u> <u>L</u> <u>E</u>. The vineyards of Nemea drifted by. Along the roadside were small stands selling wine and honey, garlic and apples. Less than two days ago she had been home in New York. Ten days before that she was in San Francisco visiting family. Why this great journey, this pilgrimage to her friends? There was the book she and Max were working on, that was reason enough. It was important work. Together they were going to make something beautiful, poem and image would become more, she was sure.

But it was more than that. For months in her studio she had found herself getting lost in the photos and totems she had brought back from Greece on her previous trips, lost in the sensations, the light, the goat bells at twilight. The warmth of it tugged at her, slowly enveloped her in daydreams of color, swimming blues, silver-green blur of olive trees, red of the earth, dense gray of stone. It was the light she felt with them, Max and Briseis, their

5

children, their home. They were a way to a deeper kind of relationship. They had no agenda, wanted nothing from her, just loved having her with them—made her part of the family. To them she was; it didn't have to be announced or discussed. She wanted that now, wanted to give herself to it.

Clifford's moonshine: S T IL L. The bus slowly ground down the switchbacked hill to Argos. She doodled alongside the crossword she was struggling with. When she came to Greece she felt she was leaving her world and life behind, that here she was a fresh person and could do and conceive anything—as though she was stronger and weighed less, could jump and float, could somehow enter the Greek air with a new array of senses—hearing color, tasting music, touching the atmosphere. It was the sun: the interaction between your flesh receiving the light and your eyes perceiving the light that let you feel with your body what you were seeing. At a beach it could be overwhelming, the warmth of air, water, and color, light combining so vividly, so completely that you felt yourself dissolving into the fused liquid color and heat, consumed in a warm, wet aquamarine. She caught a glimpse of the ancient agora in Argos. She wanted more.

She wanted that new person, that transformed, Greek Sandra, to enter into her relationships as she entered into color and light, with a freedom to blend and mix and make. Here, in the mountains, with all the baggage of her life left lying in a heap back in the States, she wanted to close the gaps, bring her creativity into living use, making, with other people, a more resonant way of being.

She sighed and laughed to herself. Slow down, Sandra. These must be jetlag hallucinations. No expectations, she said to herself, just be with your friends and have a nice, quiet, productive time. *A non-commissioned songster:* $\underline{S} I \underline{N} G$ $\underline{E} R \underline{S} A R \underline{G} E \underline{N} T$.

The bus slowed as they passed a truck laden with rugs that was stopped beside the road. Nut-brown barefoot gypsy kids were dashing about in the dust while the women perched high on the rugs and the men huddled up front examining the engine. Just beyond them was a roadside shrine, a crudely painted metal frame with glass sides and a peaked roof on thin metal legs. She had studied them on previous trips. Typically they contained a motley collection of odd icons covered with aluminum foil, candles and a lamp, old coke bottles filled with lamp oil, matches, perhaps a memento of the unfortunate who perished on this stretch of road. She found it touching and lonely, the incongruity of the elaborate effort to remember a loved one and the sloppy care given to the shrine. These objects of memory, the mana, or juju, as Max would say, given to them—this was what she wanted to explore. She wanted to create images that would give that sense of imbued power. Memory totems. With its thick mix of ancient pagan, country, folk religion and Christian traditions all sharing various shrines, objects, and saints, Greece was vivid with this kind of imagery. There was a lot of material to gather. The collaboration with Max was a good start. His energy pushed the project all over the terrain, he wasn't attached to any point of view. And although his work dealt more with the acts of man in the landscape, interspersed with the right images she could give the poems a new, subtler resonance. There was wonderful work to be done, and she grew more confident as the bus rolled on.

Opaque quartz loos: $\underline{J} A S P E R \underline{J} O H \underline{N} S$. The road wandered through vast and continuous mountains. They

7

were *her* Greece now, how they changed color by the hour, blue-gray to dun, splashes of green. And empty, for miles not one sign of a human. She tried to pronounce a village name from a signpost. Difficult, even with the same name given in Roman letters below the Greek. Eight kilometers into those mountains was a village, a gathering of humans. My god, how isolated those people must be.

The bus suddenly braked. Outside, the road was covered with goats. Two dark, lean shepherds, their trousers stuffed in their boots and wielding crooks, were slowly guiding the herd across the road. They never wear sunglasses, she thought, just squint against the glare. The hillside out Sandra's window was busy with shaggy multicolored beasts, many bearing marvelous, uniquely twisted horns. Shitting without thought, baaing and butting, eating and staring curiously at the bus, they were in no hurry. It was easy to project upon them a mythic quality, prehistoric, they seemed as ancient as the mountains they roamed. As though they had witnessed the coming of man and wouldn't note his passing—all the while inscrutably chewing, stripping the landscape of all the but the toughest vegetation. The bus eased past them and geared back up to speed. Sandra closed her eyes and kept the goats in her mind. She was going to do a lot of work with goats.

• •

THE VILLAGE HOUSE WAS 100 YEARS OLD and across the road from the platea and cafe/restaurant. It had taken nine months for Max to make habitable; for his labors they received four years free rent. The property sloped steeply down from the road the house abutted. You entered through an old metal gate onto an old stone patio.

8

Directly to your right a stone staircase led down to a dirt courtyard enclosed with high stone walls. There was a cellar off the courtyard where the chickens lived. Off the entrance patio was a door into large rooms disused save for Max's original innovation, a bathroom and shower. Before you rose another staircase, also of stone, that led up to a large wood-floored and roofed veranda, a hiati, and the main living spaces—a large living room in front, a small bedroom shared by the children, and a winter room with a large fireplace that served as Max and Briseis's bedroom. At the back end of the veranda Max had built a kitchen, which also connected to the winter room. There was a small balcony off the living room. The front of the house was shaded by a large almond tree just outside the entry gate.

Briseis creaked open the door from the hiati and entered the kitchen in her bathrobe, hair turbaned in a towel. "Oh, that was lovely. I feel really warm all over." She loosened the towel and briskly rubbed her thick black hair.

Max looked up from his book. "Did I leave you enough hot water?"

"Oh yes, there's masses." As she rubbed her hair her bathrobe fell open, partially exposing each breast, her stomach rounding down to a thickly thatched pubis, curve of inner thigh. Max involuntarily inhaled the sight of her and held it. He wanted her so often. The gift of his hunger, that's how he thought of it. For ten years now, through the pregnancy and long recovery, through the now constant illness of scleroderma. Not expectation but desire. Wasn't it just another manifestation of love? He didn't lust after other women, all his focus was on her. When queried on the meaning of life, he stated without

9

hesitation, to give and receive love. Poetry, art, music, wasn't it all an expression of this? Sex too, but with sex he honed it down, funneled it all to Briseis.

It endeared him to her, stirred her love deeper. She was charmed and flattered. It wore her out. His ardor never took a break. He was an animal this way—and yet, animals only mate when the female is in heat. He reached out and stroked her stomach, still brown from the sun of summer.

"Yeeessssss," she purred.

He circled his arm around her butt and pulled her to him and kissed her stomach, rubbing his face against her, kneading her buttocks. She sighed, let the towel drape over her shoulders, and put her hands into his unkempt bush of a head. "We have plenty of time," he murmured to her stomach.

"Time for what?"

"To pleasure the wife."

"Mmmm, I think we do have enough time for that." She turned from him and walked into the adjoining bedroom.

Max closed his book, emptied the dregs of his coffee, glanced at the clock, and followed. On the bed she sprawled on her stomach, torso slightly twisted, a knee cocked toward her head raising one haunch. He dropped his clothes in a silent heap and climbed on the bed. Without touching her with his hands or body he kissed the small of her back, worked his lips over the vertebrae down into the fold of her ass, nuzzled her there, kissing the insides of each cheek, working the spine down between the buttocks with his tongue. She murmured approval and rotated her ass to ease access, contracted and released her sphincter on his nose, his tongue and mouth. Then twisting at the waist she rolled, lifting one leg over his ducking head, and settled on her back, knees slightly raised, his face in her sex.

He ran his tongue up one clitoral lip and down the other, then lightly up the ridge while gently massaging her mons with his nose. He filled with the smell and taste of her, entangled in her hair, using his entire face, as though he could enter into her. He took the hood between his lips and rolled it, his tongue slipped out to the clitoral knob, darted about it, circled and then he brought all this mouth and tongue to bear and rolled and licked and rocked his face in her.

The sensations slowly rose. With eyes closed she could see a golden glow rising from between her legs, oozing up like rising water through her muscles, a tingle just brushing her flesh. She brought her hands back behind her head and arched her back and rolled and rotated her pelvis into him. She moaned slightly and twisted to guide him. The rising warmth flowed through and over her breasts into her neck and then was all she experienced, all of her body was centered in a point on her forehead. Her mouth dropped open and small sounds from the back of her throat whispered out. Hands still behind her head she thrust herself into him and the center of her flowed back and forth from her head to Max's face and then her breath stopped, caught in her mouth as a series of warm waves lapped from inside . . . one, two . . . seven times full and warm a rolling undulation of vibrating particles, liquid, floating, her head opened wide and the energy radiated out. Max coaxed her on, pressing with his tongue, massaging with lips, and she brought her hands to the sides of his head and stroked him back to his neck and lightly rocked, buoyant. And then she slid off and settled

11

back into the mattress and tried to replace the air she'd missed, while Max rolled his head and laid his wet face on her thigh.

Twitter and shriek, birdsong seeped back into the room, shadows and strands of light cast the old plaster walls in a shaky geometry, dust illuminated in a shaft of sun. The clop of a donkey, whine of a distant motorbike, rustle of mulberry leaves on the tree outside the window. Briseis drifted with the sounds, unable to focus with ear or eye, the distant wood-plank ceiling wavered with the birds. A sudden waft of lilac filled her head as her eyes closed and her mouth dropped open.

Max inhaled heavily through his nostrils, the stink of her sex thickened his senses. He was so full of it his head throbbed as though with the onset of a carnal migraine, a rhythmic contraction and expansion of skull. He listened to her breathing, felt her pulse in his cheek against her thigh, waited. He didn't want her to come too far off, and he lifted his head, placed a hand under her thigh, and gently turned her over while ducking under. The beautiful mounds of her ass rose before his eyes, and he crawled up onto them. Supporting himself with one hand he guided himself to her wet, swollen opening and hovered there, barely probing, working the head around and around, punctuated with the suggestion of entrance. Briseis, barely conscious, pulled one knee forward to ease the process and rotated her pelvis back and up and with this motion brought him deep inside her.

Max gasped, caught his breath, hovered in the depth of her, rocked back out, paused, took a breath, and pushed back in as far as he could go. He was so deep in her, so full of what she offered, as though it was his arm up to the elbow rather than his penis. She involuntarily exhaled, as

12

though he was pushing up through her, displacing her air. She flexed and moved her mouth as though singing, but no sound came.

Max was slowly rolling his hips from side to side, twisting his torso to alternate the friction, riding her ass that pushed back with short arrhythmic thrusts. Briseis felt her breath catching, the liquid creep once again rising up from her center, less focused but electric with Max's penetration, being filled and taken. He leaned forward, grasped her outstretched hands in his, and leaned into her. She moaned now, and her sound flattened all thought to a single wavering line. He groaned in return and reared and roared into her blind to all, all that was taken up, drawn into the new being that was the union of them.

Briseis came to first. She didn't think she could move yet, but asked, "Max, what time is it?"

"Ummm, shit, time to get up." He rolled off the bed and began pulling on clothes. "If I leave right now I can get bread before she arrives—if her bus is on time, that is. I'll pick up wine on the way back. Anything else?"

"No, that'll be fine. I'll start prepping the briami now. You're going to make the tzadziki, right?"

"I'm on it."

Briseis looked dreamily up at her lover/husband, took a deep breath of amazement that the two of them had found their way to a life in this Greek mountain village. "You're just going to go like that? You must reek of me. What will Sandra think?"

"That I was getting my licks in. What the hell, I'll brush my teeth on the way out."

• •

Syrupy village: M A P L E T H O R P E. They had passed through Tripoli and climbed still higher into the mountains. Some trees were beginning to change to orange and yellow. Occasionally she'd spy a tiny church on a hilltop. Old women in black rode donkeys along the road. Village children stared at the bus as it passed. Suddenly they crested a hill and there, across a deep valley of rolling hills, was the Tayegetos mountain range, a massive spine of rock that towered over Lakonia and disappeared to the south into the Mani peninsula. She tried to pick out Varsova, their village, but it was too far away, she didn't know the mountains well enough. The bus wound down through the village of Voutiani. She'd be there soon. She took several deep breaths while she feasted on the increasingly familiar terrain.

This was her fourth visit to Max and Breseis, to Lakonia and these wonderful mountains, but her first alone. She had always come with a mutual friend or a lover. This time she had just herself to offer and relished the idea of having them all to herself. Leonidas and Andromache would be bigger. She had science puzzles for them and hoped they weren't too easy or too complicated. She didn't know how fast children developed. Leo and Maki were eight, at the lower end of the age range given with the puzzles, but they always seemed very advanced, they'd probably have no problem. Unless, of course, they found them *too educational*. It would be great to be around children again. None of her friends back in the city had any. It was strange how people with children congregated together, and those who didn't did too. Well, the hours were different. *Inquiry after mom: Is your _____?* M O T H E R W E L L.

There were more houses all the time now. On the

outskirts of Sparti, spread along the banks of the Evrotas River was a large gypsy encampment. There were some traditional gypsy tents but many more cheap wooden frameworks covered with sheets of plastic, which reminded the sensitive viewer of the extreme poverty of the Romas. Sandra smiled at the ugly, half-finished concrete buildings that lined the streets as they entered the town—they were part of Sparti too. Then the broad main street with its large palm trees marching down the middle. The bus waited for a man pulling a two-wheeled cart piled high with what looked like microwave ovens.

The Sparti bus station was located on a narrow, congested street that added density to the screaming chaos that was Greek bus travel. There were already two other buses parked ahead of them. The sidewalk and street were a mass of pushing, shouting people struggling with luggage while cars and motorbikes attempted to bump their way through. Sandra disembarked looking for a familiar face, didn't see one, and turned to wait for the luggage compartment to be opened. It was such a naked feeling, to arrive somewhere alone and wait for friends you hope are coming to get you. The combination of anxiety and expectation brought her up on her toes to scan over the short, scuffling crowd.

There he was. Max's shaggy head bobbed as he slid and pushed through the milling travelers. Shirttails flying, baggy pants flapping, he leapt over a pile of bags, and before Sandra could decide just how to greet him had embraced her off her feet, shouting, "There you are!" She returned the hug as he spun her around. What was that smell? Over his shoulder she could see the movie house marquee. *The Piano* was playing.

"Same old bus ride, huh?" Max tossed Sandra's bags

in the back of his beat-up Renault 5.

"It was okay." She settled in her seat and pulled her mane of hair to the side. "It lets me ease into the Greek countryside. It's part of coming to Sparti. It wouldn't be the same if there was an international airport here and you could just fly in. It wouldn't feel so remote."

"Remote," he paused and looked up Lykourgou toward the mountains, "that's for sure."

"How are Briseis and the kids?"

"Great. Leo and Maki are huge. You'll hardly recognize them."

"Are they at school?"

"Yeah. Fourth grade, can you believe it?"

"Fourth?"

"They start a year earlier here. So they're eight and in the fourth grade. Now that they're fully fluent, it's all too easy for them."

"And Briseis?"

Max stared ahead for a moment. "Doing pretty well, really. The drugs she's taking now are working. She's feeling more flexible. She's teaching full-time and really into it. Besides a miraculous total remission, about as good as you could expect."

Sandra exhaled. "Oh good, I'm so glad to hear that."

Driving through a village on the outskirts of Sparti, they pulled into a gas station. Max grabbed a jug from the back seat and got out. "I'm gonna get some wine. Come on, you can see the barrels." They walked into the front room of the station, where three rough old farmers were seated around a battered metal table drinking wine and eating bread and onions. A young man entered from the back room and shouted out, "Yasou Max, ti kaneis?"

"Kala, Petro, kala. Ti kaneis, kala? You have any wine?"

Petros laughed, grabbed the jug, and beckoned Max and Sandra to follow. In a dimly lit room were four enormous wooden barrels. Petros crouched before one, then rose with a grin and held out two glasses of a wine the color of apricots. "Champagne, Max, champagne!"

"He's very proud of his wine."

Sandra and Max clicked glasses. "To love, my dear, always to love."

"I'll drink to that." Sandra felt the fresh, clean, fruity wine refreshen her mouth. "Oh, that's a flavor I remember. Wine from the barrel is an entirely different animal."

Petros looked up from filling the jug and grinned.

A kilometer down the road they pulled over. Sandra looked at the large fenced field. "Isn't this their school."

"Yeah, it is. And their class is out on their diallimah, ah, recess. Come on, I can see Leo."

They got out of the car and walked to the fence. A stocky, grinning boy ran up, leapt onto the fence, and while hanging there shouted, "Hey, Sandra, how ya doing? I scored a goal today!"

Sandra felt her entire body warm. "Hi, Leo. How are you? You're so big."

"A goal, huh? Was anybody playing defense?"

"Sure they were. It was a real game with teams and everything."

"Bravo. Where's Maki?"

"She's over with those girls." Leo pointed vaguely to an area near the school building.

Max waved, and a girl broke away from the group and ran toward them, trailing a mass of curly black hair

17

and wearing a brilliant smile. Sandra couldn't believe how happy she was to see them, to feel their exuberant energy. How life-affirming the two of them were.

"Sandra, you look soooo beautiful!"

Sandra laughed, "Thank you, Andromache, so do you."

"What do you think, Daddy, are we both beautiful?"

"Way beautiful. Too beautiful. Absolutely divinely heart-stoppingly beautiful!"

"Yuck. See you at lunch." Leonidas peeled off the fence and ran back into a brawl of boys, pushing and punching and knocking each other down.

"Maki, how's it going today?"

"Oh, same old same old. Kirios Kosmas got mad at Leo today."

"Why?"

"For falling out of his chair laughing."

Max and Sandra burst into their own laugh. "That's my son, no doubt."

"Leo can be soooo stupid sometimes!"

"Well, we can't all be as smart as you, my dear."

"Yeah, yeah." Maki was already up to speed with irony. "What's for lunch today, Daddy?"

"Briami, tzadziki, salad, feta, you know."

"Good. A vegetarian lunch." Maki turned to see her class moving toward the building. "Oh, our diallimah is over. Bye." She ran to catch up with the others.

"What, is Andromache a vegetarian now?"

"No, but she thinks it's probably cool and definitely against the grain."

"How does it happen so fast?"

"I dunno, just feed and water 'em. They do the rest."

Sandra lingered at the fence, watching the children

18

file up the stairs and into their school. She studied the raw physicality of the group, banging and reacting to each other and yet very much a unit, a throbbing, breathing entity.

• •

"MORE WINE, SANDRA?"

"Oh, no thanks, Max. Briseis, that was a wonderful lunch. It's been ages since someone cooked for me."

"Oh, you're really welcome. It's so simple. The whole thing is the ingredients. Beautiful olive oil, fresh herbs and vegetables, voilà, it's a breeze. And slow cooking, that helps."

At a table on the hiati, they all leaned back and listened to the afternoon. Bees were busy in the geraniums and petunias that overflowed from pots and old cans brightly painted and the jasmine that had climbed up over the railing. Cicadas rattled and cracked. A neighbor's lambs bleated for their mum.

"Oh," exclaimed Sandra, "there's nothing like being back in the village. I didn't know how much I missed it till this very moment."

"Varsova in October, it's the best."

"Look," said Max, "how this big bumblebee is humping this flower. He's really rocking out, giving it all he's got."

All energy, they watched the bee do his work. Finished, he slowly lifted up and away in the afternoon heat. They followed his flight until he disappeared. A swallow soared by, and then another. The birds lifted Briseis out of her reverie. "Oh, did Max tell you we have swallows nesting downstairs?"

"No, really?"

19

"Yes, it's been wonderful watching them. They've had three batches of chicks. The latest group is flying already. Come on, I'll show you." The women got up and headed down the stairs.

Max called after them, "I'm making Greek coffee. Who wants some?"

"Hey, have you guys got any homework?"

The children, sprawled in deck chairs in the afternoon heat with comic books and gameboy, looked up at their father.

"Yeah, we had to kliesi some reemas. That's all we ever do, it's so dumb."

"I know it's dumb, but have you done them?"

"I have, but Leo probably hasn't."

"Yes I have! Probably before you."

"That's not possible, I did them before we even left school."

"Yeah, yeah, so what?"

"Okay, okay, so you've both done whatever it is you're supposed to do. That's all I want to know." He turned to see Sandra smiling up at him from a deck chair. "You might be wondering what *kliesing reemas* is. It's conjugating verbs. They do masses of them, pages and pages of that bullshit. They do end up knowing them all, though."

"So what's the school like?"

"It's crap. Rote learning at its most mind-numbing."

"Doesn't that bother you?"

"Not really. Briseis and I both feel the role of schools is vastly overrated. Neither of us had very positive experiences when we were young. She was an army brat and went to a different school every year, and me, I was thrown out of every school I attended. We both remember

20

being bored to tears. As long as they learn to read and write and do mathematics, both of which *can be taught* with this grinding repetitive method, then it doesn't make much difference to us. They get their real education here at home."

"Yes?"

"Yeah. They taught themselves to read and write English here in Greece when they were five. We provide the materials—music, science stuff, history, tons of books—and we do stuff with them all the time. We take them to ancient sites, to concerts, we read to them, we talk to them about the affairs of the day. And we've lived without a TV for years, so their heads aren't filled with all that crap. So yeah, who needs the fucking school?"

"There's the social element, though."

"Right. So they attend school, hang out with the other kids, learn Greek and math, and they get a smattering of Greek mythology, though far less than they get at home. You have to realize, this is a village school. A lot of these kids come from homes that don't have a book in them. I've been to these places. Some of their parents are barely literate, if that. So the pace of the education, such as it is, is incredibly slow. It's dull stuff. Fortunately, they have very short days, sometimes they're back at 12:30. Nobody eats lunch at school."

"But Briseis is a teacher."

"Yeah, but not in this system. And she certainly doesn't teach with those methods. Her lessons are fun. She uses literature and music and games. Her students adore her, partially at least 'cause she doesn't try to pound it into their heads. If she was in the public school system, she wouldn't have the freedom to do what she does."

Children's voices shouting Leo and Maki's full names

21

rang out from the village platea across the street. They burst out of their lethargy shouting, "Bye, Daddy, we're going to the platea." They crashed down the stairs and out the gate, their father's admonition to watch the traffic bouncing off the backs of their heads.

"Sandra, I'm going to go fart around in the garden for a while. Your bed in the living room is all made. You know where everything is?"

"I'm not going anywhere. This chair is just right. I might just drift off."

She was riding a horse on a small path in the mountains. It was warm and sunny, the wildflowers looked like spring. She was wearing shorts and sandals but was bare from the waist up. The sun was wonderful on her back, like hot delicate fingers stroking her. She rode around a bend in the trail, and there was a small village strewn against the hillside. There didn't seem to be any people about but animals in abundance: goats, donkeys, chickens, a pig rooting around in a garden. Afraid that someone might come upon her nakedness, she leaned forward and hugged the horse around the neck, covering herself in his mane as he slowly walked through the village. A hen riding a goat trotted up to them. With a squawk it leapt, flapping its wings, and landed on the horse's head. Sandra sat back and stared while the hen turned its hind end to her and squatted. Soon she could see an egg emerging, and she held out her hands and caught it. Without turning around to look, the hen leapt down to the goat and rode off. The egg was warm, shiny, and perfect; she raised it to her lips and kissed it. Glancing up, she noticed that people were staring at her from doorways and windows, from behind fences and trees, and she urged the horse to hurry up. He began to gallop out of the village while she hung on with one hand and cradled the egg in the other.

"Sandra! Sandra!"

She bounced off the horse—and fell into the afternoon. The sun was an egg perched above Lazineekos, her head was listing to the left, her hands were cupped in her lap.

"Sandra, look!"

She looked across the street to the platea playground. Andromache and two other girls were hanging upside-down from a bar, giggling and waving.

• •

MAX AND SANDRA LEANED BACK in white plastic chairs at a table before the taverna, luxuriating in the warm evening. Silently they watched the moon rise out of the Parnona mountain range. They were easily silent together, always had been. Yet through all the years back to their college days, they had never once flirted, never once a hint of mutual chemistry that might lead to union. Just that they saw the world through the same filters, analyzed with the same equations, agreed.

"I'd say about the start of the second quarter. A week shy of full, maybe. Beautiful. Out here in the country, especially in this village with its location, you know the moon, you're intimate with it. Every day, just about, you know where the moon is and what it's doing, where and when it rises and sets. It's part of the life."

"In the city it surprises you. You look down a street and there it is, hanging between the buildings. Or better, when you see it on the water, the long rippling reflection."

They watched a cloud scud across it. Children were shouting in the playground. The wine was cool and fresh. Other tables murmured nearby. Across from them, a car pulled up at the house. Before Briseis could alight to open the gate, her children were shouting at her from the swings. She threw her books back in the car and walked into the platea, her loose skirt blowing about her bare legs. They waved, and she languidly moved toward them, nodding and speaking to villagers along the way.

"I see, while I'm slaving away, others are lounging at the taverna. Nice for some."

"Somebody has to do it, my dear. How did it go?"

"I had good classes tonight. The kids were really focused, and we got a lot done." She eased into a chair, exhaled. "It's such a beautiful night."

"How many classes did you have?"

"Three. I had an hour's break from six to seven, which I really needed because I hadn't gotten all my prep done today. Have you ordered?"

"We were waiting for you."

"Are the kids having their usual?"

"Souvlakia, yeah. So, lemme see, eight souvlakia, an order of patates, tzadziki, that'll do them. What do we want?"

"I feel like grilled chicken. Sandra, they do a beautiful job with their chicken."

"Sounds good."

"Okay, we'll share two orders of chicken, salad, that'll do, won't it? And more wine, of course."

"Of course."

The table was littered with the debris of dinner. The women were watching the other diners and murmuring to each other. Max had taken the children home for bed. Bats darted through the lights above, eating insects. Lulu, their dog, was begging french fries at another table. Soft, the faint evening breeze caressed their flesh. Sandra

24

was about to dissolve, melt in a swoon. She turned to an equally blissful Briseis.

"You seem especially relaxed today."

"Yes, I suppose I am. It's the weather, and your arrival—now I don't have to worry about what needs to be done before you get here. And, well, Max and I had, um, particularly extra extra-curricular activity this morning, and the glow of that can last all day."

She had smelled it on him. Now it warmed her, to have caught the scent of their love. "How nice. I don't have the benefit of that, but the village has already cast its spell on me. Oh," reaching out and touching Briseis on the arm, "I fell asleep on the hiati this afternoon and had an amazing dream." As the moon crawled up the night, she spun her dream out. "And then I heard my name being called and woke up. It was Andromache and a couple of other girls in the playground wanting me to watch them. What do you think?"

"Wonderful dream. Loaded with stuff. Where are you in your cycle?"

"I ovulate at the full moon. I'm very regular."

"Huh. A chicken riding a goat. What do all the animals mean? And the egg. I mean, there's birth and sex, but isn't that stuff in all dreams? It is in mine."

"Yes. I don't know. It's a dream I can think about for days."

Briseis leaned over and whispered, "Here comes Maurice. I think you've met him on other visits."

A slight, shaggy-haired man in his mid-sixties, dressed as a community theatre would dress the artist abroad, in whites, straw hat, scarf, sandals, came walking toward them. A woman, younger, in bright green patterned pants and yellow tunic, was with him. She moved with

25

an oddly alert bearing, given the relaxed, wine-infused atmosphere. Maurice doffed his hat, greeted them, and introduced Roxanne. He was Flemish, but his English came with a pronounced French accent that always struck Briseis as a Maurice Chevalier impersonation. He wet his lips and looked hungrily down at Sandra. "Haven't we met before? I'm sure of it."

"Yes, we have. I was here about a year ago."

"Mmm, yes, you are an artist, no?"

"Yes, I am. I paint."

"You must come to my house. It's just up the road. I'll show you my work. I am doing many interesting things."

Roxanne had assumed a flamboyant hands-on-hips stance. Her English rang out oddly, as though she was in a play. "Fascinating, what he is doing. You should see, really," she hissed.

"I'll try and come by."

"I will be expecting you. Well, we are dining with Costas tonight, so we will leave you. Enjoy the rest of the evening." They walked off to another table.

Briseis leaned toward Sandra, and she reciprocated. "Roxanne is visiting from Belgium. She's been here about a month, and Maurice is also seeing Agnes, the old English woman with all the dogs."

"Oh, I remember her. Where does she live?"

"Right below the platea here. There's a trail between his house and hers. He slips down there under all sorts of phony pretenses and has it off with her."

"Oh, you must be talking 'bout Mo-reese!" Max laughed, sitting down and reaching for the wine as he rejoined them. "The village Lothario."

"Shhhh, not so loud, Max. The kids are asleep?"

"Dreamland. Check it out, Sandra." Max raised his

wine, and they touched glasses. "He's kind of a phony and a crap artist, but you gotta give him credit. Here he is, this weird Belgian engineer, quits his job and comes to Greece to be an artist. And he's always got women! Never locals, of course, but every single, middle-aged, foreign woman in the area, just about, has made it up there to his *love studio*. I mean, he's working two right now. Brie, you talk to these women. He's actually fucking both of them, isn't he?"

"Sshhhh, Max, you're so loud." Briseis turned to Sandra. "It's quite strange really, but both Agnes and Roxanne have taken me as their confidante. I'm the only available person in the village when you get down to it. So I hear all the lurid details."

Max slapped the table. "The dog! We should send wine over to his table just to salute his virility!"

"Max, no, don't. Then they'll send wine over to us, and we'll never get out of here."

"Yeah, okay. But damn, when I'm sixty-five I want . . ."

"When you're sixty-five you're going to be married to me, husband."

"Ah, right, yes, wife, of course. But . . ."

"No buts about it."

"Actually, it's all about butts. I've always been an ass-man, as you know."

The women laughed. Max leaned back and looked at the moon.

DAY TWO

"SANDRA, BRIE JUST WOKE UP and wants to know if you'll join her in bed for a cup of tea."

She put aside her book. "I'd be delighted."

"Right, then I'll set to it."

Their bedroom was dominated by a huge fireplace and hearth with a vast mantle jutting out over it. The dark wood plank ceilings disappeared in the dark twelve feet overhead. Briseis had done the old plaster walls in an apricot wash that seemed to highlight the air moving in the room. It was an old, drafty house, the air was always moving. A window beyond the bed revealed an enormous fig, its huge leaves filling the window in rustling green, above it the tile roof of an old olive press, and farther still, the mountains. Briseis was sitting up, pillows propped against the headboard, an antique art deco affair Max had rescued from the cellar. She looked up with a soft smile, "How did you sleep?"

"Not bad considering the jet lag. I was awake in the middle of the night for a while, then I drifted off."

Briseis fluffed up some pillows beside her. "Here's your spot. Oh, are you doing a crossword too? Great, we can help each other." They giggled and pulled the quilt over their feet.

Minutes later Max entered from the kitchen with a tray bearing tea, toast, peeled and sliced pears, fresh figs.

"Oooooh, yea!" They cooed in unison, shifting to make room for the tray. Max placed it on the bed between them.

"I knows how to take care of my women."

28

"You do, it's true." Briseis reveled in his gestures of service, hoped never to take them for granted, knew she did.

"Now that you guys are all set, I'm going to dash into town and get some stuff. Anybody need anything?"

"What are we having for lunch?"

"Tomatoes yemista."

"Pine nuts, that's what we need."

"Pine nuts, that's koukounari, right?" Max scratched this in a small pad he had drawn from his pocket.

"Right. Very good. To this day he hardly speaks any Greek, but he knows food."

"And hardware store, excuse me." Max crossed his arms.

"Yes, okay, food and hardware."

"What else do you need? Nuts and bolts and nosh. Besides amour, of course."

"Interesting perspective, from a poet." Briseis raised her tea to her mouth.

"Ah, but my poetry is merely a manifestation of love, my dear."

Briseis looked over her tea and said, "Vanity cometh before the fall, beware the bear of hubris."

Max studied the floor. "How true. " He looked up, "Thank you."

Sandra found these exchanges so softly comical that she'd still be grinning minutes later. They were so comfortable with each other, and with her. They always wanted her to join in, but it took her a couple of days at least to acquire their timing and feel free with all the teasing. You were not allowed to take yourself too seriously.

They sipped their tea. Their pens scratched paper. The rising heat of the day, of themselves, was narcotic, as

29

though they were about to drift into another dimension, a parallel world where the rapturous rest. But they stayed in the room's womb, settled in with soft colors you could taste. There were books on every horizontal surface. In the corners of the room they climbed up the walls in Pisa stacks. Up the village a donkey complained. A lost bee buzzed near the ceiling. From two directions thin wands of light sheared the morning into thick, heavy Rothko shapes.

"*An off-breaking ball,* second and third letters 'o'?"

"*Googly.* It's a cricket term . Don't ask how I know it—I think it was in a previous puzzle. You must try these figs. They're from the tree out back." Briseis peled the last bit of skin from the fruit and pushed the deep purple flesh into her mouth. "Oooh, they're the best." She inhaled deeply and let the fruit melt over her tongue. Her hands dropped to her lap as she devoted everything to the sensation. Sandra watched her as she pushed her head back into the pillow, murmuring her delight, and reached for a fig.

"Andromache, would you please see if the chickens have laid any eggs," Briseis asked, coming out of the kitchen. She and Sandra leaned on the hiati railing and watched the child race down to the courtyard. The chickens scattered before her as she disappeared into the deep cellar where the birds roosted at night.

"Do they have names?"

"Oh yes," said Briseis. "That fat brown hen over by the wall is Beatrice. The gray speckled one is Bernice. That other brown one there is Bernadette. I don't know why all the 'b's, it just sort of happened. The white one is Mrs. White, after the character in Clue. And that strutting red rooster by the gate is Dr. Dan, named after our old naturopath in Portland."

"What about those two other roosters? They are roosters, aren't they?"

"They don't have names, unless you want to call them lunch and dinner. They're excess males. When we buy chicks at the market, they aren't sexed so you generally get about half and half. But you only need one rooster. It's the same in mammal societies, extra males only cause trouble."

"They'll lay without a rooster, won't they?"

"Certainly. But besides fertilizing the hens, which he does relentlessly—see, there he goes—he watches out for them, warns them of danger, finds food. He makes himself useful. But like I said, you only need one. See how the hens are losing their feathers on their backs. That's where the roosters peck them so they'll squat and they can mount. Three roosters will wear out the poor hens. So Max is going to slaughter them soon."

"He does it himself?"

"Yeah. Leonidas holds the feet, and Max chops off the head. They taste pretty good."

"How come you still have to buy chicks?"

"We don't know. Occasionally one of the hens goes broody and sits on some eggs for a few days and we get all excited, but then she gives up or loses interest or something. I don't know, it just hasn't happened yet. The eggs look fertile. When you crack them you can see if they're fertile by examining the blastoderm, the little white lump on the yolk. If it has a little translucent eye, it's fertile. At least, that's what our book says. But we have no *real* evidence of fertility. Maybe we should eat Dr. Dan and keep one of the young roosters."

"Look, they're fighting."

"Dr. Dan keeps them in line. He's still king of the

yard, but not by much."

Max entered the courtyard carrying a canvas bag, a hoe slung across his shoulders. The chickens parted for him. He was dressed in deeply worn carpenter's overalls, a hole at the knee, nothing underneath, and shod in a thoroughly abused pair of sneakers. "Hey, farmer." Briseis and Sandra leaned over the hiati railing high above him. He shielded his eyes and peered up. He was not large but thick, burled as a working man, with a density about him, a sense that he could become larger. He was erratic, mercurially insensitive, too convinced of the sincerity of his own emotions, eager to collaborate. He held up the bag. "We're still getting tomatoes."

"Great. Are there any big enough for stuffing?"

Max looked in the bag. "Yeah, these will work."

Andromache came out of the chicken house with a basket. "We got four big fat eggs today, Daddy. Three brown ones and a white one."

Briseis turned to Sandra. "The brown chickens lay brown eggs and the white ones lay white ones. I never knew that till we got chickens."

"What about the gray speckled one?"

"She lays brown ones too. When she was little we wondered."

"You want some help with lunch?"

"Sure, you can slice and dice." They moved toward the open kitchen door.

• •

A CUP OF TEA SAT ON THE FLOOR next to her along with Jim Harrison's *A Woman Lit by Fireflies*, *The Collected Poems of Theodore Roethke*, and a small journal. Sandra reclined on a deck chair and basked in the afternoon sun, slowly, barely moving her hand as she shaded with pencil a drawing of a group of fragments of ancient Greece laid out on a table nearby. Bees were buzzing in the potted geraniums and basil, parsley and petunia. The village was siesta-still, an hour had passed without a car. Every few minutes she would look up at the mountains, at Lazineekos, towering over the village, the backdrop of flawless sky, think nothing at all, take a sip of tea, and return to her meditative drawing.

Briseis had driven into Sparti to teach. The children, home from school, heavy with lunch, were on their beds, deep into their books. Max was in the living room, the saloni, working away, occasionally the clicking of the keys could be heard. She found herself grinning, laughing silently, and this made her smile widen. She was deeply at peace, utterly calm. Full, nothing was required. The vacancies, the things undone, unfulfilled, faded in the brilliant haze---she was just this body, barely clothed in a tank top and shorts, just this body in the sun. The heat floated over her, filled her to floating, and gently laid her down again. She stretched and arched her feet. A butterfly bobbed by. Faint goat bells rang far away. A lone cicada started up. A breath of air rustled the leaves of the almond tree.

An unkempt head peered out of the door. "Sandra, want to read a poem?"

"Sure, Max," she murmured.

The poet stepped out. "I think we'll open the book with this poem, or maybe with 'Only a Madman,' I'm not sure." He handed her a short, neatly typed poem. "All the poems aren't written yet, so maybe the perfect opening poem is en route even as we speak. It may arrive in the next moment."

She smiled up at him and read the poem. She sat with

33

it. Closed her eyes and let it enter her. She tilted the page slightly so that the words blurred, examined the shape it formed, read it again. Max was pretending to examine the almond tree. "It's wonderful, Max. I remember that donkey. In Karavas, right? Would you read it to me?"

Max took back the poem, righted himself, took a breath. For some, for many, the only way to receive his poems was through his voice. He naturally spoke from deep in his diaphragm—a resonant timbre—untrained, imperfect, but potent, able to push a whisper far out beyond itself—investing the work with a cadence and diction that too often the page did not reveal, a failing he hadn't come to terms with. He had announced himself to Briseis with that voice years ago. At a group reading in Portland's O'Bryant Square, he had thundered out great rhythmic incantations to whales, women, and the disenfranchised over an African drum, as loud as the saxophone he punctuated each piece with. It wasn't instant enrapturement, but he became part of her that afternoon, though it took years to realize.

> *The cocks are busy with bragging,*
> *their boasts swirl in the*
> *afternoon wind.*
> *The eaves of the schoolhouse*
> *are hectic with swallows.*
> *The drone of a distant tractor*
> *putters in and the donkeys,*
> *thick with bugs, howl and bray,*
> *"Life is unfair,*
> *Life is unfair."*
> *Through the grape leaves*
> *the sky's blue burns.*

34

Sandra sighed, "That's just like it is. Did you write that today?"

"No, but I came across the notes and put it together today."

"I've got some good donkey images. Guess I should make sure I've got some chickens too. You add so much when you read it. Maybe we should enclose a cassette with the book?"

Max grinned and nodded. "Yeah, sometimes the poems aren't right on the page—only when I read them. Brie is helping me clean them up, to make them like I hear them."

"I'll never forget that donkey in Karavas, what an otherworldly noise."

"I'm hip. Those long two-in-the-morning screams, like some kind of cosmic orgasm that went on and on. The primal conception of the universe. Unbelievable."

Sandra shook with laughter.

"I mean, Meg Ryan, get outta here! Step aside for the deep donkey! The muthafucka is getting it on with celestial beings!"

The goat bells segued from a tinkle to a gurgling stream. Max leaned over the railing and looked down the street. A large herd of goats was coming up the hill. Lulu, out of a dead sleep, leapt to her feet and raced to the railing in full bark. Sandra grabbed her camera, and they watched the herd as the bells rose to a river's roar, which Lulu frantically competed with. Some of the she-goats, laden with milk, walked with their rear legs splayed, straddling their swollen udders. At the head of the herd a tall, beautiful girl in tight jeans and a loose blouse stretched her fine, muscled legs in a long shepherd's stride, casually swinging a small switch, not bothering to see if the goats were following. She shyly glanced up at the two foreigners and their hysterical dog for the briefest moment, and then quickly looked away.

"Ah," sighed Max, "shepherd girl. What a vision."

"Who is she?"

"The best our village has to offer, that's what. She's from a village way up in the mountains, Anavriti, but she and her family live here now. Isn't she exquisite? That face and eyes, that doe-like demeanor. The body. Ah. I keep thinking of my unmarried friends. This is what they need, a simple Greek country girl, all of sixteen. Probably comes with a nice preeka—twenty goats, a piece of land with some olive trees. Ready to pop out some babies, all the while attending to their every need. They could do worse. Hell, they couldn't do better."

"Which unmarried friends are you thinking of?"

"Well, that's the problem. I can't bear the idea of any of them putting their disgusting paws on our shepherd girl, the flower of our village." They watched the herd resound up the road. Lulu was running out of breath. "I mean, can you imagine turning Pro Benway loose on that unspoiled blossom?"

Sandra burst out laughing. "That *is* a vision. How's he doing?"

"After many years of really severe hardship, he's found himself a little niche in the computer software business. He's all right. Damn, look at that billy." Max pointed to a large male that towered over the herd, great curved horns curling from his shaggy skull, his chin beard snarled and dripping. "Primal, these beasts."

"They're amazing." Sandra took several photos in quick succession. "Oh, look." The billy suddenly mounted a she-goat right in the midst of the flowing herd. He grunted

36

and rutted, standing now taller than a man, shaking his great head back and forth, while the nanny struggled to keep her feet and bleated. The shepherd girl's mother, a thick troll of a woman following the herd, looked up at them with a grin, shrugged with her shoulders and arms to say, 'tee nah kahnameh, *what can you do?* and walked on, chuckling. The billy dismounted, snorted, and slowly moved up the hill after the herd, followed by the freshly fertilized nanny.

"The lust of the goat, as Blake so astutely put it, truly it is the bounty of god," Max said reverently. They leaned over the railing to watch as the herd disappeared around a small church up the road, leaving a trail of pellets. The bells faded to a trickle. The living power of the herd, musty and fecund, hung in the air.

"They're wonderful creatures," enthused Sandra.

"Yeah, and wait till we show you a wild herd, they're positively prehistoric." He reached down and stroked the dog. "Lulu, okay, enough, for god's sake. You frightened those goats something awful. You ready for walkies?" She reared up on her hind legs and tried to dance.

"Looks like it. And so am I," said Sandra.

"Great, I'll go get the kids."

They took a road that wound down through the village. "Strati lives here, the guy who runs the taverna. His wife had a stroke a while back, that's probably why he looks like a walking ulcer. Munches Zantac like it was candy. The house behind him is the stonemason's place. *His* wife is a religious nut. This shack over here is Theofiloyiannakos, which means 'little Yianni the friend of God.' Brie tried to teach the kids—hopeless, dense as fucking stones. The father is a gravedigger, and the mother ran off with some

37

guy in Sparti." Leo and Maki and Lulu raced far ahead
while Sandra and Max examined a donkey tied to a tree
next to the road. "Not quite so big as a horse, huh?"

Sandra backed up several steps and took a couple of
shots. "Have you ever thought of having one?"

"I'd love one. I'd ride it all over the hills. But we're not
in the position to get any more animals right now. This
next house is the tone-deaf cantor's. You've heard him on
Sunday. Incredible. What a noise. Just goes to show ya—
having the spirit, which he has, ain't enough. God forgot
to give him an ear. He and his brother owned the first
piece of property we bought. They're from the generation
that came of age during the war and the civil war that
followed, consequently they got little or no schooling.
When we were giving them a down payment, we handed
them two hundred and fifty thousand in five-thousand-
drachma notes, which he dutifully counted out, one, two,
three . . . When he got to fifty he looked up and asked, *Is
that right?* No way could he do the math, all he could do
was count. There are a lot of people in the hills who never
got a chance to learn the basics."

"Nobody in the States knows about the Greek Civil
War."

"Yeah, the nationalists won because the Americans
came in and made sure they won. Probably a good thing,
too. If the communists had won, Greece would be like
Bulgaria or Romania now. The Greeks wouldn't have
had any more success with Communism than any of these
other countries."

"What's this place?" Sandra pointed to the last house
in the village, an oddly shaped modern affair surrounded
by extensive vegetable gardens and innumerable fruit
trees.

"Oh, that's Miltiades's place. He grows all his own food. A pretty interesting dude. Wait, look, here he comes up the path." A short, very thin man with long, flowing gray hair and beard, carrying a long staff and dressed in loose white clothing, came slowly toward them. He smiled broadly, raised his hand, and said, "Yasou, Max mou. Ti kanis?"

"Kala, Miltiadi, kala." Max gestured to Sandra. "E filee mou, Sandra."

The man smiled, nodding, "Welcome to Greece, my child. It is a great pleasure to meet you."

"Hi. Kali mera." Sandra gave the universal sorry-I-don't-speak-your-language shrug, which, accompanied by her smile, was quite enough. They said goodbye and moved off.

"He was a shoemaker in Athens for something like forty years, and then he dropped out and came down here. His wife refused to come so he lives alone."

"A hermit kinda guy, huh?"

"Yeah, and he really looks the part. Like the Second Coming or something."

They stopped on a bluff above the Tripi canyon, where the land drops off steeply two hundred feet to the river. The north side of the gorge is carved into terracing for olives, the steeper south bank tangled with wild vegetation. A great rock spur thrusts out from the hillside, exposing a sheer face several hundred feet high with the village of Tripi perched atop. Above that Lazineekos rises gray green toward the blue. A narrow band of the valley floor had been cleared and, irrigated by the river, was covered with the vivid green of orange orchards, a color that rose dark and heavy against the glittering dusty sage of the olives. The breeze turned the leaves, flashing their silver underside, a visual tinkle perfectly tuned to the bells of a small goat herd working the hillside far up the valley. The afternoon air grew a hazy opaline glow, as through a gauze screen. The ghosts of Greece rose with the heat of day, their spirits inflating and blurring the afternoon light.

Max pointed up the valley and said, "The Spartan army used to march through here double-time up over the mountains to Messenia to put down revolts. Imagine. I wonder where the path was? Did they chop one out of the hills, or did it follow the river bed?"

The Greek landscape speaks a human language. There is a sound in the land, in *this* place on the planet where the meeting of sky and earth is clean and sharp. We recognize the sound, it is deeply familiar. We know the cadences in our blood, but more than that, there is an identification at the level of consciousness, right there where you make connections and forge your tools in the fires of culture. They looked west up the gorge to where it doglegged to the left. A massif of rock, Messoracchi, towered some three thousand vertical feet above. On their left, the south side, a small road traversed the flank of the mountain.

"Isn't that the road to Kalamata?"

"Yeah. We should take that drive again. It's a dramatic stretch of road."

The bell in the tower at the Tripi church tolled four times as they started down the steep trail. Water and stone, stone and water and air clashed and splashed and produced a constant shushing breath of blue-white noise that cooled the visual field before their flesh tasted its refreshment. The river's rush was eating the sound of the children and dog who shouted and barked. In the thick of its roar, in the churn of its whooshing echo, their mammal sounds pierced brief holes in the dense water music.

Along the river towered a variety of oak, maple, and plane. Just above the water beneath a stand of cypress stood a tiny, white-washed church, big enough for perhaps a dozen of the faithful. Max peered in the dark at the ikon. "I don't know, Agios Souzon, it looks like. Never heard of him. But somebody has. Most of these little churches are built by individuals manifesting their faith or assuaging their guilt or whatever. I wonder what Saint Souzon did. Probably a martyr. So many of them are. I mean, big deal, so you get yourself killed." Sandra laughed, propping open the door and small window shutter of the church to take a couple of low-light shots. Lulu trotted into the church closely followed by Andromache. "What's keeping you guys? Haven't you seen this church before?"

"Done now." Sandra slipped her camera into a pocket. "What are you doing?"

"Making boats. Come on."

The path from the church led right over the river. Only halfway across did you notice that you were on an old stone bridge that gracefully arched over the water. From below it was fully visible.

"Why do they call it the Turkish bridge?"

"It was built during the Turkish occupation, which makes it at least two hundred years old, and it could be a lot more than that. It's really nice, huh?"

"Beautiful. It's so much a part of the landscape, like an organic thing. Who uses it?"

"Oh, shepherds, a few yia-yias on donkeys riding between the villages, the last few people around here who still walk."

They looked up at the rays of light that penetrated the

41

leafy canopy. The trunks of some trees were completely encased in ivy, giving them a thick green bulkiness. The light flashed off the river, off the stones and the dragonflies zipping above the rippled surface of the water. Lulu thrashed about in the shallow water snapping at insects.

"Okay, heads up, we're having a race!" Leo boomed from up the creek. Leo and Maki were crouched on the banks holding the bark boats they had fashioned, with little masts and leaves for sails. "You guys are the finish line." They released the boats, which swiftly bobbed toward the middle of the silver stream, and followed along cheering their respective craft. Sandra clicked off a couple of quick shots. Max grabbed Lulu by the collar as she was about to plunge in. The tiny boats wiggled through the spackled light.

Leo's boat caught in a back eddy. "Ah gahmoto, ella you stupid boat." He bent down to free it, but Maki shouted, "Hasta rei, ohee hehree, that's the rules!" Then Maki's caught on a branch, tipped over, and sank. "Tee? Yiatee? Gahmoto! Well, mine was ahead."

"Skase, Maki, mine is still floating."

"Yeah, way back there."

Max held up his hands, "All right, nobody's a winner, everybody's a winner." Lulu plunged in and sank Leo's boat. "They were great boats, though."

Leo shouted at the dog, "Lulu, you dumb dog, get outta there." The children ran upstream looking for materials for new boats.

Max and Sandra stood listening to the water, dazzled by the rare and delicate sunlight filtering through the trees. Max sang a snatch of Leonard Cohen:

    . . . and just when you mean to tell her

42

that you have no love to give her
she gets you on her wavelength
and she lets the river answer
that you've always been her lover.

Sandra received this in silence, luxuriating in the noise of the creek, thinking of all the years of knowing Max and the easy affection they shared.

"That's a great song. A great *poem,*" he said. "The only pop song included in the *Norton Anthology of Poetry.*"

"Really?"

"Yeah, but they don't have it exactly right. I mean, he sings it slightly differently. Maybe he approved the changes, for the page? Who knows?" He gestured with open palms, then slowly bent his head back till he was staring up through the trees. "October light filtered through alders and pine, ooouh, that's fine."

Sandra laughed. "Max, are you going to start rhyming now?"

"Maybe, who the hell knows? I just go with the flow."

The path up to Tripi started at an abandoned mill. Just the moss-covered walls remained. Much of the trail was crude stone stairs, and the vegetation made parts of it a dark, cool tunnel. After a vigorous climb of twenty minutes they emerged from the trees into the village. Old stone walls and buildings were scattered across the hillside, and the small path wandered up and down through them. Most courtyards had chickens and a dog, and Lulu soon had most of the village hounds howling in righteous indignation, even ones up-village that had only heard of the intruder. She ignored most of them, much to their dismay.

The trail ran by a rose-colored house without roof or floors, an empty row of arched openings for windows. They stopped to look. "The Germans burned this village to the ground. Every house except the informer's. Look at the plaster work, this must have been a pretty nice house. Look, there's where the fireplace was."

"They left the informer's house standing?"

"Yeah. What a wicked logic they used. But no one loves an informer. Most of the houses have been rebuilt. Like this one, the walls remained standing, so they'd just fill in with new floors and on up. This is why the village still looks old. And ya know, for the most part they do such a shitty job of rebuilding that the interiors look ancient already."

"What happened to the informer?"

"Throat cut, I imagine. Or tortured to death. If he was lucky, it was a bullet through the head. Leo, Maki! Wait up. Don't go up to the road without us. And hang onto Lulu!"

When they reached the children standing just below the road, Max pulled a leash out of his pocket and fastened it to the dog's collar. "Okay, now remember, this is the road to Kalamata, so there might be big trucks and buses and stuff like that, so don't screw around, stay on the shoulder."

Maki turned, "Daddy, why do they call it the shoulder?"

Leo turned around and Sandra grinned and said, "Yes, Daddy, why do they call it that?"

Max looked at their smiles, bordering on smirks, then at the road. He raised a hand and scratched his beard and then shrugged. "I don't know. I mean, you could invent a reason, the shoulders being to the side of the head, but we

44

don't call the road the head or the body or anything like that. So beats me. Maybe shoulder has another original meaning. What do they call it in Greek?"

Leo and Maki gave exaggerated palms-up shrugs. Click, and Sandra was already returning her camera to her pocket.

"We'll call that one *the don't-know-nothing twins go to Tripi*," Max cracked.

"Oh yeah, sure, Daddy. We know lots more Greek than you do," retorted Leo.

"Yeah, we left you behind *ages* ago," announced Maki, hands on hips.

Sandra was trying to contain her laughter as Max looked down at his sneering children. "Okay, okay. Is pravda. That's absolutely true, you guys know a great deal more Greek than I do. I'm glad about that. I depend on you two to help me out. So I'll retract the previous statement. We'll title that photo *the know-almost-everything twins go to Tripi..*"

"Right."

"That's better."

". . . *and don't get any ice cream.*"

"What??!!"

"Just kidding, just kidding. Come on, let's get going. And stay, for lack of a better word, on the shoulder."

Tripi rambles along the mountainside above and below the road, entire neighborhoods clinging to spurs jutting out over the ravine. Gardens have been planted on any vaguely horizontal ground. There is a lush, fertile feeling. At an outdoor taverna winding along a rock face, water poured out of stone spigots and rushed off down a trough. They cupped their hands and drank the fresh,

45

cold mountain water. Leo stuck his head under a spigot, then shook his head like a dog.

At the end of the village a sign reading "KEADAS" pointed toward a concrete staircase that ran straight up a very steep hill. By the time they reached the top, a small flat area before a sheer rock face, the adults were out of breath. Before them a great deep crack in the rock twisted up from where they stood a hundred feet or more. The opening at ground level wasn't much wider than a man. As Max and Sandra approached and peered into the chasm, a rush of shockingly cold air hit them and drove them back.

She shivered and asked, "They really left babies down there?"

"Yeah, that's what they say. The Spartans were something else. Fucking monsters."

"What was it? Girl babies?"

"The malformed, incomplete, and yeah, maybe excess girls. Warriors, that's all they wanted. And enough healthy females to produce warriors."

They stepped back up to the opening. "Why is this air so cold?"

"I guess it indicates how deep it goes. The legend says it connects with another tunnel down at the end of Mani. The cold feels like the spirits of the dead rushing out of the earth. Spirits who never had a chance, just born in the wrong place."

Sandra shivered again and stepped back just as the children, who had been climbing on the rocks, rushed up. Leo stepped into the hole. "Come, Daddy, we're going in, aren't we?"

"Sure. Sandra, you coming?"

"No, I think I'll pass. This is a very creepy place."

"Okay. Maki?"

" I've *been* down there. I'll stay up here with Sandra."

"You're a chicken, Maki."

"It doesn't go anywhere, Leo. What's the big deal?"

"We won't be long."

Sandra and Andromache moved away from the opening and sat on a rock in the sun. The child looked intently at her and asked, "Why did they put girl babies in there? What was wrong with those Spartans, anyway?"

Sandra reached out and touched a curling lock of Maki's hair, a great dark, curling mane that haloed a face remarkably like her father's. Max's eyes stared up at her. "I don't know. I don't know if they were truly evil people or if it was somehow necessary. To us, it's the most awful thing anyone could do. To us, children, babies, are the most precious things of all."

"How come you don't have any kids?"

Sandra sighed and smiled and stroked Maki's cheek. "I've never met anyone yet to have babies with. But I'd love to have a girl just like you."

"How come you haven't met anyone? You're beautiful. Anyway, what happened to that Roberto guy?"

"I don't see him anymore. To have a baby with someone, it has to be a very special person."

The child looked out across the canyon and then turned back. "I guess my Mom and Dad are lucky. They're special to each other."

Sandra bit her lip, leaned over, and embraced her. She kept hugging her, her eyes squeezed tight, till she was sure the tears had passed.

"Brrrrr, it's fucking cold down there."

47

"Where does it go?"

"You can only go about a hundred feet down the slope and then there's a rock slide that blocks it off. Last year I brought a friend who was visiting up here. Mo Bursts, you know him? Anyway, a Portland poet, and he really got into this place. He claimed that the whole thing was a human sacrifice, not just a disposal of the imperfect. That this cut in the rock is the cunt of earth. The Spartans were returning the babies to the earth, feeding them to Mother Earth. This is how he read the symbols. He went on to talk about death cults in Crete and said Christianity is basically a death cult too."

Maki jumped up on a rock and said, "Uncle Mo is weird."

Max laughed. "Yeah, of course he is, but he comes up with some pretty interesting shit sometimes. Another theory is that this was a myth created by the Spartans themselves, to scare their enemies. Psychological warfare. Others claim infanticide was common in ancient Greece. There's no record of large families." Max tilted his head and turned his palms toward the sky.

Sandra was staring across the ravine. She pointed to a small structure above a patch of green high above them on the opposite mountain. "What's that?"

"A shepherd's keep, can you believe it? Talk about isolation."

"How do they even get there?"

"Must be a trail, but you can't see anything from here."

"Daddy, it's time for ice cream!"

"You're right. I could use a beer myself. Come on." Max reached down and pulled Sandra to her feet. "We can take this trail here and avoid most of the steps."

Max leaned back in his chair, his feet on another, took a long drink of beer. "Oh, that's cold, mmm, beautiful." He reached out his empty hand and let the water from a stone spigot run over it. "Isn't this place great?"

Sandra sipped her beer, nodded dreamily, watched the children spooning their ice cream in. Max quickly sat back up, leaned on the table, and in a broad cockney accent said,

> *The man bent over his guitar,*
> *A shearsman of sorts. The day was green.*

Andromache looked up from her ice cream and quoted back,

> *They said, "You have a blue guitar,*
> *You do not play things as they are."*

Max came back,

> *The man replied, "Things as they are*
> *Are changed upon the blue guitar."*

Andromache, with Leo joining in,

> *And they said then, "But play, you must,*
> *A tune beyond us, yet ourselves,*
>
> *A tune upon the blue guitar*
> *Of things exactly as they are."*

Sandra clapped her hands. "Wonderful. Who wrote that? Did I hear you do that last time I was here?"

"Probably. That would be your Wallace Stevens guy there. I really like some of his. I taught that to the kids years ago, before they could read. We used to do a lot of other poems, but they've forgotten them, or claim to have, to avoid being embarrassed by their father even more than they already are. Oh, Blake, they still remember him. Ready for a little *Songs of Innocence*?"

Leo and Maki made puke faces and moaned, "Not here, Daddy!"

Max sighed. "They become more self-conscious by the moment. But Blake they'll never forget, because I sang it to them in the womb. Singing away to my little lambs."

"Daddy!"

"Okay, okay, I'm not going to sing, all right? Geesh, soon after they learn to walk they want to tell you how to act in public."

• •

"CHECKMATE, DOG BREATH."

Leonidas hit the living room table with his fist. "Gahmoto! I didn't see that!"

"Nah, you were looking to attack."

"Two more moves and you would have been begging for mercy."

"Talk is cheap, dude. Look, Leo, I'm gonna have a drink with Sandra, and then we can all play a game if you like."

"Great. Will you make popcorn?"

"Of course."

Sandra and Andromache were on the couch drawing a bouquet of wildflowers in a vase on a table before them. Max silently moved so as to see their work. His daughter's graphic abilities amazed him, and each time Sandra visited, her skills leapt dizzingly ahead. Leo could barely draw a stick man, but he was the one who had received Briseis's family's ear and way with music. It often sounded

50

like he was channeling his great-grandfather. Max loved the balance they struck.

"Andromache, it's beautiful."

"You think this is good? Look at Sandra's, it's fantastic."

It was. They were both using colored pencils, and Sandra had achieved exquisitely delicate effects, her flower petals translucent, leaves almost in motion.

"Are you guys about ready to take a break?"

Radiant, Sandra looked up and flashed her devastating smile. "Yeah, I don't think I can do any more with this now. Oh, Andromache, I like how you did the little blue flowers. That's just how they are." Maki beamed.

"How does a drink sound?"

"What are you having?"

"Ouzo."

"Mmm, yes, I'd love one."

"Let's have it on the front balcony. We can look at the moon. Maki, when we're through taking a break we'll all play a game together, okay?"

"Clue?!"

"Mister Parnell with the ouzo bottle on the balcony. Sure, if that's the one you want."

Max brought a tray with a pitcher of chilled water, glasses, a bowl of ice, a bottle of Barbayianni, a bowl of pistachios salted in their shells, another of last year's olives black and shiny with oil. Briseis had turned him into a gracious host by the deep enchantment of her style and grace. Everyone relaxed when she entered a room. Things would be taken care of. Max had paid attention. He placed it on an old metal café table.

"Oh, how nice. Mmmm, pistachios don't taste the

same anywhere else in the world."

"These are from Aegina, which is famous for its pistachios. Something about the brittle combination of wind and sun." He poured the drinks. They watched the ouzo cloud when the water was added. "Well, cheers. Here's to the moon." They looked up into the bright second-quarter sphere above them. A bat darted by. The aniseed liquor settled in their mouths, filled their heads.

"Max, I so enjoy your children. They're so much fun."

"Well, they love you. They really do. And, you know, it's great for them to be around you. It expands their sense of the possibilities of life. Greek society is so limited. There's a distinct lack of imagination and fear of risks. They have us, of course, but you give them a lot."

Sandra turned to Max. "If even a little of that's true, I'm very happy." She leaned her head back to rest against the old plaster wall. Being with Max was like a seduction. Not for sex, but for some deeper bond of friendship. He wanted her inside the family. He reached out his hand to pull her in. There was no way to resist.

As though from box seats at the theater, they watched the waiters from the taverna set up tables in the platea. Two teenage girls slowly swung back and forth on the swings, talking. The clacking of the cicadas had faded, the ringing of the crickets seeped into the air. They flung their spent pistachio shells off the balcony into the street; when a car went by you could hear them crack and crush beneath the tires. The castle at Mystras was a distant darkness, and the lights of Tripi twinkled against the mountain. They talked in murmurs, half-sentences, suggestion. Max freshened their ouzos.

"What's moon in Greek?"

52

"O feggari. Which is okay, but I prefer the Latin, luna. It's practically onomatopoetic. And, you've got lunacy, moon-madness. Moon is a good word for it, too. You've got that *ooo* sound, which mimics the shape."

Leonidas appeared at his father's shoulder. "Daddy, we're ready."

The adults straightened up in their chairs. "Sandra, I think there is a mystery to solve. Will you help?"

"Gladly."

Briseis returned home to laughter, popcorn, and pseudo-French.

"I believe eet ees Mademoiselle Blanc avec zee candleholder in zee parlor. Voilà!"

She laughed. "Max, it's good to know there is a language you speak even worse than Greek."

"Ho ho, there are so many, how to keep track?"

DAY THREE

Birds and dawn light, the bisection of makes a point of waking consciousness. Sandra breathed in the smells of the village. Grass and dung, mulberry and grape. A donkey in the street clopped by. She rolled onto her back and stared up at the wood plank ceiling so far away, dark, stained with age, as though someone had hurled wine up against it. It was the saloni, with tall windowed doors that opened onto the small front balcony. Tall windows, deep in the three-foot-thick stone walls, flanked the doors. Briseis had given the plastered walls a very pale rose wash. It cooled the light. It was always dawn in this room.

She realized, of a sudden, that she was completely awake. The day was a vibration that had entered her body perfectly attuned by dream. She had shed the dirt of travel. It was a morning for work. She glanced at the desk where her cameras lay and in a moment pulled back the thin covers and sat up. To photograph in Greece, one needed to rise early. By ten it was far too bright, and every image burned. She took her brush and began on her hair, short strokes growing longer. Untangled, she quickly braided it to a single rope down her back, pulled on trousers, a lightweight blouse, slipped into her sandals, and walked out and down to the bathroom.

Max had floored the bathroom in small colored stones he had collected from their travels in Greece. On the wall, dangling from a nail, hung a small, cheap plastic mirror. You had to take it off the nail and hold it up to use it. It was the only mirror in the house. Sandra laughed to think of it. This family and the house they lived in were a blend of aesthetics, sloppiness, and freedom. They all looked partially unkempt. The children were well dressed thanks to the generosity of their grandparents, but Briseis and Max wore an old collection of faded garments, all shirttails and sleeves rolled up, funny hats and wild scarves. They were clean but not particularly groomed. Bad haircuts. They didn't care. The role of eccentric foreigner fit so well, they'd never even bothered to consider it. Now that that was what they were, they found it a laugh. Sandra loved them for it. She was fastidious and precise in her appearance—her hair alone could take an hour a day, and her clothes were carefully selected—but she found her friends' lack of concern endearing, almost holy. She finished her toilet and went upstairs to the kitchen.

Max emerged from the kitchen and smiled with surprise to see her at the hiati table with cup of tea. She had been gazing down the valley, watching it transform with the rising sun.

"Kalimera, my dear. It's good to see you up."

She turned and smiled at him. "When I woke up this morning I was wide awake. Maybe it was the ouzo last night. I'm going to get out and shoot this morning. The light will be good, and you have to shoot early." She froze him with her smile.

"Great. I'm going to run into town early. Brie and I thought we could all go up to the Menalion before lunch. The kids are off at 12:30. It's just across the valley and a short hike."

"The Menalion?"

"It's a memorial to Helen. It's a nice site, the view is great. We'll drive down and pick up the kids as they get out of school."

55

"Sounds good. Just tell me when to be ready."

Leonidas walked out rubbing his eyes. He went to the railing, pulled out his penis, and pissed mightily between the bars. His father smacked his own forehead.

"Leo, show a little class, dude. I mean, Sandra's right here trying to enjoy her tea."

Leo looked over his shoulder. "Yeah, well, what has that got to do with me?" Andromache came out of the house and started down the stairs to the bathroom.

"See, your civilized sister is going down to use the bathroom."

"That's because she can't piss off the balcony."

"That's probably your big accomplishment for the day, Leo," called his sister up the stairs. Sandra and Max tried not to laugh.

Sandra followed a path that wound up through the village. She carried two cameras, a Nikon FE with black and white film and a small Olympus with color. She came upon a small stone hut with a sagging tile roof and three comical hay bales out front. She crouched and shot. The immediacy of photography excited her. Painting was slow and laborious—that was part of its appeal. A crude hoe and battered shovel against a stone wall were next, and then a bell hung from a rough beam jutting out of a chapel wall. It felt like the nineteenth century, or older. What had changed? If you framed correctly, the power lines weren't there. A donkey stood tied to an olive tree. Two goat kids, little horns budding from their skulls, butted heads and bounded along a rocky hillside, perfectly agile, beyond balance.

A tiny crone in black with a huge bundle of sticks on her back was coming down the hill. Sandra stepped off the path to make room. She wanted to shoot but knew better. The woman grunted past with a flicker of a glance. *A woman Sandra's age, alone, dressed as she was, it made no sense. Had she no shame? Where was her husband, her children? Where were her goats?* Sandra snapped off a picture of the receding figure, obscured by her burden. A vast, bouncing faggot with legs swaying down the path.

Chickens wandered up. She caught a rooster in full neck-craning crow, beak open wide, comb and wattle ashake. The greens were so vivid, everything glowed against them. Ants marched across the path in unending streams. She wandered between small stone houses clustered on a ridge, stones underfoot, stopped, and noticed that the stones formed a wide circle. The sun baked down on her naked arms. It grew warmer by the minute, the cicadas beginning to rattle and crack. It was an old threshing circle. Max had told her there were several in the village, always on hilltops or ridges, to utilize the wind. Disused, no one grew grain anymore. Slowly she moved to the circumference and walked the edge. Weeds were growing up between the stones, but none had been removed. So much of the Greek countryside was a process of cannibalization. Each era tore apart the previous to build anew, and each step along the way was a decline. Village houses only a hundred years old were crumbling, dilapidated, faux ancient. The children had left for the city, for Australia, for liquor stores in Chicago. The men were breaking down with the houses. The women donkeyed on, bent, indestructible. Bitter.

Vegetation burst from every crack in the pavement, every gap between stones, the gestures of man as nothing to the vegetable kingdom. Two women in a courtyard fell silent and watched her pass. A ragged sway-backed dog

57

swung wide around her. She heard what sounded like a chant far below in the village and stopped to listen, but she couldn't make it out, a grunting sort of thing, growing fainter. She was in the orchards now, each tree twisted and gnarled in a different way. Women dancing, men fighting, movement and struggle, the silver under-leaves flashed with the light wind. The whole orchard was quivering, slashed and strewn in shadow. The tall dry grass broke and cracked underfoot.

This was Max and Briseis's orchard. She looked for where they had paced off the site of their future house, stood there and looked out. It was the highest part of the ridge. You could see out over the orchards to the valley below, to the castle at Mystras, the mountains looming overhead. A perfect place, a sanctuary. They had found it and bought it. She found herself grinning over their success. A beautiful house would rise where she stood, she had no doubt. A large raptor soared over her. She instinctively brought her camera up, sighted but did not shoot. The wrong lens, the result would have revealed nothing.

She spied a distant car on the road to Kalamata. A jay shraaked and flashed in the olives. As soon as you stood still, the orchards came alive with motion. Birds and wind moved in the trees and grass, insects bounced between vegetations, the air itself was vibrating. She inhaled deeply, filling her head with the sharp, dry, cracking scents of the October hills, thyme and sage and fennel and others impossible to identify. The great sensory impact of the earth pushed the noise of mind away. She saw and shot, or didn't, moved or stayed still, just another living thing swaying on the surface of the planet. She stopped looking and raised her head to the mountain that hovered above her, Lazineekos, and let the sun and wind and mountain enter her, vivid, hot, fertile, with a tugging gravitation that pulled her into the middle of herself.

She heard a sharp cry, then another, and came conscious again, rubbing her hands on her thighs, lips parted, utterly filled and empty, dizzy. She craned her neck back to see. Barely moving their wings, two hawks scribed great circles over the hills, cried back and forth, bisected the other's arc, scoured the countryside for prey. She watched until they rotated over a ridge and sank from view.

• •

WIELDING A STICK AS A SWORD, Leonidas ran ahead whacking off the dried heads of asphodel, shouting and grunting with the effort. "Eeeeyah!" Stalks cracked and shattered. Seed scattered in the breeze. Sandra and Max watched amused and followed him up the trail.

"He loves smacking and smashing things."

Sandra laughed. "The warrior in him."

"*The warrior.*" Max saw vividly before him the warfare of his youth. With guns and swords and clods of dirt the battles raged over fences and hedges, fields and forest. "Jesus, I don't know. I was the same way. More so, really. But our kids really beg the question, are we ruled by hormones, by chemistry? Look at these two: identical ages and parents, raised as equally as possible, and Leonidas is swinging a sword and Andromache is gathering flowers with her mom." They turned and watched Briseis and daughter bending together over a clump of wildflowers. Below, the Evrotas River, much diminished after a very dry summer, flashed in the sun as it wound through the deep green orange orchards clustered to it. Beyond that, the

59

white and gray sprawl of Sparti. Sandra pulled a camera out of her shoulder bag. "Think of the culture they're in," he went on. "They get Homer at school, even at this age, a simplified version, and what is it, guys fighting—over women, among other things. In the opening of the *Iliad*, Achilles is in a snit 'cause Agamemnon has pulled rank and snatched his babe—whose name was Briseis, as you know."

Sandra, in a crouch, framed and took a shot and rose, closing her camera, shaking the hair from her face. Flash of auburn, copper. "Well, it's not as though Andromache is a shrinking violet," she said. "She certainly holds her own with Leonidas."

"With ease. It's just odd to watch them manifest so many boy-girl stereotypes when we've so scrupulously tried to avoid them. But I suppose they naturally take their lead from the same-sex parent."

"Max, they're the most wonderful, beautiful children I've ever been around. They're so bright and alert and open. You and Briseis are doing a fabulous job. If I ever have a child, I'll use you two as role models." She shifted her head and looked west across the valley. He gazed at her profile, the fine nose and lips.

"Daddy, look, look at this amazing beetle we found." Andromache held out a dried stalk with a brilliant emerald scarab beetle clinging to it.

"Fantastic. What are you going to do with it?"

"Let it go, I guess. But first I'll show it Eleni's temple."

"Andromache, hold still and I'll take a picture of it."

The Spartans' temple to Helen, a pyramid of cut stone, sat on a promontory. To the west across the valley, Tayegetos was in full view, a great range of thrust rock in myriad tones of gray and green heaving down from the north and continuing south to the sea. A switchback road to Anavriti crawls up its flank. Max and the children scrambled to the top, Briseis slowly followed, Sandra walked along the base, cameras in hand, looking.

"Daddy, is this really Eleni's tomb?" Andromache asked. Leonidas turned for the answer.

"Well," Max said, "nobody really knows. Anyway, it's not a tomb, it's a memorial built many hundreds of years after Helen and Menelaus and the Trojan War. The Spartans built it in her memory, or so they say."

"Why did she run off with old Paris, anyway?"

"Well, he wasn't old, for one thing." Briseis dropped herself onto a stone. "He was very handsome, and women couldn't get enough of him. The dude was bad. I suspect he was a lot more fun than Menelaus. He was, like, the master of love. He was once chosen to decide which of the Olympian goddesses was the most beautiful. He chose Aphrodite, which was a big mistake."

"Ah, the goddess of love. Eros, what can you do?" Max held up his hands.

Briseis rolled her eyes. "She bribed him. She promised to make Helen fall in love with him."

"They *all* tried to bribe him. She promised him erotic love, the most beautiful woman in the world. He didn't give a damn about riches and power, wisdom and all that. He wanted the babe!"

Leonidas and Andromache sat perfectly still, watching and listening. They loved prompting these discussions.

"The babe?" Briseis gave him a sarcastic grin.

"Okay," Max retreated, "what they really were were a couple of incredibly vain rich people, although Paris knew what it was like to be poor, who were being manipulated by the gods, mostly just for their own amusement, 'cause life was so boring up on Olympus."

Click. "Hey, it sounds like I'm missing the mythology lecture."

"It's fast becoming a socio-economic mythology dialogue."

Briseis laughed. "Why would the Spartans build a temple to Helen after all the trouble she caused?"

"It was her desirability. Paris steals her, and then the Trojans fight to the death to keep her; this only confirms what they already knew—she was the most desirable, beautiful woman in the world, and that was worth anything, the lives of thousands, the destruction of nations. As far as her running away, eh, that was the gods fucking around. Who is master of their fate, anyway?" Max noticed their intense attention. "So what do you think was on top of this thing?"

"A statue!" the kids cried. "A really big one. Gold, so you could see it shine from far away!"

"That would be nice. Who would make it?"

"Phidias," shouted Andromache.

"Praxiteles," shouted Leonidas.

Briseis grinned at Sandra. "They get a lot of this in school, plus we take them to all the sites."

"Giacometti! One of those skinny vertical figures maybe forty feet high. Like a lightning rod."

"Or a radio tower."

"Yeah, but it would be sending out visual waves." Max gestured with both hands out over the Lakonian plain below them.

A breeze picked up, cooled them, and each focused on a different aspect of the vast panorama before them--- an ocean of orchards, villages scattered like islands across it, the mountains a chiseled mass of peaks and ranges, a muscle of earth flexed and risen into the blue. They sat a moment in their communal silence and felt the site, reversed time and sat with the phantoms that inhabit every ancient site, every holy mound, and saw what they saw.

From the shrine they walked to a small church on an adjoining knoll. A path wound through the waist-high, golden grass. Cicadas rang and clacked. A goshawk's cry cut through the insect noise; they watched it slowly turn and disappear over a distant hill. The church was unlocked, and they entered quietly into the cool semi-darkness. Max dropped some drachma in the collection box, and he and Briseis and the kids lit candles for the dead, standing them upright in the sand below the candelabra. Max always lit one for a fallen friend—at forty-two, already so many— Briseis and the kids for her mother only months gone. Sandra studied an icon mounted on the screen. "What are these stamped tin symbols for. Here's an arm, a cow, a house. Look, and a baby. I've seen something similar in Mexico."

Briseis fingered a tin heart. "They're called tamata. You buy the appropriate image, depending on what needs healing or good luck, at special stores and bring them to the icon of the saint you're petitioning, say a prayer, and attach it. Like these. Or they can be thanks for prayers answered."

"They're wonderful." Sandra took several photos, black and white, color. She worked fast, with confidence. She had never *been* a photographer, but when her work evolved to mediums that required it, she found that all her artistic experience could be brought to bear through the lens. It was a quick way to gather images in the field,

63

materials to work with later. They would evolve when she applied her hands. The three adults gathered closely to examine the tamata. "Would you take me to one of those stores?"

"Sure. I know a couple who run one," Briseis said.

"It's like express mail to God. How did that song go, something about *Get me Jesus on the line? Lord, I need me a new refrigerator. Could ya make it frost-free?* Actually, I don't see any appliance tamata. There's a cow, but there aren't any chickens. A chicken doesn't have the value. It isn't worth enough. Hell, the tamata itself is worth more than the chicken."

Briseis looked out a small arched window, thought of the death of her mother, and let her mind go with death. The sickness and death of wild birds goes unnoted. Where do they go? Only those caught by accident or cat, but where are the millions whose demise is unseen? Food. Their carrion energy flows through the unwinged and earthbound, sears their dreams with flight.

"Sandra, do you like this Byzantine style? The flat, two-dimensional effect?" Max gestured at the ikons.

"Yes, I do. A few years ago I probably wouldn't have, but now I think I understand how it works. You enter into them in a different way. They seem to speak beyond what they are."

"Yeah, Patrick Fermor devotes a whole chapter to this in *Mani.* He says they're not supposed to look like humans 'cause they're symbols of the abstract idea of God. Something like that, as though they were ideograms."

"Otherworldly," said Briseis, returning from her musing, "especially the eyes. It's strange how they look at you. I remember being afraid of them as a child. I thought maybe they could see into me. It tied in with my fear of my father. But when I grew older I began to understand them as stoic, timeless."

"Hey, girls aren't supposed to be back here," Leonidas's indignant voice rang from the nave.

"Oh yeah, sure, like you're *so* religious. God's probably a woman anyway." Andromache retorted.

"Nah, kids, God's a swallow."

"You mean something to drink?"

"I suppose if you were thirsty enough, but no, I mean the bird."

"A female bird, probably."

"The one who lays the egg of the world."

Max eased out onto the road and pointed the car toward Sparti. Briseis was seated next to him. Sandra, by popular request, was in the back between the children.

"Daddy, what are we having for lunch?"

"Pizza."

"Yea!"

"Ah, this is an easy crowd to please." Max began to sing: *"Fly me to the moon and let me play among the stars, try to see what's happening on Jupiter and Mars, in other words, lick my shlong, in other words, won't you make it long and . . ."*

"Max, that's not how it goes."

"I didn't think I recognized that verse."

"Sandra, you've never heard those lyrics? I think it's what ole Frank used to sing to Mia Farrow. Or was it Ava Gardner? The kid cleaning the pool?"

"Oh Max, for crying out loud."

• •

THE METAL GATE ONTO THE STREET RATTLED, and Lulu exploded in yowls and barks. "Ella, Max!" boomed up

65

from the street. Max pushed up from his deck chair and leaned over the railing. Yiorgos was grinning up at him. He thrust a huge jug up in the air and shouted, "Call off the dog, I've come with wine."

"Yiorgo! Of course you have!" He called Lulu, who reluctantly trotted up the stairs, allowing Yiorgos to bound through and up after her.

"Ti kanis, Max? I've come to see the beautiful Sandra and share my wine!" He banged the five-liter jug on the table. "And this is very good wine," he caressed the neck of the bottle, "I got it from the monks at Saint Argiris, the little monastery over in Parnona." He gestured toward the mountain range to the east across the valley. "They don't normally sell their wine, but I know the abbot." His eyes darted about the hiati, sucking everything in, wanting the attention of all, even the furniture. "I didn't see the car, but lights were on. Briseis must be in town teaching, eh?"

Yiorgos was heavy, ursine, and his presence more so. A dancing bear, he pranced about on the wooden floorboards. Leo and Maki peered out from the door to confirm the source of the noise. He hailed them, crouched, caressing, and began speaking rapidly to them in Greek. How was school? Was anything interesting? What had they done today? He loved to hear them speak, marveling at their Greek, at the purity of their speech in a few short years. He produced chocolates from a pocket and gave one to each. They smiled, thanked him, accepted tribute with a naïve grace. He tousled their hair as he stood up and turned, clapping his hands together, "So, where are the glasses? And food, we should have something to eat." He was in charge, eager for the night to begin.

Max had already fetched glasses. He placed them on the table and returned to the kitchen. Yiorgos poured out

66

three glasses of wine the color of peaches. He handed a glass to Sandra, who had come to the table. Yiorgos never sat in the deck chairs, they were too low, not conducive to leaping about. He raised his glass to his nose and inhaled deeply the heavy fruit bouquet. "Ah," he clicked glasses with Sandra, "Yamas." They drank. This was wine a full year in the barrel. It had a hint of musk and filled the mouth with a progression of flavors, berry, pear, hazelnut.

He pulled up a chair, sat down, motioned Sandra to do the same, lightly slapped the table, and asked, "So, when did you arrive? . . . Monday, yes, and from where? New York." He named the city with a reverence and paused to consider the great challenge of the metropolis, his ambition questioned for a moment. Max came out of the kitchen with a tray and began placing bowls and plates on the table. There was bread and cheese on a cutting board, olives swimming in oil, onions, garlic, figs. Yiorgos leaned forward and took it all in with joy. "Bravo, Max. Perfect, a peasant's feast." He grabbed an olive and popped it in his mouth while reaching for an onion that he deftly pealed and quartered.

"Have you got your musto yet?"

"In a couple of days. I'm soaking the barrel now."

Yiorgos explained to Sandra, "It's the raw grape juice from the press." He chopped the cheese into chunks and offered Sandra a piece on the end of the knife. "Hmm, that's a little late, but it should be okay." He tore off a piece of bread. "I've got a thousand kilos fermenting up in the village." He laughed. "Not all for me, of course. I'll sell two or three hundred kilos, give some away, eh." He grinned. "I won't run out."

"Yiorgo, this is excellent wine." Max refilled their glasses. "Oh, we want to take Sandra to a panayiri. Do you know of any in the next week?"

"A panayiri, hmm, let me think. You know, ten years ago I was mad for them. I'd go to two or three a week sometimes. All over the valley. And there were a few others like me. I'd see them over and over again. And they saw me, they knew. It was just for the excitement of the yortee. For each village it's a big event. There's a lot of energy," he raised one finger, "sexual energy. The young women are all dressed up, they come with their families. The men, the fathers, in the little mountain villages," he leapt to his feet, "they're proud of their women, but they don't want you to look too hard. So they shepherd the women in like this," he pantomimed the bowlegged walk of a village man. He had a huge head and a thick elastic face which he now screwed up in exaggerated pride. "They have the women in front of them and try to walk behind them all at the same time so you can't look at their asses!" The walk became ridiculous as he swayed and crab-walked about the hiati. Max spit out his wine laughing. "Then they decide to dance. You know, if a family dances then the patriarch has to tip the band. So they reach into their pockets like this, like they have so much money they can hardly get it out. You know how they are, they carry all their money in a great roll, and they peel off a five thousand drachma note and throw it at the band like it was nothing. Ha ha! But despite their fathers, the panayiris are a chance for the young women to show off a bit. And the young men are all looking." He became a tall, thin young man craning his neck to see over the crowd to the dancing. "And the bold ones get out there and dance." He sat down and poured himself a glass. Sandra and Max were still laughing.

"So is there a panayiri coming up anywhere?"

Yiorgos gestured with his glass. "Pardali. Not tomorrow, the next night, Friday." He pawed the top of his head. "It's a good one. They'll have a band, roast pig. It's Agios Stouzon day. I could go with you. Why not? I haven't danced in weeks." Sandra and Max happily settled back and let the show go on. He leapt from problems with the in-laws to his teaching to the history of his village that he was trying to write. "Look, you can see the lights of Krysafa from here." They looked across the valley at the lights of the village constellated against the greater darkness of the mountain. "Oh, look at the moon." Yiorgos rose out of his chair and went to the railing. The olive-covered hills glowed. "See how it changes the air." He waved his hand as though the light could be grasped, could be spun into strands of music. The crickets were louder now. At the platea car doors opened and closed. You could hear Yiorgos breathing deeply, he needed a lot of air.

A car came round the bend. "It's Briseis." Max was down the stairs and opening the gate before the car turned in. He kissed her, took her bags, and followed her up the stairs.

"I see, wouldn't you know," she exclaimed, "while I'm trying to hold the attention of hormone-ridden teenagers, others are making better use of the evening, drinking wine and eating meze." She popped an olive into her mouth. "Yasou Yiorgo, ti kanis?" They kissed each other on both cheeks.

Leo and Maki emerged from the house. "Hi, Mommy." They hugged her around the waist. Maki held up a paper. "Look at the drawing I did with Sandra." Briseis took it and held it to the light. "Andromache, this is fantastic. The best you've ever done! Sandra, you're an inspiration."

"Sandra showed me how to do this bit here so it's like three-dimensional.""It's wonderful, really." Briseis sat down at the table.

"Brie, would you like a glass of wine?"

"Okay, thanks, my love. Just a little."

"Mommy, you want to hear my new tune?" Leo had been upstaged enough.

"Sure sweetie. Are you going to play it now?"

Leonidas ran back into the house and returned seconds later carrying his clarinet. He readied himself. "This is called, 'Harlem Nocturne.'" He tapped his foot twice, and the famous opening phrase purred out into the night. It was stunning to hear a child play so soulfully. The adults applauded when he finished. He acknowledged them with a nod of his head.

"Oh Leo, that was beautiful. When did you learn that tune?"

"Today."

"Today? My children are brilliant." Briseis' smile warmed them all. "Have you guys bathed?"

Leo and Maki looked at each other and then the family turned in unison to Max.

"Ah, right. Douche the children, was that part of the program?"

"It's Wednesday night."

"Yes, yes, of course it is. Well, nobody looks like they're asleep yet. Leo, you're first. Get on down there. I'll find you some fresh jammies."

"Did Daddy remember to feed you guys?"

"Yeah, we had omelets and patates."

"Oooh, that sounds good."

Later, the children sleeping, Yiorgos gone down the hill, Max pecking out a late-night inspiration, Sandra and Briseis sprawled in the deck chairs luxuriating in the end of the evening. Across the street in the lights of the platea, bats were darting through clouds of bugs. A dog barked up-village. Lulu snored at their feet.

"Oh, what a full day. Hiking in the afternoon, teaching in the evening. I'm pooped."

"Yiorgos said there was a village festival we can go to."

"A panayiri? Where?"

"I don't remember the name of the village, in the hills somewhere. It's on Friday."

"Great. We can take the kids. They love panayiris." Briseis pushed her hair back and looked up at the moon. "What's that, about two or three days till full?"

"Max and Yiorgos said four. It feels like four."

Briseis turned to Sandra, "Does it? Are you that regular?"

"Clockwork."

"Well I'm sure your body clock is at least as accurate as those two, although in certain things, like the moon, they're usually spot on."

DAY FOUR

TOWERING PALM TREES marched down the center of Sparti, each rooted in a small green island centered in a broad boulevard of concrete and asphalt. The vast sidewalks were cluttered with orange trees, cafés, motorbikes, at every corner the kiosks' ever-swelling displays—ice cream boxes, refrigerators, magazine racks. And still there was room for the milling and flow. The mothers of Sparti were out shopping for lunch. They stopped and talked without sitting down. It was eleven. The cafés were filled with men of all ages, the retired, the working, and vast swathes of unemployed young men, paralyzed with ennui, whiling away the morning—there is no work, or none that suits them—too young for komboloy, worry beads, they twirl their keys and smoke. All will disappear by two o'clock to eat meals the women have prepared.

Sandra and Briseis leaned toward the smudged window of an old farmacio. Inside, an extraordinary jumble of cultural artifacts covered with dust served as a window display. There, labels faded by thirty years of afternoon sun, were antique sunglasses and orthopedic shoes, bottles of witch hazel and snakebite ointments, canes and hernia belts, ancient apothecary vials, a mortar and pestle, a stack of denture cream packages, and signs advertising hair bleach and depilation unguents.

"Why don't they change the display? Who would be interested in any of these things?"

"It's what the pharmacist put in when he first opened his shop. He's never changed it. If one of his children ever takes over, they'll remodel, but till then . . ."

"All these hair-removal creams. Is that a big thing here?"

"Oh, yes. Greeks are pretty hairy to begin with. The women, especially middle-class women of this generation, are really into it. These are an improvement over the older methods. They used to make a paste of lemon juice and sugar, and you'd spread it on your arms or legs and let it harden. Then they'd rip it off."

Sandra shivers. "Ooooo, that sounds awful." She points. "Those pink rhinestone sunglasses have come back into style several times since they've been in this window." She raised a camera and took a shot.

They moved on to a new-clothes store where they stood dumbfounded. "My god, those are the ugliest clothes I've ever seen!" Sandra turned to regard the street. "I don't see anyone actually wearing this stuff. Who buys it? Look at that dress. Mustard. Cheap hotdog mustard. And so much of it."

"Cheap, tarty clothes, that's what they wear when they dress up around here. Only they're not cheap. Look at these prices. That blouse, that horrid green thing there, is about a hundred and fifty dollars. Last year they all had the *Dynasty* look, with great cascading locks and stiletto heels. I'm not quite sure what this year's *style* is."

Sandra mused, "I'd say 1988 or so. About four years old, but stuff that wasn't nice then either."

Briseis nodded and they smiled at each other, secure that even when rigor mortis began to set in they would not be wearing anything displayed in the shops of Sparti. Their sense of fashion was individual. Briseis envied Sandra's style, her eye for how clothes work, the assemblage of materials and cut. Sandra's look was subtle, precise without being fussy; casual and elegant, with only

73

as much elegance as the situation required, to punctuate the moment. Just so. Briseis was hobbled by indecision and inexperience. And lack of money. Having been a mother for so long, facing needs greater than her own private desires, she had put off consideration of the subject. Now she was wearing clothes Sandra had given her, which fit perfectly. They were the same size, yet their bodies were very different. Sandra had a certain boyishness, a harder, leaner musculature, broader in the shoulder, narrower in the hips and waist. Briseis was delicate, rounder. Briseis stepped lightly, cautiously, Sandra with confidence and muscle, a full rotation through the ankle. She wore a long skirt she had made from fabric bought in Italy. Sunglassed against the late-morning sun, down the walk they moved in her clothes. She pushed her hair from her face and looked up at the palm trees. They stopped at the newsstand and examined the foreign press.

They entered a religious artifact cum wedding and baptism shop. Everywhere the articles of ritual were piled precipitously, so high they disappeared in the dark near the ceiling. A young couple greeted Briseis enthusiastically. They offered to order coffees from a nearby café, but the friends begged off. Could they see some tamata? The question drew quick looks. *Why did they want to petition God? As a cultural artifact? Eh, foreigners, what can you do?* A box was placed on the counter, full of tin tamata. There were hearts, horses, men, women, houses, Thank Yous, various appendages, goats, babies stamped into thin strips just smaller than a hand. Sandra held them between her fingers, rubbed her thumb over the imprinted images, chose a hand, an arm, a heart, a baby. She also bought a hundred candles for the wax. "It's for a technique I'm

74

using, encaustic, suspending pigment in beeswax. I like the effect it creates—an odd depth as though you're looking into something, as though the image is suspended in time, that the past and future of it are partly visible. It's hard to get wax of this purity in the States."

They walked across the bright expanse of the platea and up the street to a café. They chose a table under an awning stretched across the sidewalk, then walked through the café to the kitchen to see the gleeka. Baklava, galaktoboureeko. The sweets beckoned from the glass display case. A young man intently described each concoction, everything made right here.

Sandra pointed. "What's that thing that looks like shredded wheat?"

"Kataïfi. It's got nuts and syrup. It's very good."

They settled back at their table and waited for their order to be delivered.

"Max read me a new poem yesterday," Sandra said. "It was really good. He reads his work so well. Were you familiar with his poetry before you met him?" She tilted her head to the side, took a sip from her coffee, and a slight breeze lifted the hair around her face.

"You could say that Max summoned me with his poetry," Briseis replied. "If I hadn't been moved by it, if he hadn't made an impact, we would have had no history. There's something about public performance, it's not directed at you personally, you can enter into it in an anonymous way. You can pay attention without any self-consciousness. Especially if you don't know the performer. It's a funny thing.

"I first heard Max at a big public reading in Portland. We, this guy I was hanging out with, were really struck by

75

his reading. It was unique. We had never heard anyone perform their work so theatrically, with that big voice. And the poems he did that day were good, some of his best. So a couple of months later, we were putting together the fall poetry schedule for PSU, and we thought, why don't we have that guy who read with the saxophone? Liven things up a bit. We didn't know his name. It took me half a dozen phone calls to track him down. I was talking to poets I didn't know, saying, 'You know that poet with the saxophone?' They'd say, 'Oh yeah, Max Parnell. Maybe so and so knows where he is.'"

Sandra laughed, "Couldn't you just find him in the phone book?"

"Hardly. Anyway, I finally got ahold of him, and he said sure, especially when I told him we'd pay him. I needed a signed contract that day, I guess we had to file our budget or something, so I raced across town with a contract to where he was living."

" I'd been in New York for years by this time," Sandra said. "Was he living with someone?'

"Oh yes, Abby. She's very nice. We have a picture of the reading in the park. You can see Abby sitting in the middle of the square with Elaine, do you know her? She's a friend of Teri's?"

"Yes, I think I've met her."

"Way in the back of this photo you can see me and Isaac. I look frightful, wearing an old pair of jeans and wrinkly white T-shirt, hair not washed, not really thinking about it. So we chatted a little, and I asked for a photo for the poster, and he pulled out an envelope with maybe two dozen different photographs of himself reading, which I found incredibly vain. And then I left. That was it." She shrugged. "But I guess it wasn't really, because almost two years later, when I got together with Max, I was talking to my sister on the phone, she was here in Greece, and I mentioned that I was seeing this poet, and she immediately said, 'Oh, the one with the saxophone and the whale poems?' I had mentioned Max to her after the reading, and she had picked up something I wasn't even aware of. Elektra is amazingly intuitive, sometimes she can see the future. She should have been named Cassandra. The mythic Elektra is probably the least prescient character in the *Oresteia*. Her problem is that she relies on it way too much. She's only right some of the time. She's always going off half-cocked because she got a *feeling* about something. But she was right about this. Knew right away who I was talking about. Abby said, years later, that she saw this incredible energy between Max and me right from the start. I don't know, other people were seeing what we didn't see."

"How did the PSU reading go?"

"Fine. He had all sorts of musicians and multivoice pieces. It was a pretty small audience, though. The reading was boycotted by the English department."

"Boycotted? You're kidding."

"No, Max was not a favorite of the poetry establishment, and when they heard he was going to read, they hit the roof. They wanted me to cancel his reading, but they had no authority over me so I ignored them. Professors actually told their students not to attend. Later, at an English department social event, this professor and poet, Carl Henry, came up to me and said, 'Really, Briseis, you didn't have to give him a reading just to get him into bed, did you?' What an asshole! This was two years before I got involved with Max."

"Maybe *everybody* could sense it," Sandra laughed.

"This explosive sexual energy."

Briseis laughed too. "I guess. We were meant to make our children." Foot traffic streamed past their sidewalk table. The European feel of the street, the sidewalk, people walking and talking. And Mediterranean, the pace human, made for contact. To speak was to come into real physical intimacy. A kiss, a hand along an arm, in the hair, solid on the neck. Greeks are made to rub up against each other. The polis, the village, they invented it. All piled on top of each other, talking, complaining, arguing, cheating, forgiving. Girls walking arm in arm, men grabbing each other, tousling hair, hugging, kissing. At the cafés they sit close, breathing on each other, smoking, reaching out with a forefinger to brush a lock of hair from a companion's face. It is all to encourage intimacy, bonds, relationships melded like blood.

Sandra and Briseis leaned toward each other across the small round table cluttered with copper breekis, glasses of water, demitasse cups, gleeka.

"Look at that man coming up the street," Sandra whispered.

"Isn't he wonderful!" Briseis breathed back. "A shepherd, more than likely, or a farmer from a village deep in the mountains. Look how he walks."

The man strode, no, *swaggered* up the sidewalk, erect as a soldier. A great gray bristle barely controlled sprang from his head, mustaches that resembled the horns of a bull, long, thick, working muscles flowed from his neck over his shoulders and back down to his heavy forearms and battered hands clenched around great cloth sacks of dried beans and flour. The weight of the sacks tensed and defined his body. He was short, shorter than the women who watched, dressed in the old-style wool jacket of the countryside and stiff, shiny new jeans, rolled twice at the ankles to accommodate his stature. Bright blue eyes glowed from his dark, squinted face as he marched with his load through the tables crowding the sidewalk, enjoying being in town, nodding to strangers, and to Briseis and Sandra with a grin. They returned the smile, turning to watch him till he disappeared around a corner. They sighed together.

"Those guys, they still exist. Up there with their goats."

"The energy, the . . . the vigor, I guess you would say."

Briseis nodded. "Virility. It's so different from these middle-class wankers you see here in town." She waved her hand. "Their machismo is so phony and dull, but with these traditional men, you have a manly pride, their every gesture is exaggerated, bigger than life. They have an earthy sensuality. They're really fun. But they're a vanishing breed. Not that you'd actually want to be *married* to one."

"Or have one as a father."

"Amen. Some of those qualities you want, just not the whole package."

They took their time. The coffee was thick, the gleeka divine. A sugary syrup clung to their lips, they took it off with their tongues. Briseis asked about Roberto, Sandra's recently discarded lover, who had been with her on her last visit. "We stopped in Italy on the way back to the States, remember? Roberto's family lived right in the middle of Milano. Everything was so crowded, and that Italian family thing is *so* claustrophobic. Needless to say, I was not greeted with open arms by Mama. I guess I represented the States. If Roberto and I got married, he would never

79

return. Her desire to have him near outweighed wanting him married. But I'm only guessing, she didn't speak a word of English."

"You should always see a man with his mother," Briseis advised. "It's very revealing. I didn't with my first husband, and it was a huge mistake. Well, okay, the whole thing was a big mistake, but it's one I might not have made had I seen Sam with his mum. It was a very wicked relationship." Briseis expelled the memory with a great exhalation of air. "But I got Amalia out of it, so there's something positive."

"Absolutely," Sandra nodded. "How is Amalia?"

"Fine. She's twenty-two, beautiful, spent the summer working on Paros, having a fantastic time. I don't know what she's going to do this winter, but that's her business. The scene in Milano sounds like a nightmare."

"Roberto became *Italian man* in Italy, with all that implies. A peacock, a mama's boy expecting to be waited on. I don't speak any Italian, and I was having all these odd, silent, nodding encounters with various relatives, everyone grinning like idiots. There were endless aunts, uncles, cousins, I lost track."

"Mediterranean men all revert," Briseis said. "Especially after you marry them. There are a lot of foreign women here in Sparti who married these wonderful, romantic Greek guys only to see them transform into stereotypical Greek men. They're out constantly with their male friends, don't do anything around the house or with the children, and think they should be able to have affairs. What did they expect? Almost all of them are miserable, and most of them are stuck here. Or think they are."

"Why is that?"

80

"Mostly they are young and uneducated when they have these summer romances, and they become completely dependent financially. But mostly it's the kids. They can't take their children out of the country without the father's permission."

"Really? It sounds like Iran."

"It's not that different. Plus there is really nothing for them to go back to. They've been here for fifteen years. They'd be poor single mothers back in England or the States. And to get divorced and stay here is almost unheard of. So they stay and become Greek mothers, hanging onto their children."

Sandra gave a sigh of resignation. "I'd love to have a child, but I'm not interested in marriage. Not that I have anyone in mind."

Briseis hesitated on the edge of this new intimacy, unsure where Sandra wanted to go. "Have you tried to have one?"

"No." She looked down from a great height and then jumped with a rush. "I was pregnant by Paul once, a man I lived with in New York. We hadn't planned it, but when I discovered I was pregnant, I wanted to have the baby. Paul was awful. He didn't want a child, he was vehemently against it. I was sick the whole time. There wasn't anyone to help me. And then I miscarried. It was a very dark period, the beginning of the end of our relationship. I hadn't known how much I wanted it till then. It's a bit of a cliché, but after I miscarried I felt empty. And alone."

"Hello, Miss!" A small chorus of teenage girls suddenly clustered around the table with armloads of books and grinning faces, vital and bright, a great hormonal crush, eager for a world that wasn't ready for them.

"Hi, girls," exclaimed Briseis. "This is my friend

Sandra. She's an artist from San Francisco."

"Hi." In unison amidst much shifting and shuffling.

"Hi, are you students of Briseis?"

"Yes, we are." They beamed, giving the impression they were about to burst into song in praise of their favorite teacher.

Looking up into their beaming vigor, Briseis asked, "What time do I have you guys tonight?"

"Seven to nine. We'll see you then, Miss." The girls swirled away down the walk. One turned and said, "Nice meeting you."

Sandra smiled back and raised a hand.

"They're my favorite class. They work hard, but they're lots of fun, too. I told them you're an artist because I want to give them a sense of the possibilities. They don't just have to get married and have babies . . . which is an odd way to get back to what you were saying. I'm sorry, talk about a shift in mood." It was an unprecedented moment that she felt was about to drift off and vanish before they'd gone as far as they could in this sudden clear air.

Sandra waved her off. "What can you do? You're like Miss Brodie."

Briseis looked off dramatically and said, "That's because *I'm* in my prime." They laughed together, in the same book. One reads over the other's shoulder.

"That was years ago. I'm not wandering around saying, 'If only.' But I am thinking that if I'm going to have a child, it had better be pretty soon. Almost right away, really."

"What are you going to do?"

She looked off across the street and sighed. "I'll have to have one on my own. I've thought about it, and it's time. I'm ready. I wasn't before, but now I am."

"What sort of father are you looking for?"

Sandra laughed. "That's the hard part. I want certain qualities from that end. I'm not just going to buy sperm from a fertility company or something. I want to know what kind of genes I'm getting. But I don't want to wait around to see if I can find the right partner. I don't want to be married. I just need some good sperm."

"I suppose you'd want someone who's already fathered a child, so you can look at the product."

"That would be preferable."

"Do you have candidates?"

"Not really. It's an odd thing to do, you know, to consider the men you know as potential fathers of your child. Not as lovers but as producers of seed—this guy's really creative, this one's good-looking and healthy. It's not something I've ever done." She poked at the remains of her kataïfi. "You don't really know what you're going to get. There aren't any guarantees."

"That's for sure. You just pray you're lucky. If it's healthy, that's all that matters. But how are you going to approach this guy, whoever you decide on?"

"I don't know. It's *so awkward*. What do you say? He's presumably someone you know, someone you already have a relationship of some kind with, and *what do you say?* 'Excuse me, but I think you have all the qualities I want imparted to my child. Would you mind depositing a sperm sample at this clinic.'"

"Yeah, that's not how it's supposed to go, is it?"

"It's a detached, scientific approach, but what's the alternative? And women do it all the time now. Especially gay women, naturally."

"What if the father wants to be involved with the

child? What's his relationship going to be?"

"Exactly, there's that too. Is the whole thing going to involve a lot of negotiation and everything? It gets a bit depressing when you start factoring in all these things. I don't think it will happen."

They let the noontime heat work through them, students with backpacks flowing by their table. Briseis vaguely rocked in her chair, seeking a bridge, a way to gift the moment and return in kind, to cure Sandra's singularity. What could make the circle whole? Then there it was. She looked up with a grin and spoke without consideration. "Well, you can have some of Max's, if you want. You don't need any more proof than Leo and Maki." Her words hung in the small tight air they shared across the table. They both caught and held their breaths. The street had stilled as though captured in a photograph. Briseis was dizzy, giddy, as though she'd discovered and revealed a secret many years deep.

Sandra paused, utterly unprepared for such a gesture. She felt a glow coming up through her chest. Her face flushed. She looked down at the table and then up into Briseis's smiling face. The world beyond them was blurred, out of focus; they existed in a new realm, a zone of shimmering light, of radiant heat. Just above a whisper she replied, "I'm overwhelmed, that's, that's very generous of you. Max was just the type I was looking for. I mean, I'd actually thought about him, but I never would have been so presumptuous as to ask. I don't know what to say."

"Sure, I can be its auntie. Or its stepmother or something. The relationship would be rather complicated."

"That's for sure. But I wouldn't want twins."

"No, you wouldn't. But you don't have to worry about that. It's a maternal thing, though they call it fraternal. I dropped two eggs, and they both got fertilized. It doesn't have anything to do with what Max is producing. Of course he would have to approve. But I'm sure he'd be thrilled with the idea of fathering your child. Don't all men secretly want to father great hordes of children? They don't want to raise them, just claim them as theirs."

"But how would we do it? I don't imagine there are medical facilities that handle this sort of thing around here?"

"Oh, you don't need all that. I read about it in a book. All you need is a turkey baster. You know, like a giant eyedropper. You suck the stuff up. and then up she goes!" Briseis gestured with her hands, what could be simpler. "I've never actually done it, but apparently it works."

They laughed together at such an odd nervous pitch that people at tables near them turned and looked. The sudden realization that people at nearby tables might indeed understand English made them mock-wince like guilty schoolgirls.

Sandra leaned across the table and in a quieter voice asked, "Do you have one?"

"A baster? No. We'll have to shop around. It might be hard to find one." Briseis made a comical surreptitious face, and they both exhaled the intensity of the moment out, leaning back in their chairs, wondering.

Sunglasses back on, they looked up at the sun and then back down the street. The lunch-hour bustle was waning. People were settling their café bills and grabbing packages. The two of them were transformed and newly bonded with this change, their friendship on the verge of becoming something else. Was it possible? Could they actually move from easy companionship to the communal? Could it possibly be as easy as just deciding?

A squeal of brakes without a resulting crunch brought them erect in their chairs.

"Oh, look at the time, we'd better go. The kids must already be back from school. Max is making youvetsi. All we have to do is pick up bread. We'll get some 'dirty-old-man' bread on the way out of town."

They pulled up in front of a dilapidated storefront, a constant stream of people entering and exiting with loaves. Two men covered in flour were busy loading the ovens that open on the entry. There wasn't much room. Large woven baskets on the floor were piled with bread. An old, shabby, unshaven man stood at a small table by the door. They selected a loaf from the racks after giving it a squeeze test and handed the man the bread. He wet a finger with a stamp sponge, peeled a sheet of paper, and slowly wrapped up their purchase. Under his breath he kept up a constant muttering stream of commentary.

"How wonderful, it's still hot!" Sandra said, settling back in the car. "It smells fantastic. So that's the dirty old man."

"That's him."

"What was he saying?"

"It's sort of nonstop. Basically he's saying something like *Ah, pretty ladies, please squeeze my bread, oh you're so lovely I could eat you up.*"

"That's hilarious. He really is a dirty old man."

"Yes, and they say he has two wives."

"Really?"

• •

THE NIGHT COOLED SLOWLY. Max was naked, propped in bed with the collected Robert Creeley and a notebook, pen behind his ear, sheet vaguely covering him. Briseis climbed into bed wearing a bright pink T-shirt, balancing a cup of tsai tou vounou, mountain tea, settled back, and exhaled, "Ah, another day."

"A good one?"

"Mmmmm." She sipped and smiled to herself. Her smile widened so that eventually Max turned to ask, "Is that a smirking smile or an 'I have a secret' smile or what?"

Sipped more tea. "Oh, nothing. Just enjoying my tea." Smile continued.

Max chuckled. "I see. Good tea, huh?"

"Oh, very."

Max looked at his wife feigning profound interest in her tea and thought, two adult women in the house make a conspiracy. The chemistry changes, the ions in the air or something. The moon tugs harder on their lives. Then, thinking that's not bad, he wrote it in his notebook.

Briseis set her tea down, leaned over, and kissed him on the temple and then on the ear. He closed his eyes to luxuriate in the electricity her lips generated, trace the current down his neck and out across his chest. She knew. Leaning further she brought her lips to his stomach and brushed them along, rustling the hairs. "Max?"

"Yes?" Don't talk, he thought.

"Do you ever want more children?"

His eyes snapped open. "More children?"

She turned her head to him and laid it on his stomach, pushed her thick black hair out of the way. "Yes. I mean, I know you're not longing for more children, but do you ever think that having another child, producing another, would be a good thing?"

He looked down into her face, this moment unreadable.

87

"Are you, what, talking about reversing your tubal ligation? I mean, surely you're not thinking about bearing another child?"

Briseis grinned up at her husband, two steps behind. "No, of course not. My god, what a thought!" She continued to smile while scrutinizing him, reading the expressions that flashed across his face. She had him utterly baffled.

"Then, what?"

"Well . . . Sandra and I were talking today. She wants to have a child, and she knows her time is limited. So she's thinking about getting some sperm from a good donor and having one."

"Yes?"

"And so, I don't know what came over me, really, I mean, I didn't think about it, I just blurted it out and . . . offered her your sperm." She gave him an "oops" eyebrow-raise.

"How generous of you!" Max was smiling now.

Briseis sat up. "She said that she had already thought about it. Only in terms of who would be an good sperm donor. Aren't you flattered?"

"Uh, yeah, sure. And you assumed that I would say yes."

"Well, don't all men want to produce lots of children? Like a sheikh or something?"

"I don't know about that. But, think about it, what would my relationship with this child, my child, be? Are we Uncle Max and Auntie Brie?"

"Sure, wouldn't that be fun?"

"Yeah, but I would be this child's *father*. Wouldn't I want to *be* its father? Uncle isn't the same thing. Someday the child is going to want to know who its father is. How can I be its father when the child will live in a different country? What do we say to Leo and Maki?"

"It sounds complicated, but really, why should it be? Sandra wants to have a child this way, and why shouldn't she have sperm from someone she knows and loves? Think of it as donating to a sperm bank. You wouldn't know then. Sandra will take all the responsibility. She's going to raise the child herself."

"Okay. But think of this. We assume Sandra will be a wonderful mother. Caring, giving, enlightened. But what if she gets together with some guy that maybe we don't like so well, and now this guy is the child's stepfather, and maybe we don't approve of *his* child-raising technique. Eh?"

"I hadn't thought of that. But you can't control everything. The whole thing should be about Sandra having a healthy, happy baby. That's what she wants, and I think she should have it. *You* don't *have* to do it. She can find other sperm. It's just that, you're here, you've got healthy sperm, and she ovulates in three days."

"What? You mean you're talking about right now?"

"She's only here for another week, and then she'll be gone. It's not like you can beat off into an envelope and mail it to her."

"How would this go down?"

"You get a turkey baster."

"A turkey baster?"

"Yes. You know, the big tube with the ball at the end. Like an oversized eyedropper. You ejaculate, we suck it up and then blast it up Sandra! Ta dah! I've read about it in books. It apparently works."

"So you've got it all figured out." Max stared up at the distant ceiling. "It would be fun to see what the child looked like."

"Oh, it would be beautiful! Think of the hair."

"The hair, yes. But we don't have a turkey baster."

"No. That's a problem. I'll go around Sparti tomorrow and look for one. That is, if you agree to part with some of your precious seed."

A rush of thoughts and images flashed through his head, and then his mind was empty. He looked at his wife, whom he loved more than ever. She was sitting up staring at him with anticipation, and he let go. "Sure, what the hell."

"Oh good!" She leaned over him and kissed him deeply on the lips. He caressed her shoulders. She kissed his chest, his stomach, she kissed his now swollen penis that she gripped in her hand while circling the head with her tongue. She loved its shape and took it in her mouth, massaged the shaft with her lips, the head with the roof of her mouth. He was thick, big. She could only take so much but moved her head down and up till just the head was encircled. She slid off and ran her tongue down the ridged spine of it to his balls, licked them wet. Inhaled one and then the other. Max rolled his head back and forth, eyes closed, a gush of blood churned in his mind's eye. His hand found her bottom and slid down the forgiving crack to the wet lips and tendrils of flesh. She arched and moved. He inserted two fingers, curled them, extended. She thrust her butt backward, took both testicles in her mouth and rolled them like balls of candy. He worked his fingers into her mane. She slowly brought her mouth up to his, swung her leg over and, straddling, guided him into her. They groaned in unison. He kneaded her thighs, she began to rock. Slow. Rising up on her knees, coming down on him. She draped her arms on top of her head and rocked. He rubbed her nipples between thumbs and forefingers. Slow, they took it slow. They'd practiced. The old bed creaked, joined in. She gripped his hips with her thighs, rotated her weight from one to the other. He hung onto her heels, then whispered, "Turn around." She grinned, rose up, and without fully withdrawing turned around to face the foot of the bed. Thrust. Thrust her buttocks back on him and grunted low, her hands on her knees, fully penetrated. Max ran his hands up and down her spine, worked the small of her back. Laden with saliva he worked her anus with his thumb. She groaned anew. He pushed it in. He could feel his penis moving in her. Filled, utterly, she let go. Max followed.

DAY FIVE

THE MECHANICAL TRILL OF THE PHONE cut through the birdsong for a moment. Sandra heard Max having a brief conversation in Greek. He came out the kitchen door rubbing his hands in full bellow. "All right! That was the musto man. He's bringing it this afternoon. Which means I've got to gather wild herbs ahmehsos!"

"What are you talking about?"

"This is one of the secrets of Greek village wine. Two or three hours before the musto arrives, you douche the varrelli, the barrel, with a hot herbal concoction." Max was bounding about the hiati. "I've been soaking the varrelli to get it wet and swell up the wood so that it doesn't leak. What the hot herbal douche does is, first, it heats up the varrelli, which kick-starts the initial fermentation, and then, too, it disinfects and seasons the varrelli, imparts the taste of the country to the wine. Of course, everybody's herbal mix is different, making each wine unique." Max spread his hands out before him. "It's not like you really want to taste the herbs, mind you. I mean, it's wine. It has to be subtle, hints, whispers of . . . whatever. Whatever you find and cook up. Hey, you want to help?"

"I was hoping you'd ask."

"So basically, you just wander about looking at the vegetation, smelling it, tasting it, and if it seems like something that would work, gather it up. Be excessive. We can always reject it when we're throwing stuff in the pot." Sandra and Max worked their way along a hillside behind the house, bending and sniffing, stuffing vegetation into canvas bags. The early sun cast long shadows highlighting the greens and browns. "The herb we really don't want is sage. It's too strong and oily, although it would be a good disinfectant. But the rigani, oregano, is good enough for that." A dozen species of birds sang and squawked and chirped. They were in a clearing with brittle waist-high grass waving and crackling with the wind. "Oh, Sandra, right here last spring I watched tortoises mating.

"Really?"

"Yeah, this is the third time. It's supposed to be a rare sight. I was down in the garden, and I heard a thrashing around up here, so I came up to investigate. This last time I knew what it meant. What was different was, there were three of them, two males, bull turtles if you will, and one female. And the males were fighting over her. The way they fight is to ram each other. It's really ridiculous. They can't hurt each other, but they get up a little head of steam and just before they get to the other they pull their head in. Bang. It's pretty funny. The female was watching, waiting to see who's toughest. Once in a while one of the males would peel off and try to mount the female, but the other male would ram him off. Finally, one male tortoise established dominance by shoving the other one quite a ways away. Then he came back and mounted the female. Regular from-behind style. I don't know how he gets it in her, what with the shells and everything. But he does. He must get pretty long, I would think."

"Yeah. Maybe the female can sort of extend the opening or something?"

"Probably, yeah, I'll bet that's part of it. You can't really see, of course. Anyway, it's funny, they go on and on, like twenty-five, thirty minutes, with the male making all sorts of noise, grunting and groaning, sucking air for all he's worth."

"What about the female?"

"She's just sitting there taking it. No noise, nothing. Sort of, 'Tell me when it's over.'"

"Then what?"

"I think that's their only contact. They go off on their separate ways. Don't even look back. Eventually she lays a clutch of eggs. I don't know how many. I think she digs a little hole and puts them in. She doesn't have anything to do with the little ones. When they hatch they're on their own. They're reptiles, you know, ready to go."

"Not like mammals, huh?" Twirling a green feathery stalk, Sandra raised it to her nose. "This smells like fennel. Will that be good?"

"A little bit, sure."

"Max, did Briseis talk to you, you know, about, um, this is an awkward thing to say." She looked away.

Max stood up from where he'd been examining a plant like a man with a winning ticket, a born-again Mormon, sarcastic and loving. He relieved and embarrassed her with his smile. "Yes, she did."

"And."

"And why not," he laughed, "you're welcome to it. When I think about it, I can't think of anyone else I would share it with. Just you, Sandra. It will be a beautiful child."

She felt as though the sun had suddenly got much hotter, the glow of it on her. She wanted to go to Max, to embrace him, and yet held back, shy, awkward with this new intimacy. How would it all work out? It would be her child, and yes, it would be theirs. Max stepped toward her, reached out, and gave her shoulder a squeeze. He looked into her bag. "Oh, I think we have enough. There's one other ingredient we need called skeeno. It's a type of laurel. There's some farther up this ridge. Come on."

Max turned and began hiking briskly up the hill. Sandra stood and watched him, moving with vigor and assurance. He began to whistle. The father of her child.

Max got two big pots of water boiling and scattered the herbs they had gathered on the kitchen table as Briseis walked in. "Look at all this stuff. I wonder what it is?"

"Why don't you get your book and identify some of it?"

"Good idea. The water won't be ready for another ten minutes." He went off to find it.

"Sandra, I'm going into town for a few things, do you want to come? We could shop for a baster."

Sandra turned with a grin. "Will we have different colors to choose from?"

"We'll be lucky if we find one. I've never seen one in Sparti, in a shop or a home."

Max entered with his plant field guide. "I can't think of anything else that would work, though. You gotta get it up there a ways. I mean, we're designed to do it ourselves, aren't we? Or as they say down at the feed store, never up, never in. Har har."

The women turned and looked intently at Max, who picked up a sprig of mountain vegetation and flipped open his book. After a few moments, he looked up. "This is indeed skeeno. What it is is mastic. Isn't that what they made gum or glue from, once upon a time? And there's the liqueur from Chios, Mastica." The women were still staring at him. "Yes? What? You guys look like you're considering taking a sperm sample against me will or something. What are you going to do, hold me down and beat me off?" They grinned, waved, and walked out the door. Max thought of his note of the previous night concerning conspiracy and threw the skeeno into the pot.

Sandra and Briseis sipped their coffees. The platea stretched out before them, crisscrossed by lone shoppers lugging bags and the odd pair of backpacked schoolgirls holding hands. They had not found a baster, although they had looked in half a dozen shops. Briseis was annoyed, disappointed, frustrated to the point of shouting. "This is the way it is *so often here*! You can't get what you want. All the shops have the same stupid shit. Oh!"

Sandra, resigned, "It's part of living outside of America, isn't? In the States we're used to getting whatever we want whenever we want it. It teaches you something. It tones down your immediate-gratification impulse."

"Yes, that's true, and it's a good thing, to get away from that godawful 'pursuit of happiness.' Happiness, is it something you chase down? Only metaphorically. I guess you shop for it. What are we going to do?"

"Maybe it wasn't meant to happen?"

"I don't believe that. Why shouldn't you have a child, and why shouldn't you use Max's sperm?"

Sandra looked at her friend and loved her more than ever before. She wanted a baby, she wanted the dream of *this* child, made here and now in Greece. But the path was strewn with impediment, the limitations of culture—or rather, the commercial shortcomings. It came to her in a rush that it wasn't going to happen, and her eyes began to tear. Once again. She felt a rolling contraction in her pelvis. Her body wanted to speak. Briseis reached out and took her fingers in hers. Their hands rested on the table among the cups and water glasses, forks and plates. They looked at each other, nodded in recognition of what they knew and shared. Yet they couldn't quite speak it, they were not that bold. They had both, from childhood, learned to hold back, and now, as they advanced into middle age, wanted to shed these garments of invisibility and be seen. But by only a select few, certainly, those in the tribe whose blood they recognized.

Briseis straightened up. "We still have most of two days to come up with a solution. We just have to think and be creative. It's meant to happen, that's what I think."

Sandra grinned, looked down at their hands, in her head she could see rounded shapes. "I hope so. Very much."

"Right. We'll do it." Briseis sipped her coffee. "Mmm, they make yummy coffee here."

She looked out across the platea, her eyes out of focus, she was quickly far away. "The best cup of coffee I ever had was in France, in Lille, at the Hotel de la Paix. The Hotel of Peace. It was the first place we stopped when we left England on our way here."

They had bought an old VW Passat hatchback. It had right-hand drive, and they managed, just, to get all their belongings crammed in it, leaving enough room in the back seat for five-year-old Leonidas and Andromache to sit up, flanking a huge pile of clothing, toys, musical instruments. As they drove out of Uffington, Briseis's brother's village in the Midlands, second gear began to slip. Max could feel it but clenched his teeth in silence and drove on. Briseis and the children began to sing. He joined in.

The next day, having visited her grandfather's grave in Perry Green and spent the night with an uncle, they got behind schedule and careened into Ramsgate late for the ferry. Urged on by waving attendants, they raced across vast empty parking lots toward the fully loaded boat.

They were the last car on the ferry to Dunkirk. Next stop, France. To the Old World, nothing to declare but their love.

On board Briseis found a quiet corner to deal with her motion sickness while Max walked the decks with the children. At the rail he gave them the history of the battle of Dunkirk so vividly, almost choking with emotion, that the children froze and stared at their father in awe and fear. He knew everything, and it was important. They looked out at the sea, and there was the ragtag improvised flotilla of fishing boats and yachts that Churchill had summoned by radio, with rhetoric and passion and drunken bluster, to save the British army trapped on the beaches. Through the night, back and forth across the channel they went, filled to the rails with shivering, frightened soldiers who thought they had seen their last. The German army, due to unusual confusion in the high command, didn't attack, and the Brits got out and home. "So, kids, as you've seen, the English are an odd, rather uptight group, but one thing they are is tough. Plucky bastards, don't ya know, like junkyard dogs when cornered. Or at least, that's the British mythology, what they fiercely want to believe."

Briseis set her cup down. "We spent that first night in Lille. At the Hotel de La Paix. We were so excited. Everything was new and fascinating. Lille has a very fine Gothic cathedral. Max had never been in one, and walking in, he was stunned at the grandeur of the space— so huge, dark, empty, with shafts of light coming through the stained glass windows highlighting how amazing it was, the design and craft involved. The kids got into it too. They were too young to be bored, so if we were excited, they were excited. Although the most exciting event that day for Leonidas was discovering that the French had

98

Teenage Mutant Ninja Turtles too. Les Tortues Ninja. My French was rusty, but I managed, with gestures and bad grammar, to get us a nice omelet dinner in a classic bistro. Max was no help at all. Didn't even try to speak French. Leonidas, encouraged by his father, kept shouting for more cheese.

"The staff at the hotel noticed us hauling all our belongings in—we'd read not to leave anything in the car—and asked where we were headed. On our way to a new life in Greece. They sighed, 'Magnifique! Quelle merveille!' People could tell how much we were in love. That's how it seemed, anyway. The kids were cute with their little backpacks. Then people find out they are twins and go all gushy.

"In the morning we had a beautiful continental breakfast in a little room off the lobby, the bread hot and fresh, the butter a revelation, and the best cup of coffee ever. As we left the hotel, staggering down to the sidewalk with our possessions, the staff, two elegant young women who worked the desk, an older man who was the manager, and the woman who had served us breakfast, stood on the steps and waved to us, shouting, 'Bon Voyage! Bravo, go to your new life in love.' And even, 'Toujours l'amour!' Always love."

They sighed together. Why one woman and not the other. What are the fates thinking?

Lulu leapt to her feet and raced to the end of the hiati barking ferociously. Sandra got up from the table and went to see what the commotion was about. A pickup truck was stopped at the gate in front of the house, two rough-looking men looking up. Maki ran up shouting, "Shut up, Lulu!" punching the dog in the shoulders.

"Where's your father, my child?" shouted one of the men.

"Oh, it's the musto! Wait a minute, I'll come down and let you in." Briseis turned to Sandra, "Hold onto Lulu. I'll lock the gate so she can't get at them."

Leo walked out of the house playing a Gameboy. "What's happening?"

"It's the musto, Leo, I'm going to show them where the varelli is."

"Wait, I should do that."

"Too late." She ran down the stairs and opened the gate. After checking the barrel, the men dragged a long, thick hose into the cellar, hooked up a pump, and began pumping out the contents of several large plastic containers in the back of the truck. The musto splashed into the barrel, filling the dark room with a heady, intoxicating scent that, along with the dark men moving in the shadows, the hum of the pump, the gurgling roar of the fermenting musto plashing up the sides of the barrel, and Lulu angrily barking from above caused Sandra to stagger back into Max's arms as he entered the cellar.

"Gotcha! Wouldn't you know, I'm gone for five minutes and that's when they arrive." He released her, shook hands with one of the men, and moved to peer into the barrel or, rather, to breathe its contents. "Aaahhh, that's it, that's fucking it! Get back, Bacchus!" He turned, looking wilder than ever. "Is that the most amazingly potent smell that ever filled your nostrils?! Makes you want to dance or fuck or something. Hey, kids, have you tasted it yet? Leo, go get us some glasses from the kitchen, and be careful coming down the stairs."

"What's the extra for?" There were two ten-liter plastic containers full of musto next to the barrel.

100

"Once this stuff settles down, I'll top it up with this extra. Damn, it's really gurgling. I'll bet it sat around for a day or two, which means it has already started to cook, ferment, but it'll be okay. All right, Leo, tap us each a glass . . . slowly, that's it. Okay, yammas, ya'll"

"Yammas!" They clicked glasses and sipped the frothy musto.

"Hmm, sparkling grape juice."

"Yeah, that's it."

"So what do you do now?"

"I leave it open, just covered with a cloth for about two weeks. Every day I'll tap a bucket of it and pour it back in the top. This will agitate it, keep it going, get more air in there." He inhaled deeply. "It's great, isn't it? I love the patterns of life in the country. In the fall you make your wine, 'round Christmas you pick the olives, in the spring there's the garden and pruning of the olive trees." He rubbed his hand on the barrel. "Wine is a completely natural process. You squeeze the grapes, and that's it, it makes wine all by itself. You don't have to add anything. Of course, there are things you can add to clear it, to protect against contamination, but it's not needed."

Sandra took another sip. "Will this be retsina?"

He turned, "No. For that you make a little cheesecloth bag with pine resin in it and hang it in the barrel during this first process. I did it one year, but I prefer it pure."

• •

IN THE REMOTE MOUNTAIN VILLAGE OF PARDALI they pushed together two small tables on a raised area in front of the village store that afforded a view of the platea and south down the valley, the mountains purple in the twilight. Leo and Maki ran off to an adjoining playground

101

where the children of the village were gathered, and Max went to get wine. Sandra watched the children enter the playground. "They're certainly not shy, are they?"

Briseis turned, following her gaze. "No. They've had a lot of experience entering new situations. They're ready to adapt. And more importantly, they always have each other. I think that gives them strength."

"Do they speak English to each other?"

"No. Children don't want to appear strange or foreign, they want to fit in. As you've noticed, they speak Greek to each other much of the time. English is the language of the adults in their family. Their peer relationships are conducted in Greek." She looked toward the darkening mountains and sighed. "What a beautiful night. Here comes Max with the wine. Oh, and there's Yiorgos."

The men arrived together at the table.

Yiorgos rubbed his hands together. "Just in time."

A five-piece band was tuning up, tables were filling with locals and visitors. A church bell chimed the hour. Having filled everyone's glass, Yiorgos raised his, "To the evening."

"To the women."

They laughed. "Sure, to us."

Yiorgos leaned forward with his huge head. "So, you got your musto."

"Yeah, I have high hopes."

Briseis turned to Sandra. "Did you taste and smell it?"

"I've never smelled anything so rawly sensual."

"It's Dionysian. I practically swoon." Briseis held her hand up. "I mean it, I get dizzy, it has such primal sensuality. The harvest, the fermentation, the last heat of summer. You'd think, in wine-producing country, there would be more babies born in June than any other time."

Yiorgos looked wide-eyed at the women

"Yiorgo, it's not just men who feel it."

Yiorgos slapped the table. "You see, you see! That's just it! Katrina has no appreciation of it! She looks down on it as a peasant activity, a village hobby. But who's more of the village than her?!"

"Oh, I'm sure she appreciates it." Why was she saying that? "Yiorgo, there's another meaning for the word musto, must. There's a Hindi/Persian meaning: a dangerous frenzy in some male animals, elephants in particular, I believe. It comes from their word mast, which means intoxicated."

Max raised his glass. "Here's to dangerous frenzies."

"You're getting too old for that. I'd prefer paroxysms of benevolence."

"Ah."

A clarinet moaned over the crowd, and the band kicked in behind. A dozen villagers were soon dancing in a circle before the band. An elegant man in a suit with his equally flashy blonde wife entered the platea, a native son returning to show off his big-city success. He was immediately pulled into the circle of dancers and given the lead. He danced well and with spirit. As he led the dancers around, he extracted a five thousand drachma note from his jacket, and when he passed the band again slapped it on the sweaty forehead of the seated bouzouki player, where it adhered for the rest of the tune. Panache and flash, all the village knew of his return. They drank it in, with admiration and envy. He had built his parents a house too big, his Mercedes was too long, his wife too thin.

On a sheet of wax paper, the remains of two kilos of roast pork. They had eaten it with their hands and washed

103

it down with village wine straight from the barrel. The band, after a short dinner break, began a slow, mournful tune featuring the clarinet. Yiorgos pushed up from the table and announced, "I must dance." He walked out before the band, threw some money at them, and began, with his hands held up, a slow, turning solo dance. Max went, kneeled near him, and kept time with his hands.

"Oh, a zembekiko, bravo Yiorgo! Come on, Sandra, we're supposed to kneel by the dancer and keep time by clapping." They rose and knelt near Max. Andromache and Leonidas came from the playground and joined them. Yiorgos had the grace large, heavy men are often gifted with. His head hung down, eyes closed, while he improvised with the mood of his soul. He slapped the heel of his shoe, took a small leap, bent and touched the earth, all within the rhythm of the music.

"This is great. Why aren't others dancing?" Sandra whispered.

"Because Yiorgos has seized the moment so utterly."

"Opa, Yiorgo mou!" shouted Max.

Sweat glistened on his forehead while his steps became more eccentric. Yet it all fit, larger than life, as big as the village. And then he stopped, acknowledged the band with a nod, and walked back to their table. He had refreshed their glasses by the time they returned.

"Bravo, Yiorgo, that was beautiful! Very soulful." Briseis kissed him on the cheek.

He glowed. It was impossible to praise him too much. He wanted all the love and admiration they could muster. Leonidas held up his glass of Orange Fanta, "Yammas!" They laughed and clinked glasses. The band segued into an up-tempo tune, and the platea filled with dancers.

The moon, incomplete but huge, rose from behind the church, each roof tile luminously defined, the bell tower a holy event. Yiorgos, prompted, was relating country customs for bringing luck with pregnancy. "A lot of superstitions are to conceive male children. For instance, after the women have made up the bridal bed for the first night, they have a young boy roll on it, so that the bride will have a son. And when the bride crosses the threshold of the house, she has a pomegranate. She rubs the fruit along the portal, throws it to the floor, breaking it, then holds the door frame with both hands. You can't look at these things rationally, but the symbolism is obvious, the bright red, many-seeded pomegranate represents fertility, and the juice is blood, the blood of the virgin bride. They used to hang the bloody sheet out the window the next morning to prove the purity of the bride."

"What is it with virgins?"

"It's considered a guarantee of paternity."

"Which it isn't."

"This is the same culture, though, that considers a pregnant bride a good sign."

"Really? Why would that be?"

"Because it is a sure sign that the marriage will be fruitful. Traditionally, engagements, once made, were very rarely broken, and consequently, the couple was given a much freer rein after the engagement than during courtship, when they were constantly chaperoned." Briseis cocked her head to the music. "It's a kalamatianos. Come on, let's all dance." She grabbed Sandra's hand and pulled her up. "You too. It's easy, just watch me, or better yet, watch the kids. If you lose track, just fake it. That's what Max does."

"The story of my life."

The six of them formed a line, Andromache leading, and danced their way around the platea. Sandra's brilliant hair swirled in the moonlight. She found the step easy and glided along with the rest as they bounced between other lines of dancers. She had stepped into another life. With full vibrato, the singer was moaning out his tune from the back of his throat. The clarinetist wound a looping solo around the melody while the rest of the band beat out the time. It was a perfect moment. She was between Max and Briseis, his grip firm and warm, hers light and cool. She threw her head back and stared into the moon.

• •

"How's the musto?"

Max climbed into bed. "Oh, gurgling away. Full of life, really."

"Well, that was a fun night. The kids fell asleep in seconds. It was good to get out and dance."

"Yeah, it settles all the food and wine, wakes you up before you get sluggish." He stared up into the dark wood of the ceiling hearing the band again.

"I'm still disappointed about the turkey baster. Sparti is hopeless. I can't think of anything else to use. I mean, it has to be shot up there to have a chance."

"Too bad we can't just do it the old-fashioned way."

"Well, maybe we should."

They listened to the night, to the house in the night, to their breaths entering it all and whether they could follow the question, the sound of their asking. A barn owl called and again. Lulu answered. What do they understand of each other, two creatures alone in the night?

"How would that work?" Max asked.

"I don't know, I haven't thought it through."

"Perhaps the three of us, it should be the three of us, somehow."

"Yes. How so?"

"I could start with you. And then, just before I come, I could switch over."

Briseis inspected his face. "You like the idea of that, do you?"

"You're the one who brought it up."

"I asked a rhetorical question, you have swiftly moved to mechanics."

In a corner again. He was necessary but in the way. He kept missing things in his considerations. Max turned to his wife. "It wouldn't be a romantic situation, obviously, but that doesn't mean we couldn't have a laugh or two."

"It's like some kind of fantasy for you, isn't it?"

Max exhaled noisily through his nostrils. "Let's just let it slide. You looked for a baster and didn't find it. If Sandra's going to have a child, she's going to have to make it happen herself somewhere further down the road. It's too complicated."

Briseis sat up in bed, pulled her knees up, and rested her head on them. She was wearing a large t-shirt, one of his. Her feelings wouldn't stay put. Max was right, it was too complicated. Why was she so intent on helping Sandra have a baby? Was she a surrogate, so she could, vicariously, have one more? She couldn't put it together, but a deep need throbbed warmly in her chest. She took a deep breath. "I'll discuss it with her tomorrow, and if she says yes, and it's quite likely she won't, then we'll do it."

"Are you sure?"

"Yes, I am."

The owl called again. "What language has a word for *I want you to have?*"

DAY SIX

"E<small>AT UP, YOU GUYS</small>, you don't have much time. The bus is early."

Sandra watched the children shovel in the muesli. "So the bus that went up the hill a while ago is the one that will pick them up?"

"Yeah. It goes to Soustiani, turns around, and comes back, so we can always tell if it's on time. Except if it snowed in the mountains."

"Not likely today."

"For which we are eternally grateful. Okay, now grab your backpacks and beat feet."

Andromache stopped in the doorway, "What are we doing today, Daddy?"

"Today? I don't know. What do you mean?"

"Well, Sandra's here, so we'll probably do something different."

"Ah. We'll see. We don't have anything planned yet. Now run!" She sprinted down the stairs after her brother. "Leo, is the bus coming?"

"You'll never make it!"

Lulu barked after them, encouraging haste.

Briseis took a deep breath and set the stack of papers aside. Correcting compositions was her least favorite task, but she'd managed to finish them all. She leaned back against the bedstead and closed her eyes. Kyria Voula's rooster crowed, a dog up-village complained, someone was chopping wood, a heavy buzzing came from the bees working the grapes below the window. Despite her late morning drowsiness, there was a delicious electricity tingling through her limbs. Even her perpetually cold hands were warm. She felt like a child about to attempt a small act of bravery: jumping from a rock into the sea, taking off on a rope swing in the woods, traversing a log over a creek. She felt that loud.

Sandra was on the hiati reading. Briseis, from the kitchen called, "Sandra, how about elevenzees?"

"Oh, that's sounds nice. Need any help?"

"I've got it." She took the two-cup breeki off the hook, measured out two demitasses worth of water, fetched the Greek coffee from the fridge, and spooned it in along with sugar. She lit the burner and placed the breeki on the flame while stirring the contents. It soon bubbled to the top. She took it from the flame, allowed it to settle, brought it to a boil again, then poured evenly into the cups, making sure not to diminish the frothy foam. She arranged the tray: two glasses of cold water, the coffees, and a plate of koulouraki with a hint of anise from the local bakery. The ritual pleased her. Amidst the chaos and faux poverty of their lives, it provided a welcome elegance. She carried the tray out to the deck chairs.

"What are you reading?"

Sandra held up a book. "M.F.K. Fisher, *Serve It Forth*. I've never read her before, only about her. She has a unique personal style. The subject is food: eating, preparing, the people who do it, but it's all woven into a narrative, a memoir. There's no resemblance to a cookbook. It's more like an inspired travel book where food is the geography. I've never read anything like it."

"I like the sound of that. Let me read it after you."

They sipped their coffees Greek-style, noisily. Intimacy encloses itself, makes a magnetic field. They were the story and hummed with the rhythm of the village. Twenty-five, twenty-six, Briseis was counting to herself, waiting for the number to fall that would initiate her offer, for a magical number. A rune. Forty-two, their age stopped the sequence. Yes, forty-two, there was very little time left, and each moment must count. The odds stack up, the chances of life narrow, pass through the eye of a needle only to miss the target, fall short like fireworks aimed at the moon.

"Max and I talked last night." She was holding one hand tightly with the other.

"Yes?"

"I mean about the situation, the turkey baster."

"The turkey baster?" she laughed. "Can't have been a very long conversation."

"I mean, what to do. Maybe there's an alternative."

"Such as?"

"Well, the natural way."

Sandra felt her stomach twist, the coffee almost came back up her throat. "What are you talking about?"

The faster she talked the easier it might be. "I know this must sound really weird, and you know that Max and I aren't in any way kinky. Well, I'm not, Max probably would be in the right situation, has been, but that's not what this is about. It's about you getting pregnant, having a child of your own. And because there doesn't seem to be a turkey baster within two hundred miles of this godforsaken town, and you might not be back here again for years, well, it's now or never."

Sandra stared at her friend. "Are you suggesting that Max and I have sex?"

"No. Well, yes, but we thought we could all be involved in a way so it wouldn't be weirdly intimate but sort of friendly. Max could be in me and then, just before he ejaculates he could, um . . ."

She held up her hand, "Stop, Briseis, no, that's not going to happen. I very much want to have a child, but not like this. That's just too far to go. The risk of repercussions, of strange feelings, no, I don't think so."

"I'd be there too. It's not like it would be romantic or anything."

"Thank you for the offer. It's incredibly generous, but I have to decline. It would be too much for me. I just couldn't do it."

They gazed affectionately at each other and sighed together.

"Don't say no right now. Think about it. Consider all the angles and possibilities. And then, well, who knows, you might change your mind." She took Sandra's hand in hers. They looked down at their hands together. Bri's were slightly gnarled and had a hard shine from the scleroderma.

They didn't sit together on the bus. The girls sat in a cluster near the middle of the bus, while the boys sprawled and punched in the back.

"Maki, who is that woman at your house?"

"Oh, that's Sandra. Isn't she beautiful?"

"Yeah, but who is she?"

"A friend of my parents. She's visited before. She's an artist, a really great artist."

"Where's her husband?"

"She doesn't have one."

"Really?"

"Yeah. I don't think she's ever had one."

Village-girl heads spinning like the wheels of the bus. *No husband, imagine!*

• •

THE ORCHARDS HUMMED. Up ahead came grinding mechanical noises, stone and plants breaking and crashing together. The clearing of the land for the construction of the house had begun, a violation of the earth, of the atmosphere of morning. Sandra could see the bright throb of yellow through the trees, turning and pushing, ripping, tearing. She came upon the site and gasped. Two olive trees lay on their sides, roots hanging in the air. Mounds of entangled earth, stone, and root and bundles of scrub oak littered the site. The amount of land cleared was frightening, it seemed far too much, the raw red of the clay, the tractor relentlessly pushing and digging. She saw Max across the clearing gesturing to a man with a clipboard and rolls of plans.

They walked to the center of the clearing and stood looking south over the orchards toward Sparti. Their lives had begun to change. Max and Briseis were moving into a life that felt preordained. Max's family had money— not a great fortune, but a considerable amount, earned in just one generation. He was the son of a very successful man but showed none of the anxiety of that breed. He had taken the comforts in stride, clubs and yachts, and as an adult walked away from them. The force of his energy was enough that no one bothered to try and direct him, steer him toward a career. He was obviously going to do what he wanted. He had the privilege of being rough, deliberately careless, uncaring, brutal. Twenty years ago, reckless. Now he no longer cared about risk. What was risk, unless death was involved? They limped along on Briseis's earnings and didn't worry about money. They had none, but they could get it. And that made all the difference. Medical coverage, retirement, university for the children were of no concern. Down the road there would be money. It would be okay. It made choice easy, failure less dangerous, consequence less than fatal.

That time had arrived. They had sold their house in America and begun erecting the house Briseis had dreamed and conjured since she was a nervous military brat moving every year across Europe and the Middle East, always the outsider living in a rented house, not quite English, nor Greek either, trying to sound like the others, desperate to fit in. Now she would have her place, a brilliant house gleaming in the Greek countryside, a place she would never leave.

"Brie is gonna shit when she sees this," Max said and scanned the devastation he had wrought.

"The cleared area seems so big." Men pushing the earth around, it was an elation, a power. Women were not part of it.

"It always seems like that. Every time you clear some countryside for a building, it looks like way too much. You're not just clearing for the building itself but for the construction of it. If you leave too many trees close to where the building is going to be, you just make it harder to build. We'll plant lots of stuff around the house afterward, but for a couple of years this is gonna resemble an industrial site: machinery, materials all over, sand, cement, iron, insulation. All that stuff. You gotta go through the ugly to get to the sublime." He laughed again. Nothing of her conversation that morning with Briseis was revealed. He was making something, it was all that mattered. "Right here is where the house is going to be." He stopped and looked down the clearing toward the orchard. "Oh fuck, no! Oh Jesus Christ." Sandra followed his look. Forty meters away a tractor was stopped, and standing in front of it stood Briseis, holding out her arms, Christ-like. Max started running toward her.

"Max, I can't believe they needed to knock so many trees down, to clear away all that wild bit in the back. I should have been there."

He ran his hand through his knotted hair. "Listen, you've got to keep focused on the end result, which will be this fabulous house on top of a hill. The odd bush or blackberry vine is not important. It's not like this is a pristine, untouched wilderness. This land has been worked for thousands of years. The olive trees we knocked down were truly in the way. The wild stuff that you love will all return if we let it. Any change we make to the terrain around the house is temporary. Even as we speak, seeds are dropping on that bare turf, waiting for water and heat. And excuse me, your civil disobedience gesture was crazy. The guy on the tractor is working for us! He was dumbfounded. He had never seen the like, that's a guarantee."

Briseis harrumphed with derision. "Well, I think it's a disaster." She placed a large platter of chicken youvetsi on the table. The orzo was thick with tomato and glistened with the juice from the chicken. A hint of Metaxa and cinnamon steamed off it. There was bread from Sparti, baked that morning, a tomato salad, village wine the color of raspberries. She surveyed the table, then fetched a bowl of thick black kalamata olives swimming in olive oil, bringing it all to completion. She called the children to lunch.

Max pulled the fatty tail bit from the carcass and

held it up. "Okay, Lulu, it's the semi-finals. Catch this and you're into the finals. Miss, you're out and will have brought shame upon us all." Lulu's attention on the bit of chicken in his hand was absolute. Max tossed it high. She waited until its descent, then sprang forward snapping it out of the air. "Yea!" Max and the children made crowd noises. "The crowd goes wild! Lulu is into the finals!"

The house was quiet and settled for evening. The children were reading, the adults were lounging with ouzo.

"How was it with your mother at the end?"

"Oh, it was very stressful. Mostly because of my bloody father. He was completely out of control. Drunk day and night, babbling on with no one listening to him." Briseis quivered with it.

"But that didn't stop him from yakking. Remember the zwibelkuchen?"

"Oh god, don't remind me!"

"But Sandra hasn't heard this, it's a weird bit. Actually, the whole scene was over the top. There's Brie's mom, Athena, covered with blankets on this divan in the middle of the salon. She's got some kind of scarf affair on her head 'cause she's lost her hair. She's in pain, but she has a morphine patch, so it's endurable, or that's what she wants us to think. There's nothing to be done for her at this point. The cancer had metastasized through her body. It was a matter of, well, nobody knew how long, but weeks, a couple of months.

"For quite a while the Major had been trying to take care of her—to his credit, I suppose, but the way he did it! Listen to this, his wife has goddamn stomach cancer. She can't eat anything. Maybe a little soup, a little crema.

115

Bland and thin, right? So you walk into the house, you say hello to Athena, and from the kitchen you get, 'She won't eat anything I fix her. I make these marvelous meals, but she won't touch them, has no appreciation for what I'm doing here in the kitchen. None.' That was the cue to ask what was on the menu today. 'Thai shrimp.' Thai shrimp, can you believe it? What was going through the man's mind?"

"Nothing. He was drunk all the time."

"That's for sure, and every day it was some violent dish she couldn't have kept down ten years ago. Jellied eel, curried goat, tiddly oggie, I forget some of the wild concoctions, Mongolian chicken livers. It got to be a joke. 'What's on tap for lunch, Major?' The Major's standing over his stove, pipe clenched in his teeth, puffing away, stiff drink at hand, and announces, 'I'm making a superb toad-in-the-hole. The preparation is very tricky. It has to be done just so. Nobody takes the time to make it properly anymore.'"

"What's that?"

"Oh," moaned Briseis, "it's a thoroughly disgusting English dish, the sort of thing they served you at boarding school, sausages done with a batter and then fried and you have some mash. It's easy to make, any idiot can do it."

"But only an idiot would!" Max almost rolled to the floor with laughter. "Toad-in-the-hole. Hole-in-the-head. And Athena would look up and say, in this pathetic voice, 'See what I have to put up with, darling?'"

Max stopped, the two women were staring.

"You know, my love, it wasn't really a comical situation. It was my mother dying."

Max stared intently at his wife but only saw the story, the narrative, the laugh. "Yes, of course. Your mother was a saint throughout. Black comedy, maybe, except your father had all the lines."

"We finally hired Blinka to move in and take care of her, and that was a great relief for Elektra and me. We were there every day, but this way we knew she was getting something she could eat and was taking all her meds, and Blinka would clean her up and adjust her positions."

"Yeah, and that freed up the Major to shift into *really* serious drinking."

"That's true. The caregiving had held him in check, vaguely."

"But the zwibelkuchen, let me get back to that."

Briseis looked at Max and said, "Let's leave the story where it is. Sandra has seen my father in action, there's really nothing to add. At the end of her life the situation is reversed, and still everyone is at his mercy. When we were children, in a very codependent way she would always take our father's side. She didn't protect us from him, and she should have. She tried to keep the peace by placating my father. At the end she was defenceless, but we really couldn't protect her from him either." Briseis sighed. "One more time I considered it all while I sat with her. How she had so utterly failed in the mother's primal task, the protection of her children. She didn't see it that way, of course. From a selfish point of view, I was at least able to release some of my anger and resentment. Difficult to maintain that when the object is suffering and finished." She looked up at Max, "So no, who needs the zwiebelkuchen?"

"Right. I'll get more pistachios."

• •

"Brie, let's put the kids to bed and then the three of us can take a walk in the moonlight. Walking by

117

moonlight through the orchards is great."

Alone on the hiati, Sandra could hear the cycle of life turning, turning, a slow rumble and roll. Where was it going? She was like a woman who had stepped out of the stream of life and walked along its banks till she was utterly dry. The lines of the Cohen song slid through her head, "And just when you mean to tell her that you have no love to give her…" Max's voice came from the house. He was reading *Treasure Island* to the children, giving the characters extravagant accents. She wanted to be read to—and she wanted to be the reader. What was the story, how would it turn? She could see Briseis's mother surrounded by children and grandchildren whispering out her love, her last morsel of joy held on the tongue. She hadn't begun. Where would *her* children come from if she didn't begin?

The moon, nearly full, slashed the geraniums with silver. Music from the taverna, bats carving up the swarms of bugs in the streetlight, Lulu snoring at her feet. She rubbed her bare thighs and stared into her life. The need to make, to fashion out of the material at hand, to guide the forces of the world into new living shapes, where did it lead? What lasts? What had become of her ambition as an artist? A nervous metallic taste in her mouth, like something out of childhood.

She stood up and looked across the road to the platea. Two boys on bikes were lazily scribing circles around the plane tree. Diners were beginning to arrive. Two teenage girls sat on the swings talking. The scent of jasmine filled her head. She should put on better shoes for walking, she felt like running. When had she last run? She couldn't remember. How could that be?

Briseis called from the kitchen, "Almost ready."

She would take the gift offered, she would try to make a new thing. A life. The hairs on her arm twitched. She went to change her shoes, something suitable for running.

As they left the lights of the village behind, the lunar glow intensified, casting the olive trees in a carbon-edged luminescence. Silver and spraying their lunar shadows about, the olive armies marched the humped and rolling earth. The gravel road glowed. Lulu ran ahead, barking at the moon, at any movement, fearless in the predator-free night.

"It always looks full the night before it actually is, but if you carefully scrutinize it, there's a certain incompleteness apparent. Maybe it's just knowing what the date book says. If I didn't know that tomorrow it's full, would I be able to identify tonight as one day shy?" Max stopped and stared at the moon.

"What's the Greek for full moon?" It was so bright Sandra almost shaded her eyes.

"Panselenos," said Briseis, "selene is moon and pan means all, all of the moon."

"But feggari is moon too."

"Yes, but selene is the ancient word. Selene was the goddess of the moon."

"And fucked Zeus."

"Everyone fucked Zeus," Briseis sighed. "She also bore Endymion fifty daughters, which symbolized the fifty lunar months between Olympic games."

"Fifty daughters! I'd settle for one."

Briseis and Max turned to look at Sandra, who shrugged. Lulu's barking suddenly jumped in pitch and ferocity.

"I'm going to see what's happening." Max headed

119

off through the orchard toward Lulu's near-hysterical barking. The women walked on.

"It's been too long since I walked in the moonlight." Sandra pulled her hair back from her face. "Too much urban living. The moon hardly counts in the city. It's just another light."

"I think moving from the city to the country was as significant for me as changing countries," Briseis said. "It was fantastic for the kids. It's so safe here that they can be free, like little animals. When they grow up or go to university, I expect they'll go to the city, the metropolis. They're supposed to. But they'll be grounded with their rural experience." She laughed. "At least, that's what I tell myself. Maybe they'll be completely lost."

"Not those two. They'll hit the city like comets." Sandra glowed with the thought. "Sure, they've had the rural experience, but they've traveled and received a very sophisticated home education from you and Max, they reflect your personalities and your approach to life. They must have a lot of friends."

"They do." It was nice to hear your children's praises sung, like a neck massage.

"Briseis."

"Yes?"

"I've thought about what you said, the alternative you proposed."

Briseis caught her breath.

"My first reaction was to say no, that it was impossible. But I've thought about it all day and . . . and I want to take you up on your offer." There, she'd said it.

Briseis took two deep breaths in succession. She felt a heat rising in her chest, felt the moonlight entering her flesh. "Oh, good." They turned to each other, luminescent and weightless 'neath the moon. "And you ovulate on the full moon?"

"Yes, I do."

"Then it's got to be tomorrow."

The dry October air felt rough down Sandra's throat. They embraced with the lightest of touches, as though to squeeze harder would shatter the night. They inhaled each other's hair.

From the orchards came Max singing Van Morrison.

> Well *I* want to make love to you tonight, *I* can't wait
> till the morning has come,
> It's a fantabulous night for a romance with the stars as
> they twinkle above,
> Can *I* just have one more moon dance with you,
> mmmyyyyy love?

DAY SEVEN

THE MANI PENINSULA, which forms the middle tine of the Peloponnese trident's descent into the Aegean, provides the tail end of the Tayegetos mountain range. From Gythio they headed west through a pass in the mountains, reaching Areopolis at ten in the morning, the deep blue gouge of Limeni Bay far below them, impossibly defined by the hard rock shoreline. They wandered the old part of town. Sandra photographed the odd carvings on the church. A group of old men were in full swing at a café, leaping up from their table to dance, laughing, shouting.

A slow meandering drive followed through blinding noon high sun and deafening cicada scream into deep Mani. There is no relief in Mani, nothing to break the light and heat reflecting off the unforgiving stone. A tree in Mani is truly sacred. So is enough dirt to hold a seed, accommodate root. One thinks of the moon, the land is so barren, imagines that only a hybrid species, part man, part reptile, could possibly exist on this terrain.

From a window high in an abandoned stone tower in Vamvaka, Max watched the women walking a walled pathway. They were talking and moving very slowly, Breseis beneath a straw hat, Sandra with a baseball cap. Every few meters they stopped to examine the rockwork or a bit of defiant clinging vegetation. Heat rose from the rock hallucinating the terrain, light so bright the horizon looked burnt, nothing heard but the roar of a million cicadas celebrating their short lives. The sun midday high, no shadows, nothing dark or cool in the world.

In Mani, the earth too rocky to facilitate burying, the tombs are above ground, often adorned with photos of the deceased and objects from their lives.

"Look at this one. There's a little plastic motorcycle and a bottle of ouzo. I see, and he died at the age of twenty-four." Max rose from a crouch before the tomb. "Brie, remember those great graveyards in England?"

"I do. Sandra, did you spend much time in graveyards when you were in England?"

Sandra laughed. "Not much, though I think I know what you're talking about. Old, moss-covered, semi-abandoned."

"Yeah, that's about right. Lots of carved stone, bits of scripture, stuff like *Peace at last. Gone to the final resting place.* You don't get that sort of thing in Greece. There were many *Lost at sea* stones, and children getting sick, dying in droves. Yet it's one of the things you do when you visit an English village. You go look at the church, generally the most interesting piece of architecture, with its steeple visible for miles, maybe some flying buttresses, and then you wander around the graveyard out back. It's cold, there's wind and violent gray skies. So then you go to the pub and stand by the fire."

"Did you say flying butt-resses?"

"I did indeed. Nothing flying in this heat, though."

"Amen."

Two cypress trees pierced the waves of heat, the midday sky bleached of color, a bird sounded near the cemetery wall. A bird? Briseis peeked around a large tomb and jumped back with a start, saying, "Excuse me, Madame, we didn't hear you. We were just looking."

A black-clad crone stepped into view. *Why would you look at others' dead? No one that belongs to you is here.*

123

"Seeg-NO-mee, seeg-NO-mee." They backed together toward the gate. She turned away, picked up a fatigued broom and started sweeping.

"Oops, didn't want to disturb the mourning, the grief-ridden." Max fired up the car. "The dead, okay. If we could get a rise out of them, we'd be jamming."

"How embarrassing. Exposed as graveyard tourists."

"Looked like she'd been in mourning for a long time."

"Yes, that's their role. Their mourning can last forever, or at least until they get shoved in there with the rest of them."

"How 'bout something to drink, I'm parched."

"Sounds good. Where there's some shade."

"Cold, wet, and dark, that's what we want."

A sheer rock wall rises from the bay a hundred feet or more and runs a kilometer out into the sea, providing a deep sanctuary for the fishing village of Gerolimenas. Beneath an umbrella on the dock they drank.

"There's some nice buildings in this town. Look at the three-story one there with all the stone work."

"Mmmm, I'll bet it's lonely and bleak in the winter. It's October and look, we're the only customers on the waterfront. Most of these places are going to board-up pretty soon, I'd guess."

"Does this village have any history?"

"I don't know about that, but Patrick Leigh Fermor wrote a great bit set here. He was waiting for a fisherman to take him by boat down to the end of the peninsula, Cape Matapan, so he could see the cave that's supposed to be the entrance to the underworld. While he's waiting, this other fisherman tells him that when the conditions are just right, they can hear the roosters crow on Kythera, the island south of here. Probably bullshit, but it immediately reminds Fermor of Henry Miller's great bit with Katsimbalis in *The Colossus of Maroussi* where he wakes the cocks of Attica by crowing from the Acropolis. Anyway, Fermor does this terrific riff about cocks waking each other in this pan-global concatenation until the waking returns to Gerolimenas having encircled the earth."

"Do you have that book?"

"Fermor's *Mani*? Yeah, you can look at it tomorrow. It's a wonderful book, although, as Morgan once put it, he lays the erudition on with a trowel. It can be heavy *laden-with-detail* going, but then he rescues you with something bright and brilliant. For Mani, it's the best book."

"So what do we look at next?"

"From here I thought we'd go straight to Vathia. It's only twenty minutes or so. If we see something along the way, we'll stop. But really, Vathia is the most dramatic Mani village. Part of it has been tastefully turned into a hotel. We'll check in, wander around Vathia, and then drive over to the other side, to Porto Kaigo for lunch."

"Good plan, my love."

"I'm finished here."

"Let's beat feet."

A cluster of stone towers, the village of Vathia rides a narrow spine of rock that twists off the main mountain ridge west toward the sea 300 meters below. They wandered down the gravel "streets," only big enough for a donkey or a pushcart, searching for reception. "Are we, like," Max asked as a young woman led them to their tower room, "pregnancy pilgrims?" They were still laughing as they threw down their small bags, locked the room, and leaded for lunch.

125

• •

AS THEY CAME OVER A RISE, far below was the tiny white settlement of Porto Kaigo, squeezed into a nook in a small bay. Barren hills swept steeply up from the still blue water, sun-stunned browns and orange flashed, the open sea pushed in through a sharp break in the earth. Descending the switchbacks felt like entering another world, isolate, a secret village where no one is known, an end of the world.

Several children were fishing on a dilapidated dock as they walked along the sand. Far above they could see single towers atop utterly barren hills. It was the end of the season, the town nearly empty. They passed the first two tavernas where the proprietors eyed them greedily and walked into the third. A man and a woman sprang to their feet as they entered the kitchen.

"What have you that's fresh?"

"Everything's fresh, caught today. Behold!" The man pulled out a drawer underneath the counter stuffed with ice and fish. He began singing the praises of each. Max and Briseis discussed them with expertise before deciding on marithes, a large sfireetha, and kalamarakia. Oh, and grill up little octopodi to begin, followed by a salad, cheese, patates, tzadziki. They returned to the veranda and looked about.

"Too dark."

"Yes, let's eat on the beach. It's just the right temperature."

They carried a table out onto the sand, just at the water's edge. Their host laughed approval and rushed out with chairs, bread, wine, whatever you want, just ask.

Across the bay was a walled village glowing in the afternoon. They kicked off their shoes and dug their toes into the sand. A new species, they were lighter than air and needed anchoring. Max filled their glasses with Mani wine and said, "L'chaim."

"To life." Indeed.

The tzadziki was tangy with yogurt and garlic, a hint of mint; they dug up great globs of it with bread torn from the fresh loaf.

"Brie, what's the name of that village?" Sandra pointed across the bay.

"Achillios. The principal at the kids' school was a teacher there for two years. He said he felt like a monk. Isn't it beautiful! Like a miniature walled city. These places are so isolated in the winter. No one comes, the weather's frightful."

Their collective excitement soon infected their host. He brought the grilled octopus with small glasses of ouzo. "For the octopodi." They looked at the octopus and ouzos and then at each other, their faces about to break apart with their jumpy shared electricity.

Max took the tongs and placed two ice cubes in each ouzo, speared a tentacle, grabbed a glass. "There are food items that demand a certain accompaniment. For this," he held his fork in the air, "only ouzo."

"Without a doubt," said Sandra.

The sea murmured at their feet, two gulls soared lazily over the water. They had become a romantic dream, nothing was missing.

"Pound," said Max, raising a finger, "had two women, Dorothy, his wife, and Olga Rudge. And they were both with him at the end. I think Olga is still alive, actually.

Damn, she must be near a hundred."

Briseis laughed. "Well, at least you're not a fascist."

"Certainly not, my dear, nor near the poet. I wouldn't mind my own radio show, though."

Sandra was glowing, the entire surface of her body tingled, each breath seemed to flow thoroughly through her. She was wet. "Pound had a radio show?"

"Yeah. He broadcast propaganda from Italy for Mussolini during the war. It was intended for the American troops. Complete nonsense, of course, and the chances of it turning the soldiers was nil. Still, it was treason as it is defined, and he paid for it with years in a mental hospital in D.C. But the interesting part was, after his arrest in Italy, they put him in a cage, just tall enough to stand up in, and only maybe two meters square. The poet as tiger, too dangerous to circulate. Later, after they moved him to a tent, he wrote the Pisan Cantos, his last great work. And they are brilliant." Max raised his wine glass.

> *The ant's a centaur in his dragon world.*
> *Pull down thy vanity, it is not man*
> *Made courage, or made order, or made grace,*
> *   Pull down thy vanity, I say pull down.*
> *Learn of the green world what can be thy place*
> *In scaled invention or true artistry,*
> *Pull down thy vanity,*
> *   Paquin pull down!*
> *The green casque has outdone your elegance.*

The women applauded. Max accepted with a bow of his head. "Good advice that, *Pull down thy vanity.* Oh, and a little later in the poem he writes: *'But to have done instead of not doing/this is not vanity.'*

They all took a breath, exhaled, and looked out across

the bay, to the walled village, to the mountains beyond, to the source of the wind that was whispering to them. Then the fish began to arrive.

The marithes, tiny smelt lightly dusted with flour and quickly fried in olive oil, sprinkled with rigani, came with fresh halves of lemon which Max violently squeezed over the platter, making them sizzle. They are eaten whole with the fingers, each fish a crisp burst of sea and olive. Mouths full of it. The house wine, from the barrel, cool and fruity.

"These taste combinations, the contrasts, you don't get this anywhere else in Europe."

Max picked up a small fish with each hand and held them out to the women. They leaned forward and took them with their mouths.

The kalamari arrived. "Ah," Max threw his head back, "no comparison with that frozen taverna crap you get all over Greece. They're an entirely different creature than the marithes. An ancient thing, I think. Been around for millions of years. I like cooking these when I can find them. They're easy to prepare, take minutes to cook."

"I think we're the only customers in the whole village. They've been waiting all day for us!"

"Yes. Maybe we're the last diners of the season. After us they can board up and go back to their olives in Kalamata. A small stone house high above the sea, wavering hills of silver trees, a herd of goats straggling down from above, a line of laundry snapping in the breeze.

They drank more wine. Their host hovered at the edge of the beach, everything must be replenished. The fishing children looked up at the laughter billowing down the beach. There was time for everything, to eat and be everything. The sun was flaring the top of the hill a burnt

129

orange, the beach was in shadow.

Plates were cleared away before the pièce de resistance was borne onto the beach. The sfireetha, grilled over charcoal, basted with lemon, olive oil, and rigani, filled the platter with glistening blackened silver, and they collectively exhaled an awestruck, "Ah."

The man handed Max the tools to dissect the creature. He stared at the fish, then handed the knife and long fork to Briseis. "Here, my dear, you always do it with such precision and delicacy. I believe this deserves it." She nodded in agreement, took the tools, and began.

When the fish was just a skeleton they rocked back their chairs. A cat was eating the head at the water's edge. "Oh, I don't think I'll ever be able to eat that fish again. It will never compare." Briseis turned toward the taverna, their host standing on the steps smiling. She raised her glass, the others followed. "Bravo, friend, it was brilliant! A miracle. The best ever!" Sandra and Max echoed her acclaim. He danced down the sand to their table abeam. "This is a special meal, yes?" They sighed. He whisked away the remains and quickly returned with a plate of melon, peeled and chopped into bite-sized pieces, each one penetrated by a toothpick. "Is best after the fish, you know." Max dunked a piece into his wine, popped it in his mouth, bellowed delight.

Leaving the boisterous lunch on the beach, they followed a narrow trail cut through the scrub oak and chaparral, curling up around a hillside, in single file to a stone promontory where a small, white-washed church trimmed in blue stood before the flashing sea. It was unlocked, and they entered the cool darkness now struck by the light from the door. In the nave there was a fragment of fresco exposed, a robe, part of a staff grasped

130

by a bony hand. Briseis lit a candle for her mother. They turned to see Sandra looking for a way to attach a tamata to the icon. It was imprinted with an image of an infant.

"Good idea, Sandra," enthused Max, "get the juju working in your favor. Here, here's a little string you can use." When she had finished attaching it, they all stood back and watched it sway and settle, dangling from Saint George, who was clinging to his horse while shoving a lance down the throat of an unfortunate dragon. Waves against rock murmured outside. Briseis broke the silence by observing that village women must have hung many tamata to insure the return of their fishermen husbands and sons. "What's worse, being the fisherman or the wife and mother of the fisherman?" They filed silently out of the church and watched the sea beat away at the jagged rock of the coast. As the waves pulled back, the porous stone sizzled and cracked. A small fishing boat passed the church and entered the bay helmed by a lone dark man with rolled-up sleeves, a cigarette firmly in his mouth. He took them in with the briefest of glances. What had he caught? Something for dinner, something for the empty tavernas, nothing at all?

Walking back to the village, their spirits began to rise again, and by the time they could see the beach they were laughing.

• •

THEY RETURNED, just over the hill to the other side of the peninsula, to the fortified village of Vathia, stone towers stark against the blue of the sky, the burnt yellows and browns of the hills, the quivering sea far below. The late afternoon shadows of the towers cut the village into geometric fragments of light. Up narrow stone stairs to

131

an ancient oak door, the large lock barely turned under the pressure of key and opened with a screech to a stone-floored, vaulted dream of whitewashed walls and dark wood beams. On a platform in an alcove, the bed was cool with white linens and hand-woven spreads. An old donkey saddle leaned against the wall, vast weathered terracotta urns held dried flowers, lamps, bleached sea stones.

Briseis went to the bathroom in an adjoining building, reached from a small veranda off the room. Max sat in a chair, kicked off his sandals, took a drink of water. Sandra examined herself in the mirror. Shut off from the world, it was absolutely still, cool, dark. Sandra brought a hand to her face, took a deep breath, then another, felt a charge move down her. She wanted to see herself, but the woman looking back was bolder, stronger, so balanced as to be rooted. Had she come all this way for this? How could she be so sure? Max studied the ceiling, tried not to think of what was to occur, unconsciously wet his lips.

"Mmmm, I just took a cool, well, lukewarm shower." Briseis was briskly toweling her hair. "It was so refreshing. You guys should take one too." That this shower could be taken together flitted about the shadowed corners of the room, but they were all in anyway.

"Sandra, why don't you go next," Max said, unbuttoning his shirt.

"Okay, a shower sounds great." She walked onto the veranda.

Briseis, in one of Max's T-shirts, draped her towel over a chair, turned to look at Max, and laughed. "The cat who ate the canary. That's exactly the look on your face. This must be some kind of fantasy for you. Some ultimate male vision. Isn't it?"

Max shrugged. "It feels more complicated than that. I mean, this isn't some crazed, drunken lust adventure. I've done that, as you know. This is a planned, thought-out mission to help a friend conceive a child. It's much more serious and, consequently, erotic. It feels like a very powerful moment is about to occur, is occurring."

Briseis nodded and smiled. She loved this man. "I know what you mean. We needed the ouzo and wine at lunch, which, by the way, was one of the greatest meals ever eaten, to loosen up so we don't take ourselves too seriously. I mean, it should be a joyous event, not anxious and self-conscious." She was walking across the room. "We're trying to make life out of love, what better thing to do with our energy!" She bent over Max and kissed him passionately.

"So how do we proceed?"

"You go take a shower, and Sandra and I will be ready for you when you return." She grinned and tousled his hair. "And I was thinking, don't wait until the absolute last second, you don't want to waste it. The main thing, the only thing, is to shoot that stuff up her. So make sure you've got enough time to get inside her."

"The deeper the better, I guess."

"Um, yes, I suppose so."

"From behind, then."

"Been giving it a lot of thought, have you? What, are you hoping for a little Max?"

"A little Sandra would be fantastic."

"That it would."

"Okay, Max," Sandra padded in wrapped in a towel, undoing her tied-up hair. She shook it loose and smiled. "It's all yours."

"Don't go anywhere, I'll be right back."

133

Briseis sat on the bed, grabbed her T-shirt, and pulled it over her head. "Well, are you ready?"

"I guess." She shrugged her shoulders. They both laughed.

"How's it going to go, then?"

"I'll get Max going, and then he'll switch to you and deliver the payload."

They laughed again. "Can you believe we're actually about to do it?"

"I'd have never dreamed that we would be here like this. But it's been a great day, and we can have fun doing this too! It doesn't have to be some weird thing. Max and I both love you dearly. We want this to happen for you."

"I'm deeply touched that you guys would do this. There isn't another couple in the world who would." Sandra unwrapped her towel, and they sat leaning against the bedstead, giddy, girls at a slumber party with an enormous secret.

"You'll have to be ready, though, when Max is. You know what I mean?"

"I thought of that. I'll, you know, prepare myself while you two are, uh, doing your . . . preparation." Sandra started laughing, and soon they were leaning against each other, tears of laughter dripping onto their breasts, running down their flesh.

"Damn, I'm glad you two are relaxed, anyway." He had only partially dried himself, beads of water hovered on his shoulders, he was half-erect already.

"Looks like you're near ready, my love."

He climbed onto the bed and crawled on all fours until he was over his wife and kissed her deeply. She returned it, pulled him to her with one hand, and caressed his penis with the other. They both exhaled a

134

low, moaning hum of satisfaction. Sandra, stunned that it was suddenly happening, stared, fascinated. It was a few moments before she realized she was touching herself while Max licked Brie's nipples and they played with each others genitals. She had never been so close to two people making love. Her flesh tingled, lips parted, breath quickened. They looked beautiful. Briseis turned and twisted beneath his arched, suspended body. She was ready when he turned her over and pushed himself into her, just a fraction, then another. She arched her back so her buttocks rose to him, flexed to draw him deeper. The third presence was electrifying. He began a slow stroke, lingering at her opening, teasing her need, unaware for seconds at a time of the woman waiting for him. He felt huge, every moment of her vagina was full of him moving, singing with the sliding pressure. When his hand slipped under to stimulate her, began to play with her clitoral lips, her mouth opened with a groan that rose from the core of her. The two of them together were rising through her, and she came with a pelvic bucking and rapid, gagging gasps. She sank into the bed for a long moment until the thought of Sandra flashed before her. She turned to look at her friend while reaching behind to pinch Max, jerking her head toward Sandra.

Sandra was on her stomach, rocking on her hand, amazed at how stimulated she was, how on the brink the lovemaking had brought her, when Max's hand cupped her buttock and squeezed, his finger sinking down between her fleshy mounds. She reflexively tightened her sphincter, gasped, then relaxed and opened herself. He was pushing her legs apart, his hands were moving over her thighs and ass, his finger found her wet and ready. He pushed into her.

Is this the way we look? Beautiful. Briseis reached out for Sandra's hand and took it firmly. Sandra gripped back and kept her other hand there at her center, she wanted everything. Max was slowly rocking into her, deeper with each thrust. She felt to him delicate, utterly different than his wife, tighter, the shape of her pushing against him, flexing, contracting, making room for him. A new man sliding deeper. Max's mind vanished, his body went on without thought. He held himself up with one hand and stroked her back with the other. She was jerking, gripping Brie's hand with each convulsion, "Oh, oh, oh," till Max spasmed, a bellowing roar shook the room, and he thrust as deeply as could, held it there while his sex pumped his life into her.

Crickets trilled. She was walking along a narrow mountain ridge. On both sides the mountain dropped sharply away, leaving only just room for her feet. Far below the sea stretched away until it became the sky, a sky that was slowly drained of color as it ran toward the sun. Her flesh came alive as a breath of air moved over her, curled around her body. She noticed that she was naked and descended into a curved hollow in the mountain. There was a pool of water and she moved into it until she was floating on her back. The sun was very bright, and she closed her eyes to it and floated.

Sandra slowly eased into her senses, into an awareness that her senses were sending messages. Her head was thick with the sweet, heavy smells of their lovemaking, the taste of wine in her mouth. She listened, amazed, to Max and Briseis. They were deep in sleep and breathing slowly, not quite in unison, one just behind the other, as though one inhalation triggered the other. Lying on her stomach,

136

her head was turned away, and she could only hear them, could only imagine how they fit together. One of them, it must be Max, was against her, not pressing, just touching along her buttock and thigh.

She opened her eyes. A beam of moonlight was bisecting the room, glowing as a column along the far wall. She was there, in bed with her friends, and they had made love together. She was a little sore, could still feel the last time Max had entered her. *Had entered her.* Was it possible? Back and forth she moved her head, to shake it awake. And blinked her eyes. Opened them wider, and still saw their room, penetrated by moonlight and still. Cricket trills grew in volume.

Sandra slipped one leg off the bed till it touched the floor, then gently rolled her weight onto it and lifted off the bed. After waiting a moment to listen and hearing only steady breathing, she turned and looked at them. They were a woven sprawl of limbs and hair and sheets. Max was mostly uncovered, just a leg under the sheet, on his stomach, buttocks in the air, legs and arms thrust out at odd angles. Brie was on her side toward Max with the sheet pulled up to her breasts, one arm draped over her head, her covered hip rising above the tangle. Sandra wondered over them, ran her eyes over the length of them, wanted to touch and stroke these now so intimate forms. She caught her breath, reached out, and as delicately as possible brushed her fingertips on Max's back. He moved an arm and she pulled her hand away.

She dragged her hand through her snarled and matted hair and let it fall. Never mind. Wearing sandals and a long shirt, Sandra laboriously opened the old-fashioned door latch, each squeak resounded, and slipped from the room.

She took a deep breath, and then another. The air was clean and pure, as though it was new, freshly minted. Out on the gravel path the towers of the empty village glowed and loomed in the radiance of the vast moon burning above the sea to the west. The air was still and warm. She moved without purpose till she reached the end of the empty village, where the land broke off steeply down to the sea. She sat and stared at the long trail of lunar light that ran from the moon across the gently rippled sea to the Mani and her on a rock above. The slightest caress of a breeze whispered off the sea, moved over her arms and legs and face. She opened her shirt, leaned back, and let the moon flow over and into her.

DAY EIGHT

MELODIES OF DAWN BIRDS seeped through the shutters along with a whisper of light. Max rolled onto his back and listened. Did the various species improvise together, did sparrow listen to tit? Was crow mere critic. There was no logic to the mix, just a simple, rolling sonority reverberant through the high clear air of Vathia. He studied the vaulted ceiling. Very nice plasterwork, smooth, clean, and white. Cool, that was the effect, aesthetic and physical: cool.

He turned, and there was Briseis, on her stomach, breathing heavily and likely out for hours to come. He ran a hand over her ass and up her back. She didn't move. Then he woke up. Where was Sandra, the other woman he'd been deep inside mere hours ago? She wasn't next to him, his outstretched hand told him that. He rolled the other way and peered across the room. There she was, on the small second bed. When had she moved? We're aware of such a small portion of what goes on in our life. Our eyes only see a part of the spectrum and part of the world, our ears catch murmurs of unknown musics. A tornado of activity swirls around us in a blur, and in our head we create a world out of chaos. Sandra was there now. Had one of his little sperms made it to the egg? How long did it take? Were there some still struggling up the canal? Lord knows he'd pumped enough into her. Mmmmm, he closed his eyes and was on her again. Last night would forever illumine his memories. Especially if she conceived, then it would be the beginning. A child they had made together. He couldn't imagine. What would she look like? Or he? He always thought of a girl. His child that he would not be

139

father to. How awful. To be separated from your child in such a convoluted way. When would she know? Someday she would know, it was inevitable. How would it all be explained? Had any of them considered this? Would the teenager have a fight with her mother and show up on their doorstep? *I want to live with you now, Daddy.* He shook his head, it was too much. He didn't want to have these feelings unless it was necessary, only if it was happening in front of him. Only if that pain was the avenue forward.

He swung his legs over and onto the floor. Shorts, shirt, sandals, and he was dressed and slipping from the room. If you're lucky, the first hour of the day is for silence, solitude. Having kids made that near impossible, but whenever he could indulge, he did. Far below, Prussian blue, the sea was still in shadow, but only minutes more. Up through the bird-loud village at a brisk pace, he jumped in the car and headed south to the Marmara beach, a set of sandy crescents just minutes away.

At water's edge he shed his clothes and with two running steps plunged into the sea, cool enough to completely awaken. He pulled himself through with long underwater strokes, broke surface, rolled onto his back, bellowed and roared at the sun. He echoed off the rock, as though the rock could talk and tell him where the day would go. The rock should know.

He was a poor swimmer but loved being in the sea and performed a few minutes of awkward backstroke parallel to the shore. Then he stopped and floated. The Aegean is salty, buoyant, easy to float on for extended periods. He could hear a click-tick, click-tick underwater. He'd heard it before, the churn of the sea rustling its pebbled bed. Click-tick, click-tick—the planet is in motion, all of it, a continuous surface adjustment, new connection every moment, everything is old, is part of the flux as the sea is. And he was part of it, jiggle and lap, quiver and wave, from Rio to here, Capetown to Kodiak, earth to the simmering inner edge of the whole bubbling mass. He stayed there, slowly spinning in the sea, a leaf, a star, barely anything at all.

Sandra was on the veranda when Briseis emerged. They both inwardly winced. She made herself a cup of tea, looked over the buffet, and carried the tea to the table. Sandra looked up with a smile, "Good morning."

"Good morning. I slept like the dead. How 'bout you?"

Sandra looked off toward the sea, "Well, actually, I didn't sleep very much." Pause. "Too much, " she waved her hand vaguely, "much too much."

"Are you okay?"

"I'm fine. Really. It's just a lot to process, to make sense of it. I've just begun." She paused, listened. "Are you going to eat?"

"Oh yes. What are you having?"

"Honey and yogurt, which is fabulous, and a couple of these fresh figs, and I'm thinking about this piece of coffee cake."

"That all sounds divine, I'll be right back."

Max appeared still dripping from the beach. Sandra and Briseis were the only people on the dining veranda. He joined them with coffee and a plate laden with rolls, fruit, cheese.

"Been swimming already?"

"Yeah, it was fucking fantastic, if you'll excuse the expression."

141

Briseis rolled her eyes, Sandra watched a hawk riding the wind, a silence wafted from the coffee and enveloped the table. Bees busily worked the jasmine dangling above their heads, the cicadas were beginning to drown out the birds, for the first time in years Max felt like a cigarette.

How incredibly awkward, Briseis thought. Are we the same three people who laughed through lunch just yesterday? I don't suppose we are, ever. We ebb and flow, tugged by the moon, by gravities in opposition, random elements. Our steps are never retraced, moments as brief as the lives of bees. The party ends, the shutters close, the sweat dries on the flesh and is washed away. What happened? They had come together, and in a month or so Sandra would know if it meant anything. It had been very exciting. Her head was full of their smell, sweat and wine, fish and ouzo, sexual juice of them a mingle, smeared on each other, it throbbed through her head, swelled and subsided like waves. She trembled. The act is easy, but the ramifications spectrum out forever. Who would it be, this child? If a child came . . .

They were looking away, their eyes on anything but each other. Sandra was sunk deep into herself, trying to divine any chemical reaction out of the ordinary, listening to herself, her deep self, for the noise of the new. She was too mature to fool herself, knew how easy it would be to imagine that she felt conception had occurred, and so listened with a clinical detachment, unsure what she was hearing. If only you could will it to happen, if it was a matter of concentration, she would like her chances then.

Max returned with more food. "Damn, I'm hungry." He broke open a roll and lathered it with butter, bit it in half and chewed. "Brie, you want some more tea?"

"Oh, yes, thanks, my love." She held out her cup.

"Sandra?"

She turned to him, "Thanks, no, I'm fine."

The women sipped their tea, Max his coffee, bees gathered nectar from the jasmine entangled in the railing, the sea continued to wear away the mountain they were on.

"I suggest we cross over to the east side of the peninsula and return that way. It has a different look."

"How so?"

"There's no level ground. On the west side you've got this plateau above the sea that's what, a kilometer or two wide, but on the east side it's sheer mountain down to the sea. Very rugged, even more harsh than the western side, except it doesn't have that sun-baked feel, being in shadow in the late afternoon."

"Okay then, I'm done."

Dotted with dwarf oaks and diminished heather, the harsh rock of East Mani serrates the Gulf of Lakonia. Well above the sea they wound past ghost villages, towers clinging to cliffside, reached only by footpath, hollow and whistling in the wind.

Max drove and rhetorically observed, "Like the space inside a broken vase."

Briseis turned to him, "Yes?"

Max gestured toward a village below. "The society is broken, shattered, it's the space we see, the echoing space vibrating against stone and sun, against the ghosts of maniacs and the power of the clan, the blood of it all spilt, drained away."

Briseis nodded. "The towers are phallic, of course, it was a warrior culture, after all. Mothers referred to their sons as guns."

143

"Then they were sons of bitches."

"Not much different than the Spartan mother's command, 'With it or on it.' It's the same mentality. Some claim they are the true descendants of the Spartans."

"Not much of a life for anyone, was it?"

"Fuck no. Hey, that village is called Exo Nimfio? What, outer nymph?"

"Yes, that is what it means."

"Damn. But why?"

"Maybe they kept their hot babes down there?"

"Yeah, right, leathery old Mani women probably looked fifty at twenty-five, like the gypsies. By the time gypsy women are twenty, whatever joy and spirit they had seems to have been squeezed out them. By then they've had at least a couple of kids and their husbands probably thump 'em regularly." They let that settle upon them for a kilometer.

"A very rough life. Not many choices. Not like us." Briseis stared across the gulf toward the hazy outline of the third, east finger of the Peloponnese and thought, these people could spend their whole lives without having ever gone over there, within eye's range but utterly out of reach.

"Brie, what you want is to get in touch with your inner nymph."

"I think I have."

"Joy is my name."

They were fifteen minutes early at the school.

"I've got a real thirst. I'm going over to the café for a beer. Anyone want to join me?"

"I think I'll just sit on the bench under the tree."

"Me too."

144

They watched him cross the road. He had moved out of the circle, already he was reentering the world, from the intimate to the public without a thought. The stark emptiness of the deserted playground spread before them, gravel flashed in the midday sun. Across the road along the small river flanked by vast plane trees, birds were singing the joys of cool, watery shade. A tractor worked a nearby field.

"Men are, in many ways, like dogs. Domesticated, but still animal, still capable of behaving at that level." Briseis turned to Sandra. "How are you doing?"

"I feel strange, awkward, like I don't quite know how to relate to either of you. And that's very weird." Sandra shrugged, stared out at the playground. She was sore but didn't mention it. "It's as though nothing is quite the same now, our relationships have shifted and don't fit together as they did before."

"Maybe we were naïve to think that you and Max could have sex, even with me there, and everything would still be the same."

"I suppose we were. I mean, we weren't really considering what came after, besides my hoped-for pregnancy." Sandra watched Briseis massaging one hand with other.

"Thinking, so much thinking . . ." Briseis muttered. "I'm always thinking, always considering the worst possible outcome and working up a way to fear it." She was staring at her gnarled hands. "Since I was a child I have been worrying things to death. This is possibly the most spontaneous thing I've ever done, in as far as the inspiration for it was followed by the pursuit, the resolution of the impulse. Without worrying about all the details." She held an ulcerated finger up to her face.

145

"Now I suppose I'll work myself into a tizzy about all the possible repercussions of what we've just done."

Sandra squirmed on the bench. A dog was sniffing around the swing set, a crow alighted on the jungle gym, a door banged open and a flood of children poured down the stairs with a roar. Leo and Maki broke off from their friends and ran to the women.

"Hi, Mommy, hi, Sandra, how was Mani?" Leo was as loud as his father. He hugged his mother.

Maki looked around. "Where's Daddy?"

"He's over at the café."

"Can I go get him?"

"Okay, but watch the traffic."

She ran down the walk and, after exaggerated checking for cars, bounded across the street.

"How was school today, Leo?"

"Okay, same old same old, as Daddy would say."

"And last night at Elektra's, did you do anything fun?"

He shrugged. "We played video games."

"How original."

"Pssst, Leo."

Leonidas looked up from the notebook he was scribbling verb conjugations in. The kids were dutifully doing their homework at the kitchen table. "Yeah?"

"What's with the old people?"

"What do mean?"

"Well, don't you think they seem weird? Like they're not really here or something. I mean, they've hardly talked all afternoon. Mommy just corrected papers and left to teach. Sandra's out on the hiati reading, and Daddy's down in the garden with Lulu. Nobody's doing anything together."

146

Leonidas considered this information. "Maybe they're just tired from the trip to Mani?"

"Mani's an hour away, it's not like they went to Spain. Or Athens, even."

"I dunno. They're grownups, who knows?"

"We should all play a game tonight."

"Yeah, okay. Which one?"

"Monopoly."

"Hearts."

"You just think you can beat Daddy at it, but you do only if he lets you."

"Tonight I'm winning."

"Fine. We'll get Daddy to make popcorn. You almost done?"

"I've got one more verb to do."

"Slowpoke, I'm done."

"Yeah, yeah. If you're so fast, here, do my mine too."

"In your dreams, Leo." Andromache slammed her notebooks shut, grabbed her drawing pad, and went out on the hiati.

Sandra looked up into the beaming Andromache. "Finished your homework already?"

"No sweat. Leo's still doing his."

"Girls are faster, huh?"

"No doubt." She sat down. "Sandra, how do you draw an empty glass, you know, so you can see through it but still see it? I tried but it doesn't look very good."

"There are a couple of tricks." She placed her book on the floor and took up her drawing pad. "Here, let me show you."

• •

A FOX FURTHER UP THE ROAD stopped and stared

147

into the car lights, then leapt into the bushes, luxuriant tail following. To witness the wild was the gift of the countryside, where everything was a matter of killing, eating, mating. How had we tangled ourselves up so, where every act and gesture involved a complicated web of connection and consideration? Animals act, they don't consider. Briseis sighed to herself. And I waste my time trying to pound English into heads as dense as concrete. A group of teenagers at eight o'clock at night, having been in school for the previous twelve hours, what could you expect? Tired, bored, hungry, hormonally distracted to the point of seizure, it was necessary to seduce them into learning, trick them by making the subject interesting, funny, pertinent. If I don't make the effort, they might go through the entire day without one person really caring. Maybe I'm giving myself too much credit, or others not enough?

She entered the lights of the village and pulled up to the house. I wonder if everyone has recovered, emerged from shamed silence? Have I? Lulu burst into noise, giving voice to her best impersonation of a fearless guard dog, a beast with no shame.

She entered the kitchen to a card game.

"All of the rest of the tricks are mine." Max displayed his hand on the table.

"What?!" Leonidas was dumbfounded. "Are you sure?"

"Sure. I lead this and then these. You're most likely holding the queen of clubs, right? Remember, most people are trying not to get hearts, that makes it easier to run them. You have to learn to read your hand, then watch how the tricks play out. First thing I do with a hand is figure out if I can run it."

148

Leo stared at his father's cards and then his own. Max thought, it's about time to start teaching him poker. They both shoved a great fistful of popcorn into their mouths. Briseis shook her head at her barbarian males. What was shame to them?

Andromache looked up. "Hi, Mommy, you want to play? We can start a new score. Daddy won the last one, by sheer luck."

"Let me dump all this stuff and get my coat off first. Isn't it time for you guys to get ready for bed?"

"Brie, I made you some oatmeal with walnuts and honey. It's ready."

"Oh, thanks my love."

"Ablutions, pedtheia." Max shuffled the cards several times and put them in their box..

"Maki first."

"What, you can't brush your teeth together? And who is supposed to shower tonight?"

"Leo."

"Ah, I don't need one."

"Dude, you always need one. Listen, it's been a long day, if you guys want someone to read to you, get it in gear." They marched from the kitchen.

"Brie, whose turn is it?"

"I don't know, my love, but can you perform the duties?"

"All right, where were we?"

"Jim Hawkins just met Ben Gunn."

"Aye, that's true enough. Now then, Ben Gunn's just told Hawkins that he's been on the island for three years and Hawkins says,

"'Three years!' I cried. 'Were you shipwrecked?'

149

"'Nay, mate,' said he, 'marooned.'"

Max drew out the word and let it hang there before them. His children peeked out from under their covers, wide awake.

Briseis looked at the pile of compositions to correct, sighed deeply, and walked out on the hiati. Crickets were trilling, sweet jasmine hovered, the taverna was playing the same Dalaras tape. Sandra was curled in a deck chair.

"What are you reading?"

Sandra showed her the cover. "Frank O'Hara. Max handed it to me earlier tonight. He's really good."

"I've read a few of his things Max has given me. I read some of them out loud to Max when he was in the hospital, after his motorbike accident. He was in a lot of pain, couldn't read or anything, and wanted me to read to him. Poetry, of course. We had this anthology, *The New American Poetry*, it's a famous collection, and Max would ask for poems by certain poets. I remember reading O'Hara's poem about Billie Holiday, and one about the movies."

"Were you in a private room?"

"Are you kidding? This is Greece, Sparti, there were six other beds in the room and several people around each one."

"Intimate."

"A communal experience. Max dictated a poem while sprawled on the bed, have you seen it?"

"What, he told you what to write?"

"Yes! It's quite funny. You should put it in the book. Wait, I have a copy in a folder in the bedroom." Briseis rose and quickly returned. "He put the title on afterward."

150

POEM MURMURED TO BRISEIS WHILE WAITING FOR A SHOT IN THE BUTT TO PULL ME BACK FROM A SCREAM

. . . too much joy . . .
mustn't let anyone know . . .
God notices . . . he sez
"Think you got it dicked, eh?
(God uses verbs like that)
. . . and then
"Well, take this, dickhead."
Zap.

Sandra laughed. "This is verbatim?"

Briseis glanced at the paper in Sandra's hands. "Remarkably enough, yes, except, as I said, for the title. I think that should go in your book."

"Absolutely. He didn't have anything seriously wrong, did he?"

"No, thank god. One doctor tried to tell us his back was broken, but that was bullshit. He was just banged up pretty good. We were lucky."

Max sat down with a glass of wine. "We've been lucky since we met, my love, and we're still on a roll. Does anyone else want something to drink?"

"Couldn't possibly."

"No thanks, I'm still recovering from yesterday's lunch."

"Yesterday's lunch, ah yes . . ." Max exhaled long and slow.

Briseis held out the poem. "Do you remember dictating this?"

"Oh yeah. Us poets, you know, we're always working," he said with a wide grin.

"Yeah, yeah."

• •

"DAMN, BRIE, give those compositions a break."

Briseis was seated in bed with a pile of compositions scrawled on lined paper torn from spiral notebooks. Max picked one off the top and read: "Having a dream or goal is important in life, especially for young people. My dream is to go to Naples and dance in strip clubs while studying music composition. In order to achieve this dream, I keep my body always in shape. My experience with the music helps my dancing."

"It doesn't say that!"

"If only it did. I would help you correct them if they read like that."

"The dreams of these children are mind-bogglingly banal, 'have a nice car,' 'get a civil service job,' 'bring honor to my family.'"

"'Honor to my family?' What is this, the Middle Ages? *There* is someone who fears the father."

Briseis looked up at Max. "Yes, that's probably what it means. The fear of shame, fear of the father, lots of fear in traditional societies now burdened with all the junk of middle-class life as well." She felt a chill swiftly run from her neck to her toes. "I remember lectures about this sort of thing, especially from Mummy. Everything was tied to the status of the family, or, really, the glorification of Daddy, which the wife gets to share in a reflected way."

"'Daddy, Daddy, you bastard, I'm through,'" Max hissed.

"Don't wake the kids."

"They're out, hiding in the stockade with Hawkins and the rest."

"You're lucky, you get to read Stevenson. They insist I read those dreadful Redwall books with the talking beavers and the rest of that garbage."

"It's your own fault. You do too good a job with the text. I hear you in there giving the different species different accents. Yorkshire foxes, for crying out loud!"

"I have to do something. They are so turgidly written."

Max handed her a page fresh from his printer. "Here, this is something better than turgid, I believe."

"New?"

"Moments old."

She read it through, and then again.

> *The silence is a slow draining away*
> *a tap inserted in the veins of joy,*
> *the tools that love and loss employ*
> *compress a life to just one day.*
>
> *'From this moment on it will all be different'*
> *we think, we mourn, lose track, forget*
> *that this truth is far less important*
> *than 'give much more than you will get.'*
>
> *Things of earth wait out the weather*
> *we cannot see inside the other,*
> *but birds return after hurricane*
> *and when they sing the song's the same.*
>
> *It's best sometimes to just remember*
> *what after every winter came.*

He had only begun to work in forms, and found them a delight. It was connected with having left America, with leaving his audience, tiny as it was. Here, without the readings and small publications, he was truly writing for himself, and Briseis, so everything was allowed. Sonnets, villanelles, why not? Briseis found it curious. And it was thrilling, to see it all pushed through words.

"It's very good, my love. Beautiful. And you wrote it tonight?"

"Yeah, just now."

"I don't know about this last couplet. Shouldn't it be with the previous four lines?"

Max looked at the poem. "Maybe. It felt like it should stand alone, but I'm not that sure."

She nodded, wet her lips, smiled. "Sometimes I think you're living this life in order to get material."

"Just the opposite. The writing is a manifestation of the life, just as the children are a product of the love. The poems are a love product."

She chuckled. "Laying it on pretty thick, don't you think?"

Max shrugged. "Okay, they are merely constructions of words with no meaning beyond themselves, and I do it because it gives me pleasure and a wee amount of recognition, which is also pleasurable."

She paused. "You enjoyed it, didn't you?"

"Are you kidding? Of course I did. My two favorite women naked and writhing beneath me!"

"What was it like?" Briseis leaned back and scrutinized her man.

"Well, first, I haven't been in another woman since before you and me."

"Yes."

"But it was odd, too, in the sense that Sandra and I weren't really making love as we generally think of it. I mean, we weren't caressing and kissing, touching in the way two people do. All the foreplay was with you, and then bam, I'm shoving it up Sandra."

"You put it so delicately."

"That's what I'm saying, there wasn't any delicacy. That part was missing, but it was more than compensated by the physical sensations, which were, um, terrific." Max pulled a hand through his hair. "The point was to deliver the payload, not to have some long erotic session. So I tried to stay with the program."

"I see. But you were in her quite a while the second and third times, as I recall."

"Yeah, well, that's the nature of the beast. When a man has more than one orgasm during a sexual encounter, he doesn't usually come as readily as the first time. You were urging me on, I remember."

"I wanted her to have as much chance of conceiving as possible." She could see them before her, Max riding up on her raised buttocks, Sandra bracing herself, gasping with each thrust. She would have liked to be him.

Max switched off the light. On their backs they examined the streaks of light from the platea, fragmented by the fig tree, splash the wall and move with the wind. The taverna was slow tonight, they had turned off the music already. Crickets wound away in the dark.

"The end of your poem, it reminded me of something Christina Rossetti wrote."

"Hmm?"

> *I heard the bird sing in December,*
> *We're nearer to spring than we were in September.'"*

"What will spring bring?"

"What it always brings."

DAY NINE

THE BUS BRAKES SIGHED and the vehicle began to roll downhill before Andromache reached her usual seat next to Sophia. She looked out the window in time to see her father waving and gestured back. The bus disappeared around the hill. Max walked back through the house to the kitchen to retrieve his coffee, then out onto the hiati. Sandra was in a deck chair, book in her lap, tea on the floor beside the chair. She wasn't reading but staring out at Lazineekos. He came up behind her, placed his free hand on her shoulder while looking to see what she was reading.

Sandra glanced up and then away, saying, "Look." They watched the silver mottled ball of moon, brilliant against the morning blue, slip into the Tayegetos, and they were lovers no longer. Their erotic connection evaporated, vanished into the morning, and they were friends again, the product of some fusion, some elements of spirit bonded, as though the living energy of the day cohered within them and grew.

Max peeked into the bedroom. Briseis was stirring. He turned back into the kitchen and put the kettle on, sliced two pieces of bread and put them in the toaster, pulled down a mug and put a tea bag in it. He opened the fridge and got out the butter and raspberry jam, poured boiling water over tea bag. The toast popped, and he swiftly buttered it, trimmed the crusts, extracted the tea bag, stirred sugar and milk into the steaming mug. He placed it all on a tray and carried it into the bedroom. Briseis, having heard the rattle of his labors, was sitting up in bed.

"Ooohh, thanks, my dear. That looks yummy. How is everyone today?"

"Kids are great, made the bus. Sandra and I just watched a beautiful moon setting, and God is, oh, who the fuck knows where she is."

"A mystery to me."

"And to her."

"God is a mystery to herself?"

"Yeah, that's good, huh?"

"Very, my love."

"It's Sandra's last night, what should we do?"

"We could go out and eat."

"Yes, but where?"

"Music, where is there some music? I'll call Yiorgos and ask if he knows."

Max walked slowly through the courtyard, then peered out the gate. The back orchard throbbed with energy. A million insects busied the vegetation. Birds landed and lifted off among gourds and late tomatoes. Outside the great circle of his garden, tall, pale grass waved in the breeze, vast fig trees faintly quivered. He held Lulu's collar. "Quiet, Lulu, we're going to watch where she goes." Fifteen meters away gray, speckled Bernice waddled along a path, then ducked under the foliage of a pomegranate tree. "So that's where she's laying them." A minute later Bernice emerged and waddled back to the courtyard while Max and Lulu, pretending to examine the figs, went to her lair. In a hollow beneath the tree were six large brown eggs. Max took five. If he took them all she would find a new hiding place, this way he merely had to check twice a week or so. He walked up to the house.

"Briseis, look what I found out in the orchard."

157

"Who is laying out there?"

"Bernice. I thought we were missing some eggs so I watched her this morning, and sure enough. She's laying under the pomegranate. I left one so with any luck she'll keep laying them there."

"Do they do that often?" Sandra asked.

"Occasionally."

"They have the instinct to hide them, protect them, but won't sit on them." Briseis lifted her hands in bewilderment. "I mean, they're deeply stupid but surprise you sometimes. When they lay an egg, they often don't even turn around to see it. They just walk off like they've taken a shit. And then, at other times, like this, they exhibit all this concern, hiding and hoarding. They're fun to watch. You don't normally get to observe creatures at length like this. Dogs and cats don't count, they're too influenced by us."

"Yeah, Brie, you think they're fun, but you don't feed them at sunrise and put them away at night, clean out the henhouse, and all the rest."

"True, my love," she sighed, "but remember, I've already laid and hatched my eggs."

• •

A MAN AT THE NEXT TABLE suddenly leapt up from his chair, which crashed with a rattle behind him. Swearing continuously, calling down all evil on the heads of the current government, he wadded up the newspaper he had been reading, threw it to the ground, stomped on it, then kicked it over the heads of the men at a nearby table. One of them, laughing, raised his hands and shouted, "Goal! Don't worry, Kosta, the king will return!" This made Kosta even more furious, and he stomped across

158

the platea, untied his donkey from a mulberry tree, and rode off.

Max, Sandra, and Briseis unsuccessfully stifled their laughter. "What was that about?"

Briseis said, "Kosta is a right-wing nut who absolutely hates the current socialist government. He usually keeps it to himself, but sometimes it is more than he can bear."

"The Papandreou government has raised the farmers' subsidy, so what's his beef?"

"Not enough, my love, not enough."

"How much would that be?"

They all took a simultaneous slurp of their coffees. They were taking their elevenses at the village kafenion, enjoying the shade of the great plane tree that towered over it.

A small Renault pulled up to the platea and honked. Max leapt up, "Hey, the mail." He returned with a handful of envelopes.

"Anything interesting?"

"*New American Writing*, a postcard from Dick and Scarlett, they're in Costa Rica, and some junk. Oh, and he gave me a letter for Agnes. I'll run it down there when we're finished."

"You won't have to, here she is."

A short, ethereal, bird-like woman in her sixties, very lightly dressed in a peasant skirt, flip-flops, and diaphanous blouse, entered the platea. They waved her over to their table.

"Mail call, Agnes."

"Oh, thank you, Max. I knew I was going to miss him. It's so bothersome, this mail system, or lack of one."

"Yes, but it does have a certain personal touch."

"But what if you don't get on with the postman? You'll

159

probably never receive your post."

"Good point, Agnes, which is why I'm extra-friendly."

"It's most annoying." She turned to Briseis. "Briseis, how are you, my dear?"

"Fine, Agnes. We're just enjoying this beautiful morning. Would you like to join us?"

"That's kind of you, but I'm afraid I must decline. I have to get back to the dogs, and Maurice promised to come by and fix my kitchen sink."

"How are things going?" Briseis couldn't resist.

"I have a yeast infection, of all things. At my age." She sighed, "Oh to be a woman."

They watched her walk away.

"'Oh to be a woman?'"

"Can you believe it?"

"Must be this clean, clear country air."

They heard a dirge-like chant coming from further down the village, and it was getting closer.

"Then bo-roh, aieee, aieee. Then bo-roh, aieee, aieee."

Max and Briseis smiled to themselves.

Sandra asked, "What is it? I've heard this before."

Max leaned on the table. "It's Sisyphus, or our village equivalent. His name is Thyestes, but we call him 'Then Bo-roh.'"

"What's he saying?"

"'I can't.'"

"It's like Beckett, 'I can't go on, I go on.'"

An old man in pajama pants, torn shirt partially tucked in, longish hair in wild disarray and wearing one slipper shuffled into view, wailing out his chant with metronomic frequency. "Then bo-roh, aieee, aieee! Then bo-roh, aieee, aiieeee!"

160

"My god, what is his story?"

"His story," Max said, "once you know it, the whole thing takes on a certain mythic quality. We asked about him, and what they told us was, he had several children he used to beat mercilessly. The wife, too. So the kids grew up and left the village, never to return except to rescue their mother. Now he's old and sick and crazy, and his children won't have anything to do with him. Nothing. So he's condemned to march through the village bemoaning his fate while everyone who sees him thinks he deserves it. Amazing, huh? It's like something the gods would force upon you. Some of the stuff that goes on in the Greek countryside is hard to believe." They could hear him further up in the village getting fainter.

"Does he ever say anything else?"

"Yeah, once in awhile he shouts, 'Petheno,' 'I'll die!' Alone and unloved, that's for sure. One night I was driving into Sparti in a cold, horrible storm, and he came lurching out of the darkness with this obsessed look in his eye. He appeared to be shouting or roaring. It was like Lear or something."

"But no Cordelia."

"Amen."

• •

THEY PARKED TWO BLOCKS OFF THE MYSTRAS PLATEA. Briseis pointed to a small stone house. "That's my uncle Orestes's house. His step-mother whacked him upside the head so often as a child that he went deaf. Can't hear a thing." A little farther along they passed an old bakery. "This bakery is owned by a violin player, and while his loaves are baking he plays. Look, there's his violin." They all peered in to see the violin, bearing a smudge of flour,

161

resting on the wooden counter next to the cash register. High above them loomed the Byzantine castle of old Mystras, its battlements stark in the lunar glow.

The children led the way, pushing through a door into the noise and smoke of the taverna. A quartet of musicians on a small, raised dais were drinking wine and talking while children ran between the tables. At a table near the musicians Yiorgos was waving.

"Leonidas, Andromache, what a joy to see you. How are you my children?"

"Hi, Yiorgo, we're great."

"Yeah, me too.""Yiorgo, my friend, thanks for getting here early and copping a table. We won't have any problem hearing the band from here."

"I didn't have much choice. It was already filling up when I got here." Yiorgos stood up, trying to suck in his stomach. "Good evening, Briseis, Sandra."

"Where's Katrina?" Briseis mischievously asked.

"Huh? Katrina? Why would I bring her?"

"Some husbands actually take their wives out."

"Yes, yes, and I do. But this way we can all speak English and nobody is left out."

"How thoughtful."

The English with their irony, what can you do? Yiorgos slapped his hands together. "So, I've ordered wine. They have pretty good wine here.

What should we eat?"

"Tzadziki!" shouted Leonidas.

"Patates," chimed Andromache.

Getting some air the men stood outside the taverna. "We went down to Mani a couple of days ago."

"Mani?"

"Yeah, Sandra took a lot of photos. She'll probably use some Mani images for the book."

"The book? When will it come out?"

"This will be a long-drawn-out process, I'm sure. Sandra does not work fast, *and* she's very meticulous. So you just have to wait. We had a fantastic lunch in Porto Kaigo."

"You went all the way down there?"

"Sure. It doesn't take very long. We spent the night in Vathia."

"You spent the night? Why didn't you just drive back?"

"Ah, for fun."

"With the kids?"

"No, they stayed with Elektra."

"Just the three of you, eh."

"Right. We didn't think of asking you to come along. Sorry."

Yiorgos stared at Max. It was all too easy for this man. and sometimes it was almost too much to bear.

Max laughed and slapped him on the shoulder. "Next time, for sure, Yiorgo mou."

"Will there be a next time?"

"How does it go, Yiorgo, 'You can't step into the same river twice'? The ground beneath our feet is shifting, the repercussions of even one act are infinite, 'Across the morning sky, the birds are leaving.'"

"What? Was that a song lyric?"

"Yeah, Joni Mitchell, I think."

"You're being too abstract, man. I can't follow where you're going. It's like you're saying this stuff just to hear how it sounds."

"That's partially true. Too, what I'm saying is defined

by what I'm not saying. The echo in the margins, if you will."

Yiorgos shook his head. "You tell me nothing. It's all just word play, like juggling."

"Sure, why not?"

Andromache appeared in the taverna doorway. "Daddy, the music's about to start again."

Leonidas was leaning forward in his chair, listening with rapt attention to the clarinet player, nodding his head, tapping his foot to the music. He had quickly deciphered the player's tricks, what riffs he usually used in his solos. Not that he could play like that himself, not yet, but he could hear where it was going, could guess where it would end. At eight he was first chair clarinet in the Sparti Philharmonic and was actually paid a monthly stipend. Soon he would be a soloist.

"See, Daddy," Leonidas pointed, "these demotic players have an extra section before the mouthpiece. It gives them that low mellow tone."

"Oh yeah. Do you need one?"

"No, I'm not playing this kind of music. The philharmonic wants a sharp clear tone. You know, Bolero and that stuff."

"Yiorgo, your father was deaf and mute, right? So when you used to interpret for him in the village taverna, how did you tell him what people were saying?"

"Well, he was a smart man, remember. He read lips a bit, and I would use sign language."

"Of your own invention?"

"Yes."

"For instance."

164

"Okay, we're in the taverna, and let's say two guys at the table are having a typical village conversation. One guy says, 'If it rains tomorrow, I won't plow the fields, I'll prune the trees.' First I do this." With one finger pointed out he turned his hand over away from himself. "That means tomorrow. If I reverse the gesture," he turned his hand toward himself, "it means yesterday. And if I had two fingers out that would be not tomorrow but the next day. Then I go," he raised his hand, palm down, wiggled his fingers while lowering his hand, then shook his head while moving his fist horizontally, the thumb sticking out like a plow, and finally made a scissors gesture.

They all exclaimed. "That's great."

He acknowledged their praise. "Well, that's an easy one. Sometimes it would be too complicated for me and we would have to call Andreas over."

"Who was he?"

"My mother's brother. He was the closest to my father, but more important, he was a man of infinite patience. He would sit there until my father got it, no matter how long it took."

Max loved these stories. "But Yiorgo, how would you know he got it? I mean, maybe he was interpreting the signs completely differently?"

"Ah Max, we weren't discussing existentialism! These were conversations in a village taverna. Simple, basic, and the same thing over and over again. So he knew a lot of what was happening, and he could make intelligent guesses. Like you do. You don't understand what people are saying, but you can guess from the context and what you know of the person. So," he turned his hand in the air, "you use some of the same tools as my father."

"You never learned a formal sign language, did you?"

"No, we were peasants in a village, where would we get that kind of instruction."

"What I find fascinating," Briseis was in her element, "is that every language has its own sign language. Before I studied linguistics, I thought, as I assume most people do, that there was an international sign language, but there isn't. Obviously, there are certain gestures that cross over. 'I love you'"—she performed the movements—"would probably be understood anywhere."

"Except in a village plagued by river blindness."

"Thank you, Max. But there they could probably hear."

"Yiorgo, I know you've explained some of this stuff before, but I think Sandra might like to hear. Your father could make a variety of sounds that you could understand and then explain to people, right?"

"Oh, yeah, I think there were about two hundred."

"But nobody else could understand them."

"No, only me. My mother, my brother, they didn't have, I don't know, the inclination, the need to know. They could understand commands. Beyond that was a gray zone."

A song entered his head, and he tried to shake it out. "Oh, why do they play these tunes?" he wailed, and slapped his hand on the table. "This song, it is too tragic, it carries too much weight with it! There are certain songs that follow you around, that won't let you go! Just when you are fine and relaxed, here comes that song to rip your heart out!" Everyone listened to the mournful clarinet meander and peal its way through the melody. The string instruments were sitting out, only the drummer added the odd beat, abstractly so, the singer warbled out in pure demotic vibrato his melancholia.

"Oh, I'm sweating, " cried Briseis as she wiped her forehead with a napkin and dropped herself onto a chair. "Sandra, you've really got that one down. Next time you can lead."

"Not yet. I'm very content to follow. It's really fun once you've got the steps down."

"Mommy, can we have ice cream?" Leonidas spoke for them both.

"Sure sweetie. But I don't know if they have any here."

"There's a Delta box at the kiosk."

"Okay. Ask Daddy for some money."

"What? Gimme a break, you guys don't want Pagoto."

"Yes we do!"

"Really? Oh, well in that case, here's five hundred drachs, that ought to be enough."

They ran out the door of the taverna to the kiosk in the small Mystras platea where they studied the embossed graphic on the side of the ice cream box. Every offering was considered but they generally made the same choice every time. Andromache wanted chocolate in a cone, Leonidas strawberry on a stick, so the more esoteric choices such as banana in the shape of a monkey were finally dismissed as frivolous. The clarinet moaned out the opening of another melancholy song. Yiorgos sighed and murmured the title of the song, "Tis Evdokeeas." He began to rise from his chair, but Max held out his hand, "My turn, Yiorgo."

"Really? Well, this is a special occasion."

Max went to the empty dance floor and began tapping his heel to the music. His arms hung at his sides, but his fingers were snapping in time. The children, surprised, quickly knelt on the floor and clapped to the music. Briseis

167

turned to Sandra, "This is most unusual, we should lend our support." They knelt with Yiorgos around the slowly moving Max and brought their hands together.

Max saw them gather at his feet, closed his eyes, and gathered himself into the music. He wanted to say something to himself, to his family and friends, about their lives together. Something he couldn't express in words, something only the body could tell. He straightened his arms out to his sides, lifted a foot and spun. They wouldn't get it, he wasn't near articulate enough, his feet illiterate, his time merely adequate, yet he danced on, bending to slap the floor, twirling, hesitating, a short hop into the future, and back.

They gathered for goodbye in the street before the taverna. The children ran to get a drink from a spigot on the trunk of an enormous plane tree in the middle of the street. They exchanged embraces, kisses on the cheek, laments for times together already lost. Yiorgos looked up at the moon, glowing above the castle. "Hmm, two days past full, is that right?"

"Yes," came in unison from Max and the women.

Yiorgos looked from the moon to his friends, back to the moon, thinking, I'm missing something here. The moon tugging and pulling something beneath the surface of things.

DAY TEN

Sunrise. Sandra rose early one last time, quickly dressed, grabbed her camera, and slipped from the sleeping house. It was gray, cloudy. She hadn't shot the village in this light and opened up the f-stop as she walked up the road. Roosters were crowing, nothing else stirred, not a breath of wind. It smelled like rain on the way.

She took a path that led down to the lower part of the village, brilliantly awake to the vividness of the world, to the life of this morning yawning before her. She framed an old plow leaning against a hut, shot, moved on. A magpie swooped across the road and disappeared into an olive grove. She photographed because she was a painter. She did not paint moving objects nor, generally, did she photograph them. Her pursuit was the vibration of the stationary object, the multiple meanings of any moment in time and where the connections may lead. Static did not mean frozen, in her vocabulary; rather, she applied the audio meaning to the visual, white noise became the interference of color, the electrical current emanating from anything existing in three-dimensional space.

Beneath an olive tree she found a dead jay, its coverts of blue, white, and black radiating beneath the wings. She knelt and examined it, turned it over. Perfectly whole, unblemished. What caused its death? She took several shots. Soon another creature would eat it. A loud *baaaraacckk* startled her, she looked up to see a crow on a power line. It was soon joined by another. Often with mammals you had the illusion that you knew their thoughts, their motives, but with birds the mystery was complete. Was there anything there but hunger and the

169

desire to mate? A chill passed by, and she stood to shake it off. The crows watched, nodding to themselves. Beyond, Lazineekos rose up against the gray. When would she return? It might be many years. What would happen?

Leonidas staggered under the weight of Sandra's bag. "Yo dude, you want a hand with that?"

"I can do it, " he barked, swaying along the sidewalk.

"Now, you have everything, right?" Travel was Briseis's only organized time, the only time it seemed to matter. You can't fly back to get something, they won't let you on the plane without your passport.

Sandra grinned. "Yes, mom, I've double-checked."

"Oh, sorry, it's just a habit I have. And you wouldn't believe the number of times asking that question has saved the day."

"Briseis is late for everything except the plane. For that she's bloody hours early."

"I can't believe you're already leaving! Write and tell us any news. I'll even try and write back. Max will write, anyway, maybe I'll just add notes to his letters."

"I will, you can count on it. I'll send photos, too." She turned to Max, "When you've made the final decisions on the manuscript, send it by courier, and I can start loading it into my computer."

A man opened the bay doors of the bus, shouted "Athena," and they handed him her bag. Sandra looked at them all, sighed, this was it. They all moved to hug her at once, got entangled, and laughing, waited their turn.

"Good luck, Sandra, however it works out." Briseis was tearing up.

"Thanks for everything. I had the greatest time. And take care of yourself, that's the most important thing.

Leonidas, give me a hug." She lifted him off the sidewalk.

"I'm going to send you drawings."

"Andromache, I'll send you some too. Max," she accepted his bear hug, "thank you. It was my best visit ever. We'll be in touch about the book, and I'll send you copies of images I'm considering."

"Goodbye, Sandra, we're going to miss you. You bring a wonderful energy into our funny little tribe."

Sandra found her seat and looked out the window at them, at the soft ragged humanity of them—old shorts and flip-flops, hair askew—and her heart broke in a sob. Max held Andromache on his hip, Leo, holding Briseis's hand, was jumping up to see in the window, all of them held up a hand to wave as the bus groaned and wheezed into motion, and her heart broke open to imprint this image, the radiant love of their up-turned faces. They would be scattered in the years to come, but this moment's bond she would carry forward. It wasn't just this moment but all of their time together brought forward to this beaming wave, this was hers forever.

"I wonder what will happen," Max mused out loud.

Briseis looked toward him with an odd half-smile.

"What do you mean, *what will happen*?" Maki asked.

"Oh," Max sighed, "just that Sandra is in flux. I mean, yes, we are all in flux, all changing, you kids the most, obviously. It's just that Sandra hasn't found her place yet. I know this only because she's still looking."

"Maybe she has lots of places."

"Maybe. If that's the case, then one of them is here, with us."

The bus turned the corner, and they all watched its absence, the lack of bus and what it had taken. Max looked up at the heavy gray sky expecting a bird, but it was just miles of dense cotton. Leo tugged on his arm, and he looked down into a toothy grin.

If her horny feet protrude, they come
To show how cold she is, and dumb, he shouted.

Maki and Max loudly joined him.

Let the lamp affix its beam.
The only emperor is the emperor of ice cream!

Briseis felt her whole face open in a smile as she watched them. No matter what, he would always be father to these children. Max reached out with his spare arm and pulled her to him, and they moved off down the sidewalk, a jiggly eight-legged creature with a nose for something cold and sweet.

Part Two

2001-02

A MOTLEY OF MUTTS

When you come down a country road with four beasts
bounding, folks give way, tits and sparrows and
magpies burst from the maquis and scrub oak
in full shrieking terror and the dogs scatter in pursuit,
the tall grass in the orchards quivers and bends before
our rush our pure bouncing energy,
the energy of going,
the pursuit of nothing but blurs in the twilight.

Eleven years ago today we landed in Greece,
in midnight Patras on a boat from Ancona—two nights
and a day gliding down a glassy Adriatic, to the east
the humps and rocky darkness of the Balkans, quiet,
on the verge of explosion, our young children slept
through customs, stuffed in the back seat with
saxophone and typewriter, gecko blaster and books,
nothing to declare but our love,
a sum far greater than the parts.

And Lulu, our oldest beast, was being born about then
to a wild bitch in a cave just down the road from here.
Shepherds found the litter of eleven, dropped seven in
a barrel of water and found homes for the other four.
Lulu carries fortune with her, through the years
dodging death with dumb luck and strength and will,
to be, to be with us, to roam the hills pushing herself
upon all manner of creature. She loves a fight,
goes out of her way to find one, even now,
old and arthritic, she's ready to mix it up.
Sticks her nose in badger holes, comes back

175

a bloody mess, next night,
what the hell, goes out and does it again

The chain of command is loose, not really a chain
but a frayed old rope in my whistles that bring them
plunging out of the bush for new direction.
I don't talk canine, they listen human, they listen
and respond en masse a moment before scattering
along the tracks of lesser mammals, snouts to the
trail and traveling low they savor the vapor
of hedgehog and kounavi that clings to grass,
that wafts amongst wildflower, that saturates the earth,
they see this gaseous form sharp in their
mechanical minds and when one hits a fresh scent
they roar in their joy and
the pack converges again as one.

In these years we have pushed ourselves out onto
the edge of human into more animal and less,
much less, we cannot run, we are dead meat on open
ground, we have discovered a bad gene or two, have
turned on ourselves and watch our limitations multiply
so that the horizon is dense with the wreckage
of incomplete and out of reach gestures, tasks, and
manners of being. We will never climb that mountain,
never ever swim out to that island; we cannot believe
our good fortune—we can still dance, after a fashion,
and the dogs, ecstatic with this news, dash into the hills
where they roll in copria and carrion returning so
pungent we lock them out and turn on the hoses.

They have marked our time here, these animals we
have gathered and lost and found again.

They catch us out and witness our every,
our turns of silent cruelty, our rage at their constant
needs, our rolled up newspapers, our lunch leavings
tossed in the air for them to catch and catch, they give
us this small connection to the wild, to the too small
place in us that glows with this contact with spirit
without guile, to hunger and what is greater.
They go crazy, and I follow.

1

EARLY MORNING. Leonidas and Andromache had just left the house, walking down the hill to the main road where the bus would pick them up. Max was at the dining room table with a steaming mug of green tea that he was vaguely sipping while reading Cormac McCarthy's *Cities of the Plain*. He looked up, out the glass doors and across the valley to the east just as the sunrise burst through a bank of clouds hovering over Parnona. A spectrum of brilliant orange flashes rayed out of the cloud gap and randomly illuminated wooded hillocks across the broad valley. Motionless, empty-headed, he watched the silent sun blaze away at the clouds, and then, without any preliminary or connective thoughts, picked up his pencil and wrote:

> *I believe I am in exile now*
> *from something more than country*

Just that. The beginning of something. It felt like it came from deep inside and carried with it a big meaning, like an omen or maybe the advent of deeper understanding. Something more than country. Beyond nationality, beyond culture, outside of language. Where was he? Not in Mexico where John Grady was pursuing his doomed romance. In Greece, here, he didn't belong here either. It didn't matter. He had no need to belong, to attach himself to a particular geography. Where was this exile beyond country, beyond the landscape? You probably couldn't get there on horseback.

The phone rang and he picked it up. The voice of

Briseis's doctor filled his head. "Max, this is Panos, how are you?"

"I'm fine."

"I have some bad news. We got back the biopsy, it's lung cancer."

It wasn't so much like being punched but as though a giant, placing one hand on his chest and stomach, the other on his back, had pressed its palms together, squeezing out every ounce of air in one violent exhalation. His field of vision had narrowed to the cover of the novel, a fire in a distant wheat field, flames and billowing smoke rising from a flat horizon toward which plowed rows streamed.

The doctor was talking. "The way to approach this is that the survival rate is about five years, which is the same as with the scleroderma, and so, this might not shorten her chances."

"You think so?"

"I'm sorry, Max. We just have to move forward on this. I'll set you up with a friend of mine. He's the best oncologist in Greece. She'll need to start chemotherapy right away."

"Have you told her?"

"No. We thought you should be here. That's why I called so early."

"Right." Max looked at the clock on the wall. Nine. "I'll leave now and be there by noon."

"Noon. Okay, Costa and I will be there shortly after that."

He pushed the off button and slowly laid the phone down on the table. His free hand still held the book, closed on a finger marking his place. He stuck a scrap of paper in the place and set it aside and thought, this is the end, how long will it last? He closed his eyes and looked,

179

there was only darkness, no image appeared, and listened to the air passing in and out of his nostrils. He picked the phone back up, punched in a code. He would call his son, who wouldn't question him, wouldn't sense in his voice the sagging weight of it, the vertigo of death blurring their lives' horizon.

Leonidas answered in a whisper, "Daddy, we're in class."

"Yeah, I'll be quick. I'm going back up to Athens."

"Is everything okay?"

"Yeah. I'm going to bring your mom back. Eat lunch in town and I'll pick you guys up from frontistirio as usual. I'll call if I'm late."

"Kalo taxidi."

"Thanks." He clicked off and exhaled wearily.

Leaving Sparti, north to Athens, requires crossing over the lone bridge spanning the Evrotas River. Briseis used to sing her grandfather's song, *Yasou Evrotas*, every time they crossed over, encouraged the kids to sing along. But the last years, with all the relentless trips to Athens, round after round of medical treatment, the river had remained unsung. Max glanced at the large Roma encampment along the river: not a traditional gypsy tent left, instead a rickety village of wood frames covered by plastic that shuddered in the wind. To be sure, no one there knew the song.

The road quickly climbs out of the valley, Voutiani the first mountain village, houses piled upon each other, olive orchards spread out in every direction, a lone church on a hilltop and the first panoramic view of the Tayegetos, bald and gray, defining the sky, a great rock grumble sharpening its teeth on cloud, pushing south toward the sea.

A dead fox along the road, a herd of goats working the chaparraled hillside, mountains to the east, hazy layers of blue crisscrossing, swelling like waves, uninhabited, inedible. It was all the same, so many mornings to the city, every curve and dip in the road. Yet this morning had a hollow core, there was no hope at the end of it. He didn't believe that a cure lay ahead. Had he ever? Is it ever possible to know what you thought at any point in time, completely stripped of what was later learned? There was no way to gloss over the carcinogenic doom. How would she take it? Had she already resigned herself? They always discussed these issues indirectly, feeling that positive thinking was, if not healing, if not actually impacting the connective tissue, the assaulted organs, at least more pleasant, a light cast on a pretend future. They juggled hope that way, knowing they couldn't keep it in the air for long, that it would bounce off their awkward hands and crash at their feet. Sprayed on a concrete retaining wall were the slogans of the Communist Party, bewailing the march of history. How could she fight cancer, half-finished as she was, surely?

Down a long curving slice through the earth he unconsciously leaned into the turn. In a short flat valley lay the memorial to the 118, a particularly Spartan remembrance. Throughout Greece were other markers, testimonials to the swift cruelty of the Nazis. A plinth engraved with the names, adorned with roses, punctured the air. In order to control the community and deter resistance, the Germans rounded up 118 prominent Spartan citizens and kept them incarcerated. Briseis's grandfather, conductor of the local orchestra and choir, music teacher at the high school and prominent composer, heard the night before the roundup from a friend, the

German teacher at the high school, who had been pressed into service as a translator, that he was on the list. An hour later he and his wife left, hidden on a wagon full of watermelons bound for Athens. The captives were moved about but eventually, as reprisal for resistance activities, brought to this desolate valley and executed.

Each year the Sparti Philharmonic was bussed out to play the national anthem and a funeral dirge. It was always cold, the wind whipping across the heather, scrub brush, and stone as each name was read, and after each name another shouted, "Present!" "Paron!" echoed out over the scattered relatives. It was a litany that never failed to chill. Four men from one family perished on that awful day. To Leonidas on clarinet it was just another gig, a short one, but Max always found himself staring out over the landscape wondering where they fell, imaging the shackled prisoners facing the firing squad, the order given and how they fell. Paron! Last year Briseis hadn't gotten out of the car, too cold.

Further up in the mountains the leaves had changed, were falling. At this altitude winter was near. Two winters back he had driven through heavy snow, only one lane open for many miles, police with phones at each end letting one direction through, then the other. Briseis had been at the hospital in the city enduring massive cortisone treatments to bring her inflammation down. With each crisis he had to balance the needs of Leonidas and Andromache with hers. Her sister Elektra helped, sometimes spending a week in the city, or feeding the kids. He could hire attendants at the hospital. She needed him most, but the kids were in their last year of high school, racing around all afternoon and evening to private schools, and needed support. Briseis often insisted that he return home. A tree

182

growing up through an abandoned house. He passed an old quarry, a great white and red rock gouge torn from a hillside, he was probably driving on it.

He stuck Moby's "Play" in the CD player, and the car filled with "My honey come back, sometime." It was as though his mix was designed for this very drive. "I'm going to find my baby, whoa, 'fore that sun go down." Heartstruck lyrics moaned out relentlessly. He wept through Alepohori, fox village, and rolled down into the wide Tripoli valley. They had loved driving around the Peloponnese. Just shove the kids in the back, grab the map, and hit the road. They might drive a couple of hours just to see what that village looked liked. When they were young the kids loved it, stuffing the back of the car with pillows, stuffed animals, comic books, Gameboys; as teenagers they slept through the departures and feigned interest when their parents returned chattering about their dull adventures: the old-fashioned kafenion in this village, the church in the cave, the remote beach at the end of ten miles of dirt road. "When can you drive us to Sparti?" was often their only response.

They saw different parts of the whole, focused on dissimilar detail, and then put it together, reminding each other of what they had seen but not noted. Often they did it while looking, pointing out the odd tool hanging behind the counter, the gecko peeking out from the wall, the tortured shoes of a village yia-yia, adhered to a windshield an icon dangling from a suction cup. He could see her before the birth of the children, vigorous, beaming, unwound from all the constrictions of pain and deformity. "Why does my heart feel so bad? Why does my soul feel so bad?" pleaded a soulful man from the CD. Because I

183

want to hang onto this life, answered Max, because the suffering of those I love is gnawing away at me. Because I don't know the way forward. She never really recovered from birthing the twins. Not completely. So much of life we don't recover from, so much leaves us diminished. Nietzsche was wrong when he said, "That which does not kill, strengthens." Life is a slow grinding down, each blow weakens, till you have nothing to resist with. Exiting from the Artemisium tunnel you realize how high up you are, with the long valley descent below you, down to Korinth and the sea. "Why does my heart feel so bad?"

They had stayed with Brie's parents in Porto Rafti, a seaside village on the east coast of the Attica peninsula, forty-five minutes from Athens. All the family were there, in various rented houses, preparing for the big event. Briseis and Max had never thought much about getting married. Then Max figured they could probably get an extended vacation in Greece if it was presented in the proper fashion. Max's parents flew the entire tribe to Greece. The twins were a year and a half old, Briseis's daughter Amalia was an exquisite sixteen, they were thirty-five, and they daily hiked over the hill to Avalaki Beach to swim and sun, everyone deeply tanned.

• •

THE YOUNG WOMEN WITH THE MOPS were in the hallway. Short, squat, strong, Albanians, Ukrainians, Eastern Bloc diaspora cleaning up the oozing filth of Greece. Several times a day. A good job. First the broom, then the wet mop. She admired their powerful backs, their strength, able to work all day at this steady, methodical pace. They were outside the regular hierarchy of the hospital. Everyone, nurses and doctors, got out of their way. Minutes later

184

they were gone, pong of ammonia in their wake.

Briseis sipped her weak hospital tea, looked out the window at the trees in the park, vaguely listened to the old women at the next bed. "Panayioti fell off the mule, they say he won't be able to work for a week! A week! How will they manage!" Fine, I'm sure. A week off, seegah. Try the rest of your life. Briseis reached for her journal and thumbed it to the day. Sighed and looked at the previous days.

5 October

Took 8 mg Medrol today to see if I perk up at all (plus want to get house clean). Well, didn't perk up too much. Groggy in the morn—tired & furious because of Amalia's phone call at midnight last night. She went on and on shouting at me about sending her rent money to go to school & she owes money everywhere. I can't figure out her math at all. Tried to explain that I couldn't commit to an amount until I know results of test next week—maybe I'll need an operation or something. She couldn't get it. I got enraged & shouted back at her. Still furious this morning cause couldn't sleep well. M gave me Kornfield's Meditation on Anger. Very interesting but obviously going to be a lot of work. Took Leo to doc (Ionnides)—has bronchitis in right lung. I knocked over a motorbike as I was parking—to L's huge embarrassment. Everyone watching from balcony. Gave guy my #. Crummy old thing it was. On way home Leo complimented me on my hair & outfit, so am not a complete loss.   Felt really bad, forgot to get Max newspaper and chocolate. Did some embroidery but had to keep changing stuff as didn't look like I thought it would—cannot figure out border at all. Also typed recipes so not totally unproductive in spite of grogginess.

6 October

Fat face again this morn—think I'll go back to 4 mg Medrol. What's a little lethargy comp. to not having a fat face. Sore from sex last night. Got stuff ready for tomorrow. Made a plum/apple crumble. Swept liv rm & dusted a wee bit—was sweating like crazy & exhausted afterwards. Am reading Poisonwood Bible— really good. Incredibly well-written—distinct voices of the narrators & you feel you are in the jungle.

7 October

Go to Athens. Make egg salad for L & A. We get to Athens— Don calls on the cell and we arrange to meet at the entrance to the Tower of the Winds. We get there on time, 2:30 & wait, then grab a restaurant table right opposite—great spot. After waiting a while we order food & around 3:30 Don calls—is waiting somewhere else entirely. Finally meets us by which time we've finished eating. We had a nice time anyway but then I had to go check in at the hospital. It's always weird going into a new ward—everyone stares at you & you ignore them. But later everyone gets to know about everyone else—way more details than you could possibly want to know.

8 October

Scan 8:30 a.m.?? Didn't sleep much. Hospital noises & goofy woman talking all night & getting up & pulling her IV out. Got up at 6 and had shower so I'd be ready. M came early. Then waited till noon getting more & more apprehensive. Finally went down. Was ghastly, had to lie on stomach w/arms overhead for almost an hour it seemed like. Hands went completely numb & I was worried they'd get bad bits on them from no circulation for so long. Actual thing hurt only briefly but there was endless going in & out of the cat scan & them yelling at me not to move. Afterwards I was furious & told Panos they should explain what they are doing & not treat me like a piece of meat. Had to stay prone for the next few hours & not eat anything cause some air got in my lungs. Was starving. Cheated a few sips of tea, which was wonderful.

∙ ∙

THE TRAFFIC UP LEOFOROS ALEXANDRAS was already slowed to the pace of a brisk walk. Max put on John Coltrane's "A Love Supreme" and drifted with the waves of notes that poured out of the man's tenor sax. Jimmy Garrison thumped out the melody on bass. A conversation with God, obviously, there being nothing supreme about human love, grounded and walking with a limp. In that apartment building on the right, Brie's grandparents had had an apartment. He first met them up there, on their wedding trip. Everything covered with dollies. Papous, already in his eighties, had bought strange little marionettes for the kids and spent a long time trying to make them work, to no avail. Yia-Yia fussing about, afraid the kids would break something, which, a mere eighteen months old, they were very capable of doing. Papous had written them songs and went to the piano and sang them. Leo and Maki, to their credit, did not burst into tears but smiled angelically, even clapping afterward. The old egomaniac lapped it up. Applause from his great-grandchildren, his due. Tough being a genius, but it has its rewards.

The national police headquarters towered above the street, fat cops loitering on the sidewalk, protecting the building, in theory. Coltrane was moaning. It must be nice to have a god, Max thought. One that could answer your requests, prayers, whatever. You listening up there? How 'bout a little of that cure stuff down here? Turn up the love beam and heal my wife, huh? Yesterday would be soon enough. When a taxi tried to cut him off, he gave a long blast on his horn and sneered at the driver.

Max slipped through the mess of intersections at the

187

end of Alexandras and up the hill past the children's hospital. Kiosks festooned with balloons and stuffed animals and whatever other cheap children's crap they could think to overcharge for. He took a right on Mikras Asias and cruised by the Laiko Hospital, fully locked into the circling search for on-street parking. He lucked out, finding a spot a mere two blocks away, grabbed tea and pastries at a croissant shop across the street from the entrance, and pushed his way through the milling crowds. Besides patients and staff there's again as many people and more roaming about the hospital halls, smoking, talking, waiting for news.

The cleaning ladies had taken over the ward, all visitors banished until the mopping was done. They bent to it, wagging their peasant asses down the hall, that thrusting arm gesture, back and forth, just right for working the soil, or a floor. They always seemed to be around, but the hospital was never clean. Chipped paint, cracked marble, exposed pipes, broken furniture, the entire building sagging with fatigue. Drug reps in double-breasted suits, glistening shoes and freshly coiffed, loitered in the lobby, waiting for a chance to stroke the doctors with free samples. Max found their position a peculiar fence-straddle, salesmen without an order book, who never made a sale. A phalanx of lab-coated doctors swooped through the swinging doors of the ward and disappeared down another hallway. They must be late for their coffee. New doctors, mostly young women, jeans and sport shoes beneath their lab coats, healthy, full of success, no children yet, powerful futures ahead. Maybe.

Max rotated the inevitable sentence in his head. He couldn't possibly wait for the doctors to arrive, couldn't imagine being with Briseis and not telling her. They were too much together, the bond too thorough. He could never have had an undiscovered affair. She would have known with his first step through the door, they were adhered in so many places, at hip and heart and head. The doors of the ward swung open, and the families of the ailing groaned to their feet and shuffled forward.

• •

SHE SAW HIM IN THE DOORWAY, waiting for two heavy women to squeeze in around their aged mother. Was Max supposed to be here today? She couldn't remember. Wasn't he supposed to come tomorrow? Oh good, he had tea and croissants.

"Hi, my love, what a pleasant surprise!"

Max pushed aside the debris on her side table, set down the sack with the tea and pastry, and sat down on the edge of the bed. "Kalimera, my dear. How you sleep?"

"Oh, not bad. Rula the night nurse gave me a warm sponge bath, and after that the ward was quiet and I think I slept for hours. Then, about five in the morning some frightful woman somewhere down the ward started wailing, Lord knows what about. She went on for a bloody hour, I swear, and it didn't sound like anyone was helping her."

Max picked up her hand, examining, stroking. "Panos called me this morning." He looked up into her face. "It's cancer. The prognosis is five years. Oh god, I'm so sorry." He put his head on her lap and began to sob. She stroked the back of his head. Cancer? What, I have cancer? She couldn't grasp it, it wouldn't stay put in her mind. Tears were streaming down her face. What does he mean, cancer? Max raised his tear-stained face from the sheets, reined himself in, stopped shaking.

189

"I don't know what to say. I'm so sorry, Brie."

"Well, there's nothing for you to be sorry about. So this is why you're here. They called and told you, didn't they? And when are they going to tell me?"

"They'll be here by noon or so, I think. They wanted me to be here."

"But why, why do I have lung cancer, I don't even smoke. This is what caused all the coughing, isn't it? It sure took them long enough to make this call. Fungus, *fungoose*, they kept saying!"

Infuriated, she looked around the room. Hair a vivid orange, a bloated yellow diabetic woman groaned in the next bed. She was doomed to lose her toes, though she didn't know this. The examining doctor had turned to the assembled students only yesterday and told them this in English. Her dreary daughter was there twenty-four hours a day with the bedpan and brow mop. Near the door was a frail, ancient village woman on oxygen. Every hour or so she raised herself up and chirped out a series of tiny bird calls. She's calling her long-dead husband, said her granddaughter, who came every afternoon. Everyone here is doomed, Briseis thought. A woman in a nightgown dragging behind her a bag of urine, IV hose dangling from her arm, stuck her head into the room. "How do you get out of here? I'm leaving! You stay here, you're gonna die!" She snorted and shuffled down the hall. There was no arguing with that. Truth, oozing and sick and lost.

2

October 15

People calling all the time. I'm so tired of telling everyone I'm even sicker than before, of people catching their breaths, trying to think of something positive to say. Daddy told me to "just bat on." This afternoon sitting on the hiati watching the light change on the mountains I suddenly realized I didn't have any resentment against anyone—it's all magically gone. But then I realized I am incredibly resentful that my body has done this. Also afraid of pain, etc. And also realized that I had been feeling sorry for the doctors having to tell me I had cancer instead of feeling sorry for myself. Not that that would have done any good. Last night my back hurt where they did the biopsy. We made love this morning, it was very nice—life in the old bag yet. Maki and Leo being very sweet and attentive. They have no idea what's to come. Neither do I.

October 17

Dark in the morning now, dawn just starting to come up with a stripe of pink and purple over the top of the hills. Max and I both tired and blue—the bad news is finally hitting us! Now realize all the warning signs were there—high lefka (white blood cells), getting more anemic, diarrhea, fatigue, sweating (Medrol hid the fever). Now I am really very mad that this wasn't diagnosed earlier. It was on the scans, although the bronchoscopy showed negative, for some reason.

Very sad all day. In the early evening took a walk with Max and the dogs, it was very beautiful, everything so vivid and bright and clear. The dogs were snacking on dried figs and pears they found on the ground. Then I found a few blackberries and further up the dogs found some grapes on the vine. Foragers, the lot of us. I couldn't walk that far, but it lifted my spirits and I feel much better. Played cards with Maki in the evening while Leo and Max played some awful computer game full of shooting and people screaming with pain. And this was from his office at the other end of the house. What is it about males?

22 October
Horrible day. Awful traffic in the city, took us ages to get to Kifissia. There was a horde in the doctor's waiting room and we waited for an hour and a half and then see this youngish doctor w/ very blue eyes who tells me that this may be a secondary cancer, with the primary being in the womb or ovaries. He examines my belly but doesn't say what's there. He doesn't give us any info about the disease or prognosis or possibilities, just do the scan and do the chemo. I'm totally freaked out when we leave and we fight traffic all the way back in to town and the hotel. Later I call home and Maki says Dimitra and Katarina are spending the night and that Leo is at Socrates's. Don't have to worry about them, anyway.

23 October
Wake feeling ghastly. The Alexandra Hospital is a maze of broken decaying buildings and we have to wander around for quite a while trying to find the place for the CT scan. It's in a temporary building (that's obviously been in use for years) in the back yard, completely unsigned. You're just supposed to know, I guess, because no one could give us directions.

We wait for hours. Max looks up at a sign in the room, ANAMONH (ana mo nee) and asks, "What does that mean?" "Waiting." "Just that, waiting?" I nod and he gets out his notebook and begins scribbling madly. The head nurse calls me into her office and asks me how I first felt with scleroderma. She has it too. Says she went to John Hopkins and they didn't help her at all. They finally do the scan and afterwards they have us wandering all over the hospital getting papers signed, little stamps affixed, and nobody even wants to do the job. They act like you're imposing on them!

192

Finally get the scans and they are clear except for some crystals on the ribs. Then the doctor starts yelling because I don't have my IKA book, which the hospital that did the biopsy has kept, says I'll have to pay! The head nurse comes in and tells him to stop bothering me, to just let me go with my scans. Bless her, we are sisters in the skin.

We call the other hospital about the IKA book and they say first that it's not there, then that they aren't finished with it.

October 24

At 8 AM we dutifully present ourselves at the blue door. But disaster—they absolutely have to have the IKA book. The doctor says do it tomorrow but then relents and says if we're back by 9 AM we can still do it. We race out and luckily catch a cab to the other hospital. They've lost my book! And try and send me away. I stand there forcing them to keep looking and finally they find it. We have good cab karma and make it back just in time. Whew. But the system is unbelievably stupid. While I wait for my treatment Max has to dash all over with papers and then drive about twenty minutes to another IKA building. He gets lost twice and has to call and get better directions. There he waits in line to get the chemotherapy drugs. Whereupon he returns and delivers them to the staff. Huh? They don't use those actual drugs on me, what he's doing is replacing what is used. But why don't they have the drugs at the hospital? It often seems they've made it as difficult as possible, but that's probably giving them too much credit. More likely it was created haphazardly over the years by many different people who were not coordinating with each other. And everyone just accepts it. It's a tremendous relief when we arrive home in the late afternoon.

• •

MAX CAME INTO THE SALONI and held out a piece of paper to his wife. "Here, my love, a new letter poem, to Dan Raphael. Remember I told you about the window-

193

washer at the Alexandra?"

"Vaguely."

"Yeah, well I use that image."

TO DAN: THE VIEW FROM THE HALLWAY

Dan, read your greatest hits while hanging
in the hallway outside the cancer ward,
sunshine streaming in the windows,
Athens a hazy glow below, pigeons leaping
into space, beating the air—afunction with
the crumbling Athenian architecture.
A man was washing a window
on another part of the building,
he had no scaffolding, just reached
his arm out and squeegeed the sliding window
but couldn't get it all, finally climbed out
on the four inches of sill and perched
above forty feet of air ending in concrete,
he closed the window and while gripping
a bit of plaster trim squeaked it clean.
I reached out of my window and felt for the handhold,
no purchase. A breath of wind, oh,
and he would be with the pigeons.
Some sit, some pace,
some search for greater danger.
Not a lot of laughs in that hallway.
It's not a matter of knowing anymore.
Come, look at the pigeons, look at that man
perched there without wings. You see,
we risk everything here
that we might clearly see.

"It's very nice. This has longer lines than most of

194

this series. *Squeegeed*, what a great sound. Do you want 'afunction' to be one word?"

"I thought maybe. The longer lines are probably 'cause it's to Dan, though they're not like breath lines."

Briseis went back over the poem line by line, looking mostly for the extra word. She handed the poem back. "Read it, I want to hear it."

Max, still standing, shifted into his big poetry voice. Briseis closed her eyes and let the words pound into her skull. This was what was happening while she had poison flowing into her veins. Max was reading poetry and watching pigeons and window-washers. While she sat in a mental fog he was trying to more *clearly see*. From her flight chair in the chemo room there was nothing to see, just other wingless creatures taking the treatment. Earthbound. What does he see when he looks at me? The old me, I hope, the thirty-year-old me. How awful if he saw me as I am, twisted and swollen, hair falling out, suffering, and not very gracefully at that.

Later, she looked at the poem again and wondered, would she have fallen in love with him without the poetry? A stupid question but still, it wasn't the first time she had asked it. This musical language was a great seduction tool, for her anyway. Then again, bad poetry was extremely off-putting. Well, one had to have some standards. Couldn't go about boinking any old bard spouting erotic couplets. Just wouldn't do.

195

3

Uᴘ ᴛʜᴇ ʀᴏᴀᴅ ᴛʜʀᴇᴇ ʜᴜɴᴅʀᴇᴅ ᴍᴇᴛᴇʀs past the end of the village was a big blue American style mailbox that bore the legend:

PARNELL
ΒΡΟΜΟΓΟΥΡΝΑ
ΑΓΙΑ ΕΙΡΗΝΗ

From the box a paved road led sharply up through the olive groves some fifty meters till the trees opened on a house perched on the highest point of the hill; you looked up, only the tile edge of the roof visible. The land fell away in every direction. It was two stories of building cut into the hill. Around both floors wrapped a wide covered balcony and, below, patio. The house was covered in a plethora of climbing plants that reached the roof: white and yellow jasmine, wisteria, honeysuckle, bougainvillea, trumpet vine, and roses. From a circular parking area a stone staircase curved up through a garden to the upper floor and the main entrance. The house was designed to face south down the valley to Sparti eight kilometers away and east toward the Parnona mountain range, twenty kilometers distant. The Tayegetos loomed directly above. The Byzantine castle at Mystras appeared beyond the closest foothills. A formal entryway on the south front of the house opened to a large living, dining, and cooking space. Many windows and double glass doors opened onto the hiati from both the dining room and the living room. On the north side of the upper floor were Briseis and Max's bedroom and Max's office. The childrens' rooms were downstairs. All four bedrooms had double glass doors that opened onto covered outdoor areas. From every vantage point were olive trees and mountains.

Sunrise was still a ways away, but the birds were heralding its approach. Max kept his eyes closed and took it in. Sparrows and tits twittered about their dreams, a dove cooed, and there was Brie's little owl with that peculiar call, like a puppy's bark. Maybe it was speaking to Brie's subconscious mind, conclusion to a healing dream. A power chord resounded from an electric guitar, then another followed by an unaccompanied signature bass line, and Rage Against the Machine roared into "Killing in the Name of." Leo used his music as his alarm clock. Five days a week at 6:30 in the morning, the house thundered with his playlist. He'd been waking to this tune for the past two weeks. Max listened to the opening cut and soon knew all the lyrics. Sometimes he'd rather not. Limp Bizkit, for instance, was true excrement, but Rage Against the Machine he had come to like, especially this track. *Some of those that burn crosses, are the same that hold office.* Very clever. How the refrain, *Now ya do what they told ya"* eventually changed to the ending chant, *Fuck you, I won't do what ya tell me.* Max felt it was completely appropriate that this children left for school with this ringing in their ears. He'd had the same attitude, without the song. He rose and shuffled off to the bathroom.

Leo hated to be late and miss the bus. It amused his family that he displayed no discipline in any other aspect of his life: music, studies, cleaning or picking up after himself. This and personal hygiene. He'd no more go to school without showering than he'd open a schoolbook over breakfast. He just wanted to get there on time, then he could go back to sleep, or torment the teachers. By the third tune he was up and moving toward the shower. Upstairs his father was making tea and coffee, in the next

197

room his sister was groaning.

Andromache did not wish to rise. Though Leo's music had the desired effect, she felt she'd been dragged from sleep, her fingers dug deep, furrowing the soil of dreams as she entered, reluctantly, the day. She'd been late for something there, too. She was supposed to show some drawings, they kept falling out of her portfolio, and people were stepping on them, the bastards. She peered across her dimly lit room toward her open closet. What could she possibly wear that would lift her into the day?

Their parents over the years had refined their response to the mediocre chaos that was the Greek school system. In high school everything was aimed at passing the panalinions, the university entrance exams, university being essential for a civil service job, the holy grail of Greece. Because no one trusted the public schools' ability to prepare their little darlings, an entire alternative school system, the frontesterios, had developed, a bewildering collage of private schools teaching language arts, the sciences and maths, history, and on. From two in the afternoon till sometimes ten in the evening the children of Sparti, and all across Greece, would dutifully troop between schools getting the information required pounded into their skulls. Rare was the child who could succeed without the benefit of the frontesterios, which drained the pockets of Greek families, down to the working poor scrambling and scraping to come up with the funds. The entire system, public and private, emphasized rote learning over everything else. Creativity, analytical thought, had no place, precise regurgitation was the order of the day. If they had known just how bad it was in the beginning, Max and Briseis might have moved on, but the primary-school experience, a class of twelve in the village school, had lulled them into complacency, and then it seemed too late. They had investigated private schools in Athens but couldn't bear the idea of moving to the city. Over the years as they spoke with many teachers, students, and parents, their contempt for the system had only grown along with their resignation. Max didn't like the idea of mass education. After learning to read and write and do basic math, the rest was a crock: expensive mind-control baby-sitting. For him the knowledge and experiences that were useful in life occurred outside of schools. Briseis was not so extreme, but her memories of her own schooling, as an army brat with a different school nearly every year, and her suffering at the hands of teachers and fellow students could still send a chill through her.

So they told their children, learn what you can, make sure you graduate, and then go abroad to study, if that's what you want to do. They had no doubts about the intelligence and abilities of their children. Their Greek was good, their English was at a very high level, they had availed themselves of the large private library their parents had accumulated, they had traveled and been exposed to a variety of experience far beyond their contemporaries. All these privileges would open the door to the next level if they knocked. So besides math and science, which they both enjoyed, they bypassed the frontesterio system. They took music lessons and Andromache found a local artist who would critique her work. It was enough.

Max saw and heard the bus roaring up the hill. It went up two villages above, turned around, and came back down. Took about twenty minutes.

"Bus up!" He shouted down at them.

He plopped the milk down in front of Leo, who poured

199

it over his muesli and began to shovel it in.

"Is Maki up?"

"Yeah."

"Do you think she wants coffee?"

"Don't know."

"Okay. Right." He called downstairs. "You got time for java?"

"Probably not, Daddy." Maki changed her scarf and undid her hair. She was too groggy and hazy to shower every morning. It was enough just to get up. She looked in the full-length mirror, stuck both hands into her hair and tousled it a bit. Looked again. Shrugged and grabbed her bag. Out the window she saw Leo walking down the road. She opened the window and shouted, "Leo, wait just a second, gawd!" She could leave from the downstairs but always came up to say goodbye. She ran upstairs, kissed her father as he opened the door, and ran down the stairs. Max looked uphill, saw the bus rounding a bend. Just in time. They rarely missed it, though it was entirely Leo's doing.

• •

Andromache walked down Paliologou with Katarina and Effie, another day of high school bullshit over. It was such an utter waste of time. She couldn't wait to be done with it. Six more months.

"Maki, what are you doing for lunch?"

"I got physics and math starting at two. So pita, sandwich, the same old shit."

"Where?"

"I'm not sure, the Ritz or I don't know. I got to meet Leo at the platea. He's got the money."

"God, you're so lucky you don't have to go to

200

frontistirio all day. I get off at nine."

"That sucks."

Andromache was aware of the privileged position she and Leo occupied. It was a freedom. All they had to do was graduate, not worry about scoring high enough to get into university in Athens or Thessaloniki. Come September she would be painting at the Art Student's League in New York City and living at Sandra's apartment in the East Village. She sometimes found herself looking around Sparti thinking *not soon enough.*

She walked up to a group of boys in the platea and exchanged hugs, handslaps, caresses, the habitual physical intimacy of Greek culture. "Where's Leo?"

"He coming, he's just over at that kiosk." Adonis loved speaking English and always tried to use it with Andromache. She encouraged him.

"Adoni, did you burn me that program yet?"

"It's right here in my bag."

Leo walked up. "Maki, what are you gonna eat?"

"I don't know. I'm so bored with what's on offer here on the fabulous Sparti platea. How much money do we have?"

Leo reached in his pocket and pulled out a wad of bills and coins. "Twelve euros."

Maki stared across the platea toward the usual fast food joints. "I wish they had pizza by the slice here. I mean, good pizza by the slice."

"Yeah well, they don't. I'm going for a pita."

"Okay, get me one too. And some fries, and a coke."

"Why don't you just come with me and get it yourself."

"Okay, okay. You gotta smoke?"

There was no sign they were twins by their walk. Leo had developed a hands-in-pocket street shuffle that he considered quintessentially American. Maki walked with a full hip rotation that had been garnering the attention of men at cafés for the past two years.

"They're coming back tonight, right?"

"That's what Daddy said. We can call them after classes. Do you have music tonight?"

"Harmony and piano, six to eight."

"I'm going to go over to Carlos's for a while. I'll meet you at the Enigma afterwards."

Carlos was Andromache's occasional lover. Chilean, he had arrived in Sparti a year earlier and opened an import shop. Handsome, charming, divorced, with a child, he spoke Greek with a Spanish accent that softened and made musical everything he said. He was very kind to her, gave her clothes from the shop, did not try to possess her.

Maki had told Briseis about Carlos soon after she'd gotten involved, and her mother had understood right away.

"You're being careful, of course."

"Yes, Mom, and Carlos is too. He doesn't want a mistake pregnancy on his hands. He knows what that means. And lots of other stuff too. It's not like being with some teenage boy who can't wait to get it out of his pants."

They shared a laugh. "Believe it or not, I do remember that."

"He's turning me on to all sorts of new music. He's been everywhere, India, Thailand, Bali, and the States too. His Greek is better than his English."

"I love his accent."

"I know. At first you don't even think you're hearing Greek. He's a man, he takes care of himself, has his own place. And he's not clingy or anything like that, he's just happy any time I come by. And gives me a kiss when I leave. It's really nice. I know it's not some permanent relationship but right now, I like it."

Briseis gave her daughter a hug. "I'm happy you're having this experience, I really am. It will broaden your perspective. There is one thing, though. I'll have to tell your father." She could feel Maki's shoulders slump.

"Do you have to?"

"Yes. We don't keep stuff like this from each other. That's not how we do things."

"He's not going to like it, is he?"

Briseis took a deep breath and starting coughing. She motioned toward a bottle of cough syrup. Maki poured a spoon, ladled it into her mouth, and then rubbed her shoulders till the spasm passed. "Like it? No, he probably will never like it, but I think I can bring him around to acceptance, though it may be grudging at first. I'll think about it for a while before I bring it up. You know how Daddy is, he can really pinpoint the weak parts in your argument. You are going to keep seeing Carlos, aren't you?"

"Yeah, what do you mean?"

"Well, if it was just a brief fling, you know, maybe it wouldn't be necessary to get him all excited."

"Mom, what did you just say?"

"I'm kidding, of course I'll tell him. I don't look forward to the conversation, but that's part of adult life, sucking it up and facing the music. And it will be okay. Daddy's a very understanding man, but you know, he adores you. You're his girl." Briseis paused, lost in thought for moment. "It's fascinating, really. He loves you and Leo very much, as you know, but his relationship with each of

203

you is so different. He and Leo are like pals, hanging out playing video games, drinking beers, guy stuff. Whereas with you he's very solicitous of your needs. He's always wanting to smooth your path, make it easy. He's much more nurturing. With Leo he's more, 'Come on, don't be a wuss, stand up and take care of business.' Which is a good attitude to take with Leo, otherwise he tends to slide. You don't require that, except for getting up in the morning."

"Tell me about it."

"And maybe I'm just the opposite?"

"Yeah mom, kinda ying-yang."

"More like ding-a-ling. Make-it-up-as-you-go-along parenting. Toss the dice and hope for the best. We were just really lucky and got you two, who make it look like we know what we're doing."

Max came in from outside, poured himself a glass of wine from the jug in the refrigerator, and plopped himself down on the couch opposite Briseis.

"Did the dogs enjoy their walkies?"

"Immensely. They got on the trail of something wild for a while and were howling like coon hounds. Not that I know what coon hounds sound like. I think they bay, actually. Isn't that the word? I don't think you could call what our dogs do proper baying."

"Proper baying? Our mutts are more prone to raising a cacophony."

"That's for sure."

"Um, did you know Andromache has a new beau?"

Max looked up. "No, I haven't been informed. Who is the lucky guy?"

"Carlos."

He tried to let that settle in, but it was no-go. Like pouring oil into water. "Carlos. Carlos? You mean the Peruvian guy with the shop downtown? The guy who is old enough to be her father? Doesn't he have a child?"

"He's Chilean, actually."

"I don't give a fuck if he's from Kathmandu. How old is he, anyway?"

"He's thirty-four."

"Thirty-four. Twice her age, in other words. Why does a thirty-four-year-old man want to hang out with a seventeen-year-old? Besides, of course, the obvious reasons. Jesus Christ. When I was in my thirties I didn't want teenage girlfriends, I wanted women."

"I think certain men want to play the, um" (don't use the term father-figure, she thought) "wise man, mentor role to young women. But I do know, from the other side of it, that young women are often attracted to older men. Andromache is just at that age. They're far more mature. The boys are still just boys, but she's a young woman, and they often are looking for something more than what the boys can offer them."

"Did you have a relationship like that?"

"I did, one summer while we were in Greece. I was eighteen, and Elektra must have been, fifteen, is that right? Well, you know Elektra, she was advanced in that department. And we met these two guys. Men. They had a car and money and took us to places in Athens we'd have never gone to. It was great."

"And you were fucking them?"

"Of course. What do you think? And then summer was over, and we went back to, where were we then, Germany. And we never had any contact with them again. A summer fling."

205

"But Carlos lives here, in Sparti. He's not going anywhere."

"But Maki is. She's going to New York in September. She's very sensible about the whole thing. She knows it's not a permanent arrangement. She's not trying to play mommy to his child. She's not moving into to his apartment. She's just with him sometimes."

"With him."

"Yes, Max, they have sex, among other things. They're lovers."

He was running his hands through his hair. Staring at the floor. Putting the brakes on his imagination. She felt a sharp pang of compassion.

"Come here, my love, sit here next to me."

He did. She took his hands.

"You don't have to worry. He's a nice, gentle man. They practice safe sex. Nothing's going to happen except that she'll have a better idea of what she wants out of a relationship than she did before. That alone makes it a valuable experience. She'll be more prepared for the world."

"I hope you're right." Everything was accelerating. It wasn't possible to stop anything, or even slow it down. It all roared off toward the horizon and vanished. People grew up or got sick, right before your eyes. It was as though you'd bought a ticket to a show and had to stay in your seat and watch. He wanted to heckle, he wanted to challenge the narrative, the whole goddamn direction of the universe. Everything broke down, everything failed, eventually.

"You'll see. I know this story, Max, I know how it plays out. It will be Carlos who is left and filled with longing."

4

November 9

Told M about Carlos yesterday. Didn't like the idea, of course, but it wasn't the drama I anticipated. Typical, my life isn't nearly as dramatic as I assume it will be. Dreamed of Sandra last night. We were walking along a street, maybe New York, and we hear someone shout, look up and see Little B, the way she looked when I last saw her, five? She's standing on a window ledge high above us and she just jumps and floats down laughing, light as a feather, and we catch her together. Then I woke up and just lay here remembering her birth, so long ago. Is everything 'so long ago' now? Was it really my last holiday alone? Without the demanding horde? Now the only time I'm away from them all is when I'm in hospital—don't know if that's ironic or just pathetic. We knew a girl was coming, she'd had an amnio. But the part I love is she didn't reveal the name till after she came, she kept it secret! It's somehow the greatest honor I have ever received, to have a friend name her child after me. Oddly enough, I was named after a friend of my mother's. That seems a good lineage. Good it was a girl that looks like S. What if it had been a boy that looked like M? How awkward. I must call her soon and see what's up with them. Drat. I want to talk to my old friends but I hold back—all I have is bad news, like I'm seeking sympathy when I just want to hear them. Oh, I'll never get over myself—everything has got to be so complicated. I just get paralyzed.

November 10

Rose feeling ghastly. Phone call from Amalia last night. Everything a disaster! She's lost her job, she doesn't have any food in the refrigerator. If only she could go to school. Then go to school, I say. Oh, but it's so difficult and nobody is helping her. I try to explain that she has to find out about the school, fill in the applications, go through the procedure. She changes subject and begins shouting at me. It's all my fault! And I suppose, in the grand scheme of things, perhaps it is. I tell her to take responsibility for her life, that blaming me is counterproductive. But this just makes her say I don't care. There just doesn't seem to be a way to get through to her. I have to get this out of my head and focus on healing. It's not healthy for me at all. I try to meditate & pray for forgiveness and compassion in my heart. Visualize my spirit owl carrying away my bitterness and bringing me back a green jewel—I swallow it and the green spreads to my heart.

Max came into the bedroom with a fresh cup of tea. "Ah, the hot and strengthening. Thanks, my love. You know, I think that little owl is my spirit creature."

"What's that?"

"The little owl that comes outside the bedroom window and talks to me."

"That makes the odd sounds, like a puppy barking?"

"Yes, that's what it's like. It makes a *kiu* sound too. Sometimes I think it's talking to me."

"What's it trying to tell you?"

"I don't know. I suppose that's the riddle of spirit creatures, and to come to an understanding, to an interpretation of their message is to, oh, I don't know, more fully integrate yourself in the natural world."

"An interspecies dialogue?"

"I realize it's New Age nonsense, but haven't various indigenous groups worked with this? Didn't some Native American tribes believe in this sort of thing? Vision quests and all that? And the names, Crazy Horse, Sitting Bull."

"Oh yeah, the Lakota Sioux were into all that. Still are. Back during the Wounded Knee occupation I met a guy named Black Crow, old guy, probably the age we are now but had done some hard years on skid road, who claimed to have been lost in the Badlands and followed an eagle for three days and found his way out. Okay, he might have just been spinning a story for whitey's benefit, but he seemed authentic. Have you read *Black Elk Speaks*? He talks about this sort of relationship with the natural world. Not all the names have to do with animals or birds, though. In Black Elk there's a Red Cloud, a Dull Knife, oh, and my favorite, he had a cousin named Hard-to-hit." Max laughed. "Isn't that great?"

"Especially if you were a warrior. What would your name be?"

"I don't think you got to choose your name, any more than we do, but I think as an animal I wouldn't mind being called Laughing Bear."

"Laughing Bear, that would suit you."

"Or Chuckling Beaver?"

"You don't chuckle, you laugh. I'm not sure what my name would be."

"Some type of singing bird, I should think."

"Hmm, yes."

"Skylark-at-Twilight."

"You think so? Lovely. I'll consider that one."

"This reminds me of a bit in a Jim Harrison poem, about the attraction of women to the Crazy Horse type of man."

"Have I read that?"

"I can find it immediately." Max walked out of the room and came back seconds later. "It's part of his long sequence, 'Returning to Earth,' it's short, here it is."

Abel always votes.

Cain usually thinks better of it
knowing not very deep in his heart
that no one deserves to be encouraged.
Abel has a good job & is a responsible screw,
but many intelligent women seem drawn
to Crazy Horse, a descendant of Cain,
even if he only gets off his Buffalo pony
once a year to throw stones at the moon.
Of course these women marry Abel but at bars and
parties
they are the first to turn to the opening door
to see who is coming in.

"Bravo Jim Harrison! I married *my* Crazy Horse. My friends thought *I* was crazy."

"Yeah, but I feel more like Abel every year."

"As it should be, my love. To be like that at fifty would take a great deal of effort, and that would be pathetic. And you, husband, are not pathetic."

"I see. I believe the term is damned by faint praise."

Briseis started to laugh, but it turned into coughing. Max went to fetch the codeine syrup.

• •

MAX PULLED OVER to the side of the road below the village, grabbed a pair of pruning shears, and got out. Lulu, who had leapt out further down to run behind the car, came panting up. He scratched her head. "You still got it in you, don't you? Damn." He cut low branches from the eucalyptus trees that stood along the road. The village had planted them a few years earlier, and they already towered over everything. The pips from the tree crunched under his feet. He looked up across the canyon toward the mountains as though a flock of birds had suddenly taken flight with the memory of a bit from Hugh Kenner's book on Pound and his compatriots. In 1945, as Pound was being escorted by armed guards out of Rapallo with a book of Confucius in his pocket, he stops and picks up a pip, a eucalyptus seed, and puts it in his pocket. He and the tree were foreign to Italy, yet this was to be his synecdoche in the tiger cage, "Pisan Cantos," and mental hospital that lay ahead. Looked at endwise, it does resemble a cat. It took forever to kill that old bastard. He threw the boughs in the boot and drove home.

She watched him move about the room setting steaming pots of eucalyptus leaves around the bed. The windows fogged, she inhaled, it felt good, the relief in her lungs, and thought, why? Why does he do it? What does he get out of it? She was sure she wouldn't do the same. At least not with this enthusiasm. It would annoy her, she would grow resentful. How much did she believe in love and duty? Or duty to love? "Thanks my love, it helps a bit. But that's enough, really."

"Just one more pot."

One more pot. If that was all it took. Just a little more eucalyptus fumes and my lungs will be scrubbed clean and I'll take up jogging. She closed her eyes. I'll rise up like a great feminist phoenix, the true female response to Lawrence, and I'll, what? What would my creative act be? How would I manifest resurrection? She could hear Max outside with the dogs. Tramp had dug up something again and was being berated with a great stream of obscenity.

Another sunset, Briseis alone on the hiati, her owl out on the phone pole. What are you trying to say to me? *Kiu,*

211

kieeuuu. What might that mean? That I shouldn't worry about other people's problems? Surely it must be something more mystical than that old pop-psychology slogan. She had a brief laugh. She could hear Max mocking her with, "Use the force, Brie." He should talk, with all his Buddhist imagery around. The owl was looking at her, rotating its head in that strange fashion. They must be able to see in the dark. The dogs came running up the road. Lulu spied the owl and began to bark, and the bird swooped off and with several powerful strokes of its wings whooshed through the twilight orchards, a final *kiu* lingering where it once had been.

"Lulu, hush, you flaming nuisance! I was trying to communicate with my owl."

Max came up following the dogs. "Did you get any dialogue going with your bird?"

Briseis sighed. "No. I haven't been able to make the interspecific leap, if that's even possible."

"Konrad Lorenz, you know, the Austrian guy, an ornithologist or something who was all the rage in the sixties."

"Yes, vaguely. Imprinting was part of his studies, right?"

"Yeah. He apparently had amazing relationships with birds of all types. They would swarm around him when he went out. Ride his shoulders and stuff. He was in a Russian prison camp during the war, and when he was released he returned to Germany with his *pet starling.* I've read that he was fantastic in person, could talk on for hours about birds and animal behavior."

"Well, my love, we're not going to meet those sorts of people out here in the Greek countryside, are we?"

"Alas. Just means we need to observe more closely.

And take copious notes."

"Copious notes?"

"Sure, otherwise how are we to benefit from our experiences?"

"Who is this we?"

"Myself, and Leo and Maki. Or Maki anyway. Leo seems to think the natural world is a superfluous sidelight. Something that has to be tolerated but doesn't require any attention."

"Raised in the country, but you'd never know it."

"He used to help me kill the cocks."

"Yes, we certainly misinterpreted that behavior."

Nov 15

Woke up way too early. Lot of coughing and feeling parched so have to get up and have tea. Then can't go back to sleep. Very cold and rainy again.

A little less tingling in my hands and feet. Heard my owl, it sounded like it was in pain, but that must be my projection. Carry it away, little owl, carry it away. I realize how much I define myself by what I've done and feel like a failure and useless because I haven't done things. Of course, I have done things, some useful, creative, or good, it's just the 'I'm a useless bad girl voice' in my head. And besides, it's enough to be. Now I will just be, and whenever I can do something I will. Was starting to get all wound up about 'list of things to do before Xmas!' I could feel the old crap gearing up for another round—refuse to do it—will do things as I enjoy them.

5

IT WAS HAPPENING, she'd been fooling herself. Denial, whatever. She was losing her hair. It was coming out in clumps. There was no way around it.

"I think I want big hair, " she announced over lunch.

"Meaning?"

"Like Dolly Parton, or like they have on 'Dallas,' maybe."

"Oh cool, Mom, why not go for it!" Maki said. "When are you getting a wig? Can I come and help you choose?"

"That would be fun, but it'll probably be on a weekday, that's when they're open."

"No problem, I'll miss a day of school. Big deal."

Leo's ears perked up. "Hey, if you guys are going to Athens, so am I."

"You want *country-western* big hair?" Max was still trying to imagine this.

"Something like that. Something completely different than I've ever had."

"Okay. What color are you thinking of?"

"I want to say red, but maybe that's too over-the-top."

"No, Mom, red's no good for you. And blond would be stupid. Maybe a dark henna kind of thing might work. Or auburn, like Sandra's. You're thinking like cascading curls, the whole works?"

"Yeah. Sort of a you-only-live-once type gesture."

"So has this been a longtime fantasy of yours?"

"No, not at all. I always liked my hair. But now there's nothing to like, is there?"

"I'm having a hard time visualizing it."

"Oh Daddy, that's just cause you're a man."

"You both go to a male hair stylist, excuse me."

"But that's Panos, Daddy. And he's gay."

"Eh, that's stereotyping. Being gay doesn't make you less of a man."

"Okay, okay," Maki conceded, "but it's not stereotyping to point out the obvious. There's a certain percentage of gay men who are really into and good with fashion and hair, interior design, all that kind of stuff."

"So when is this big hair expedition going to take place?" Max asked.

"I suppose we should coordinate it with a chemo treatment."

"You're not going to feel like shopping after your treatment."

"We'll go the day before and get a hotel," said Maki.

"Now you're talking." It was a coordinated assault that the parents had walked right into.

"But that would mean you were missing *two* days of school."

"So what?" In chorus.

Max tried to head them off. "How many absences, appurceas, do you have, Leo? I don't imagine you have many, Maki, but what about you?"

"Oh man, I'm cool. I hardly have any."

Andromache rolled her eyes.

"Chill, Maki, I haven't been thrown out of *that* many classes. And think about it, you'd have masses if I didn't wake you up every morning."

"You don't wake me up in the morning, Rage Against the Machine does."

"Same thing. Anyway, you can get one of those doctors to fill out an absence form, and we skate free."

"Got it all figured out, huh?" Max did like how Leo

improvised on the fly. If only he'd put that energy into his music.

"How did my getting a wig get to this? Suddenly we're spending the night in the city, getting fraudulent documents from doctors, and who knows what else you guys have planned."

"Come on, Mom, we haven't spent time in Athens all together in ages. I can't even remember when it was. You guys are up there all the time, but we hardly ever get to go."

"Yeah, Sparti is a wasteland, man. We gotta get some of that urban juice."

"Spare me."

"It's true, the beat of the streets and all that."

"It could be fun, though." Since her cancer diagnosis, Briseis found herself letting go of some of her adherence to rules. A 'why the hell not' attitude was seeping into her approach to life. It was all contracting and expanding simultaneously. The amount of life to be lived and her way of living it. What was important? That was the only question left.

On the roof of a building above the road on the outskirts of the city—they had noticed it each time they had passed it over the years—was a sign with the heads of several cheery sixties-sitcom type people with lots of hair and the words **TOP HAIR**, in English. Now they were going there, though typically, it wasn't as easy to get there as it looked. It was a small place and chock-a-block stuffed with wigs.

Max and Leo wandered the isles laughing at hairpieces while Briseis and Maki got serious. The woman working the shop was kind and patient, willing to get down all sorts of ridiculously inappropriate tresses. Brie's national health care would pay for the wig, and Max suddenly realized that this must be the great majority of trade for this shop, chemotherapy victims.

The attendant was good at her job, even more than they first realized. After many wigs and much laughter, Briseis ended up with the first wig the woman had had her try on. Same color as her own, a bob-type affair. Everyone agreed that it looked great, though Briseis was a little disappointed that her big-hair fantasy had come to naught.

"I guess some people aren't meant to have big hair."

"Mom, it looks great! Those other ones just looked too fake on you."

"Easy for you to say, my dear. You have big fabulous hair."

"Yeah, but my daddy gave me this." Maki shook her mane dramatically.

"Okay, enough with the flaunting."

The Carolina Hotel on Kolokotronis street, clean and adequate, two blocks from Monastiraki Square, in the heart of the city. They window-shopped up Ermou to Syntagma Square. A band from Peru playing on the pre-Christmas streets, electric with shoppers. The Acropolis illuminated above them. Then back down Mitropoleos past the cathedral and into the warren of shops that is the Monastiraki bazaar. Shopkeepers outside their narrow storefronts barking their wares. They shout in English, Maki and Leo respond in Greek. T-shirts and sweatshirts for Leo, boots and a handbag for Maki.

"Tell me, my love, is it true that a woman can never have too many boots?"

"Absolutely. I think this is carved in stone somewhere around here. It might have been Pericles's wife."

Dinner in the Plaka. They supplemented their simple village life with restaurant extravagance. Maki and Leo pored over the menu like the young gourmands they were becoming. First a table full of mezes. Max turned to Leo, "Dude, we really need some salingaria bourbouritsa."

Maki made a face. "Snails, yuck. They're just slugs with a shell."

"Don't be a wuss. Ya just suck 'em right out of their shells, mmmm."

"Brie, is it true that most Greek recipes for snails come from Crete?"

"That's where they specialize in them. They feed them on barley and thyme, imagine. The ones they're serving here are probably from Crete. Oh look, they have taramokeftedes. We have to get those!"

They ordered with abandon, they wanted everything. Salonikia mythia yemista, Salonika-style mussels stuffed with baby shrimp, rice, onion, parsley, garlic, dill, and sage, cooked in white wine. Saganaki, kefalotyri cheese quickly fried, then hit with fresh lemon juice so it sizzles. A kalamata olive paté. Followed by patsaropatatosalata, beet and potato salad with anchovies; and horta, wild greens. And main courses of katksikaki sto fourno: goat kid in the oven; kalamari stuffed with rice, pine nuts, currants, parsley, dill, mint and tomatoes; barbouni: grilled red mullet; and moussaka. Max and Leo drank a robust Nemean red, Maki and Briseis an Assyritico, a crisp white from Santorini.

Only blocks from their hotel and thankful for it, they staggered through nighttime Plaka.

"That was one of the top meals, folks, really first-class," Max announced.

"Exceptional. You rarely see so much variety done so well."

"Maki, you should have had some salingaria. They kinda burst when you bite into them."

"Oh shut up, Leo. I dined divinely without them."

"I was sorely tempted by the sheftalies."

"Oh Max, that would have been overkill."

"What's that, daddy?"

"Aha, my son. This you must try sometime. They take the stomach lining of a lamb and soak it in water for a day. Then they mix pork, onions, garlic, tomatoes, herbs and all that stuff, including a raw egg. They lay out the stomach lining and cut it into squares. Then they put the pork mix in the middle of the squares and fold them up like dolmathes, right. The final killer touch is that they grill these puppies over charcoal! Muthafucka, you feel like you're on the beach about to pillage Troy!"

"How much of that Nemean did you suck down?"

"As Geoffry Firmin in *Under the Volcano* liked to say, 'The proper measure.'"

"I see. A revealing example. Next you'll be quoting my father. Are you kids going to go out?"

Leo moaned. "I don't know. I'm so stuffed I can barely put one foot in front of the other."

"Same here. It's been a long day. We'll probably just stretch out and watch some TV."

"Television! A city luxury."

"It's not a luxury. Everybody in the world has a TV except us!"

"Oh, break my fucking heart. You guys are so deprived."

"Deprivation was not Leo's point, Daddy. He was merely pointing out that it is highly unusual in the modern world to be without a television."

"Excuse me. Who have you guys been listening to?" The children and their mother stopped in the street and stared at Max. "I see, it all comes round, doesn't it? But think about it. If we'd had a television you probably wouldn't be able to make this argument so succinctly."

"We wouldn't have to, Daddy. We'd have a television."

"Oh sharper than a serpent's tooth."

"Not allowed! No Shakespeare!" cried his children.

Briseis burst into laughter. And they all joined her, and their laughter echoed up off the broken balconies of old Athens to a pale three-quarters-done moon.

Max and Briseis stretched out on the hotel bed.

"Do the kids really recognize Shakespeare quotes?"

"Well, my love, I'm afraid you telegraph them with the theatrical English accent."

"Next time I'll use an Alabama twang."

"Something to look forward to."

"Are all families as ridden with irony as ours?"

"One can only hope."

• •

THE ALEXANDRA HOSPITAL, set back from Vassilis Sofia Boulevard, specialized in obstetrics and, oddly enough, also had a cancer treatment clinic on the top floor. There was a locked blue door separating the hall from the cancer treatment clinic. And, unusually for Greece, the *No Admittance But Patients* rule was actually enforced. Elsewhere, family members just burst through any door, shouting and yelling, pleading and bribing.

Briseis passed through the blue door, Max and the kids sat on a set of broken plastic chairs outside. Up and down the poorly lit hall were friends and family of patients receiving chemotherapy.

Leo took a long look around. "Wow, this is a really grim scene, isn't it?"

"No shit. The people who go through the blue door are fighting for their lives."

"What are Mom's chances?" whispered Maki.

"She could get better." Max stared at the dirty marble floor. People were smoking. "Look at it this way, she's not going to live to seventy-five. What we hope for is more a matter of years. She's got cancer and scleroderma. This," he paused, "reduces her chances. But she still has one, and that's what we work with. So she does all these extra things, visualizing healing, diet, breathing exercises, meditation, and who knows, maybe something will work, or several will in combination?"

"I don't really think about Mom being sick that much, but being here is a harsh reminder."

"Yeah, this place is awful. Come on, she'll be at least two hours. We'll go find a café, maybe up around that little park past the U.S. Embassy."

"Plateia Mavili?"

"Yeah, that little triangular thing with a fountain. There's a foreign newsstand there too."

It had turned sunny. They sat outside, ordered, and sat back with their fresh periodicals. Leo had a copy of *Kerrang!*, the British new-music magazine, Maki had the latest *Art in America,* and Max had the boring old *International Herald Tribune.*

"Daddy, look at these Gerhard Richter paintings. He

221

is the master."

"Hey, System of a Down is coming out with a new album."

"Okay, I can play that game. The Americans are bombing Afghanistan."

"Really?"

"Why?"

"They claim that Osama bin Laden and his gang are holed up there, and they are convinced that he was behind 9/11."

"But why bomb the country, if it's just this guy?"

"Valid question. U.S. foreign policy is a blunt instrument, and right now Americans, so they say, are anxious to see some fireworks, payback and all that, so Bush and the guys are letting the Afghanis have it. Poor bastards. Oh, and dig this. The Pentagon, the U.S. Defense Department, always gives these attacks names. This one is called Operation Enduring Freedom."

"What?!"

"Oh shit, look at the time. You guys stay here, I'll go get your mom and bring her back."

"Cool, dawg, we'll hold onto the table."

"Leo, your true passion."

"Check it out. I do way café."

Andromache watched her father walk away. "Way café?"

"That's right. I'm working all the time. Being café man is not just about drinking frappes and smoking cigs. You gotta give something back. You have to create new terms and phrases to define the experience."

Maki laughed. "Leo, you are so full of shit."

Leo raised his palm. "Scoff if you will. The true café philosopher scorns recognition."

"Conveniently so."

Briseis walked out of the blue door, saw Max, and managed a smile. "Another chemo treatment."

"How did it go?"

"About the same. No worse, anyway. I met this poor young woman in there, twenty-five, two kids. You don't have to look very hard to find someone who has it worse."

"Certainly not in the chemo clinic."

"Amen. Where are the kids?"

"At a café in Plateia Mavili. Just up past the Embassy."

"Well then, what's for lunch?"

"You're hungry?"

"Yes, astonishingly enough. All this poison has given me an appetite."

6

TO NATE, A YOUNG ACTOR IN NEW YORK

When you leave New York, Nate,
come here and we'll haunt ancient theaters
and play to empty centuries rising
into bat-swirled darkness.

Blind Oedipus and righteous Kreon
crashing through the murdered,
temples and palaces piled high
with the justly slain or not;
what authority, permission given,
who claims to know the geometry:
where State and soul do intersect?

Of Eros and of dust we
emerge to shattered dramas,
ill-suited fates allowed to
drag the action into gore,
always the father is killed,
always the daughter smeared
in his blood, an incubation
of vengeance at work.

Carved from hillsides
these rooms to hold
our compositions wait.
This is where murder belongs,
rape and patricide, all
the slaughters we can conjure
are revealed as need,
requirement of heart,

pulse of species pushing
against the gravities
of body and planet.

You come here to act,
to embody rage and keen lament
that those remaining disperse
purged to render the torment
of love's vendetta.

"That's a vividly romantic view of the theater, public catharsis, and all that. If he had any sense he'd get on a plane shortly after receiving this."

"But he won't."

"You're certain?"

"He's struggling with substance abuse, as they say. That's what his mom says. And I get the impression that he's filled with self-doubt."

"He and Jeffrey never did anything with the play you wrote for them, did they?"

"No, the ungrateful bastards. I think it was perfect for them. One act, three characters, no set, essentially, and one costume. You could get it together in two weeks."

"Horses to water, my love."

"Pearls before swine."

"*'Tis a tale told by an idiot.*"

"*Full of sound and fury.*"

"*Signifying nothing.*" They finished the quote together and gave each other self-congratulatory nods of the head.

"Does it count if we're brill but nobody's around?"

"You mean in a tree-falling-in-the-forest sort of way?"

"Yeah."

"It doesn't have to count. If we amuse each other, that's enough."

"And we do."

••

BRISEIS WAS SLIDING DOWN INTO THE DAY. First she noticed that her hands weren't throbbing. What a relief, the absence of throb. A plump robin hopped across the bedroom veranda floor, she could hear Max in the kitchen. In her dream she had been climbing in the olive trees. She could talk to the birds in their language, their songs. They were all chatting away merrily, light-hearted orchard gossip. Someone was complaining about the crows. And then her voice flew out of her mouth, flapped its wings, and soared over the orchard. She couldn't make a sound and woke up. If only she could fall back asleep, if only she could make those sounds.

Max peered around the door and then walked away. Five minutes later he entered with a tray with tea and biscuits.

"Oh thanks, my love. 'The hot and strengthening.'"

"How'd you sleep?"

"Not bad. My hands weren't hurting, for whatever reason. I had a marvelous dream. I was singing with the birds."

"Really? Fantastic!"

"Yes, it was. I was up in a tree sitting on a branch, but I still had human form. I've decided I'm going to start singing."

"How so?"

"I'm going to have Leo ask Praxiteles down at the school if I can take lessons."

"But you already know how to sing."

"Not really. I mean singing scores, doing scales. This will make me do it. And it's about healing my lungs too.

226

I'm sure he can give me exercises and the like."

"Hey, Skylark-at-Twilight, spread your wings."

08 December

Leo asked Praxiteles about singing lessons, he agreed, and this morning after my massage I made arrangements for twice a week lessons. This is a good idea—imagine that I've spent so long not singing. I can hardly do it anymore. It will be good for my spirit as well as maybe helping my breathing. Am so glad Leo wasn't embarrassed with the idea of me going to his music school. Leo showed me scale exercises. Amazing how competent and relaxed he is with the technical aspects of music. We sang the scales together and then Andromache joined us. It was wonderful, our three voices together, each different but blending nicely. Guess we were cruel not inviting Max to join us, but he's often off-key and, of course, louder than anyone else.

13 December

Couldn't find a present for Leo, but scored fabulous jewelry for Maki. Had lesson with Praxiteles, v. difficult—discover I can't actually sing at all. He sez I'm singing with a pseftiki foni, a falsetto, and I must develop my real voice. V. interesting from a psychological/philosophical pt. of view. Should I consider my entire life in these terms? It would certainly fit my impostor complex. The exercises were v. difficult. Praxiteles really liked "I'm afraid the masquerade is over." I realize how hard it is to sing. He has a great voice. In eve had good massage—does armpit muscles—v. painful—cause of curved back, my head goes forward, then my arms go back, all imbalanced. Zack sends email about healing soups? Why not, I guess. Later Leo, Maki and I watch "Runaway Bride." Dumb.

• •

What kind of moron wants Christmas lights that play

the same damn horrible tune over and over again with that cheap tinny fidelity? Deck your balls, jingle your bloody bells. Max and Brie were at opposite ends of the Christmas tolerance scale: he abhorred it, and she loved it.

The children had been terribly cute when they were in first grade and just learning Greek. They had adorable accents, the result of being exposed to Max's appalling Greek pronunciation and Brie's non-Lakonian speech. That first year they came home singing traditional Christmas carols in Greek translation. The translations often had nothing to do with the original lyrics, they just used the tune. *Scorpee san pan doo*, went a line from "Jingle Bells," scattered all around, which certainly wasn't any more inane than "a one-horse open sleigh." Maybe in the Austrian Alps that line had resonance, but here, or nearly anywhere else? But what was scattered all around? He couldn't remember, some sort of religious joy.

Now the children spoke like proper Spartans, not a trace of their parents in their Greek. Bah, he thought as he glanced at his Christmas shopping list, when is coming the Christmasless December? It amused him to use Greek sentence structure in English. They always went overboard and gave the kids too much stuff. But they were so appreciative and genuinely excited, it was hard to resist. They had already bought them new luggage for their college departures next fall, and Brie took care of the clothing end of things. She knew what Maki would like, and Maki would tell her what Leo fancied. This left their passions to be attended to by Max. He had scored an MP3 player for Leo, but Maki was still a toss-up. There was a very cool portable fold-up easel, but he couldn't quite pull the trigger on the purchase.

It started raining again. He cut across OTE Park, jogged across Lykourgou to the fence around the Sparti museum park, then under the arcade that ran along the park. Up ahead was the back patio of the Enigma Café and, despite the weather, Sparti's youth, slouched about in deck chairs, smoking and sipping frappes. He knew the gang and waved as he walked past. Some nodded or waved back.

Through the double front doors of Tyrtaïos, the music school, was a hallway with a few chairs along the wall. From a room in the front of the building someone was playing classical guitar scales. Then from the back he heard a familiar jazz piano intro followed by *Hush now, don't explain*. The voice was female, deep, with a raspy edge, breathy, and he recognized it. It sounded like Briseis's grandmother on the recordings they had when she was doing her husband's songs, with this Dietrich smoky texture. He held his breath. It was his wife. Was this her *real* voice? Was she channeling her yia-yia? They finished the tune, and Praxiteles began another number on the piano. She came in slow, behind the beat, and stretched out the phrase, *Someday he'll come along, the man I love*. Max closed his eyes, lowered his head, let as much of the music enter him as possible, listened with his whole body to the heartbreaking song washing over him. She was singing their life, the whole of it, beginning to end. *Maybe Monday, maybe not.* Tears were streaming down his face. He was having trouble breathing. The discoveries of love are entwined with music, and then they enter the body and seek out the muscles that can contain them, that can grow the memory of that impossible invention. *Until that day, I'm waiting for the man I love.*

229

7

MAX'S PASSAGE INTO THE DAY was confused, he couldn't tell where he was. He looked about. It was a room in the Riva Hotel, Briseis was asleep next to him, but something was wrong. A strange light was seeping in beneath the curtains. He looked at the clock, eight a.m. What was going on, why the sense of emptiness, lack of solidity? He walked to the windows and pulled back the curtain. The world was white and only the white moved. A heavy falling white covered everything and nothing was moving. Not a car, human, bird. It was utterly silent. Athens, empty and unmoving, covered with ten inches of snow, was holding its breath and waiting. The city mute, it was unimaginable. Noisy, screaming, belching, wheezing Athens struck dumb by a winter storm from somewhere far to the north. A Serbian winter, a reminder of Romania, of worlds of black and white hibernating till spring.

He stood for a long while at the window, hands on the glass, four stories above the street, up in the swirl of it, imagining he was a bird soaring through it, down the white and silent canyons, all the broken ugliness buried in a thick, soft, still pristine density, absence of color, light flashing off an infinite mix of water crystals, each unique and indifferent and grandly, visibly impermanent.

Briseis slowly woke into the silence. She opened an eye and saw her husband before the window. "What is it?"

"You have to get up, Brie, you won't believe it."

She staggered to her feet, blanket around her shoulders, and crept to the window. "Oh my god! Is that really Athens out there? It's so quiet! That's what was confusing me when I woke up." She shivered, "God, it looks cold out there." She looked further. "I don't think we'll be able to drive home today, my love."

"Doesn't look like it."

"I'll get dressed and we can go down to breakfast and see what we can find out."

The TV in the hotel dining room was full of snowed-in Greece. The entire country was heavily blanketed and only just beginning to dig out. The highway to Korinth was closed. They were snowed in, in the city.

Briseis waited until noon to call the house. As she knew she would, Maki answered.

"Wow, Mom, do you have snow up in Athens?"

Briseis assured her they had.

"There's masses here, like twenty centimeters or something. It's like a fairyland out there. We're all about to go out and play around in it."

"Who all is there?"

"Oh, everybody. They all spent the night. Katarina, Ephi, 'Mene, Calliope, Dimitra and Yiorgos, Odysseus, Adonis, Socrates, Panos. The regulars."

"Is it cold?"

"It's bloody freezing! Leo screwed up the furnace somehow and we can't get it to work. So the only heat we have is a fire in the tsaki. We all just slept by the fire last night."

Briseis laughed. "All of you."

"Yeah, kept us warmer, I guess, all piled in there."

"The road to Korinth is closed. We're not going to be able to make it back today. It will be tomorrow at the earliest. Do you have enough food?"

"No problem, Mom. And Odysseus's mom is making us a pastisitio. I'm not sure how she's going to get it up here.

231

I think they have a truck. I'll make pancakes for lunch."

"Bravo. Is Leo still sleeping?"

"Believe it or not, Leo is carrying up firewood at the moment."

"Oh, well don't interrupt him then. Sweetie, I'll call you tomorrow when we know what's happening. Oh, and Daddy says to leave all the faucets dribbling at night. Just a little so they don't freeze."

Max returned to their table with more tea.

"Leo screwed up the furnace somehow and they all slept by the fire."

"Screwed up the furnace? How?"

"I don't know, but they're managing. With hormones or something."

"Who's there?"

"Oh, all the regular pa-*ray*-a. At least a dozen, from what Maki told me."

"All sleeping by the fire?"

"Yes. You know how they are, like a pack of sled dogs, they just sleep in a pile. It's what I love about their group. Nobody's paired off, they really operate as a group and look out for each other. Maybe that's one of the reasons Maki went outside the group to find a lover."

"What, Carlos isn't there?"

"No, he stays away from these group gatherings. Probably makes him feel like an old fart."

"My daughter's lover is an *old fart*?"

"Never mind. Take a couple of deep breaths, meditate, whatever."

• •

LEO FOUND SOME CARDBOARD IN STORAGE, and they took turns riding down the steep driveway. Snowballs

232

were flying in all directions, a snow goon ala Calvin and Hobbes was being constructed. Every few minutes a great whoosh of snow fell from an olive bough. The dogs were berserk, tearing through the orchards, cutting great leaping arcs in the snow, chasing the sledders down the hill. Barking for the hell of it.

Maki threw a snowball and managed to hit Leo in the head. She roared with satisfaction while her brother nodded and leaned over to form a response from the deep mid-calf snow. Most of them had never been in snow this deep, certainly not here in Lakonia. If pushed, down they went, and if not, they fell deliberately, just to roll around in it.

Surrounded by flour and eggs, baking soda and milk, Maki perused the recipe to make sure her portions were right. Pancakes for twelve. Say five per person, that was sixty! How much batter do you need for sixty pancakes? Oh, here it was, okay, she just had to triple the amounts. Leo and Adonis stomped along outside on the hiati carrying firewood. They had a big blaze going already. Before the hearth was a sea of cushions and mattresses and blankets. The boys were competing on who could roll the longest joint.

"Leo, how much firewood do we have?"

"Oh, we're cool. If we burned it like this for a couple of weeks, then we'd be sweating it."

"Great. I'm going to start making pancakes. I'll keep them warm in the oven, so maybe in twenty minutes we can eat."

"Cool. Adonis and I are just going to do one more load of wood for now."

Maki loved having all their friends at the house for

these overnight gatherings, parties, whatever you wanted to call them. Away from all adults, they could do whatever they wanted, make as much noise as possible. As her mom had gotten sicker, there were more opportunities, and this was the Christmas break so everybody could come. She liked being the host, and Leo liked it too. They took charge and kept everything running, maybe not smoothly but close enough. Taking care of their tribe, as her father would put it.

• •

THE PHONE RANG, and Briseis chatted merrily for a few minutes. "That was Miltiades. He and Elizabeth are going to walk over to the hotel, and then maybe we could all go out for lunch."

"Terrific. We can go around the corner to Papayiannis's, it's close and they've got all the traditional taverna dishes. I'm already thinking hirino me selino."

"That sounds good. Fish soup, that's what I'd love."

Miltiades was a true Athenian, though he had spent much of his life in the U.K., first at boarding school and then university, where he ended up with a classics masters and met Elizabeth, a South Carolina poet pursuing the same degree. Miltos became a journalist, and two years previous they had moved to Athens. He was now the editor of a daily newspaper, and Elizabeth was doing translations from Latin and Ancient Greek for Penguin. They stomped into the hotel lobby shaking off the snow, heavily bundled, glistening with vigor.

"I've never seen so much snow in Athens," Miltos exclaimed. "We're taking pictures to show our children. Otherwise they won't believe it."

"What children?" Briseis asked.

234

"Seegah, seegah," laughed Elizabeth.

"Don't delay, Milto, impregnate your wife today!"

Miltos looked down at Max and smiled. "Soon. We don't want to put it off too long."

"'Too long' is not usually an impediment to fertilization. Might lead to a male child, though, as they're the weaker swimmers, the male sperm. So if you're too . . ."

"Thank you, my dear, I think we got the picture."

"This is science, Brie. Which is why rear entry is . . ."

"Let's go to lunch, shall we?"

"Sheesh." Max turned to Miltos. "You don't have any preference, do you? We were lucky. Got one of each, bang, right outta the gate."

"I don't think I want twins."

"You're right, Elizabeth, you don't. It's great now, but the first three or four years it's a lot of work. They keep each other company though, which is a big plus. How old are you?"

"Twenty-nine."

"Oh, plenty of time. I was almost thirty-four when I had the twins."

The streets were still mounded with white, the sidewalks treacherous. Miltos and Max helped push a car from a drift. The grateful driver produced a bottle of brandy, and they shared a drink in the street. Papayiannis's, low-ceilinged, long and narrow, was dense and steamy with the din of noisy diners. It was an impromptu holiday, only restaurants and cafés open and everyone expansive with feelings of community. They found a table in the back and ordered wine.

Miltos, burly, self-assured, brought a tremendous appetite to any table. He wanted everything, would ask other tables about their meals, and often got detailed descriptions of the preparations from the chef while visiting the kitchen. It wasn't enough just to eat. What was the background story of this bass in the kakavia? Where did the goat come from?

Both deeply literate, they often competed with each other over the meaning of a phrase from Socrates or Horace. Briseis sometimes joined in, but Max, whose adventures in formal education had avoided language studies, especially ancient ones, was utterly lost. Just the same, he paid rapt attention, waiting for the word or phrase that he could connect with. Something to give a distant resonance. He liked knowing that Thucydides was not just writing for his contemporaries but creating *ktema es aei,* a possession for all time.

Miltiades surveyed the laden table and sighed. "*Metron ariston,* that's hardly what we're practicing, is it?"

"What's that?" asked Max.

"Moderation is best," said Briseis.

"Diogenes said it. but he was quoting someone else, I can't remember."

"Cleobulus."

They all turned to Elizabeth. "Bravo Liz!" said Briseis.

Elizabeth continued, "Sixth century B.C., from Lindos, I think. He proposed the education of women."

Miltiades made his recovery, punctuated by a firm palm-slap on his forehead. "Of course, one of the seven sages of Greece. A radical in some regards. He said, *Freedom is the right of every sentient being.*"

"Sounds like the Buddha. So ariston means best?"

"Yes. You know the word. When the kids do well on a paper they get an arista."

"Oh, yeah. The same as the Pindar quote, *Ariston men eedoor.* Ed Sanders, who taught me the line, translated it as *Water is the greatest.* The hipster version."

"Metron actually means measure, but also the mean between extremes. You know the word. When you order your coffee *metrios.*"

"Cool. The middle path. Just like Mahayana Buddhism. The same insights are in many cultures, though the Greeks want you to think they thought of it all first."

Miltiades laughed. "Of course, you're in the center of the world. Let's have more wine."

• •

SILVER FLASHES across the soft white world. Covered with snow everything is bigger, denser and glowing in the moonlight. Above, swirled by illuminated cloud, the sharp flanks and ridges of Lazineekos and the Tayegetos shimmered a stunned alabaster. Adonis, Leo, Maki and Katarina stood on the hiati smoking, watching the moon move over the mountains.

Adonis pointed to the nearest peak. "Has that one got a name?"

"My father says it's called Lazineekos. He's got maps and shit. Plus he gets all this name stuff from Yiorgos Katsakis. You know, the English teacher."

"You can't see the Prophet Elias from here, can you?"

"No way, it's too far south, hidden behind the others."

They drank more light. A shadow swooped through the orchards.

"What was that?"

"Probably an owl. My mom thinks she has a relationship with one of them."

"Really?"

"Yeah. It's kind of weird. The owl comes outside her bedroom and makes these really strange sounds. Not like a bird, and nothing like whooo, whooo. It does hang around the house a lot, so who knows? I think she talks to it sometimes."

Leo flicked his cig out into the air. It dropped in a glowing arc till it hit the snow with a sizzle. The dogs stared through the wrought iron railing to where it hit. "Our mom is a lot more susceptible to this sort of thing since she got cancer."

"Attitude is important for healing, Leo. That's why she's doing all this stuff. You can't just sit back and depend on doctors and their chemotherapy."

"Yeah, I guess so. Two thousand and two. I wonder what happens this year? Something different, I figure."

"Guys, in nine months *we've all* got to be leaving Sparti. That's the main point. We have to graduate, and we have to get the hell out of here."

"Truth."

"Amen to that, Maki."

Faces glowed golden in the light of the fire. Sprawled before it on a sea of mattresses and cushions, everyone draped over each other, drinking wine, stoned. He could stare at her profile for hours, but Adonis didn't allow himself that luxury, it would only annoy her. He took the warm friendship she offered, took it in and made it something else, a different life. Andromache loved Adonis the way she loved all her close friends, emotion manifested in hugs and kisses, a genuine concern for their welfare. She had known for years about his infatuation, enjoyed it, but couldn't ever remember being attracted to him, it

238

never entered the equation. He was Adonis, she'd known him forever, she couldn't imagine her feelings changing.

She sat up enough to cradle her great-grandfather's guitar on her leg. She was not the musician her brother was and didn't care. She liked to sing and could play simple folk arrangements, and she had learned songs she could sing with her mother. She began the guitar intro to John Lennon's "Working Class Hero." Leo stepped over to the piano and without sitting down played a simple chord accompaniment. Katarina joined in and they sweetly held the last phrase, *A working class hero is something to be.*

Adonis, a child of lifelong members of the Communist Party and well-versed in the dialectic, said, "Maki, don't you think it's rather ironic, you singing that song here in your big house in the hills?"

Maki flashed him a grin. "Actually, my parents say it was ironic when he first sang it. He's mocking the fact that he *is* a working class hero. He came from the working class and succeeded beyond anyone's wildest dreams."

Still standing at the piano, Leo felt the music needed a drastic update. He knew his sister's repertoire and softly began the opening of a Pixies tune. Andromache turned and gave Leo a look Adonis would have killed to receive. Leo didn't really like playing with her that much, which made the odd occasion of it a real treat. She counted off the beat and entered on the chorus. *Where is my mind?*

8

WHEN THE MAESTRO POINTED TO LEONIDAS, he stood and took an eight-bar solo on "Take Five." He was a lazy improviser and took the easy way in and out. It baffled his music teachers. They had rarely encountered such a natural musician who could also learn the technical aspects seemingly without study, as though he already knew. Yet he seemed to play only because he could. He could excel with a minimum of effort. It drove them mad. Where was his passion? Why had this gift, this genetic fluke, been made to someone so disinterested?

It was the same in math and sciences. The boy would yack and screw around in class, a real trouble-maker. Then, just for fun they'd put a difficult, advanced problem up on the board, and while most of the class would be stunned into silence, Leonidas would come to life and propose an eccentric yet valid solution. But it was obvious he wouldn't progress much further. He could occasionally dazzle at this level, but beyond this it would require work. Work that would never be done.

Oddly enough, though, music was an obsession. He listened to it constantly, controlled his world's soundtrack, read every music magazine, could go on about obscure sidemen and record producers. His room was festooned with posters of angry black men. Max was fascinated with this phenomenon: that young white kids across the U.S. and Europe loved to listen to furious African-American street poets telling them they were going to kill them and then rape their mommas, or maybe the other way around.

What would Leo do? His parents had concluded this was a mystery to which they hadn't a clue. It was a matter of waiting. They had noticed his facility with music at a very early age, and since then he'd had every possible lesson and workshop available. Instruments were purchased. Summer music camps in America, master classes in Athens had managed to create a very competent, blasé young musician. His experiences outside of Sparti had convinced him that the inspired musicians were passing him by. It didn't bother him. He was plenty good enough for this hick town, the first soloist with the Sparti Philharmonic, paid a monthly stipend which he sorely depended on. He didn't actually care about being a soloist, but the money was better. On a night when the orchestra was playing well, that soaring collective feeling, he enjoyed that. And he loved hanging out with musicians. At the music school were several serious rock musicians, and he would sometimes sit in with them, add a little keyboard fill, tell them where the chord progression they were using would lead or write out their compositions as they were being played.

Niko, if you go a half-step up on that you'd harmonize with what Yianni is doing."

"This?"

"Yeah, and then, uh, doh minori."

"Cool."

Leo was dubious about the idea of university but realized it was the way out and so had participated in the process enough that he now had a position in the U.K., in Manchester, for the coming fall in a program called Music Technology. Recording studio stuff, a little composition and playing. He could do that. He had loved Manchester when he visited for an interview. An American with a British passport who had lived his life in Greece and was

241

entering a British university, that was exotic compared to a boy from Barrow-in-Furness or Chipping Norton. They liked all his music theory studies and managed to ignore his less than sterling academic record. He had slipped in. Just enough.

Leonidas had a comfort zone and didn't like to stray from it. Not too up, not too down, cruising along, nice and easy. Getting high facilitated this. He plopped himself down in a café chair on the covered walkway behind the Enigma Café and lazily slapped hands with Yiorgos, who was already in full café slouch. "What's happening, man?"

"Nothing."

"Is this the same nothing, or are you working new nothing?"

"Same old, man, same old."

They stared across the narrow street to the palm trees and vegetation of the museum park.

"Check out this new Tool cut." Leo handed his headphones to Yiorgos, who began nodding along with the punchy rhythms.

"Their drummer is fucking great."

"Tell me about it. They got it all going. Compositions, playing, great singer. I wished they'd come to Athens."

"Maybe they will?"

"I checked out the itinerary of their new tour. No such luck. Rome is the closest they get to Greece."

Odysseus and Adonis dropped themselves into chairs. Hand slaps and grunts around.

"Leo, anything happening at Tyrtaïos?"

"Christolakos came by and was doing some neat shit on keyboard, getting all these cool effects. And Praxiteles started drumming. They jammed a little."

"Did you play?"

"On what, clarinet?"

"Why not?"

"Wouldn't work. Not with what they were doing."

Adonis shrugged. "What's Yiorgos listening to?"

"New Tool. Fucking rocks."

"Great, I got next listen. Where's Maki?"

Leo stared into the night sky above the museum.

"Leo, where's Maki?"

"Oh, she's . . . I don't know. Either at Carlos's, or maybe she's with Katarina and Effie." Leo twisted his hand in a don't-know gesture. "Call her and find out. She's in Sparti somewhere."

"Nah, that's okay."

"Don't be intimidated by Andromache, comrade. You want to talk to her, call her up."

"Some other time. I don't want to call her if she's with Carlos."

"Especially if she's with Carlos and doesn't pick up," added Odysseus.

"Ooo Odysseus, that's some cold shit. You got your cruel shoes on today?" Leo peered under the table. "Adonis, that's what text messaging is all about. Just send her a yo, what's up?"

Adonis wrung his hands. Leo feigned a yawn, picked up his phone. and called his sister.

"Hi, Leo. Daddy's not already there, is he?"

"No, don't sweat it. We're just chilling behind the Enigma."

"Really? I'd have never guessed. Who's there?"

"Yiorgos, Odysseus, and, oh yeah, and Adonis."

"The usual suspects. I'll be there by nine-thirty, at the latest."

243

"Cool. I'm not going anywhere." Leo clicked off and put his phone back on the table. "She'll be here by nine-thirty, if you want to wait."

"Where was she?"

Leo slapped himself on the forehead. "I forgot to ask. Should I call her back?"

Adonis dismissed Leo with a *nah* gesture, an open palm thrust toward the one you're dissing, and reached out for the headphones Yiorgos was passing to him.

"Suit yourself. Are we going to have a beer or something?"

• •

SEVERAL DAYS A WEEK, depending on their schedules, Max drove into Sparti at 1:30 and picked the kids up and brought them back to the village for a true and hearty lunch. Then, often, he drove them back into town later in the day, and so on. Today Briseis had whipped up a pastitsio with a red lettuce salad finely chopped and tossed with fresh fennel and their own vinegar and oil. Leo and Maki ate quietly without a lot of eye contact. Max and Briseis waited them out. Finally, Leo cleared his throat.

"Aum, you guys have to come into school tomorrow."

"Really, are you receiving an award?" His father asked. Andromache tried desperately, unsuccessfully, to stifle a laugh.

Mom was not laughing. "What? Why? What happened now?"

"It's completely stupid. You won't believe it. But I got kicked out of school, and they won't let me back in till you come down and chat with the headmaster."

"Kicked out of school! What on earth for?"

Max, smiling, "Been there, done that. More than once."

244

Leo grabbed onto that. "See, Daddy's been there. It's not the end of the world."

"Max, please! You know he has to finish high school before he can get out of this ridiculous system. Try playing the concerned parent for a moment."

"Okay, okay. Leo, what heinous crime did you perpetrate now?"

Briseis rolled her eyes. Sometimes it was three against one around here. In the grand scheme of things she agreed with Max, but in the here and now, the girl fearful of authority and desperate to please took possession of her. She was never far away, just under her skin, twitching. And too, she was a teacher, had been, and felt a certain solidarity with them when they had to deal with bright, smart-aleck, underachieving kids like her son.

"Well, you know that gummy, sticky kind of stuff? Kind of like Gummy Bears, only you can't eat it. Sticks to things?"

"I think so."

"Well, I stuck this thing on the side of a computer, and the teacher just went ballistic."

Maki held a hand over her mouth and stared out the window across the olive orchards.

"There's got to be more."

"Okay, yeah, it was shaped like a penis."

"Oh Leo, really."

"And they didn't execute you right then and there?" Max said and turned to Brie. "See, I was right to scoff."

"This was a woman teacher, right?"

"Yeah."

"And at what time is this dreaded meeting with your headmaster to take place?"

Leo hung his head, this was probably the worst part.

"Before school starts."

"Oh, lovely. How very nice. An eight in the bloody morning meeting with some man who thinks our son is a delinquent. And what, we have to plead your case, convince him to allow you back into school?"

"I think you just have to show up, you know, and I say I'm sorry. That kind of thing."

"Gee, can't wait. Sounds like a lot of laughs."

Maki controlled her laughter, and her mother gave her father a frustrated glare.

Maki gave her brother a punch of solidarity on the shoulder as he and their parents filed into the school building. Headmaster was not a full-time position, and the person who filled it also took on a full load of classes. It was a boost in pay. A forty-year-old man with a goatee greeted them warmly. He gave them the standard talk. He didn't understand it all, but Max had been hearing the same since he was what, ten? Dreary, boring people pronouncing that the child was scintillatingly intelligent but bored and disruptive in class, unfocused, loud, always that, and needed to control himself. It wasn't fair to the children who were trying to learn. As if they had anything to teach, besides all the prejudices of societies built on exploitation and racism. They had taught him one thing: remove yourself from the hierarchy, avoid situations where anyone has power over you.

Mister Kallonis was droning on. Briseis was squirming as though she was the culprit, and in a way she felt she was. This was her son, and he was causing trouble. Why did every authority figure begin to sound like her father? He was ready to pop up in any situation and make her whole body tense with fear. Her stomach twitched. She glanced at Leo. He was slouched to the side pretending to be attentive.

Finally, with a flourish, the headmaster produced the evidence of the crime. It was wrapped in paper, and he turned it to the side out of politeness so that only Max could view the scandalous item. Max bent over and peered at the little squishy penis in the man's hand. It had little balls attached. Leo suppressed a grin. Briseis found herself saying a prayer to the air: please, Max, just let it go. Max reached out and picked up the little penis in his hand, Brie held her breath, and then with one swift motion he slapped it onto his forehead. The others recoiled slightly. The penis was stuck to Max's forehead, dangling down over his nose. Briseis felt herself falling and grabbed hold of Leo.

A bell had rung and the students, scattered across a vast stretch of concrete, began shuffling toward the building. Andromache studied her family for a clue of what had gone down. Her father was talking to her brother. Max patted Leo on the shoulder. "Just chill. I know the system is bullshit. I know the lessons are mind-numbingly boring. But you chose to come, so see it through. You've got what, about three months to go. Just be cool. Sleep through the classes. Whatever. But we don't want to go through this crap again."

"God, I was mortified." Briseis exhaled. "I was sure you were going to do something outrageous. When you picked it up, I knew it. I almost screamed. What stopped you?"

Max paused for a minute, turned to his wife and said, "You did. You're right. I was on the very brink of either throwing that stupid thing across the room or, and this flashed through my head, sticking it to my forehead. Which would have been superb."

"Dude, that would have crushed."

"But then I thought of how you would react, how painful the whole situation would be for you. And, too, I realized that would have been it for Leo, more than likely. Mostly, I could see you frantically trying to salvage the encounter, and I didn't want you to go through that."

"Thank you, my love. That was a great kindness." She sighed. "It would have been the appropriate gesture though. Pity."

9

9 March 02

Most depressing day. Didn't sleep all night—first heater was making such a noise I turned it off. Then was cold—feet & face like ice. What a dump the Riva Hotel is—the stale smell—crappy carpets, shoddy furniture, grubby curtains, no heat, no remote control, phone not working. Then fingers throbbing like mad all night. In morn, totally groggy & can't touch anything. Have shower, revive a bit at hosp. café—then pick up exams—rigamarole of getting it typed up—it says tumor on right lung bigger & on left lung smaller—how is that possible—doesn't make sense. But nothing on upper abdomen, that's good. Take them to Meletios who, without even sitting us down in his office, says, "Well, it's about the same. If you want you can do 2 more treatments. It's up to you." I tell him I'm weak, my hands are screwed up & haven't recovered from last treatment. He says, "If it was doing something, making a difference, I would be more forceful." Then stands there waiting for me to hurry up & decide this important thing about my treatment. I am so bummed by the whole thing I tell him no, don't want it—feeling like I'm being a naughty girl trying to get away with something, instead of making responsible decision about important health problem. M & I sit in hallway thinking what to do next. M reminds me that info we read says usually no benefit after 6 treatments anyway. Makes me feel better. We go home & are depressed all day. Don't feel like calling anyone but talked to Elektra later. She has all her usual problems, of course. We missed the 50th anniversary party of the Athens News, couldn't face it. And, I pooped in my pants. What a day!

Briseis studied the computer screen. Surely there was some play to make. How could it be over so quickly?

"Nine of clubs on the ten of diamonds." Max said over her shoulder.

"Oh, why didn't I see that?"

"Fresh eyes, my dear. I do find it deliciously ironic that having scoffed for years at people playing solitaire on computer, here you are."

"I can't handle the cards anymore, my hands are too fucked up."

"Yeah, that does make the irony a bit less piquant. Seven of hearts on the eight of spades."

"Oh quiet, I would have seen that. I won yesterday."

"Yesterday? I win all the time."

"What horse crap. Nobody does."

"Well, first, I don't play every hand that's dealt."

"What do you mean?"

"If you don't have a good initial deal, the odds of winning are almost nil. So I don't play the crappy deals, I just redeal."

"But that's cheating."

"No it isn't. Here, observe. You need to have several moves before you go to the deck or you don't have a chance. Plus, like, see these twos, they're no good."

"If you get aces . . ."

"If, but if you don't, you can't play anything on a two, so for instance, here you only have five rows to play on instead of seven, because you have two twos. That's a big reduction in odds. I don't play these hands. Redeal. Ah, here's a good mix with lots of plays." He furiously moved the mouse.

"Ten of diamonds on the jack of clubs."

"I don't make that move unless I have to. Maybe the ten of hearts will come up and I'll want to move it. This way I have that option, 'cause you can't move the ten back to a blank space. If you pay attention to what cards are in the deck, 'cause you see them all, you'll have an idea of what's coming. Okay, king, so I move the ten."

Briseis looked anew at her husband. Solitaire strategy, what next, stamp-lick theory? "I do it to relax. I have no desire to make it that difficult."

"What's difficult? Your brain is already turned on and working. It doesn't take any extra energy to consider these things."

"Ha, now what are you going to do?"

"Umm, lemme see, right, I'll bring back down this seven of hearts, which means I can move the six of clubs. And . . ."

"Hey, you can't do that! That's cheating!"

"Brie," Max looked up at her, "if it was illegal, the computer wouldn't allow you to do it. If it does, it's legal."

"Well, it shouldn't be."

"This is the Brit in you, right? The great fair-play culture, the honor system, the fields of fucking Eton. Utter bullshit, of course, but everyone has bits and pieces of it. So that you, for instance, create *more rules* that you can strictly adhere to."

"Oh, nonsense. Just let me play the way I want to."

"And there, see, I won!"

"Aren't you going to put all the cards up?"

"Nah, there's no need. I don't keep score or points. I just play to win or lose. I guess that's the American in me."

Briseis looked at her smirking husband and thought, *Oh, just shut up.* "Very clever, my dear. Now move over and let me play."

"I'm having second thoughts or something."

"About what?"

"Max, I'm worried about Maki going to New York. I just don't know if she's ready for that pace. She's only seventeen."

"She's a very sophisticated seventeen."

"She's a girl who's grown up in a Greek village and in Sparti, whatever that means."

"I think she's ready. She thinks she's ready. She wants to go, and that's what she's going to do. Where else?" He paused. "I mean, you're the one who thought boinking Carlos was a good idea."

He just couldn't let that go, could he? "I still think so, but if she doesn't like what Carlos is doing she can walk out the door and be on the streets of Sparti, where she couldn't be safer, where we are ten minutes away. Oh, I don't know. It just seems like too big a jump from here to there. I know, I know, you're going to say that she'll be living with Sandra, and believe me, if Sandra wasn't there, I would really be digging in my heels on this one. Her being there is what tipped the scales for me. And the Art Student's League, it's a really unstructured place. Most of the students will be far more mature than her, won't they? It's not like some little liberal arts college where they hold your hand and look after you. And it's so far away."

"Look, it's going to be incredibly exciting for her. And yes, she'll get homesick and maybe even think she made a big mistake, but that's just part of moving away. The first thing she'll discover is that she doesn't know shit, that everybody is a better painter there than her. But I think that'll just get her going. Everybody from the sticks who goes to New York has to go through that. She can do it."

Briseis sighed. "If she has even half the confidence in herself that you have in her, well, maybe. But nobody in New York is going to think the sun shines out of her

252

asshole like you do."

"Say what you will. This time next year, next spring, she'll be rocking the Big Apple. You wait and see. And I won't even say I told you so."

Briseis looked up at Max and thought, *this time next year*. What about that?

• •

March 14

Slept some last night and so feel a bit better. Still wondering how to love my cancer & want it to go away at the same time. Guess I should take care of it so it will get better. Got call from Amalia in late morn. Sounding pathetic & helpless. Asked how I was & I told her—didn't pretend to be all fine. Asked after her job search but she said she was without skills & limited in hours she can work. Was bit depressed after call especially with hands so screwed up. Then remembered how she makes everything sound difficult & awful. Went out in the afternoon and looked at the trees. Quince in full blossom & plum & cherry. Apple tree w/ gorgeous blossoms just starting to open—most delicate aroma. Cut some purple lilac, white lilac may bloom for first time. The air full of new life.

"I think Leo has a crush on some girl," Briseis said.

"Really. How do you know that?"

"Increased appetite and a certain sort of mope."

"Beyond the general mope? How do they differ?"

"It's more, I don't know, melancholy."

"Have you asked Andromache?"

"No. I'm hesitant. It feels like a breach of trust or something. If my hunch is correct, she will know, but probably won't want to reveal any details or maybe even confirm. Mostly I don't want to put her in that position, where I'm asking her to betray a confidence."

Max shrugged. "Okay. And really, what has it got to do with us? We don't have to get in a sweat about making that phone call or whatever. Risking that rejection. It's not like these kids go out on formal dates or anything."

"Did you?"

"You mean in high school?"

"Yeah. Hi, Betty Sue, you want go bowling with me on Friday night?"

"I did very little of that. I can remember only once where I called up a girl that I wasn't hanging out with and asked her out."

"What was her name?"

"Alice Lipsink."

"Lip-sync?"

"Kitchen, not synchronized."

"How did it go?"

"It wasn't very exciting, so we didn't go out again."

"Where did you go?"

"The movies. I can't remember the title, a period piece."

"But you had a car and picked her up at her house and everything."

"Yeah. It was America in the sixties. A small town in the West."

"Just like 'Happy Days.'"

"Too close for comfort, I'd have to say. But this was the late sixties, remember, and everything was in flux. Marijuana was showing up, and other drugs, and people were getting arrested for it. The war was raging in 'Nam. Long hair was an issue, but not for much longer. 'Happy Days' was dissolving before our eyes. I think it went on in small towns in the Midwest for a long time. Nothing like that for you, huh?"

254

"Oh god, no. We were shuffling back and forth from Germany to England. I was supposed to be studying for my A-levels, and my bloody parents really couldn't have cared less. I thought they wanted me to fail. Expected it. I was a girl, marriage fodder. Girls didn't go to university."

"Wow! We're the same age but grew up in entirely different environments. Middle-class girls all went off to college in the States. It was part of the routine."

"It makes me furious to think of it. Those years I wasted carrying around all that crap in my head. I had to wait until I was in America on the dole. A welfare counselor suggested I was suited for university!"

"Ah-mer-ree-ca, land of opportunity! Give us your dysfunctional children, and we will turn them into magna cum laude scholars!"

"Scoff if you will, child of privilege. For me it was true. I was suffocating in Europe. In the States they even loaned me the money to go."

"So getting pregnant and marrying a G.I. was your ticket out of there, out of Germany and away from your parents?"

"Oddly enough, yes."

18 March Clean Monday
  D coming for lunch
  Made potato salad, lettuce, tarama. Had fava and marinated octopus all ready. D didn't come, not feeling well. Elektra called in morning saying she had nothing for her kids. The four of us had a nice, mellow & delicious lunch. Kept feeling guilty about not inviting Elektra but didn't have enough food, except screaming masses of tarama & couldn't bear idea of the hoohaw & tension that accompanies them. Knew I shouldn't feel guilty but it kept nagging me.

255

In the eve Max and I took mezes to D who went on & on about his blood pressure & showed us his charts. Didn't bother to tell him that lowering alcohol intake & increasing exercise would help. Never once asked how I was. What a nutty family. So glad just the four of us had our lovely lunch together. On the way back from D's we saw a hedgehog crossing the road. M stopped & put the headlights on it—it got confused then waddled into ditch and disappeared. And then we both remembered the Athenian cab driver telling us that 'the wild' in boiled hedgehog would cure my sclera-derma and Max sd, Maybe I should have run it over?

10

Someone in white hands you
the lab results and looking out
at the audience of the world
you tear open the envelope,
smile, and announce that
the patient will live!

and everywhere the just too eager
recoil, deflated and plotting a recount.

In a Boulder bar of inebriated Buddhists, Max turned to Maez and said, "We've got to get out to the coast, man. We'll put on this show and get out of this dharma ghetto for a while. We just need a ride. Has anyone got a car worth shit?" Maez grinned, raised his hands like a priest at an altar, and examined the ceiling of the bar, which was done in old-gold-miner chic, tin tapped in ornate patterns that repeated and throbbed. They turned on their stools and gazed out through the clouds of smoke.

"How 'bout the Ginz?"

"Nah, he never has a car. Matter of fact, I've never seen him drive. That's his image, isn't it? Sitting talking into a tape recorder or scribbling mind breaths while someone else does the driving. And why not?"

Just then who should walk by but the man in question. Max reached out to him. "Allen, you know anybody who could loan us a car for a couple of weeks?"

The Ginz turned, reached into his jacket pocket, and pulled out a set of keys. "Here, take the Growler's ride. He's doing a retreat and won't be back for a month." He grinned and raised a finger. "Bring it back in good shape and all's well."

They got off their stools and embraced the great bard, and then they were driving through a densely dark Rocky Mountain night. Maez was at the wheel. Max asked, "Aren't you going incredibly slow?"

"Yeah, we ran out of gas a few minutes ago and I've been coasting."

"Ran out of gas?!"

"Yeah, what can you do? We're a long ways from anywhere."

Max looked out into the darkness. "Fuck, man, this is the far side of nowhere." They coasted to a stop. "Now what?"

Maez giggled, turned, and reached into the back seat. "Not to worry, Max. I brought my wings. I'll fly up ahead and get some gas and bring it back." He stepped from the car, adjusted his wings, and flew off.

The wind exhaled over the car and Max could see nothing. Shards of light flashed from minute stars, and then nothing. He opened the glove box to see what the Growler had left. What's this, a copy of *Zen Flesh, Zen Bones,* the collection of Zen stories by Paul Reps. He opened the book and read a story. Tanzan and Ekido, two monks, are traveling down a muddy road. They come upon a beautiful young woman all done up in a kimono and unable to cross the road. "Come on, girl," says Tanzan and lifts her up in his arms and carries her across the road. The monks travel on in silence until they get to a temple for the night. Ekido can't restrain himself any longer. "We monks have taken vows not to have anything to do with females. Especially beautiful young ones," he tells Tanzan. "Why did you do that?" "I left the girl there," says Tanzan. "Are you still carrying her?" Max closed the book, put it back in the glove box, and woke up.

He brought his wife her morning tea. "Brie, I had the greatest dream."

"Really?" He told her the whole thing. "Remarkable. Who is the Growler?"

"That's Miller Muirhead. Old friend, from Mt. Angel College. The nickname comes from his disposition. His practice just makes him grumpier. The more he sits, the more he growls and snarls."

"Lovely. And flying?"

"Yeah, like something out of Castenada. You know, brujos changing into birds and flying through the Mexican night. I've got to check my Paul Reps book to see if the story exists."

"So you're left behind in a dark empty place by a friend who can fly, but you can't."

"Interestingly, there wasn't any sense of anxiety, no dream panic. I just looked around, and then read the story."

"I find it ironic if not hypocritical that Chogyam Trungpa, the brilliant, enlightened Tibetan guru, drank and smoked to excess, and, if I'm not mistaken, was fucking his female students."

"Guilty on all counts."

"Well?"

"Well what? I didn't surrender to the guru. And anyway, have you ever learned anything from someone who is less than virtuous?

"Of course."

"You got to make your own mix, and get what you can where you can."

"Humpf."

Outside Lulu was barking her head off. Jocasta the cat was curled up at the end of the bed. Countless buds

259

were forming on the olive trees. There were swaths of pink crocus in the orchards. She could see steam rising, drawn from the earth by the morning sun. Max went out to see what Lulu was so excited about. Briseis reached for her journal.

April 13

Another sleepless night. Started yoga but was interrupted by Lena going on about another stray dog in the village. But what does she want me to do, we have four already. What a silly woman.

Maybe I got ill so I wouldn't have to feel guilty about not dealing with my relatives' problems? Daddy ranting on the phone about his blood pressure and some sort of hives on his back, and then Elektra hysterical about her kids. But all I could do is listen. But by 'dealing,' what do I really mean? I've never actually solved any of my family's problems. How could I? They cling like shipwreck victims to the cause of their problems. I know all about that.

Can't let my hands get cold, the pain is absolutely paralyzing. Or worse.

April 15

What joy, what bliss, a night's sleep. Am so grateful to the powers that be. Woke up 3:30 as usual but was amazed to realize no finger throb going on, just minor tingling, so went back to sleep until Blink-182 rocked us awake at 6:30. Woke up with a chill of fear. Death, I feel afraid of death today. It seems closer somehow or why do I say somehow? It is closer. Sky lighter this morning. Wisteria and white lilac blooming gloriously.

M sd wld take me to massage w/hands wrapped in hot sock. I realized today that my 'sins' are pretty meager & insignificant & that my greatest wrong is to myself. I have inflicted so much needless damage on myself, like scorpions stinging themselves when trapped. Was I trapped? Hard to put myself back into the situations where this might have been the case. Mostly I trapped myself.

At massage Y did v. painful stuff down ribs of back—sd it was v. special massage. Sd most therapists don't believe in it but he's opening roots of nerves that open up the blood vessels. Sd the knocking noise was my weak muscles "trying to hold the spine in a position of apelpisia—despair." Gave me a jolt, apart from the pain. Afterwards, my hands were warmer & looser. Despair? Have I really reached despair? Is that what my body is saying? Then at 8:30 Elektra called & sd Agamemnon had told Thalia that 99.9% of men had mistresses outside their marriages. (What a thing to say to your 15-yr-old daughter!) Thalia was horrified & despairing. (more despair) Elektra told her it wasn't true & think of Max, he doesn't do that, nor her uncle George. Was touched.

April 16

Woke up thinking about what Y sd about my body in despair posture. Is it that obvious or does my body know something that I don't. Probably, how could it know less about itself than I do? It's certainly not cooperating. I only learn what's happening after the fact. And it's always bad. What was that line Max quoted the other day? "Bad news is always true." Can't remember who sd it. Kosmas came in the morning and started beavering away, building a little stone wall around the willow, just like I've always wanted. Tried to do things around the house, but my hands wouldn't allow it. They're useless claws. Frustrated at how helpless and dependent I am, utter loss of autonomy, so I resent M trying to do everything for me. Leo has a new piercing! It's awful. A great bloody bar of metal through his eyebrow. The eye is all bruised w/ red bits radiating out from it but he refuses to take it out. Was horrified & upset that he didn't care about his health. The earrings are nice, Maki's wee nose stud is adorable, but this! They don't have to go to these extremes to get our attention. Reminded of Amalia's frightful tattoos. Is there a self-destructive streak in my children? Why? Life hurts us enough as it is.

261

The hillside was brilliant in wildflowers. Max brought new bouquets in every day. Each week brought new species, new colors, pinks and yellows and hyacinth blues. Swallows were building a nest above the front door. Red-rumped swallows, said Max, consulting his bird book.

"They don't have a red rump," complained Briseis.

"Yeah, but that's definitely what they are. Due to the coloring, especially in the back. Does a bird really have a rump? And the tail is shorter. Their flight is more acrobatic, the barn swallow is way faster, just a blur, whoosh. But the biggest difference between these guys and the other swallows and martins is the nest. The red-rumped is one of the genius architects of the bird world. They make this upside-down igloo kinda thing with a long entrance tunnel."

• •

In May Briseis began to have dizzy spells. She would stagger when she got out of a car, be overtaken by sudden headaches and fatigue. What was it, hay fever or something? The physical therapist said the dizziness came from the neck and how she was holding herself. She found it difficult to write in her journal, her penmanship suddenly deteriorated. The idea of a brain tumor returned with every new headache. Her greatest fear in life had always been this.

The doctors in Athens told her over the phone to get her head scanned, and they dutifully presented themselves at the clinic in Sparti. Looking rather glamorous, Antigone, a local neurologist they knew, came out and took Briseis into the back of the building. Her husband, Takis, swept in through the front door and entered his office. They were both doctors and shared the clinic.

Takis was a notorious philanderer, according to the Sparti grapevine. Years ago the doctor duo had decided that Elektra and her husband Agamemnon were the epitome of new Greek chic and begun visiting them relentlessly, as Greeks do. Max laughed remembering them. They would sit off from the rest of whatever group was gathered at Elektra's and watch in silence. He figured they were either taking notes or found the company too exotic to rub up against, or who knows? His social engagement was so limited. He was closer to people ten thousand miles away than half a mile down the road. The web did not break, he fueled its elasticity with a stream of words.

Max began reading the *Herald Tribune*. Forty minutes later Antigone came into the waiting room and motioned Max into her office. He sat down, but the doctor remained standing, as though waiting for a cue. She studied some papers on her desk and then looked up. "The scans are conclusive, Max. The cancer has metastasized. Briseis has several small brain tumors."

Revolver please, thought Max, so I can shoot the doctor. So I can answer with violence and terror, instead of nodding, pursing lips, taking it like a good trooper. Fuck bravery. She was droning on about how sorry she was. Treatment was required immediately, the commodity of hope had not lost its value. Yes it had. Knowledge was stronger, pain was greater, loss was draining the light from the room, the glass was less than half empty.

"I haven't told Briseis yet, but I can if you'd like me to. I've called Elektra."

Max stared up at the doctor. Bands of light from the blinds highlighted her from behind. She wore a lot of makeup, her eyebrows were finely etched. That Briseis's sister was the first to hear this news dumbfounded him. "You called Elektra?!" He began to rise out of his chair. then dropped back down and waved her off. "Never mind. I'll tell her. When do we get the pictures?"

"They're being prepared right now."

He slowly rose again, the husband of the patient, the bearer of bad news, eulogist-in-waiting. He felt like he'd doubled in weight. He thought of George's daughter Sybil when she was very young and, having learned about the damage the freon that came in refrigerators was doing to the ozone layer, would tell people in her crisp English accent not to linger with the door open, because "You're making holes in the sky." Holes in your head, holes in your life, in your love. Everything porous and leaking. When will the drilling stop?

He walked back to the waiting room and waited for his wife. They walked out to the car in silence.

"Did she tell you anything?"

Max leaned his head against the wheel and managed to say, "It's a brain tumor." Before out of control sobbing took over.

What? A brain tumor? How was that possible? So her lifelong fear of it was not unfounded. All these years it had been seeking her out, and now it had found her. She put the back of her hand to her forehead. The dizziness, the headaches, the difficulty writing. Brain tumor. A bloody brain tumor. As though all the rest wasn't enough. A scene from "Fawlty Towers" appeared in her head. John Cleese shaking his fist at god and exclaiming, "Thank you, thank you very bloody much!" What is sadder than comedy without laughter? What would she do now?

264

TO TERI, MORE AND LESS

Ah Teri, the days drag on,
they are far too short.
Thanks for the pictures.
We never got back to Italy
to France, twelve years ago
we dreamed at our leisure
Rome and Venice would
melt in our hands,
Provence would begin
to bore.

We were like everyone else,
we didn't know how little remains——
journeys fade, names
no longer attached——
see Florence drift, just a glossy
of mother and son
in the platea walking away.

These documents of when
add up to less than zero,
a ticker-tape walk in the sunshine,
floating images of life flash
and fall, swirl and twist till
trod underfoot they await
the man with the broom.

We are bigger than the wake
we have cast and are afraid
and hold each other that
the spinning will abate;
revolutions ago we saw horizons
as the moment's edge

265

temporary limitation,
a blurred portal out.

Now the distance is near
definition distinct,
the doors are marked,
we do not queue
but loiter
with intent.

23-V-02

11

MAX ENTERED THE BEDROOM with a tub of clean laundry, dropped it to the floor, and began putting the clothes away. Briseis, on the bed reading, looked at him with a critical eye, wondering what she'd think if she'd just met him.

"What will you do?"

"What?"

"When I'm gone. What will you do?"

Max looked up. "You're not gone yet."

"Come on, indulge me. We both know I'm not recovering. It's a matter of months. What will you do?"

"I don't know. The kids will be away at school. I'll be alone. Maybe I'll go to the States, travel around, visit old friends."

"Yes, and . . ."

"What?

"What kind of woman?"

"Oh, I see. Well, I can't imagine going backwards, hooking up with an old lover. What I mean is, the woman I may be twained with in the future I haven't met."

"So you've thought of it?"

"You can't help imagining what's coming. I mean, you've had an incurable terminal illness for years."

"Tell me about it. How much younger?"

"Come on, Brie, I don't know. I don't have an image in mind, if that's what you're driving at."

"She shouldn't be younger than Amalia."

"Amalia is what, thirty-one. Thanks. That gives me a lot of leeway."

"But she should be hot."

"Uh . . . hot, yeah, sure. Why not? Hot is good. Why exactly do you think that?"

"I just feel bad that you've been nursing me along all these years and think you should have someone healthy and hot. You know, and have lots and lots of sex."

Max looked at his wife, laughed, and loved her even more. Someday there'd be another, certainly, but now and tomorrow and till her last breath she was what he wanted. He caressed her head and kissed her eyes, her nose, her mouth.

"We should have boinked more, over the years. I know you wanted to, but sometimes I just lost my desire, and it would take ages to find it again. I should have paid more attention to it, should have made it a bigger priority. I got lost in that damn teaching. I see that now."

Max continued to stroke her head.

"And there were the kids, though I realize you did most of the work with them. When I finally quit working, they didn't really need my attention anymore."

"Not true."

"Okay, but they'd become teenagers and were moving out into the world. Their social life outside the house took precedence. I mean, they didn't want me to play games with them."

"They got plenty of game-playing in. Hell, Leo still does."

"Oh, those awful computer games."

"Watch out, you'll sound too much like an old fart."

Briseis shrugged, laughed. "Too late to worry about that now. Look at me. I *am* an old fart, nearly hairless, with bloody cancer. There's no chance of me becoming young and with-it again. If I ever I was."

"Did you feel you were when you were younger?"

Brie looked toward the ceiling. "I don't know. Maybe not so cool and hip, but I can remember feeling smarter than other people."

"Ah, the flip side of the imposter complex."

"You're right, that's it. Along with fearing that you'll be discovered, found out as a fraud, is the feeling that the people around you don't know anything, are utterly incompetent."

"Often the case."

"Yeeesss, but if you approach people that way you won't get a very good result. It's better to be curious about what they are capable of achieving."

"That's why you were a good teacher."

"I suppose." She reached out and stroked his arm. "But we've had some great times too, haven't we? Remember that time, back in the old house? It was late morning, and I was in bed grading bloody composition papers that were turning my brain into mush."

"Go on."

"And you came in and said, 'Brie, I've been thinking.' And I said, 'Yes, my love, what have you been thinking?' And you said, completely out of the blue, 'I think I should fuck you in the ass.'" They leaned against the pillows and laughed.

"And you said."

"What a jolly good idea!"

"And then I did!"

"You certainly did. Thank god for the Albolene!"

"Aye, to be sure, nothing like a well-greased bum!"

They leaned back, eyes closed, and laughed and laughed.

• •

FOOLS FOR LOVE

I.

Strange rhythm to the daze
parts lost or in a haze
don't move or leap to faze.

Yes, it comes dropping slow,
but there's too much to know
for peace to linger so.

How much time is stored
in our love's reservoir?
No matter, we want more.

But never demanded art
Nor insisted from here to start
The story of our human heart

Told from the moment met
with all that's still to happen yet
played slow as August sunset.

II.

years wedded
it's not an idea

parts imbedded
not panacea

entanglement
kept in the light

full of moment
the cycles tight

these places of weight
pushes of work

promise of fate
into the dirt

yet made one till
to earth return

grist for the mill
last thing you learn

3 VI 02

• •

BUELL SHOEMAKER must have dyed his hair himself, or
else Marlene did, but it was obvious that professional hair
care was not involved. It was always a horrid, unevenly
done red, and every time it was a different shade or tone,
magenta, raspberry, geranium. The impression was that
he was trying to get it right, one failed experiment after
another. Although he never spoke directly to the claret
stain clinging to Buell's head, Max couldn't help staring
at it. A work in regress.

The Shoemakers had suddenly appeared in Sparti,
having bought a house in the mountains above the castle
at Mystras without ever having been in the area before.
Just picked it out on a map. Buell was an emergency room
physician from Oklahoma who had worked in Canada,
New Zealand, and South Africa but was now apparently
retired, in his early fifties. His baby face and everything
about him was soft and flabby. He dressed like a boy scout
troop leader, in shorts and hiking boots. All he needed
was a ranger's hat and a scarf around his neck. Marlene
was short, wiry, abrupt, and practical. She was at least

ten years older than Buell, English, retired after forty years in nursing, and spoke with a hard East London accent. Elektra, with her style of instant intimacy, *You are my best friend,* had a habit of collecting peculiar foreigners, and the Shoemakers were quickly added in. Briseis and Max couldn't figure out why you would want this couple hanging out in your living room sucking down the wine, but never mind.

Briseis had returned from two weeks in the city having her head blasted with radiation to no apparent effect. They were drifting in a late afternoon swoon on the hiati, feet up, coffee, chocolate.

"Have you seen my little owl?"

"Just the other day, late morning, one was on that pole over there watching Sarandos's chickens. I didn't actually see it attack. You've seen one on that pole before."

"'Hello lunch.'" She laughed.

"Yeah, they're smaller than the chickens, but they kill them instantly, bang. Sarandos put mesh over the top of the chicken pen. They were going to wipe him out. They can't get at them now. I don't imagine any found you at the Hotel Alexandros? Maybe sitting on the window sill tapping at the glass."

"No such luck. Now *that* would have been weird."

"I don't think owls live in the city. Crows, pigeons, starlings, the improvisers, the garbage eaters." They heard a car rumbling up the drive. Max got up to see. "Jesus, it's the Shoemakers. Who invited them?"

"Really? Oh well, maybe we'll get a laugh."

Buell and Marlene settled into deck chairs that they pulled around so they were facing Briseis and Max, their backs to the railing, and nattered on over coffee about the new dogs Elektra had found for them in the oblivious way childless couples do.

"Oh, Reggie has been very naughty of late. Chewed Buell's slippers up, he did."

"Yeah, well, that's what puppies do." Their dogs were lingering about waiting for strokes and biscuits. Both of which the Shoemakers were generous with. "If one of these bastards chews a shoe, I'd take a stick and bash them upside the head. They know it too."

"Oh, we could never do that. Not to little Reggie and Alice," Marlene said.

"Then buy cheap slippers. But you have to wear them for a while, otherwise they aren't saturated with your scent."

"We heard about your latest setback, my dear. It must have been a shock." They began, very slowly, to lean forward in their chairs.

Briseis sighed. "Yes, it was. Oddly enough, it was always my worst fear, brain tumor. And here I have it."

"And you've just had radiation?"

"Yes, but it didn't really have any effect, besides making me feel ghastly."

"You poor thing," cooed Marlene. "What's your plan now?"

"I don't have one. I'm going to sit here and try and enjoy my time as best I can."

Max noted that the two of them were now straining forward, their elbows on their knees, eyes glowing and staring intently at his wife.

"You know, " Marlene said, "we might be able to help you."

"What do you mean?"

"Well, we specialize in endcare." She lingered on that

last word, then blew it out into the air between them. The hair tingled on Briseis' arms. Max watched the two them gear up their pitch. "We have lots of experience."

"We know how to manage pain," Buell said. "What you must know is that you don't have to suffer. This is why we have," he paused, "morphine. It is a very effective drug and easy to administer."

"Morphine," said Briseis.

"Yes, we can handle everything."

Vermilion, that was the word for today's hair, Max thought, and almost said out loud. Or maybe he did? It wouldn't have mattered as the Shoemakers were very focused.

"The important thing is not to suffer. There's no need. And what's the point, really, when we have the pharmaceuticals to relieve?"

"You mean, like morphine," Breseis said.

Buell smiled. "Like morphine, certainly. And there are others, but morphine has a long track record."

Max abruptly stood up. "Any more coffee or anything?" Syringe, perhaps?

Breseis exhaled. "Actually my love, I think I need to rest. I'm a bit knackered."

The Shoemakers rose from their chairs. "Don't get up, my dear. We'll toddle off and let you rest. You mustn't overdo. Everything slow and easy," said Marlene. "And don't forget our offer. Think it over. We're just a phone call away."

Max watched them back up and head down the road. He turned to Briseis, began rubbing his hands together, and in a Boris Karloff voice said, "We specialize in eeeee nnnndddccccaaarrrrrreeeee."

274

"My god, it was like something out of a Bette Davis movie. Could you bring me the phone?"

Elektra answered on the second ring. "Hi, what's up?"

"Elektra, did you send Buell and Marlene up here?"

"No. What? Were they there today?"

"They just left! And it was really creepy. They went on about endcare and morphine and how they were experts."

"No, really? That slimy bastard!"

"What?"

"He's an addict. That's why he doesn't practice medicine anymore, they won't let him! He kept helping himself to the morphine in the emergency rooms!"

"How do you know all this?"

"Oh, Marlene tells me everything."

"So that's why he was going on about morphine!"

"Sure, he probably figures he can skim a little off the top, or a lot."

Briseis shivered. "What frightful people! Tell them I do not want any more visitors and that I'm declining their generous offer. Imagine. It's not enough that I'm dying of cancer, no, I've got to put up with this! And you have these people at your house all the time?"

"Oh, I can get a laugh out of them. Maybe they make me feel less neurotic?"

"And that accent of hers! How did she retain through all her years abroad?"

"It's fantastic, isn't it? Sounds like she just got off the bus from Bethnal Green. They are right out of a horror movie, aren't they?"

12

Heat rolled up the hills through the orchards to the house. Briseis and Andromache, barely dressed, let it caress them. Iced tea. Chocolates, which they kept in the fridge and then allowed to warm to just below melting. Leo and Maki were finally finished with the Greek school system. They had slogged through the endless final exams, which went on for weeks. The release was such that they almost took flight. Within days they were camping on the islands, Maki and her girl friends on Amorgos, Leo and the guys on Paros, and later they all hooked up on Ios. Days of testing body limits. How much alcohol and pot and sun before combustion? Sleeping till the heat of the day woke you, whenever that was, and plunging into the glittering sea. The islands, where everyone spoke to you in English, were aswarm with young Greeks who had run the exam gauntlet and survived. Many students were so poisoned by the ordeal, by the relentless memorization, that they avoided books altogether. The final results wouldn't arrive till August, after which parents scrambled to find housing for their children in a university system that was scattered across the nation. Leo and Maki's arrangements were already made. They were leaving soft cuddly Greece and reentering the English-language world with all its opportunity and violence.

She rubbed her knuckles across her daughter's leg and cursed her hands, these gnarled claws, for the ten-thousandth time. Couldn't even stroke her child. "You're a lot like your father, you know."

Andromache turned, smiling. "Yeah, how?"

"The way you take in experience, how you process it. You make something of it. You see an event, you hear a piece of music, and you start thinking, what can I do with this, how can I use it?" She gazed out at the mountains. "You like hearing that you resemble him, don't you?"

Her daughter examined the tiles that stretched across the veranda and looked out across the olive orchards that quivered in a hot afternoon breath of air. The insects were roaring, everything else was asleep. She wanted to announce a solidarity with her mother, she wanted to give her that, but said, "Yeah, I do. I mean, of course I do."

Briseis gave a short laugh. "Don't worry, my dear. Your father and I aren't in competition for your affections. It's wonderful when a father is his daughter's hero. Especially now. And then as you grow older, you'll become more and more aware of his faults. It's inevitable. You'll see him with the eyes of an adult. He won't be so heroic. It happens to everyone."

"Grandpa wasn't your hero, though, was he?"

"I didn't have any heroes. I didn't have any good examples of how to live my life. But your grandfather, no, certainly not. I was afraid of him. You never knew what he was going to do. He was physically violent with everyone around him. The number one family rule was *Don't upset Daddy.* When he went into a rage, you just looked for somewhere to hide. And generally there wasn't anyplace."

"Daddy gets into a rage too sometimes."

"Your father and your grandfather could not be more different. Yes, Daddy does get absolutely furious on occasion, but first, he's sober, and it isn't aimed at the family or, generally, anyone in particular. The mediocre hypocrisy of the Greek system, inanimate objects, the dogs

277

when they dig up his plants, and computers, good lord. But he doesn't take it out on anyone. Well, sometimes he can be very rude to the representatives of the bureaucracy, in a bitter, ironic sort of way. Mostly he shouts at the sky or the mountain or takes long walks muttering to himself. He releases it and it's done. Unfortunately, your grandfather would be drunk and mean when he turned on his family, and he took it out on us."

"That must have been awful."

"It was. It's taken me my whole life to come to terms with it. But now I'm okay. I've given up all that fear. I forgive him everything." Briseis shook her head. "I told him that recently, you know. He was drunk, of course, and couldn't figure out what in the world I was talking about. As though I was talking about some other family."

"You know, Mom, you're my hero, too."

"Oh, that's kind of you to say. But I don't think I'm anybody's hero."

"No, you are, and to all of our friends. They remember when you stood up to all the teachers and parents." The beginning of the school year had brought student strikes across the country. Nearly every high school was occupied by the students, who demanded that a greater percentage of the national budget be spent on education to improve the dismal situation of the schools. Leo and Maki had been active participants, sleeping at the school for all the nights of the strikes. A conference of parents and teachers was called to discuss the situation. After much berating of the students and denunciations of the strike, Briseis rose and, to the shock of all, suggested that the state of the schools was indeed appalling, that the student concerns were valid, and that instead of condemning them, the parents should join them in the strike. This was met

278

with first silence and then an uproar. Word of her public support had swiftly passed into the occupied schools and given her an unlikely radical sheen.

Briseis laughed. "My radical moment. I wasn't much of a rabble-rouser, though. Don't think I convinced anyone in that room."

They listened to the Lakonian afternoon. A hawk's cry cut through the hot air. They looked up and saw it soaring high above, motionless and moving.

"What about Leo? Do you think he's more like you or Daddy?"

"What about Leo? I really don't know. His noncommittal nature certainly smacks of my teenage approach. Sometimes he acts just like Daddy. Mostly though, he's a mystery to me. He'll find his way, but it will take longer than you, I imagine. But, you know, you can't predict. Who would have predicted what has happened to me? If I'd heard it, would I have believed it?"

• •

LEO AND MAKI TRUDGED UP THE HILL to the house in the late afternoon heat wearing backpacks, carrying their towels. They were returning from three days at the beach in Vathi, forty-five minutes away.

"Did you hear? Lia's coming."

Leo turned to his sister. "Really? When? How do you know this?"

"Mom told me on the phone earlier today, but you were throwing a Frisbee on the beach, and then I forgot to tell you. She'll be here in a week."

"Wow, that's great."

"Yeah. Mom said she talked Grandma out of the money."

"*Our grandma*? That must have been some serious shmooze."

"I hear that."

Their big sister Amalia, fourteen years older, had left home when they were only three, and since then they had seen her less than once a year. She had been living in Greece when they first arrived but had returned to the States years ago. Amalia was fragile, nearly always troubled, and they loved her in an almost parental way, wanting somehow to take care of her, to heal the wounds that she and her mother always opened.

They dropped their bags and towels to the hiati floor and headed in through the dining room to the kitchen. They didn't eat well at the beach, fast food, snacks, whatever, and were ravenous upon return.

"Hey, Mom, we're back."

"Hi, kids, how was the beach?"

"Way mellow. Perfect weather, and the sea is really warm now."

"Oh, I wish I could go swimming, but it seems like such an ordeal."

"We could do it. We could all help, even if it's just for two or three hours. What's stopping you?"

"Oh, let me count the ways. The constant coughing, fatigue, I'm utterly weak. And, I hate to admit it, but look at me. I'm emaciated and misshapen, I have a little skull stubble instead of hair. I can see myself staggering through the sand like some dying creature struggling to return to the sea. Even now, I'm afraid, I haven't shed all vanity."

Her children stood before her with their arms crossed. She looked from one to the other. They had enough Greek in them and tanned beautifully. "Yes?"

"Mom!" they said in unison.

"Oh, I know, I know. Feeling sorry for myself. Maybe it all got to me a little this afternoon. I'm okay, though I do believe my days at the beach are behind me." They were still looking. "For now, anyway. Maybe next month? But you guys must be famished. How about eggs and tomato?"

"Mmmmm, that sounds great."

"Okay, help me up. Maki, you peel some potatoes, and we'll have some chips too. Leo, ask Daddy if he's hungry."

"So when is Lia coming, exactly?"

"Next Wednesday. She lands at one in the afternoon. Daddy will pick her up."

"Cool, I'll go with Daddy."

Andromache almost tried to join them and caught herself. "I'll stay here with you, Mom."

"Thanks, my dear. I don't want to be here by myself."

"Where is Lia going to sleep? I can share my bed."

"She'll be down at Elektra's."

"Why not here?"

"It's easier this way. I need everything calm and quiet around here, and you know how Lia can get things stirred up. You'll see her every day, I'm sure. It'll be fine."

Leo and Maki exchanged a look that spoke to the mysterious energy their sister and mother's relationship generated.

• •

MAX WENT INTO HIS OFFICE, sat down in a straight-back chair pointed at a wall, and picked up Jack Kornfield's *A Path with Heart*. He liked to start his morning meditation by reading a passage from a Buddhist text. In this way he reread near all of his books on the subject. Today he read the story of the old monk on his way up

281

the mountain for the final push for enlightenment who meets an old man coming down carrying a big bundle. This is actually the Bodhisattva Manjusri. The old man asks the monk, "Where are you going?" "I'm going to the mountaintop to meditate until I get enlightened, or die!" replies the monk. Then he thinks, this old guy looks pretty wise, maybe he knows something. "Say, old man, do you know anything about enlightenment? How do you get it?" The old man let go of his bundle, and it fell to the ground. Instantly enlightened, the monk slapped his head and exclaimed, "Wow, you mean it's that simple?! You just let go of everything and not grasp anything?! All these years, fantastic!" He looked around at the world with new eyes, then turned back to the old man and asked, "So now what?" The old man reached down and picked up his bundle and walked down toward the town. Max grinned, what a perfect story. After enlightenment you re-enter the marketplace and begin the work.

He put the book aside and set his timer for thirty minutes. He rocked sideways several times to settle himself and took a breath, then another, and everything slowed down. In years previous he had closed his office door to avoid disturbances, but no longer. Now, no matter how he concentrated on his breath, a part of his consciousness listened for Briseis, heard every cough. It was not ideal, this split, but this is what life asked. He listened for spasms of coughs, for the continual rasping gag, and when he heard it, he rose and went to her. She was sleeping easy this morning, there were no coughs and his monkey mind raced on to other concerns, the full smorgasbord of desire and fear, a lifetime of confusion to draw from.

· ·

BRISEIS SET HER TEACUP ON THE BED TRAY and stared across the room at the house charm Dan Barker had made them. It was a lovely arrangement of fabrics and threads, very Tibetan, with the Sanskrit for *Om* embroidered on a rectangle of gold in the center. House charm—had it brought good luck to this household? How did you analyze luck? What the hell was luck, anyway? Was it merely a prejudicial view, an interpretation of the events of one's life? Good luck, bad luck, what did that mean? Why did anything happen? Okay, because something happened before it. Max said this was the law of karma, cause and effect. If you plant an apple seed, you will not get an oak. But if that was the case, why did she have two rare lethal diseases? What had she done to bring this calamity and suffering down on this house, on herself and her family? Law of karma, my ass! Where was the cause? All these doctors, all their science, they didn't have a clue. Where was the event, or chain of events, that led to this? Coughing and gagging, taking ten different drugs, some to lessen the effect of the others. Life curtailed, reduced to ever-diminishing cycles, the geography of it constricting. Besides the continual trips to Athens for treatments, she didn't stray beyond the horizons on view from this hilltop. This was her world. More than likely, it would only get smaller.

From her bedside table she picked up a simple unadorned cross of wood. It was very smooth and fit the hand easily. A childhood friend had sent it to her, talisman for her awakened spirit. She exhaled deeply. Now you get spiritual, now that death is heading up the road. Was there really a higher power? Or was it merely making connection with your better, kinder, more generous self? The idea of God was ridiculous, at least in the traditional

283

sense. Some patriarchal bastard who gets pissed off when his creations don't do what he tells them. But what was that other bit? Good news, God is love. She closed her eyes and held the cross with both hands. I'll try to pray.

In the afternoon Max came out to the saloni and handed Briseis a freshly printed poem. "It's another of the letter poem series."

TO MITSOS, THE POSSIBILITY OF GRACE

She needs a miracle.
Do you believe in miracles, Mitso?

I believe in the inexplicable.
In the face of such fate
you have to believe
the coin has another side.

Religion does not explain
but like fog
gives shape to the invisible.

Imperfect from a single piece of wood
an unadorned cross came in the mail.
She cradles it in her tortured hands
and wonders how to pray
how to say Give me strength
and I surrender in the same breath.

Not who but what to pray to,
something bigger and beyond,
something in us all, remembered.

Miracles, I don't know
but I believe in the unexplained

and the possibility of grace.

17-VII-02

She left the poem in her lap, closed her eyes, and leaned back in the couch. It was uncanny how he could enter her mind and describe what was happening there. Unsettling. She was never sure where her thoughts left off and their conversations began. It all blended together, and some of it was condensed into verse. Into these little messages Max sent to the world.

13

THEY WATCHED THE CREDITS SCROLL down the screen while the sappy theme song played again. It was a still July afternoon, cicadas ringing, cats and dogs snoozing in whatever cool corner of the house they could find, the children at the beach, hints of a coming thunderstorm in the air, that electrical smell, and Briseis and Max sprawled on the bed. She turned to her husband.

"Can you tell me why every romantic comedy has someone dying of bloody cancer in it."

Max laughed. "I don't know. It's weird, isn't it? I swear, it's like eighty percent of them."

"Excuse me, Hollywood, I'd like to be amused and charmed, not reminded of what my life's become!"

Earlier in the summer, as her condition deteriorated, they had acquired a television, as she was finding it increasingly difficult to read. Briseis's father had volunteered to buy them one, and Max and Leonidas decided to accompany him and purchase a video player to go along with it.

"This one here should be fine."

Max and Leo peered at the diminutive screen and agreed telepathically that no, that wouldn't do.

"Actually, Major, we're thinking something more this size is in order. Brie is going to have to watch it from the bed so she won't be that close, so bigger is better."

"Humph, I'm not buying that."

"That's okay, I'll buy it."

"Oh, I see. Here's one hundred and fifty euros. That's my contribution."

"Thanks a bunch, Major."

"I'll be down at that café having a beer."

"We'll be there soon, grandpa."

They settled on what they wanted.

"Okay, Leo. I guess the way to get the price reduced is to bundle the video player and the TV together for a price less than their separate parts."

"Yeah, okay, so how much do we offer them?"

They added the amounts and decided on an opening offer, figuring the store owner would come back with a counter offer. But they did the math incorrectly and made an offer higher than the two machines separately amounted to. The clerk suppressed a giggle, took pity, and made them a deal anyway.

Laughing, Max turned to Leo. "We certainly played that one smartly. What fucking rubes!"

"I should have noticed that your math was fucked up."

Max tapped his temple with an index finger. "Kidneys."

"You're giving yourself too much credit, Daddy."

Max got off the bed and looked out the window. It was darkening quickly. He said, "I've got another movie, but we should save that for later, don't you think."

"I couldn't watch another one now. It'll probably be more terminal cancer patients or cancer victims coming back to haunt their loved ones."

"Seems to be the formula."

"My love, if I can come back and see what's happening, I will. But don't let that deter you."

"Thanks, I'll remember that."

"I suppose if there was consciousness after death, you might not really care about what the living are doing. All these stories are just the vanity of the living, aren't they?

As though our lives were so interesting that those who had finished with it would want to come back and watch others suffer."

"Good point, still some gray matter functioning. Speaking of the living, is there something I can do for you? How about I give you a complete body massage with this oil here?"

"Oh, that would be lovely. My skin is so dry."

"Okay then, nude up."

Briseis adjusted her scarf. With summer the wig was too hot, but she couldn't bear to go about with wisps of hair dangling. Max had her lie on her back and began rubbing oil into her neck and face. Oh, that felt divine. Her skin was soaking it up, every swirl of his fingers enlivened her flesh. She noticed her mouth was hanging open and closed it. You could taste the coming storm.

Max moved to her arms and began slow, gentle pushing motions starting at the gnarled hands and then slowly sliding up the arm with both his hands. The oil made the movements fluid and watery, his fingers working her thin muscles, the flesh in between. She was sinking into the bed. He was entering her with his hands. He was working through the years of disease and pain, coaxing the woman within out.

He moved to her chest and breasts. Lifting them up, nipples between thumb and forefinger, he was using masses of oil, under her arms, along each rib. Pushing, pushing lightly against her breastbone and up to the neck. She heaved a deep breath and took another in. She was full of air, or so it seemed, expanding, her chest lifting. And slow, slowly to the stomach, an easy, kneading clockwise swirl. Oil and more oil, he was drenching her in it. He had her by the hips, lifting her ever so slightly off

288

the bed and then down, rotating hands over her abdomen and thighs. They heard the patter of rain beginning.

He worked each leg from foot to crotch, ignoring time. Was it possible to go more slowly? He lingered on the knees and beneath them. His hands could nearly encompass her diminished thighs. With every stroke he was reminded of how far along they were. He caressed her mons, he worked it all. A flash of light blasted the room, followed swiftly by a crack of thunder that rattled the house. He spread her legs, he oiled her everywhere. The rain increased, slapping the roof. She moaned.

Another flash, a tremendous boom. Max rolled her over and began again on her neck and shoulders. It was pouring. Briseis felt her body rolling. She was on her stomach. He was working where her neck and head met. His fingers were making their way into her skull, into that brain that wasn't working anymore, he was moving down her spine. A crash rattled the windows, there was NO lag between sound and light as the storm was right over the house. Shutters were banging in the sudden wind. It was better than any romantic scene she had ever read. Max was pushing and easing and working the small of her back and slowly bringing her buttocks into the motion. She was as slippery as a seal, he thought as he worked the crack of her ass. More oil and more, he moved to her feet and ankles again and up the back of her legs, one hand each upon her thighs to her ass, thumbs coming up from vagina to anus she moaned again and reached back with a hand, searching for him. She found his penis and gave it a squeeze. Thunder and lightning pounded the house as though they were under attack. She squeezed and stroked with her tortured hand.

Max's surprise was complete, his joy more so, and so

easy, easy he climbed upon the bed, his hands kneading her ass. He bent over and kissed her along the spine. She spread her legs and pushed herself up to him, and he slid into her oiled opening. She felt him in the top of her head. The being of him in her began there between her legs and filled her all above, she felt it in her face. It was a swelling. Another flash and boom. Very slow, he moved very slowly, from near withdrawal to fully mounted on her ass. An extra push, the idea of deeper penetration, a dream of completion, his hand on her ass sliding down to the small of her back, over and over. She lost track of the thunder, but the lightning entered her closed eyes. A series of strobelight flashes, photographs, he was long and slow now, she could push back, she could raise her ass to him. The storm was moving on, and from far away she felt herself coming to this room, from across the valley, from years ago. He kept his rhythm slow, reached beneath her hips and gave her clitoris one stroke with his oiled finger. She jerked with an electric charge, an animal cry burst from her. He touched her again and she began to spasmodically quake, she thrust herself back toward him and he rode her into the still pounding rain. Crack of lightning, then a lag, then rolling thunder till he roared and bellowed the storm into her, six, eight, ten erupting strokes. Oh, oh, she joined him, he was collapsing, falling, to the side, not on her, she could not bear the weight.

The storm moved east across the valley, as almost all storms did, the rumbles and flashes growing fainter. The garden outside breathed its wet renewal into the room. He idly stroked her oily back and heard a sound, not quite human. What could that be? Never mind. The rain had slowed. A light thump began. Max raised his head and peered over Briseis and began to laugh. "Brie, just look to your left, on the floor." She opened her eyes, and there were their four dogs huddled close to the bed, still quivering from the terror of the storm and peering up at them like lost orphans. She joined Max and they laughed and laughed, reached out and stroked their beasts on their heads, they couldn't stop.

"So, did you guys enjoy the show? Humans fucking, did it temper your terror at all? Did you find comfort in it?"

"I'm glad I didn't know they were here."

Max clapped his hands. "Okay, out you go now. The show and the storm are over, and in just a little while we'll go walking."

They hung their heads, chastised, and didn't move.

"Now!"

With furtive looks, they filed out.

The glass doors to the veranda were open, the white curtains trailed the tile floor and the jasmine and honeysuckle dripped from the storm, a lost bee buzzed above them and exited.

14

AMALIA OFTEN CHANGED the color of her hair. This year she was a blonde. It was long and straight and suited her. Her head was long and narrow, her features sharp, her neck an elegant extension from thin, squared-off shoulders. She rotated that neck and viewed the world with a faint look of derision. It never quite measured up. She was always disappointed. The moron seated next to her on the flight from Amsterdam had tried to engage her, chattering on aimlessly. It's difficult to ignore someone seated so close, but Lia was capable of it. Alas, the effort involved had left her churned up and anxious.

The carousel was taking forever. What, was her bag going to be last off? Finally. She pulled it off the moving track and turned to find the way out, following the crowd and emerging through automatic doors to the waiting throng of relatives and tour guides holding signs. She scanned the crowd till she saw Leo waving. He was standing next to Max, who was holding a sign: LIA POPS. It was a nickname from childhood, and despite her mood, she broke into a smile and hurried to embrace her brother.

"Leo, hey, you're taller than me? How did that happen? How can my little brother be taller than me?"

Leo, proud of his new size, lifted her off the floor.

She turned to Max. "Whose idea was the sign?"

"Your mom's and mine. I've always wanted to hold a sign at the airport, and she came up with the words. How was the flight?"

Her embrace of her stepfather was half the gesture of that toward her brother, yet genuine enough, and he

292

received it warmly. "Same old same old, except I was seated next to some asshole on the flight from Amsterdam." She lowered her voice, "Wait, there he is." They all looked to see a rather nerdy man in his mid-thirties shuffling along with a little woman who must have been his mother.

"He looks pretty harmless."

"Extremely," added Leo.

"Well, okay. Maybe he wasn't an asshole, but he wanted to chat, and I just wanted to chill, so I had to make an effort to ignore him." They left the air-conditioned illusion of the airport for the afternoon wall of heat. "Oh god, does that feel good! Sometimes it seems like Portland never gets hot."

The Attica sun flashed off windows and pavement as they eased out of the airport complex. "So, how is Mom, anyway?"

"Uh, not too good. And really, saying that is ridiculous. She's got cancer in her lungs and her brain. There aren't any more treatments. Her hands are fucked from the scleroderma. So, not good."

"You mean there isn't any treatment?"

"Essentially, no. She's got drugs to manage pain and her various discomforts. She coughs a lot." Leo was leaning forward from the backseat, his head between Lia and his father. He didn't like this kind of conversations and at home would ignore them. Now he was getting the latest update, which sounded far worse than he had imagined.

"Shouldn't she go to the States and find another treatment?"

"She doesn't want to chase any more cures, and really, there aren't any. She's never wanted to be, what she calls, a medical refugee."

Lia sunk back into her seat, "Wow!" And with that one sound all the air left her and the fatigue of travel descended. Along with a horrible, maturing, most unwelcome knowledge.

But Leo could always forge on. "Hey, the guys and I went out to Paros last month. Wasn't that the island you worked on?"

"Paros! Yeah, I rocked Paros for two summers. Were you in Naoussa?"

"Yeah, that's where we were. In this campsite on the edge of town."

"Cool. My baby brother partying in Naoussa. Keeping up the tradition." They high-fived. "How's Maki? Did she go too?"

"She's great. She and some girls went to Amorgos, and then we all met up on Ios. Which is a total party island."

"And you guys are all finished with high school?"

"Been there, done that."

"That's so cool. I know Maki's going to New York. Where are you headed?"

"The U.K. Manchester, really cool city."

How could her younger siblings be leaving her behind? Fourteen years younger and leaving home, when all she really wanted to do was move back in. Be taken care of. Drop the load of life on someone else.

Briseis heard the car coming up the hill, struggled out of her chair, and went to the railing to watch their arrival. Maki came out of the house and joined her. The dogs were raising a tremendous racket, trying to herd or head off the car. Max was honking the horn, trying to get them out of the way, and Leo was shouting out the window at them. Now Maki ran down the stairs shouting a welcome.

What a cacophony! Why was her family so noisy? She laughed at the obvious answer as she watched her first-born emerge from the car.

She was struck anew with how Amalia looked like her grandfather, like the Burrows. The nose, eyes, the body shape, only she had a far more refined look. And she was so thin! She bounded up the stairs while the dogs went berserk.

"Hi, Mom. Oh, I'm so glad to be here!"

They embraced. Her older daughter one of the few people in the world who would not hug her too hard, who wouldn't evince a wince or a twinge. Just right, and she gave up thinking.

"Oh, so am I, my dear. So am I."

Amalia walked through the expanse of her family's house. The views from every window, the art on the walls, the great spread of tiles and cushions, wicker and wood, and nodded to herself. *This was never my life.* She'd been fifteen when Briseis and Max had decided to bestow some legitimacy on the twins. She'd been a bridesmaid. The big house in Portland was bought in her last year of high school, and soon after she'd left for Greece. Leo and Maki had had an entirely different life, and she couldn't help resenting it. She knew it was petty, unjust, but there it was. She had been the child of a single working mom: daycare after school, the long nighttime bus rides in the rain across town, tight budgets, the absent father. Her life should have been different, she was convinced of it. Yet she loved Leo and Maki with a devotion that bordered on obsession. She had been a child alone, her mom's friends mostly childless. How often she had wished for the company of other children. They'd just come along too late. And soon they'd be on either side of the Atlantic, farther away than ever in many ways. And where would Mom be? Her appearance was stunningly depressing. Emaciated, misshapen, weak and teetering. She hadn't really believed it till now. Her mother was dying. Where did that leave her?

The mountains quivered in a burning haze. Amalia, Andromache, and Briseis luxuriated in the afternoon swelter. They all loved it hot. Maki was deeply tanned, no more than her mother and sister in their day, and Lia was darkening quickly, sprawling daily next to Elektra's swimming pool. Briseis sipped her iced tea. "Have you heard? George and Megan are coming next week."

"Really?"

"Yes, the whole clan gathered."

They let that seep into them. The wrought-iron railings of the hiati were deeply entangled with jasmine and bougainvillea and bees and butterflies whirred and hovered through them. The dogs were sprawled panting in the shade. A faint tinkle of bells drifted in. They could see Achilles with his goats working a hillside observed by a hawk circling high above, working the heat with imperceptible adjustments of wing and tail.

"Sybil too?"

"Of course. They're driving, of all things. They leave in a couple of days. They did the math and can save a slight amount over flying and renting a car. Which sounds so much easier. It's not like they're going to sightsee on the way. It's a family trait. Great contortions in pursuit of illusory savings. What a ridiculous family I come from! And sorry, my dears, but it's yours too."

Lia lifted her head from a cushion. "It's not ridiculous.

A little weird, but way cooler than most families I meet."

"Yeah, mom. Just take a look around Sparti. There are people down there acting like it's the nineteenth century."

"That's kind of you both. I suppose no family bears up under scrutiny. Look at Max's. From the outside it appears to be a model American family, brimming with health and success. And it is. But try spending a few days inside of it with his mother and you will go stark raving mad. She's profoundly obsessive-compulsive, and they've let her do and say whatever she wants. So she does, of course. There's nothing worse than being the outsider inside one of these situations. You have no way of defending yourself. And it can feel like you're going crazy." Briseis took what she intended as a deep breath but started coughing. Her daughters sat up and watched, ready to fetch the codeine syrup. Maki got up and fed her mother a spoonful. It worked, and Briseis recovered with a few short breaths. "She's been trying to visit for the past year but I just couldn't bear it, having her in the house for days on end. It's excruciating. I don't have the strength."

Max had driven Leo and Maki to Sparti, the lights of which were twinkling in the valley below. Briseis and Lia were at the outside dining table eating pistachios and throwing the shells over the railing. Jocasta was on Brie's lap, Menelaus on Lia's. An eclectic mix of music Leo had left on was playing from the house.

"I want to go to school and learn to cut hair. I mean really learn, coloring, perms, all that stuff."

"Good idea, why don't you?"

"Well, I'll need help. It's going to be hard."

"Okay. What do you need?"

"It's going to cost plenty, I think, though I've heard

297

there are scholarships and stuff. And I won't be able to work while I'm doing it, or not very much."

"Lia, if you want to do it, go and find out what's needed, and then we can figure out how you can do it. You have to take the first steps. But we aren't just going to send money. We've done that, and you're in the same place a year later."

"It's not easy. I've had a hard time. You have no idea."

"I don't suppose I do. When it was just you and me I had to push on, I didn't have a choice. You don't want to . . . oh, listen. It's Edith Piaf. Where did Leo get this? That voice is so passionate."

"What is she singing?"

"Non, je ne regrette rien. No, I regret nothing. *I regret nothing*. Imagine? A life without regret. Hers was very unhappy, as I remember."

They listened as Piaf rang out through the Lakonian night, drowning out the crickets.

"Do you have regrets, Mom?"

"Masses. Or rather, I used to. Now, I seem to be losing them. I wake up in the morning and it feels as though some have drifted away while I slept. And they don't return. It's very strange, but I like it."

15

ON A HILL ABOVE THE TOWN, the Sparti hospital has a large veranda from which you can see back into the rooms through generous windows and glass doors. Shabby, in need of a paint job, floors fatigued, it was equipped much like a well-stocked American or British hospital in 1950. Attempts to modernize nearly always meant running more cables and pipes along the walls near the ceilings, which were now an indecipherable warren of wire and gas, oxygen and data. New regulations had decreed that smoking in the rooms and hallways was apagorevménos, forbidden, and surprisingly enough, this rule was actually enforced. So the smokers congregated on the veranda, which, facing south, afforded spectacular views over the valley and the mountain ranges to the west and east. The Byzantine city of Mystras sprawled up a Tayegetos foothill. Sparti simmered drowsy in the heat, thousands of air conditioners competing with the cicadas.

Before he moved to Greece Max had had little experience with hospitals. A friend wrecked his motorcycle, another stapled himself to a roof. Accidents, broken bones are another country from illness, from the unseen under the flesh working through internal organs, collecting, multiplying. In this you had to trust the professionals, the body is opaque and does not reveal itself. A cardiologist, after running a few tests, had told them there was liquid around Briseis's heart that should be drained. They made phone calls. Fiona had a doctor friend at the hospital, she'd arrange it. It turned out the friend didn't have the advertised authority, and now a large group of doctors was milling about Briseis's bed, watching as a young woman doctor prepared to drain the fluid. The other patients, it was six to a room, sat up wide-eyed, grateful that it was someone else facing the needle.

The doctor felt around her back for a few moments and then dramatically inserted a long needle. Though the windows were closed, Max could hear his wife scream. No fluid emerged so she tried again. Again the scream. And again. The doctors, including the senior physicians on the ward, exchanged looks, shrugged, and filed out of the room. That was it.

Max caught up with the doctor in the hallway.

"What was that?"

"It was causing too much discomfort to continue."

"But you didn't hit the fluid anyway. Have you ever performed that procedure?"

"It wouldn't save her anyway." She turned and walked into the nurses' station.

"Thanks for nothing, you quack." Several patients turned to look. Max entered the room and went to Briseis.

"Oh, there you are my love. God, that was excruciating."

"They're not going to do anything for you, even if they could. Let's get out of here."

"Good idea. My clothes are in that bag there. Help me get dressed, it will be faster."

Max called Dr. Kazantzakis, an English-speaking physician who had been a help in Brie's mother's final days. It was he who had, at a glance early in their days in Greece, diagnosed Briseis's scleroderma. He agreed to come that afternoon.

He shook his head and muttered while listening to their latest Sparti hospital tale. The good ones were

300

swimming against the current, a flood tide of malpractice and corruption. He had Briseis sit up, put his ear to her back, and lightly thumped with his forefingers till he located the liquid center. He turned to Max.

"Hold this pan under the needle while it drains. And have another ready." He painlessly inserted a needle and the flow began. Three pans filled, with Maki emptying them in the sink as Max handed them to her.

Briseis sighed. "Oh, thank you, Doctor. I hardly felt that. I feel better already."

"They didn't drain anything at the hospital?" Incredulous.

"No. It didn't seem like they could find it, for some reason."

He gritted his teeth and loaded his bag, took his payment from Max, and said, "Call me if you need any further help." He shook Max's hand and added, "Good luck." The dogs, who had been closed out of the house during all this, raced in as the front door opened. Dr. Kazantzakis shook his head again and headed down the stairs.

Max pulled her out of the bath and wrapped a towel around her. Briseis slowly walked back into the bedroom, turned, and looked at herself in the full-length mirror.

"God, I look like Dachau."

Max winced. There she stood, emaciated, ninety pounds or less, bald, very sick. Yeah, Dachau, just like the pictures from the camps. Sometimes he looked into her eyes and thought, My god, my lovely wife, my wonderful woman is trapped inside this wasted form. How did she get in there, afraid, and peering out?

Briseis nodded at her reflection and sat on the edge

301

of the bed. She looked down at her hands, which were trying to hold each other. There isn't anything else ahead, I'm just shuffling toward the end. Death, how had this happened? What bullshit. If only there was someone or something to hold responsible. But then, what good would that do? A god to blame wouldn't stop this coughing.

Everything will just go on without me: Maki, Leo, Lia, what will happen to them? What will they do? Max, he'll be okay. Probably have some sense of liberation, the anchor cut loose. And he'll write about it. He'll write about this. I know he will. She gave herself a silent, one-note laugh, that's my life after death, Max's telling of it. She leaned back into the pillows. "How *will* you tell it, my love?"

"What?"

"How will you tell the story of this, of the long decline? A series of poems, prose? You know how it ends."

Max sat on the edge of the bed, rubbed her feet, and thought sardonic didn't suit her. "I don't know. Haven't given it any thought. It may demand the density of prose. We'll see."

"No, *we* won't."

"True. But that's down the road somewhere."

"I don't think it's much longer. How could it be?"

How much more broken, the heart?

• •

HE WAS AN ATTENDANT, a faithful family retainer. No longer lover, it didn't feel like husband anymore. That connection blurred—which only made his attention more pure. Several times a day he burst into short spasms of tears. He kept them from her, he didn't know why. He was so obviously knotted with it. Lia would arrive at noon to sit with her mother and Max would run to Sparti for food, the *Herald Tribune*, the odds and ends life still required. And just not to be in attendance. A half-hour at Takis's with an ouzo and octopus, the paper, the stream of life on the street without beginning or end. It goes on. And never slows down.

Maki and Leo arose around two in the afternoon and had their coffee with their mom, who might have moved to the hiati. Elektra and George came up in the late afternoon. The three siblings talked of their lives together. The past drifted in like dust from the orchards and settled over everyone. The children charged past events with dramatically different meaning, highlighting little triumphs, the failures of adults, and rounded the edges, brightened the colors. The weather then was just right, the laughs were louder, and the melons impossibly sweet. Elektra had forgotten so much. Briseis saw the pain and fear trailing away, the order of occurrence was fractured, sometimes it was a new life she was hearing. They eased into enjoying her as much as possible. And she them.

The coughing increased. Greater amounts of codeine syrup and painkillers. There was no plan, no place to go. She woke him at two in the morning with the cough. Max gave her syrup, no relief. He gave her pills but she couldn't swallow, shaken with a harsh retching and gagging, dry gravel on paper. He kept giving her syrup, continued trying with the pills ground into powder. The low, pale light of dawn seeped in through the glass doors and found them shattered, Briseis heaving and wracked, Max gagging with tears, hands full of useless drugs. The sun spilled orange over Parnona, and Briseis slipped into a fitful sleep, with a coughing spasm every twenty minutes. Max made himself tea and sat watching her.

Some things cannot be put back together. The great lord Humpty Dumpty presides over the fallen. We sift through the pieces, we miss some.

By mid-morning she was awake and gagging. He checked her temperature, she was burning. Enough. His daughter was home, and he went to wake her. She awoke to her father's tear-stained face and was on her feet talking.

Daddy, what's happening?"

"I can't stop your mom's coughing. It's getting worse, and now she's running a high fever. I don't want to try and get her into the car. I want you to call an ambulance. The number's right here. Be precise in your instructions, you know how they are. After that call Elektra and tell her what's happening. I'm going to get dressed so I'm ready."

The ambulance arrived with just the driver. Max turned to Andromache and said, "What if there wasn't anyone here to help him? How the hell would he get someone out of a building and into his rig? Over his shoulder?" They carried Briseis out on a stretcher. Max and Maki rode in the back with her, both of them weeping uncontrollably while Brie, reeling with delirium, attempted to comfort them. Max broke down, the weeks and months previous emptied themselves in a blubbering gush that lasted several minutes, and then he came to. He stopped crying, raised his head, and looked out the window at the sun-smashed olive orchards flowing by. He felt purged and began to review the previous hours and prepare for the coming ones while he stroked his wife's head. He'd had his tears and was ready again.

• •

SHE WAS HORRIBLY COLD TO THE TOUCH and the sweat

304

was pouring off her as though her connection to the primal sea was abandoning her. They got a stack of sheets from the nurses and changed them every hour that first afternoon. The hospital IV'd the drugs in, and in the late afternoon the fever broke, the sweats ceased, and everyone let out their breath.

She was in a small room with two other beds at the end of a long, gloomy hallway. There was a small waiting room next door. Word of her crisis quickly bled through the veins of Sparti. Rumor was an instantaneous event in the community. Bad news carries a ring of authenticity. Greeks are inveterate hospital visitors. It is part of the life, part of knowing, of the improvisatory nature of being in the world. Nothing is planned, and suddenly you must visit the hospital. You meet many people you know in the hallways, visiting mum, their uncle Elias with his prostate, cousin Chrysoula's mysterious swelling. Soon there was a small crowd outside the room milling like petitioners.

Late afternoon of the second day Max stepped out onto the hospital veranda. He looked east toward Parnona and could identify the ancient memorial to Helen, the Menalion, could see the pyramidal hump shadow dark in the sun. A snatch of poetry drifted in.

> *Brightness falls from the air;*
> *Queens have died young and fair;*
> *Dust hath closed Helen's eye.*
> *I am sick, I must die.*
> *Lord have mercy on us!*

He nodded to himself. How appropriate, *A Litany in a Time of Plague*. He never knew what the library of verse he carried in his head would throw out. He said it out loud, "Brightness falls from the air."

"Who is that, Daddy?"

He turned to see Leo standing next to him lighting a cigarette.

"Thomas Nashe, sixteenth-century England. Contemporary of Shakespeare. Remembered for one poem of which that is the most famous line. Justly, I might add."

"So are you wandering around thinking, what's the appropriate poetic line for this occasion?"

Max laughed. "No, no, they come unsummoned. And sometimes they fit or add perspective, a musical accompaniment."

"Musical accompaniment?"

"Sure. Poetry is the link between music and language."

"Give me System of a Down any day."

"Okay, but can you sing it for me?"

Leo pulled a small piece of technology from his pocket. "I don't have to, I got an MP3 player."

Her voice got smaller and smaller, a whisper as though she was afraid who might hear. As though angels of death were in the air over Lakonia searching for the next departure. They took turns on the chairs each side of her bed. They leaned in close to hear. They squinted their ears. In the evening Leo, Maki, and Lia sat around holding her hands, touching her head. She felt secure, bound to earth by her children. She couldn't be taken, not like this.

Her ultimate fear, greater than brain tumor, was to be buried alive. It was late in the evening, most of the visitors had left. Family members were taking a break, Elektra was bringing something to eat.

"Max," she whispered, "you know what to do with me?"

"What's that?" He brought his face inches from hers.

"I want to be cremated. You must promise me this."

"Then that's what will happen."

"You'll have to take me to England. They won't do it here."

"Don't worry, Brie. I promise. If I have to throw you in the back seat and drive you there."

She squeezed out a laugh. "Might have trouble going through customs."

"'What's in the bag, sir?' 'My wife. We're on holiday.'"

"The ashes."

"Yes?"

"Do whatever you want with them."

The coughing, they can't stop it. Briseis veers in and out of delirium, frantically conscious and wanting to know everything that is happening. Where were the children, Max, her long-dead mother? What was being done? Maki, terrified, unable to leave the room, peered into her mother trying to see what was going on in there. Lia too rarely left. They were going to hang on. Leo found it difficult for long stretches, came and went several times a day, kept in touch by phone. George, his wife Megan, and Elektra brought food, sat relief, met the visitors, few of whom were allowed in the room. All expected Max to be the last man standing.

Another dawn. In the pale coming light her daughters drooped over the bed. How long had she been here? What day was it? What was in this liquid running into her arm? She was with her daughters at the sea, they were all the same age and hiding behind a rock and whispering. Someone was looking for them, seagulls were crying out a warning. A long, harsh fit of coughing brought her back to the room. Her bleary daughters looked up, awake with concern. Where had the seagulls gone?

Hours of wheezing coughing that night. A death rattle racketing out of her. She was leaving, what else could it be? No one could speak as they stroked her with fear and awe. Give her a word, thought Max, give her a word, and he leaned forward and whispered in her ear, "Go toward the light"—as the Buddhists say. But she shook this off and a little while later murmured, "I want to come back." What did it mean? Surely not a sudden conversion to the idea of reincarnation. She looked about desperately as though tormented by demons, her eyes impossibly open, and Lia pleading, "What do you see?" And then, "Are you afraid?" To which her mother distinctly whispered, "Not anymore."

After hours of rattling descent she returned, wanted everyone about her: brother and sister, children and husband crowded around the bed so she could see. She looked from one to the next and said, triumphantly, "See, I came back. I came back to see you all. It's wonderful to see you all . . . I came back. See?" A smile, alert and conscious again, able to whisper, and they took turns sitting near and breathing out their secrets. Not yet.

George and Max stood on the veranda in the night. Max wished he still smoked, just for this moment.

"I thought that was it," said George.

Max nodded, looked up at the third-quarter moon and said, "'The book of moonlight is not written yet.'"

They were all used to it. "It that yours?"

"No, Wallace Stevens. Sometimes I feel he's giving instructions from the great poetic beyond."

Later that night again just Briseis and Max. He massaged her hands, gently working each gnarled finger.

She smiled, closed her eyes, and said, "I love your hands. I have always loved your hands." She drifted into sleep. Last words, they are not known till later.

• •

SHE COULDN'T SPEAK THE NEXT DAY. The mouth wouldn't work, her head shook with the effort. She gestured for a pen and paper but couldn't make a letter, kept trying, hanging onto the pen, but the hand didn't understand the brain's messages, or was too feeble for the task. They longed for the tiny voice of yesterday. George wrote out the alphabet on a card and tried to get her to point out the letters of the words she was trying to form, but she didn't want to do that, and a sad and pleading game of charades was played out around the bed. Their team always lost.

Past midnight Max and Leo drove back to the village for some rest. Lia and Maki remained with their mother. Before dawn the phone rang. It was Lia. "You'd better come quick. Mom needs you." Max leapt into clothes and was at the hospital in fifteen minutes. Briseis was asleep and didn't look any different.

"She started shaking and sat up, her eyes were spinning, and that's why I phoned. Then the seizure or whatever it was stopped. I tried to call you back but you'd left already."

"That's okay, I'm glad you called. You girls go lie down, get some sleep." They stretched out on benches in the lounge, and fatigue swept them away.

Max sat on the edge of the bed and studied her in the coming dawn. Little breaths, such little breaths. And slowly, in distinctive little stages, she faded away. The breath just got fainter and fainter. He held her little head in his hands, kissed her, and said, "Goodbye, my love, goodbye." He was inches from her face, overcome with wonder and loss, and took the last tiny breath from her lips.

He listened for several minutes trying to discern any movement of air or beat of heart, but there was nothing. Gently he shook Lia and Maki awake.

"Your mom's stopped breathing."

They started to their feet, went to their mother, and then began to keen and wail. Max walked down the hallway to the nurses' station and explained in his crippled Greek that his wife had ceased breathing. The morning sun was streaming in the window as he walked down the hall toward Amalia and Andromache's tortured cries. It was eight a.m.

Minutes later a young doctor with two assistants wheeling an electrocardiogram machine entered the room, and they stepped back into the hallway. Lia was curled over in despair, Maki clung to her father, he blurted out his sorrow in short gagging waves. When she was hooked up he watched the machine print out a flat unwavering line. The doctor turned with a fatalistic hand gesture and said, "She's dead." They unhooked her and pulled the covers over her head. One of the other beds in the room was occupied by a tiny crone attended by another. They stared in silent horror, so stunned they forgot to cross themselves.

Minutes later orderlies arrived with a gurney and lifted her out of bed. With each step, Lia wailed anew. They held each other, the three of them, and watched her roll away down the long hallway and turn the corner for the elevator and the descent to the morgue.

310

Max made the phone calls, and by the time they were at the outside entrance to the morgue, Fiona, Sally, and Elektra were there. They stained each other freely, the weeping was so easy. Max started with the sense that he'd never embraced these women with this lack of restraint and need. An hour later Maki and her father drove back to the village. They sat on Leo's bed and gently tugged him awake. Max left them there, Leonidas comforting his sister, and sat on the hiati with coffee before the expanse of Lakonia, his dogs at his feet.

16

ELEKTRA, WITH AMALIA AND ANDROMACHE, parked in the shade in front of the church. Elegantly done up in black, made up to hide their sleepless fatigue, in sunglasses, they were a striking trio, stunned in the afternoon light, utterly out of place in the rundown village. Although two were sisters, they were as three generations, the same blood a flow. Andromache hadn't decided what to wear till the last moment, then borrowed a black cocktail dress from Amalia. They were the same lean height, though Maki had a slightly fuller figure. She felt awkward in high heels. Too tall.

They were early, though there wasn't a coffin to sit with. All three of them were glad of this as the coffin is always open in Greece, and that would have been too much. Maki stared across the platea at the old house, where she had lived for five years. Hard to believe. It looked small and shabby, very rundown now that no one lived in it, but they'd had a lot of fun there. She could see that now. Everything seemed simple and easy then. Mom wasn't really sick, there wasn't any frontesterio, it was like their whole lives were lived right there in that house. Popcorn and Clue, fires in the tsaki, hanging out on the hiati in the warm weather, the playground right across the street, bedtime stories every night. Swallows were darting around it; Daddy would know what kind. She began to sigh, but it turned into a cry. Elektra gave her a hug. "There, there."

They looked up the road through the village and saw Leonidas and his friends Yiorgos, Adonis, and Odysseus, in jeans and T-shirts, walking down. Bounding about them were four dogs.

"Oh my god, they've brought the dogs, " Amalia exclaimed.

"They won't bother anyone."

"They'll probably walk right into the church."

Elektra grabbed her nieces, who towered over her, round their waists and said, "Well, it's our ceremony, and if the dogs want to join, I say bloody well let them."

Amalia grimaced and Maki almost laughed, thinking you always knew where Elektra stood when it came to dogs. For the third time that day the church bells began the death knell. So many times they had heard that hard, aching sound over the years. It resonated in your bones, that dreadful rhythm. And now it was their turn. Cars from Sparti began pulling up and parking along the road. Over at the taverna Stavros and Maria were setting up tables for afterwards. Sally and Fiona, good friends of Briseis, American and English, came with armloads of flowers.

"I guess we should be up on the terrace by the entrance," Elektra said.

"Yeah, that's usually where they stand."

"Okay, girls, you don't have to talk to anyone if you don't want to. Just a little *Thank you* is all that's required."

"Not even that. A nod of the head will suffice. Anyway, it's afterwards that you're supposed to receive condolences." Sally busied herself with the funeral arrangements, such as they were. Many years go she had come to Greece and wound up marrying the undertaker. The bread, the stari, lilies, here and there. What kind of a turnout would there be? Already some of the villagers were arriving on foot. Papa Dimitritiou pulled up in a pickup, put his hat on his head, and stepped from the cab. He quickly offered condolences to the women and

313

whisked into the church to make sure all was ready.

Yiorgos was huddling with Serena, another English friend with a fluency in Greek. They'd been given the task of delivering Max's address to the memorial in his absence. "I'm not going to try and translate that poem into Greek," she said, "no way." Yiorgos was studying the text, murmuring the words to himself. "I'll do the English and then you can do the message, the prose here, in Greek, and that will be okay. Is anyone else going to speak?"

"Besides the Papas, I don't know, though anyone who wants can. Isn't that the way it works?" No one mentioned the oddity of the arrangement, Serena, an English woman, doing the translation into Greek and Yiorgos, a Greek, delivering the English. Yet who else but Yiorgos, his closest friend in Greece and a poet too?

Elektra, Andromache, and Amalia entered the church and lit candles for Briseis. Elektra was grateful she had the girls to buck up, to focus on, and couldn't give herself over to her horrible grief, some keening public disaster like her namesake. The church was ablaze with candlelight. In here they could avoid the crowd.

Leonidas sat on the terrace wall with dozens of his classmates and exchanged hugs with the arriving stream of teenagers. He wasn't sure how he felt. Numb, weirdly detached. Empty. His mom was gone. He knew how he was supposed to feel but couldn't seem to get around to it, not in the way everyone else was. His sisters and aunt were weeping like mad. Some of his friends were even crying. It felt like it wasn't really happening to him, that he was watching a rather badly made home video, everything burned out in the afternoon light. He wished his father was here, not that he'd feel any different, he didn't want to be *the* male representative of the family. Just then

314

Briseis's father arrived, and he no longer was. The Major was being shepherded by George, Megan, and Sybil. Leo watched his grandfather, puffing away at his pipe, walk across the terrace, gauging his level of inebriation. Not bad, but he looked awful.

He was drunker than he looked. The Major was using every bit of energy he had to hold off the booze he had consumed that day. If he wasn't careful he'd bite right through his pipe. First his wife, now his first-born. What bloody next? Fucking world! He marched over to Leonidas. Held out his hand.

"Sorry, lad. Tough luck. How are you holding up?"

"I'm okay, grandpa."

"That's the stuff." The Major scanned the crowd. "Not a bad turnout." He turned back to Leo. "Well, chin up. I'm going to find a place in the shade."

Megan came up and gave Leonidas a hug. She was wet with tears. Past his aunt's head he could see Sybil slipping into the church. The dogs were terribly excited, dashing about sniffing everyone. There were lots of his mom's former students. People he didn't even know were arriving, and every English teacher in Sparti was there.

Yiorgos kept going over Max's text. It was thankfully short. He had read the poem before, in the little book of sonnets, he was sure of it. More time to prepare would have been nice, rather than the phone call at noon. But what the hell, death, what can you do? He had walked up the stairs from the terrace into the old graveyard. Below was the small valley and river that ran through the village. Yes, it was beautiful, but why, why had they come to Greece, and why had they stayed? It baffled him, he who would give anything to return to the States. He turned

315

and looked at the old graves with their white marble and carved names. Most of them weren't attended to anymore. Weeds were growing up, marble was cracking. Everyone is forgotten. He wiped the sweat from his forehead with a handkerchief, wished he still smoked, walked among the old graves, and thought of Max with his John Donne quotes. How did it go, *every man's death diminishes me?* True, as far as it went, but really, every death just reminds us that we're doomed. That we'll follow soon enough, and not of our own choosing. Just random. Pfffft. Gone. Life doesn't care. Yiorgos shook his head. He was muttering to himself. He looked over the wall. The crowd on the terrace was moving into the church. He looked over the paper in his hand one last time and descended the stairs.

As he entered the church the Papas and cantor began intoning. Without thought, completely out of superstitious habit, he crossed himself, kissed the ikon, and dropped some money in the tray. He selected a candle, lit it, and stuck it in the sand with a hundred others. The small church was packed. He knew most of the young people, had had them in classes. As he maneuvered his bulk through the crowd he shook hands, nodded to others. It was a different feeling without the corpse and coffin in the center of the church. The dead was missing, but the tears were flowing just the same.

Amalia kept her sunglasses on. What did it matter, she was blind with weeping. The chanting and incense was making her dizzy. She squeezed Elektra's hand. Everything was over. What was she going to do? Staying in Greece no longer seemed an option. Everyone was gone or leaving. Mom's death changed everything. She would have to return to the States, but where? She didn't have any money. She staggered, and Elektra steadied her.

Leonidas stood near his sisters and looked around the church, which was packed. Okay, it was a small church, it didn't take many bodies to fill it, but there were a lot of people. Somehow the tone-deaf cantor had been replaced, for this event, anyway. He'd forgotten all about that guy once they'd moved to the new house and were out of range of the Sunday service, distorted through loudspeakers on the bell tower. Thank god for that. This was Vassili, a big improvement. Dad had written a poem about this guy.

Andromache realized that she and both her siblings were wearing their sunglasses. She slipped hers off. The candles blazed up. She was certain her heart would stop, break down, give up. She missed her mother horribly. Why did Daddy have to go to England? She knew, she knew. It was a promise to her mother that he had to fulfill. The Papas was speaking to the crowd now, droning on about life taken too soon, God's will, and other bullshit. Sometimes she understood why her father clung to his ignorance of Greek, just these situations. He stopped now and was signaling. Yiorgos and Serena were moving toward the altar.

Serena had decided she should speak first, and Yiorgos was happy to defer, to gain another couple of minutes. Serena ripped through the text in her amazingly precise Greek. Heads were nodding and murmuring. And then she was done.

Yiorgos straightened himself and walked to the lectern and microphone. "Good afternoon. I'm going to read what Max wrote in English now."

"'I am not with you today because I am accompanying Briseis's body to England to honor her cremation request. This is, inevitably, consistent with how our lives in Greece emerged. Briseis reached out to the world and intimately

317

touched all of your lives, while I narrowed my focus to her and Leonidas and Andromache to the exclusion of most everyone else. Lives aren't led according to grand plans but bump along, one part improvisation, one part quirk of fate. Many years ago we heard a wise man say, 'Follow your bliss.' And armed with that truth, twelve and a half years ago we came to Greece without much money or a clue, just a desire for the freedom of starting from scratch.

"'No one here knew her as thoroughly as I did, no one in the world knows me as she did. It was a knowledge incubated in love and nurtured by friendship, admiration, and respect. Together we were able to expand beyond ourselves. I like to think that the depth of our bond, of our union, and how we manifested it, is our true gift to that little bit of the world we encountered.

"'Here is a short poem I wrote for Briseis years ago. As is often the case, it now has a different resonance.

> *The silence is a slow draining away*
> *a tap inserted in the veins of joy,*
> *the tools that love and loss employ*
> *compress a life to just one day.*
>
> *'From this moment on it will all be different'*
> *we think, we mourn, lose track, forget*
> *that this truth is far less important*
> *than 'give much more than you will get.'*
>
> *Things of earth wait out the weather*
> *we cannot see inside the other,*
> *but birds return after hurricane*
> *and when they sing the song's the same.*
> *It's best sometimes to just remember*
> *what after every winter came.*

Yiorgos looked up from the paper in his hand. Many of the English-speakers in the crowd were choking back sobs. Amalia had sat down in a chair and was holding her head in her hands. Elektra was standing over her, face streaming. The whole church exhaled, and the candle flames flickered and danced, ghosts of fire in the incensed air. There would be no more speeches. Leonidas nodded his head, truth, Daddy sure could do it, and went outside for a smoke. Andromache was right behind him.

Leo and Maki stood smoking on the terrace. People were beginning to leave the church. Sally was shoveling kollyva, a traditional funeral snack, into bags and motioning to them. Maki muttered, "Oh god. Come on, Leo, this will only take a few minutes."

"I hate this shit."

"Nobody likes it."

They lined up as though for an execution. Elektra, the Major, George, Amalia, Leo and Maki, godless the lot, stood and shook the hands and received the condolences of each and every one of them. Even Leo and Maki's friends got into the line. There are traditions that are followed without thought. That is the benefit of ritual. No one has to think.

17

AN HOUR BEFORE DEPARTURE he queued with the mob in front of Olympic Airways. It was out of balance, the world. Briseis had always insisted on hanging onto the passports and tickets, just to make sure. The airport was the only place she ever got to on time. Probably got here hours ago, thought Max. Olympic ran all flights through the same queue, and as the departure time neared for destinations, clerks would call out Istanbul, Frankfurt, and those headed there would get to jump the queue. There was a Greek logic to it, regardless of efficiency. And everyone got on the plane. Or nearly. London was called, and Max and another man moved to the desk, where a cheery woman informed them that there was only one seat left. The other man began to open his mouth when Max announced, "The body of my dead wife is on that plane. I *have to* be on that plane." The other would-be passenger was walking backwards, the check-in clerk was looking intently at her keyboard as she produced the boarding pass. Nobody had anything to add. Max felt he radiated a gnawing emptiness, a vast incompleteness. A rather rough amputation had been performed.

He grabbed a coffee and *The Guardian* and walked toward the gate. Thanks, Brie, you got me on the plane. All had been arranged. A special crate had been built, a refrigerated truck would pick it up at Heathrow and take her to a mortuary in Stamford, a midland town that George and Megan lived just outside of. Death was dense with procedure. There were people who knew their way through. Sign this paper, and this one, and pay the man who does these things.

He drove through the overcast afternoon gloom of England. It began to rain. The end of fucking August, cloudy and wet. How do they live here? He took the A1 north to Stamford. It was him, probably, but England looked drearier than usual. Perhaps a brief stop in Biggleswade, but no. At this time in the afternoon you couldn't get a bloody sandwich in this country. The memorial must be going on now. Strange. He had written something for it this morning but was completely detached from the event. Maki and Leo would be okay, with each other, with Lia, Elektra, and the rest. He had his own, unique passage, alone, with the remains. A truly practical person would have ignored the deathbed promise and just buried her in Greece. She was utterly dead. He wondered if they run another test in the morgue, just to make sure. And what's the difference, you come to and you're in a box you can't get out of, whether it's in the ground or not. You could knock on the lid. "Don't bury me 'cause I'm not dead yet," Elvis Costello had once sung. Yes she was.

He drove through the medieval market town of Stamford to Uffington, a wee village in the shadow of Burghley House, one of the grandest country estates in England. There it was off to his right as he drove through the farmlands. Turrets, pennants flying, great lawns fanning out, what bullshit! They'd had the civil war and had lopped off the king's head, but alas, never a real revolution with a thorough purging of the aristocracy.

There weren't many working farmers in Uffington anymore. It was a bedroom village and emptied out in the morning. George and Megan had a beautiful stone house with a slate roof, extensive garden, even a pig sty. He went next door to get the key from a neighbor,

Virginia. Middle-aged, full-figured, with a great mane of brown hair she opened the door and warmly embraced him. "Oh, Max, how are you doing?"

"Okay, okay. Bit shattered, of course, and still in a daze." She knew the story, had been told he was coming. They had met on previous trips, and then it hit him, her husband had died of a heart attack only the year before. They were widowed kin, left behind in the land of the living.

He walked through the house. They'd made changes. Everyone was remodeling. New kitchens, floors, additions. What was enough? And could it be better? It's an investment! How about a convection oven and a hot tub? Max laughed. He still hadn't finished his house. If ever there was a remodel, it would be someone else's job.

A short walk away was The Bertie, a classic village pub. Fifteenth-century building, thatched roof, low ceilings, a fire in hearth, and a couple of capped geezers in the corner arguing about pheasants. He ordered a Laphroaig neat and a pint of Guinness and sat near the fire. The publican came out, stirred the fire, sat down near.

"American, are ya?"

"Yes, I am, though I live in Greece."

"Greece? What brings you here?"

The weather. "I brought my wife here to be cremated." Max had no feeling for what it sounded like. He didn't have the energy or wit to invent. That's why he'd come. He wasn't looking for sympathy. The geezers had been listening to the exchange and now were staring. The publican recoiled slightly.

"I'm sorry to hear that."

Max nodded.

The old coots couldn't resist. "You brought her all the way here for that?"

"They don't do it there," Max said.

"Do what?"

Max nearly said barbecue. "Cremate. The Orthodox Church still has a lot of power and doesn't approve of it, for some reason."

"Bloody hell, you don't say?"

"I don't give a fuck what they do to me. Why should I? I'll be dead!"

"That's generally how it works, yes." Max couldn't take them seriously.

The three locals stared at him for several long seconds and then kept right on going.

"Nigel, they'll probably just bung you out back on the compost. Let the worms have their way with you."

"Aye, Jeff, can't imagine the cheap bastards springing for a proper funeral. They're counting the days and wondering why I'm still getting up in the morn. I swear, if I didn't own the place, they'd have chucked me out by now."

"Bugger them, Nige, nobody's got any respect anymore."

Max rose and said goodnight. They looked up as though he'd just come in.

"Sorry for your loss, lad." Nigel said.

"Was she English then, your wife?"

"Yes, yes, she was."

"Hmmm."

The sun was back, the countryside had a hallucinogenic quiver. A rush of geese lifted off the river with a great beating of wings and swung wide over a meadow. Max breathed deep, ah, now this was England. He had studied George's Ordinance Survey Maps over his morning coffee and figured he could walk into Stamford on public footpaths in just over an hour. Half a dozen young rabbits leapt through the grass in a field across the river. It looked just like those English children's stories, Beatrix Potter and *Wind in the Willows*. Briseis loved those stories and made sure the kids got a full dose. Hell, they had plates with scenes from *Peter Rabbit*. "Peter ran straightaway to Mr. McGregor's garden and squeezed under the gate! He ate some lettuces and some French beans." And then Mr. McGregor bashed his bloody head in.

The church spires of Stamford poked above the green as he began to penetrate the town. A sign informed him that he was on Melancholy Walk. The center, full of eighteenth-century buildings and bustling in the sunshine—get it while you can—was disconcerting. He could understand what everyone was saying, always a shock after the immunity from comprehension that Greece offered him. According to his map, the morticians, R. J. Scholes, were up the High Street. He looked at the new books in the window of W.H. Smith's, was getting thirsty already.

• •

THE EXPENSES WERE ITEMIZED. The coffin, storage, six hundred pounds to transport the body to the crematorium. Six hundred fucking pounds. What if he offered to take her there himself? Not allowed, no way, you cannot ferry the dead about. The grandma attending him, a welcome change from the guys in suits, produced a pen, and he signed away. You don't get any choices, before or after.

Outside he thought, there you go, Brie, the last thing

anyone will ever do for you. He looked around. What now? A widower, alone in England, job done, nothing to do.

> *Death be not proud, though some have called thee*
> *Mighty and dreadful, for thou art not so...*

Nonsense, Mr. Donne, what could be more mighty and dreadful than this, that sweeps away everything? He thought of Maki and Leo. They had talked last night, Maki in full mourning, he could see her swollen face, Leo in denial. Was denial the right word? He clung to his equilibrium, maintained his balance. Perhaps he listened to an interior dirge, worked with a mournful chord progression that no else heard. Max's tears came again, so easily. He wiped with his sleeve and took several deep breaths. Okay, clear-eyed, ready. Staniland, his favorite used bookstore, was just down the street, and he headed there.

Experienced book buyers can scan shelves like radar. There's so much chaff, so little wheat. What's this? A hard-bound first edition of Ted Hughes's poetry memoir of his life with Sylvia Plath, *Birthday Letters*. He had read about it but never had a copy in hand. Six and a half quid, not bad. He sat in a chair by the window and thumbed it open.

> *And it was the you that escaped death*
> *In the little woven vessel*
> *On the most earthly river*
> *Of that Paradise.*

"Oh, excuse me."

Max looked from the page to the floor, boots, and up the jeaned legs to a young woman peering down at him through large glasses. Her blond hair spilled over her shoulders, she looked a good deal like Gloria Steinum. Bookstore dust drifted in the shaft of sun. He was crying and didn't speak.

"Oh, Ted Hughes. I loved that book. It's so sad, isn't it?"

"It's not *that* sad."

She managed a smile, turned on a heel, and was gone. Max stared a while at the space she'd left and looked back to the poem:

Escape incognito
The death who had already donned your feathers,
The mask of his disguise.

18

THIRTY YEARS AGO, seated on a railroad dock in Weiser, Idaho, letting cold beer flow into them while bluegrass fiddles wailed in the distance, a poet friend, Chaz Lafferty, told Max that bards in old China on the ninth day of the ninth month would pack up copious amounts of wine, along with paper and ink, and head to the hills for an all-night drink and poetry-writing binge. Magic number nine again. He had never found this story in print, but it sounded true to the history of poetry in old Cathay, to the Pound translations of Li Po and Tu Fu, to poets drunk on the moon. He tried to carry on this poetic tradition and took a hike each year to see what the landscape offered. Hardly an all-night binge, but where he lived now, there were no other poets about.

Morning of the ninth had him on the cusp of reneging, dropping the poetic quest, the vanity of it. The moment was greater. He wasn't up to deploying the energy required. To what end? Who would know besides himself?

After lunch he stared out across the orchards waving beneath a threatening sky and turned. If not now, when? If he didn't bring his lifelong practice to bear on this hardest reality, what did it mean? It was the only tool he had. The dogs were ready, and he set out. Tender to the elements, he quickly found his poem.

ONE-TON MAN

There's a lot of trouble in the world,
You don't have to look for it.

Coming storm pounds the mountains,
roll and rumble drawing near,
beasts berserk wheel thru the orchards
on the heels of phantoms nipping;
but my heart is heavy as the hills,
belovéd wife dead twelve days.

Lightning strobes the olives,
grumble of rolling thunder
announces rain, and to the
dogs' relief I turn back
toward the home our love built.
How will it stand now,
mere brick and concrete and steel.

The soulmates of my life
scattered over the world
and far away and only I
am out in this chaos,
heavy as the rain
that washes nothing away,
a thousand pounds brought down
with each footfall.

9-9-02

In a deck chair on the hiati Max stared out over the ache of a fading September afternoon. The blue was burned out of the day, south along the Kalamata road the cypress blurred and bent. There was a stack of journals and notebooks on the floor. For days he had been inside Briseis's head as she relentlessly examined her life. There weren't many surprises, but the reading of them overwhelmed him, brought her back, right here, talking, in his hands. He picked up his notebook and wrote: *September works hard for the clarity of October and fails.* The sky was birdless for a moment, then two swallows cut across and landed on the power line. They'll soon be off for Africa, he thought. How many weeks does it take? He tried to remember where they wintered. Lake Victoria? Those who made it. Death awaited a large percentage of the migration, consequently they mated like mad while in Greece, sometimes three loads of chicks, or swicks, let's call them. Lazineekos was splitting the sun, rays of light flashed the foothills and sharpened the shadows. He reached over and picked up John Berryman's *The Dream Songs* from the table and randomly opened it.

> *All souls converge upon a hopeless mote*
> *tonight, as though*
>
> *the throngs of souls in hopeless pain rise up*
> *to say they cannot care, to say they abide*
> *whatever is to come.*
> *My air is flung with souls which will not stop*
> *and among them hangs a soul that has not died*
> *and refuses to come home.*

He exhaled. Too much. Berryman was too much for the afternoon, though by reading him one felt far more sane and emotionally stable, in comparison, anyway. Max fanned the pages and found a copy of the poem he'd written imagining he had been with Berryman at the end.

"I SAW NOBODY COMING, SO I WENT INSTEAD."

A cold Minnesota wind tore
our faces as we made our way
across the Washington Avenue bridge.

Morning, Berryman was silent,
below, the Mississippi churned a
raw heartless gray. We stopped
and stared down at it.
"'Tis a strong brown god," I quoted.
"Fuck Eliot, he said, gimme a smoke."
I patted my pockets to no avail
and said, "Oops, you're out of luck."
He turned to me, eyes burning out
of that great head of hair,
"I wept without control when Dylan died,
who will weep for me?" And then
he was over the rail and
into the air,
a twisted package dark
and diving to the frozen
bank of the river.

Who will weep for me? Who wants the answer to that question, who would ask it? Briseis was huge in this regard, tears being shed across the planet. Phone calls from the States, friends tenderly dancing, their voices pitched to what they thought was a soothing murmur. It didn't, yet every time someone reached out, he expanded back into the world. Just a bit. And then another. He looked at the end of the poem. "Bank," as though he was making a deposit in eternity.

His tear-streaked daughter came out of the house and collapsed in the deck chair next to him. He took her hand in his. A tangled chaos of hair framed her swollen face. Each day was harder for her. She shambled about the house in T-shirt and baggy shorts. His chic daughter had descended to the floor of her closet, there to find her grief garments, the anti-style of despair. She had been chewing her nails. He wanted to take her on his lap, but she was too big, too old, too much a woman.

She pushed the hair from her face. "Daddy."

"Yeah."

"Have you heard what Leo wants to do?"

"Ah, yes, I have."

"Well . . . ? You're not going to let him do it, are you? Mom's only been dead for two weeks, and he wants to throw a party!"

Max stared out over the still, twilighting hills. The cicada rattle was waning, early crickets were tuning up. There was no balance to be struck. How to coax Maki out of her hole?

"Maki, sweetheart, there isn't an official way to mourn, a specific allotted time. Sure, in Greece there is, but we don't care about that. With this kind of thing, everyone has their own path, their own way to get through. 'Cause that's what it boils down to, getting through. We will carry your mom in our hearts for the rest of our lives. This is a good thing. I imagine there will be times when you feel she's right there with you." He paused for a breath, took a sip of beer. "Loss is a constant in life. From this moment on you will be dealing with loss of one sort or another. It might be some small totem that's important to you, or you'll be betrayed by love. But there will be loss. It's the hardest, maybe most important part of growing up. You and Leo have gotten the big advanced lesson. That's the way it worked out. Leo is just approaching it differently."

"Differently?! He's pretending it didn't even happen!"

"Oh, I think that's a little harsh. It's true, Leo doesn't want to deal with it right now, but he's got the rest of his life. Yeah, I think it would be healthier if he let it out, but

331

that's not his approach. He doesn't want to reveal himself that way. He's not ready for that, not now. You can't force him to. The important thing is to help each other. We help Leo by being kind to him, by appreciating that he's had the same loss that we've suffered. He's not expressing it the same way, but she was his mom too. None of us owns this loss. We suffered it together. So right now I think we let Leo find his own way to deal with it, or ignore it, or whatever."

"So you mean you're going to let him do it? It's just over two weeks."

Max looked at her, so torn apart. It broke his heart. "Look. You guys are leaving Sparti, hell, you're leaving Greece, and won't be back for months. It might be good to get together one more time, with everyone. It doesn't have to be riotous happy. It can be on the somber side, but everyone being together. You and Leo have this great gang of friends, being with them all together one more time is not a bad thing. It doesn't insult the memory of your mother. On the contrary. You can celebrate what her life gave you."

Andromache raised her eyes toward her father, annoyed, relieved to agree with him. "Will you make pizza?"

"For the party? Masses of it!"

She sighed. "Okay, I guess."

"I think the chances of it being a good event, something positive, are pretty high. So," he turned and took both her hands, "do you need to do any more shopping before you leave?"

She rolled her eyes. "Daddy, I'm going to the center of the world. What can I possibly get in Sparti that I can't get in New York City?"

332

"Mosquito bites?"

• •

HEARING THE DINGER ON THE OVEN, he leapt up and walked through the house to the kitchen. System of a Down throbbed from the speakers. Greek teenagers, Spartans, stood around smoking and talking. Clouds of cigarette smoke were already drifting through the rooms, though the doors to the hiati were all wide open. It was a great house for a party, open, expansive, with many different areas to gather and not a worry about neighbors and noise. Max pulled the pizza from the oven, set it on the counter, and slid the last one in. He turned the timer to twenty minutes. He was precise when cooking, far more than in any other activity. He thought it was because the feedback was so swift, the reaction to his gestures so easy to interpret. They ate it or they didn't. Reactions to poetry were far subtler, and generally the creator was not privy to immediate impressions. Then again, this was a forgiving crowd who would, eventually, eat everything.

Andromache stuck her head in the door. "Hi, Daddy, whatcha watching?" The music throbbed behind her.

"Ed Harris movie about Jackson Pollock. It looks good. He looks a lot like him.

She sat on the edge of the bed. "Cool, who directed?"

"Ed Harris. It's his movie, starred and directed."

Andromache pointed at the screen. "So that is how he painted before the drips?"

"Yeah, they aren't as interesting."

They watched for a few minutes as Pollock developed his style and made most everyone around him miserable.

"So he was crazy?"

333

"Yeah, bipolar and an alcoholic. A lethal combo. Dead at forty-four, driving drunk."

Andromache, staring at the screen: "Oh, I like that one. What's it called?"

"He's no help in that department. He often gave them names like 'Number 13.' Rothko is just as bad. 'Red, blue and green.' Okay, at least it's descriptive, but damn. You are missing an opportunity when you ignore the title. Same with poetry."

"What was Rothko like?"

"Deeply depressed. Slashed his wrists and bled to death on his studio floor."

"Yuck."

"Yeah, making art is certainly no guarantee that you'll feel good about yourself."

"Well, it makes me feel good."

"Then you're one of the lucky ones. Hey, don't hang out here with the old man, go back to the party. You can watch this tomorrow, or late tonight, whenever."

She pushed back her hair, killed him with her smile. "Okay. But people keep asking where you are, why you aren't joining in. They think you're back here suffering alone."

"That's sweet. Soon as this is over I'll be out to hang with y'all."

"Don't fall asleep."

"Promise."

The sound of the party flooded the room and squeezed off with the closing of the door. The Pollocks had moved to Long Island.

Later the door opened with a roar again. Leonidas walked in with a beer in one hand and a very long joint in

334

the other. "Dude, you want some of this?'"

"Bring it on, dawg. Thanks."

"What are you watching?"

"An Ed Harris movie called *Pollock*. It's about the painter Jackson Pollock."

"Who is he?"

"Abstract Expressionist. He did the drip paintings."

"Oh, yeah, I remember. Didn't we see some of them in New York. At one of the museums?"

"At several of them. He's a huge name in 20th century art."

Leonidas watched as Pollock tipped over a laden Thanksgiving dinner table. "Whoa, he's fucked up, isn't he?"

"No shit, man."

"Hey, people want you to join the party, man. They're demanding your presence. They're hoping some of your cool will rub off on them."

Max laughed. "You don't say? This is almost over. Then I'll come out and press the flesh." He handed the joint back to his son.

"Cool, dude. There's plenty of party left." He turned at the door, "Oh, the pizza went down a bomb. It was great."

"They've eaten it all?"

"Inhaled. It was too good."

Max wandered through the party with a beer. The kids that had been at the house many times called him Max, though it had taken years to get them that far. To the others he was Keerios, Mister. The beer and wine were holding up, someone had ordered pitas delivered from Sparti. People were still arriving, by cab or parental taxi.

Everyone knew where the Parnell house was, it had been party central for years. Some of the girls began crying when they saw him, gave him a hug, tried to blubber out condolences in English, gave up. Mostly, they felt thin, as though he would break them if he squeezed. Some of them were beautiful, perhaps more beautiful than they would ever be again.

He emptied ashtrays. They all smoked too much. There were hardly any who didn't. His too. Even their mother couldn't stop them. Even her death. Name your poison. But what's the hurry? He sat down on a couch with Adonis and Dimitra, two of his favorites. Soundgarden was roaring from the speakers. A new tune started up, that unmistakable bass line, and Chris Cornell was intoning, "I fell on black days." To be sure, these were black days.

• •

HE ENTERED BIRDSONG as he entered the day, following a melody. He listened more carefully. Along with the birds was a guitar, acoustic, faint but sure. Someone was idly picking, out on the hiati, probably. He opened his eyes, the morning sun flashed through the honeysuckle and jasmine, their shadows stretched across the bed. He went back to darkness and tried to pick up the guitar again.

Leonidas and six other young men were sprawled on the deck furniture sipping frappes, lazily smoking. They had arranged the chairs so they could prop their feet on the wrought-iron railing while they gazed out over the orchards. Yiorgos had a guitar across his knee.

"Good morning, comrades," said Max, "As they say on the golf course, play on through."

Heads nodded, some murmured salutations or just looked, vaguely, up.

336

"Leo, did Andromache crash?"

"Yeah, a couple of hours ago. Couldn't keep up." He offered his father a joint. Max waved it away and walked back into the house to make tea. The living room hummed with the sleeping, on couches, on cushions on the floor. Some fetal, others expansive, mouths open and rumbling. The kitchen was a mess but not too bad. Some attempt had been made to sort it out. Greek kids were accustomed to mothers following around behind. No moms here.

19

COMING BACK FROM THE AIRPORT NEWSSTAND with the *Herald Tribune* and *Guardian,* Max stopped twenty meters from the queue and looked at his children. Life didn't afford many opportunities for undetected observation, for seeing them in the world. Did they look like teenagers whose mother had just died? They looked like all the kids, albeit ones who had spent the past months in the sun, though their style was deliberately more American than most Europeans. Leo slouched in the basic uniform: baseball hat, hoodie, baggy jeans, big shoes, earphones framing the slightly dazed look of someone far more involved in his personal soundtrack than in the flux that swirled about him.

The line advanced, and Maki nudged him to move his bag. His daughter had considered her look the night before, perhaps even earlier. The desired impression was a *whatever* nonchalance, but one mustn't think she was trying, that would be too gauche for words. Not that she'd ever use that word. The look was vaguely disheveled, partial, and could, it appeared, be changed, tightened up, on the spot. Her mass of hair was held from her face by a brilliant scarf Mo Bursts had given Brie years ago, but naturally or by design, the odd strand of hair was hanging over, giving her something to push out of the way. Another scarf hung around her neck. A short jacket, sleeves rolled once, exposing various bracelets, was open over a little tank top that afforded lots of tummy exposure. The pants, velour or something similar, were cut low, fit snuggly above, but when they arrived at her short boots couldn't decide whether to be stuffed in or draped over, a little of both. She stood with her arms crossed, feet at right angles, second position in ballet, and watched the airport crowd with an intense curiosity.

Max was struck with a consideration he had never had before. What if his children were ugly and stupid, instead of bright and attractive? Would he feel the same about them? The cliché answer was, of course you would, they're your children and you love them. You nurture and care for the children you get, your initial wonderment of love slowly transforms into an emotion deeper, some meeting of heart and mind, or you hope that occurs. It often doesn't. So many wounded walking, the concourse full of them. Just then Maki spied Max watching and gave him a smirk and a nod, while Leo rocked on, and a disembodied voice reminded them not to take the carts on the escalator.

Arriving in the U.K., his children, with their British passports, smugly left him to wait in the alien line. Getting those passports when they were still small had paid many dividends. It allowed them to live and work anywhere in Europe, and it provided an escape from National Military Service in Greece for Leo. If they were trying to do all this with just U.S. citizenship, everything would be more complicated. Max was living proof, the alien with no excuse.

A train took them to the university campus, and after some confusion Leo was properly registered. Groaning under their luggage they staggered several blocks to Leo's high-rise digs. The building looked like some bleak Eastern European holdover. Leo's apartment was on the tenth floor, with a common kitchen shared by four dorm rooms. He was delighted with the space, dropped his shit on the floor, where it would likely remain, and was ready to explore the city. Back on the ground Maki said something to Leo in Greek, which caught the attention of several young men smoking in the parking lot, who called to them in Greek. Introductions all around. They found out there were "masses" of Greek students about. Downtown Manchester was full of modern buildings and bustling. They ate Pakistani and Indian food for two days and gawked.

Once Leonidas was fully settled in, Max and Andromache booked a train for Peterborough, where Briseis's remains awaited pickup, before they headed on to New York. Leo and Maki went out to a club the night before and noticed, to their amusement, that their conversations had switched entirely to English, to blend in, to gain the safety of anonymity.

Maki told him, "Remember, you can call me anytime you want. Just to talk."

Leo shrugged. "I know that, but I don't imagine I will very often."

"Probably not. Well, email at least. And I'll call you once in a while. Just to check in, speak Greek or something. Daddy said we can visit each other once during the year. There are cheap flights all the time."

"I'll definitely be coming to the Big Apple."

"Yeah, it'll be really cool. Come in the winter, by then I'll know my way around. And maybe we could meet in London. Megan has a sister whose flat we could crash at. Wow, London and New York. Goodbye Sparti, hello big city."

"Wow, look at that mohawk!"

"You're gonna do that to your hair, aren't you?"

"I dunno."

"You *so* are, I can tell. You haven't got any secrets from me!"

"I might." Leo, for the first time since they'd arrived, suddenly realized he would soon be without his mirror, Maki more a constant in his life than their parents. He shivered with the thought.

"Yeah, like what? The skin mags under your mattress? The pot stash in the battery compartment of your ghetto blaster? The . . ."

"Alright, alright. Do you have to know *everything*?" It might be good to go solo for a while. And then he thought, it's not for *a while*, is it? They were starting their lives apart. He felt a tear, and then many.

Andromache's heart started, she grabbed his head in her arms. "Oh, Leo, that's okay. Let it go. You can cry with me. I've been crying since she died." She could feel her heart in his head, throbbing.

They separated. Leo wiped his eyes with his sleeve. "I wasn't crying about Mom but that tomorrow you won't be here. And for a lot of days after that." Andromache tried to hold back her sobs. They hugged again and listened to the sound of each other, inhaled their collective scent and let their connection, forged in the womb, flow without restraint. The club disappeared and they were in the back seat of the car with their secret jokes, making knowing faces at each other, laughing at the absurdity of their parents.

Then a familiar riff brought them back. "Oh, Queens of the Stone Age. I love this song. Come on Leo, let's dance." She pulled him off his stool and into the crowd.

• •

341

"It's Lawrence country," Max said to the window. Andromache turned from her magazine.

"What?"

"We're nearing Nottingham. This is the countryside D. H. Lawrence was born in and wrote about in many of his books: *Sons and Lovers*, *Women in Love*, *Lady Chatterley's Lover*."

"That's a *whole lotta of love*."

Max laughed. "You're right, I hadn't really thought of it. He wrote many books that didn't have love in the title, but relationships, between and within the sexes was his main theme." He looked back out on the Derbyshire countryside. "A good poet, too. You should read one of his novels, Maki."

"Which one?"

"*Women in Love*, I think. Or you could read *The Rainbow* and then *Women in Love*. It's a continuing story. Your mom loved Lawrence and had some interesting things to say about the structure of his sentences, the rhythm of them . . ." Max trailed off and stared out the window as the suburbs of Nottingham began to eat the farmland. Andromache reached up and kneaded the knots in her father's neck, thought he should get his hair cut, and the train rattled on.

In the check-in line at Heathrow Max began to whistle a famous melody.

Maki pivoted around exasperated, "Daddy!"

"Huh?"

"*New York, New York?*"

"Oops," Max brought his hand to his mouth, "unconscious, really."

His daughter put her hands on her hips. "I don't know

why you pretend you're a hick. I mean, you are so far from being a hick, so why do you insist on the just-in-from-the-horio routine?"

"I don't know. I have a fondness for that type of naiveté. That sort of innocence, I guess."

"Yeah, sure, but if you were in some literary gathering in Manhattan you wouldn't do it."

"How perceptive, my dear. You're right. I only do it in anonymous public situations like this."

"So you can embarrass the hell out of your children."

"Among other things, yes."

Maki rolled her eyes.

"I wanna be a part of it . . ."

She chilled him with a look, and then a grin. The line was moving again, and they tugged on their bags.

"Did you put Mom in your suitcase?"

They wrestled their carry-ons into the overhead storage.

"Yeah. I don't intend on scattering her over the Atlantic. I think it's pretty difficult to throw something off the plane. At least I hope it is. I imagine it's frowned upon, these days, talking about throwing things off the plane. If we looked Middle Eastern, we'd already be in trouble."

"So is all this craziness about 9/11?"

"That's the front, certainly. The Bush administration used it as an excuse to go mental with all sorts of security paranoia, the bombing and invasion of Afghanistan, and it looks like an invasion of Iraq."

"What has Iraq got to do with it?"

"Nothing, as far as I can tell."

"Wow! They can just do that?"

"The Americans have more guns than anyone else,

343

which makes them the neighborhood bully. That's where you're headed, girl."

I'll be painting, she thought, and I'll stay out of skyscrapers.

Maki nodded her head to music flowing from her Discman, studied the flight magazine's film listings, sipped from a ginger ale.

Max nudged her. "What are listening to?"

She smiled, pulled the phones from her ears, "It's a new-metal mix Leo did. It's really good."

"He gives good mix, doesn't he?"

"The best."

"But you don't tell *him* that."

Maki gave her patented eye-roll and laughed, "Of course not. That's the last thing *he* needs to hear. But," she dropped to a stage whisper, "I tell everyone else."

How would his children cope, motherless and separated from each other for the first time? Perhaps it was all too much? They were only seventeen. Maybe they should have just taken a long trip, the three of them, to India or South America? Wandered aimlessly for a few months bartering for sandals and rugs, visiting yogis and artisans. But that was his fantasy, not theirs. They were thirsty for the juice of the city, to assume adult roles, to disappear into the urban mob, an English-speaking one, just another face, another note in the machinery's music. He looked past his daughter's face, for a moment he could see her mother sitting next to the window instead of the woman from New Jersey, an architect, burrowed into John Grisham.

They traded items from their dinners, cheese and

cracker for chocolate pudding. Do you want that roll?

"Daddy, all I want to do in New York is make art, look at art, and think about art. Oh, and go hear cool bands."

"There will be plenty of those. But even though it makes me sound like a complete old fart, I can't reiterate it enough, the streets of New York are not the streets of Athens, let alone Sparti. You have to develop a new level of awareness."

She sighed. "Daddy, I've been in New York."

"Yeah, but you were with me, Leo, your Mom. Pay attention to Sandra, how she does it. Being as beautiful as she is, she attracts a lot of attention, but she knows how to slide through situations untouched. She puts out this neutral-but-firm vibe that keeps people away. Only when required, of course. And she knows where she shouldn't go. And let's face it, Maki, you are going to attract attention too."

"I'm nowhere near in Sandra's league. If you weren't my father, you'd be aware of that."

He looked at her and smiled. Great curling strands of her hair had pulled free and were hanging about her face, her fine arched eyebrows, deep pool of her eyes, golden glow of summer coming from her flesh. Not now, maybe, but in six months, a year...

Images from Briseis's journals had multiplied, it was all he could think about. In mid-Atlantic, he had to say it.

"You know, Maki, there's no balance in love, no equilibrium, and even if for a brief while there is, it won't last. Nothing lasts. You can't worry whether someone loves you as much as you love them. We all want to be loved, but the real power of life, the true energy, is to love, to give love. Your mom's and my relationship, for

345

instance. Maybe from your point of view it was a great example of equilibrium. It wasn't. I'm only just realizing that now, having read her journals, being able, now, to look back on it all with at least a modicum of detachment. With your mom, I was lucky to be the one who loved the most. That's what you want to be. The one who loves the most. That's in no way a critique of her. I'm convinced she would agree. She loved as she could, which was plenty. Love is not static but in flux, it changes all the time, and how we manifest it evolves, or degenerates, for that matter. You give what you can, you take what is given. There will be plenty of situations where somebody loves you but you can't reciprocate. Happens all the time. It will happen to you. Probably already has. All the stuff your mom did, the meetings, the ACOA twelve-step stuff, all of this was toward a greater love, a deeper, more complete feeling. But this has to do with adult relationships. With you and Leo her love was complete. Which doesn't make it perfect or absolute. Even there, she got lost in her work for a couple of years. She needed some affirmation outside the home, that kind of success. If you want to understand her more, talk to Amalia. She had a very different childhood than you did. Your mom was young, nineteen, barely older than you, and a very difficult relationship developed."

"Daddy, I'm seventeen. Mom was almost twenty when Amalia was born."

"Details. Anyway, she was young, inexperienced, still entrapped in the codependent insanity of her family. She had no way of going forward except on her hands and knees. She was a foreigner in America, married to a man she discovered was crazy, dangerously so, and had to escape. Did your mum tell you about this?

Andromache nodded, "Some of it."

"Really dramatic shit. She seemed fearful and wimpy at times, but when decisions needed to be made, she was ready to take responsibility and make them." Max wondered if this was really true. Was he making myth for his daughter? It was night, thirty-three thousand feet of night to the pitch-black Atlantic, and he was painting bright colors on their loss. And why not? Technicolor, surround sound, 3-fucking-D? Everyone who knew her will make their own myth movie, and it won't have much to do with the way it was. Fading, fading faster than night in Europe. It will be morning in New York. To Andromache it must still seem like the New World, full of promise and possibility.

"Your Mom summed it up best: 'All human relationships, except those concerning infants, are a process of negotiation and compromise.' This in no way diminishes love, but rather, love is a dynamic thing to be earned, nurtured. and tenderly carried into the world."

His daughter stared at him, a tear streaked her cheek. He closed his eyes, reciting,

> So we too,
> not lost but drifting
> in the veins of the world,
> know not the distance
> but the force that drives us.

"Who is that?"

"Oh, that's from one of mine. You and Leo were inside your mom when I wrote it."

"Good one, Daddy."

He acknowledged her with a nod. They streaked west, six hundred miles an hour through utter darkness.

• •

THE TAXI STOPPED on a tree-lined street in the East Village. It was a sharp, clear morning, Andromache leapt from the car, looked up, as every new arrival does, and then spun around.

"This is your new 'hood, girl. Check it out," Max said.

Even the cabbie, an actual New Yorker, amazingly enough, couldn't resist Maki's enthusiasm. He stood for a moment by the trunk lighting a smoke and said, "Welcome to New York City, young lady. And good luck." Max tipped him twenty, it was too good a day, and they humped the bags up to the door and rang the bell.

They entered in tears as though Briseis had died that morning, as though Sandra was hosting a wake. She embraced them, one after the other and then back again. She had been suffering alone. Her husband, Francisco, had met Briseis, but he didn't know, had no history to mourn, couldn't shape his grief into stories and looks and touches. He wasn't part of the family, hadn't had that luck. They stood breathing hard by the door, faces wet, hands on each others shoulders, bags only partially in. A cat rubbed itself against their legs.

"Right," said Max, giving his two favorite women a squeeze, "tears shed. How 'bout a cup of coffee and, uh," he gestured with his hand, turning his wrist, "something sweet, something New York, Jewish maybe."

"I picked up some rugelach earlier this morning. Sit down in the living room and I'll put the water on."

They sprawled and tried to stretch seven hours of flight out.

"Come on out, honey, Max and Andromache are here. Why are you being shy?"

A moppet's head peered around the corner. Andromache burst out, "Briseis, come here!" and the eight-year-old ran and leapt onto her lap. "Wow, how did you get so big? We could practically share clothes."

"No we couldn't. You're way bigger than I am." They rolled on the couch in a hug.

"Mommy, why is Max crying?"

"You remember what I told you, about what happened?"

"Oh, yeah." She climbed off Maki and walked to Max and stroked him on his lowered head as he tried in vain to restrain his sobbing. "Don't be sad, Max, you still have us." She looked up. "Why is *everybody* crying. You just got here. We should be happy."

Sandra reached out for her. "Oh, we are honey, we are. It's a grownup thing. Sometimes tears are the only thing you have. Why don't you run and tell Daddy that Max and Maki are here."

Sandra turned to Max while Andromache went to the loo. "Wow! The pictures you sent didn't do her justice. Has it really been two years since I saw you guys? The transformation is breathtaking. That hair, I'm glad she's kept it long."

"Yeah. It'll probably be purple and spiked before Christmas."

Sandra laughed. "Right. You don't want to be too attractive. How's Leo?"

"He's settling right in. Right away he met some Greek kids, so he's not really alone. He hasn't really dealt with Briseis's death, sort of pushed it way back in his mind and just doesn't think about it." Max shrugged. "So somewhere down the line, it will be waiting for him. I mean, she'll be dead for the rest of his life."

Sandra felt a wrenching chill flash through her body. This was Max's talent, wielding a cleaver without sentiment.

"Maki has been in full mourning," he went on. "The first two weeks she and Lia just sat around in long T-shirts weeping, smoking cigarettes, and eating junk food. But then Lia flew back to the States, and the preparations to leave started to pick her up. And then they had a party."

"A party?"

"Yeah, it was Leo's idea. A going-away party, and I think it brought Maki back into the world."

"What about Amalia?"

"Wrecked. Afraid. An orphan at thirty-one. It's impossible to predict the long-term effects."

"And you?"

"I have a strange emptiness, the core of me feels hollow, though I'm constantly on the verge of weeping. I feel emotionally drained. The tears I'm shedding are part of this emptying process. It will go on for months, I expect. But I'm okay with it. It was a long time coming, and I was prepared. I guess."

"So what about this studio arrangement?"

"Well, a couple of years ago Francisco was making a Jazz documentary, 'Still Free.' Have you seen it?"

"I'm afraid that sort of thing doesn't make it to the Sparti video store."

"We have copies, I'll give you one. It's really good. Anyway, I was helping out a little, doing whatever, and we both became friends with Rashied Ali."

"Wait a minute, *the* Rashied Ali? Who played with 'Trane and Ayler?!

350

"Yes, that one." Sandra broke out the big smile. "He has a building down here, used to have a club in it, Ali's Alley, but that was years ago. He still lives in it. I had just lost my space, and he had masses of room and offered to let me have a corner. Francisco did all the work, electrical, soundproof walls. I pay him, it's not free, but it's a great space, and I can walk there. So I was talking to him about Andromache, and he said why didn't we just build on a little space for her. Et voilà!"

"That's fantastic. Rashied Ali, wow! Does he rehearse there?"

"That's why I needed soundproofed walls. He has a quintet now. They're terrific. We can hear them while you're here."

"So we need to build her a space?"

"Yeah, but Francisco has it all figured out."

"Great. You know, Andromache has money for rent, food, studio, expenses, everything. My father took care of both of them. They should be good through grad school at least, if that's the route they take."

Sandra turned to Maki, who was talking with Briseis. "You weren't interested in a full university program?"

"I just want to do art for now, immerse myself in drawing and painting and see where it takes me. If I want to learn something else, I'll bet I can find a class in it. Isn't there masses of stuff happening all the time, classes, seminars, things like that?"

"There are too many to count. And there's plenty of things that hardly cost any money." Sandra gazed up at a Clemente silkscreen on the wall. "I didn't get a degree, you know. I never stayed at one school long enough. I was a very restless student. It doesn't matter unless you want to teach. When you go into a gallery, they don't really give a damn where you studied. It's the work that counts."

The table was covered with the wreckage of dinner. The third bottle of Chianti was nearly drained. Francisco was casually snapping photographs while they drifted. "So Max," he asked, "are you going down to the World Trade Center site?"

"I don't think so. It doesn't really interest me. I'm more interested in the repercussions than the event itself. What was it like? Sandra, you were here, right?"

"Yes, I was. Francisco was on a job in Boston."

"A PBS thing with Noam Chomsky, which was canceled. It was terrible. I was supposed to fly back, but all planes were grounded. The phones were all fucked up. I couldn't get through to Sandra for hours. I finally got on a train at ten p.m."

"Sandra, what was it like?"

"I'm beginning not to trust my memories."

"How so?"

"I've talked about it so much and read about it endlessly, and I think my memories are merging with the collective memory of it. The Manhattan memory, the one all of us who were here are sharing. As you've probably read, there was a powerful surge of collective feeling, like nothing I've ever experienced. But here too, I'm suspicious of my memory regarding how long it lasted. Then Francisco got back and immediately began shooting, documenting what was happening, so that changed my perspective too. It's still a jumble and I haven't made any art that directly relates to it. What was it like for you in Greece?"

"Well, it was early afternoon, we got a phone call from Elektra saying you won't believe what's happening on TV, you should come down and see. So Brie and I drove down to her house, it's just two minutes, and we got there before the second plane, so we saw that live. What a vivid act! Oddly, though, I didn't feel any special connection with people who were in the disaster, I mean, some linkage because it was happening to Americans. I did not feel personally under attack, which I've read many Americans did. We watched for maybe two hours, and then we got tired of seeing the same footage over and over, the second plane crashing, the collapse of the buildings, the roiling clouds of debris rolling down the streets, and we went home." Max took a sip of wine. "In the aftermath I felt less American than I did before—mostly due, I'm sure, to the hysterical reaction of the Bush administration. All this militant rubbish. But like you, it's hard to isolate what you were feeling and thinking at the moment and what you've added on. One would hope it's the death knell of American exceptionalism, but I don't have my hopes up."

"Max," Francisco said, "my point exactly. At first, I did feel under attack as a New Yorker, even though I'm not American and have no interest in being. But then this whole nationalistic drum-beating began, this sense that Americans have a unique destiny and role in the world, and my sympathy drained away. There's no difference between an American's suffering and a Palestinian's or a Rwandan's. Except that the American government can make the world pay for that suffering, can extract a price."

• •

Mid-morning Manhattan, muffled, faint, came with the sun though the kitchen window. Francisco off to work, Briseis to school, Andromache slept on. Sandra and Max lingered over coffee, the *New York Times*, the last months in the Parnell house, the projects going forward. They

353

slipped so easily into the hours, everything preliminary was past. The ground was firm, they understood the sky, and the weather was whatever they imagined. They had never competed.

"Briseis is just fantastic. What a wonderful child. There's no mistaking who her mama is. Her energy and curiosity. She seems so at ease with herself. She reminds me a lot of Maki at that age, actually."

"Thanks Max, that's a high compliment. But I think she's got lots of her daddy in there too."

"You think so? Time will tell." What would it tell? What would happen to his mystery daughter? Would she ever know? Of course she would, sometime. Max closed his eyes and tried to imagine Briseis at Andromache's current age.

"Max, you want more coffee, or is jetlag getting to you?"

He came back to the kitchen in a rush and shook his head. "Oh, yeah, sure. With all this drama in my life I hadn't thought much lately of little B, I must admit." He glanced back at the doorway to the kitchen. "My daughter and not my daughter." He looked down at his coffee and then up again. "Francisco is a great father to her, she's really lucky to have him."

Sandra smiled. "Me too."

Would Mr. Grumblebit on Delta Airlines flight 452 to Miami please proceed immediately to gate 15.

Max gestured toward the ceiling. "Did you hear that? JFK is a shit airport, but I love hearing announcements in a New York Jewish accent. Something you won't hear anywhere else. Well, maybe the Tel Aviv airport, but I wouldn't know."

"Why? It's just another accent," Maki said.

"But it's not. So much twentieth-century American literature and humor is tied up with the Jewish diaspora's encounter with America in New York City. The Lower East Side, Brooklyn. Then they went to L.A. and took over the movies." Max shifted into dialect. "Irish, Italian, what? Are you kidding? It'll be a cold day in Miami when we let the goyim get a word in!"

Andromache looked at her father and smiled. He was so many personas and only one, a man trying to absorb and use the stimulus overload of the modern world. He carried the failure of this effort like a sandwich board announcing the end of the world, or pizza by the slice.

Max gestured toward the ceiling again and quoted from the poem that had been in his mind for weeks, Ginsberg's "Kaddish":

> *Ai! ai! we do worse! We are in a fix! And you're out,*
> * Death*
> *let you out, Death had the Mercy, you're done with*
> * your*
> *century, done with God, done with the path thru it—*
> * Done with yourself at last—*

His tears ran freely and soaked the shoulder of his daughter's jacket as they trembled in the concourse, oblivious and unnoticed. Just another weeping couple. He was still her hero.

20

Max sat in the car and waited. He could see Yiorgos on the balcony above performing the dance he always did slipping away from the family for a few hours. Everyone must be reassured, hugged, kissed. It won't take too long, he promised them.

It'll take bloody hours, thought Max. And look how he's dressed, slacks and polo shirt. This is how he goes to the mountains? Maybe it was a sign of respect from the man who would soon be the only one who knows, the only one who knows the names and stories, who has huddled with old shepherds in caves listening to what the mountains have told them. The only man for this holy mission.

They waved goodbye to his wife and youngest, hovering, innocent, above the car. What was their connection to the task at hand? Since he had awoken that morning Max felt on the edge of a song, a piece of music or the wind, how it moved across the earth, something older than music maybe, a harmony. What would that be?

They drove across the valley toward the Tayegetos backed by a stunning October blue sky, every tree distinct against its stones, shadow sharp. October, a light that cuts, highlights the landscape with a razor edge. Vivid, inhuman, of itself. The Byzantine city of Mystras spilled down a precipice, a welter of crenellation and churches, tile roofs and Cyprus punctuation.

They switchbacked up, Yiorgos at the wheel, to the village of Pikoulyanika, where they asked directions.

"You're going where?"

"Up there, Lazineekos. We have, you understand, a

rendezvous with the mountain."

They followed hands pointing further. Soon they were high above Mystras and traversing north past lonely chapels, through dust and gravel into the clear pine-thick air. To the east, Lakonia yawn-stretched in the sun, to the west, you could not see the mountain you were on.

At road end Max hoisted the canister of ash on his back, heavy, dense, no resemblance to wood ash. Mammal remains, a female animal out of a female animal who drank of her mother and suckled others. She settled on his back, and up they went.

Pine forest, the air reeking of resin, they traversed and climbed a needle-softened path. Hard work of the mountain empties the mind, it's just the mountain and the body, working. Round a bend a river of goat bells sang the silence up. The herd below, invisible, working down and ringing a clatter music that filled first sunlight, then shadow, then mind, all of it the sound of belled goats moving and eating. Yiorgos and Max looked at each other, they were both hanging onto a tree, panting. They nodded wide-eyed, astonished. It was the music in the stream of the day.

The path became vague, mere suggestion, but Yiorgos knew the way, up, always up. The sun climbed with them and the morning rolled away down into the valley. They broke out of the forest, past the tree line, and there were the Tayegetos, spine and hump hard geometry. Max turned and gaped, the mountains he had studied for twelve years bent beneath him. Lazineekos was beneath them, it had a bald spot. The valley below a patchwork dissected by river and road. Sparti, a great white mass sprawled and flashing in orchards of orange and olive.

The ridge widened and dipped to a saddle, and there

357

where the pommel would be, a knoll with a stone semi-circle. "It's an andarte, windbreak. Not even the Germans would come up this far." They shared a lunch of one boiled egg, two peppers, bread, cheese, one apple, and the merest kiss of wine. "That peak above us," Yiorgos gestured over his shoulder, "Koufovouni. Deaf Mountain. It doesn't make any sense. It's wrong, I think. It must have been *kourforvouni,* mountain peak, and it just linguistically drifted."

"Mountain peak? What a boring name."

Yiorgos threw up his hands. "They're illiterate shepherds. They go months without talking to anyone. That ridge down there, Prioni, saw. That bit over there is Herovouna, hand mountain. They're peasants, what do you want, poetry?"

Greater, older than their names, the mountains sat, still in the breathless midday sun, while they gathered stones for a stupa. They piled the stones into a pyramid. Max tied brightly colored scarves sent to Briseis over the years by Mo Bursts to the ends of sticks and inserted them into the mound. He poured ash over the stupa and scattered it on the earth around. He offered the canister to Yiorgos, who recoiled, then pointed at it saying, "Look, she's made of the same stuff as this mountain, the gray and white stone."

Max pulled a paper from his pocket. "A poem, Yiorgo. I wrote this years ago, but sometimes they come back to new situations. Or it's all the same life, and the rest."

LAKONIAN SONG

It isn't right, perhaps, to say
endure, if the sun shines so sweetly;
nor to mark the length of day

358

so filled with attention to birdsong.

Anything out of the blissful ordinary
is duly noted, pondered, forgotten;
if asked to explain, we say sanctuary,
and beckon outside, out of what we are.

The earth is indifferent to our efforts,
nothing remains of our labors.
Each fingered dawn reveals
that only the mountain remains, still,

changes calibrated in aeons. A great
geologic inhalation marks the time of man,
and now this mass of rock begins to exhale
and all of time and what comes after time

will play itself out
in the shadow of its silence.

Then a fragment of Ezra Pound tumbled into his head, and he opened his mouth and let it go.

What thou lov'st well remains, the rest is dross
What thou lov'st well shall not be reft from thee
What thou lov'st well is thy true heritage.

They poured a wine libation over the stupa and drank to her memory, her spirit, the mountain that received her. Yiorgos pulled a pennywhistle from his pocket and improvised a dirge, it hung there in the still air. Unmoving, a breath caught, everything still.